Praise for *L*
by Maggie Osborne

"Witty and wild . . . [with] the most enchanting heroine I have encountered in a long time. I loved it!"
—Patricia Matthews, author of *Sapphire*

"Delightful and poignantly endearing . . . sure to win every reader's heart. I absolutely adored it!"
—Rebecca Brandewyne, author of *Heartland*

"A delectable love story you'll devour."
—*Romantic Times*

"I thoroughly enjoyed reading LADY RELUCTANT. The characters were so captivating and so much fun! Maggie's written a beautiful love story and I really hated for it to end."
—Julie Garwood, author of *Guardian Angel*

St. Martin's Paperbacks by
Maggie Osborne

LADY RELUCTANT
EMERALD RAIN

MAGGIE
OSBORNE

EMERALD RAIN

Cover art by Lisa Falkenstern Charles.

ISBN: 0-312-92513-1

Printed in the United States of America

St. Martin's Paperbacks edition/June 1991

10 9 8 7 6 5 4 3 2 1

Chapter 1

Brazil, 1897

Shortly after the mid-afternoon rain, a message arrived from the wharf informing March Addison that the *Victoria,* in from London, had dropped anchor in the Pará harbor.

"Damn." He scanned the message, crumpled the paper and tossed it toward the office waste bin.

The possibility that Miss Eulalie Pritchard might actually be aboard the *Victoria* had impressed him as so improbable that he had made no preparations for her arrival. He had not shaved this morning, trimmed his mustache, or dressed to receive a lady. He hadn't given a thought to arranging his next voyage upriver to accommodate Miss Eulalie Pritchard.

Now it occurred to him that Miss Pritchard might in fact be aboard the *Victoria* as she had written that she would. Scowling, March glanced at the crumpled message in the waste bin, feeling an unwanted burden of obligation. Annoyed by the necessity of interrupting his work, he pushed back from his desk, buttoned a starched high collar, and donned the hated tie he kept in a drawer for unexpected occasions. He pulled on a rumpled linen waistcoat then stepped outside to the veranda, lit a cigar, and leaned his elbows on the veranda railing. He decided to wait five minutes before returning to the orders and invoices piled on his desk.

The veranda shading his office offered an unobstructed view of Guajará Bay and part of the wharf area. Hot afternoon sun sparkled on the bay waters, churned to a silt-laden coffee color by the afternoon rains. From this vantage point he could glimpse the tall black stacks of the *Victoria* rocking with the tide.

A sudden unnerving feeling tightened his shoulders. In contrast to his earlier belief, March would now have wagered his ivory-handled machete that Miss Pritchard had indeed docked with the sea-going liner. He felt it with the same strong, intuitive sense that warned him when an unseen squall came rushing down the steep canyons of the Urubamba. Moreover, the same disquieting feeling warned that Miss Eulalie Pritchard was going to be trouble.

March rolled his cigar between his fingers and cursed under his breath, annoyed that he had been unable to respond to Miss Pritchard's letter.

Any response would not have reached London before the *Victoria* docked in Pará. Plus, he still wasn't certain that Miss Pritchard's letter was anything other than a girlish prank. He couldn't imagine that Dr. Frederick Pritchard would permit his daughter to travel unescorted anywhere, not into London for a day of shopping, and certainly not across an ocean to Brazil. It was impossible, March reassured himself. Miss Eulalie Pritchard would not appear on his doorstep expecting him to ferry her up the Amazon to Hiberalta.

But damn it—there she was. His frown deepening into a scowl, March fixed his gaze on the muddy ruts leading up from the wharf, watching as Miss Pritchard came into view. It could be no one else. Head bent, holding her hem up and away from the street filth, she struggled up the muddy incline guiding a donkey cart bearing more trunks and luggage than March would have thought it possible for one woman to own.

Standing away from the veranda post, he narrowed his gaze and exhaled a stream of smoke into the hot air. Although Miss Eulalie Pritchard had her head down and the wide brim of a felt hat shadowed her face, he could see enough to confirm that she was going to be a headache.

To begin with, she wore a wool traveling suit that was no doubt stylish in England, but in this broiling climate was ludicrous. Such attire indicated an appalling lack of foresight.

His critical gaze dropped to her trim ankles, which were revealed when she raised her hem above the mud. Slowly, March lifted his eyes to a provocative curve of hips and small waist. He stared at the swell of a full, ripe bosom, then at her milky-white skin. She was so pale she reminded him of a young girl's china doll.

Most of the women settling in or passing through the booming trade town of Pará fell into three categories. By far the greatest percentage of European women along the Amazon were whores, women seeking their fortunes in paint, perfume, and fleshly pleasures. Next came the wives of businessmen who had been lured to the Amazon in search of fast fortunes. And finally, there were a few adventuresses who defied simple definition.

Virtually none of the three groups could be said to possess a genuinely feminine demeanor. The tropics and the river discouraged daintiness and gentility. Heat and humidity eroded delicate qualities, not an asset in any case in March's opinion.

Yet here was Miss Eulalie Pritchard, placing each step as gracefully as if she strolled in the Queen's garden, her parasol tipped at a precise angle above her silly felt hat. March suppressed a sigh. He estimated she would last about two weeks in the tropics before she joined the many dispirited souls jamming the lobby of the decaying Hotel

Central, while awaiting transport home to Europe. In the meantime, he would have to deal with her.

He watched as, pausing to catch her breath, she pulled off her hat to fan her flushed face and turned back to look at the bay. The river was wide enough at Pará, the gateway to the Amazon, that one could not see the far shore even when the haze lifted. Still the scene was colorful. Trading vessels crowded the channel vying for space with passenger steamers, cargo rafts, barges, houseboats, and assorted small river traffic.

The moment Eulalie Pritchard bared her head, March sucked in a deep involuntary breath. The hair coiled at her crown was a deep, rich auburn color, shot through with golden coppery tones that caught the sunlight like flame. Immediately, he noticed he was not the only man to be struck dumb by the sight of her.

Two men stopped beside an open doorway to stare at her. One of them murmured something in Portuguese that March wasn't close enough to comprehend. But he understood the man's tone well enough. Flexing his shoulders, March strode toward the veranda steps, his gaze hardening. The men glanced at him then shrugged a quick apology before walking away. She hadn't comprehended at all.

March cursed softly. Eulalie Pritchard was the most beautiful woman he had seen in a long time. Breeding defined her thin, sharp nose. The line of her throat and jaw was simultaneously strong and delicate. Hot sunlight caressed sculpted cheekbones and a high forehead before she replaced her hat and adjusted her parasol. Her blue-green eyes reminded him of bright jewels.

It was clear that Miss Eulalie Pritchard would require constant protection until he could get her on a ship returning to London. March suspected he was facing two weeks of aggravation. The only thing checking his temper was the certain knowledge that Eulalie Pritchard was not the type of woman to make the voyage upriver once she learned of the hardships such a journey would entail. A few anecdotes regarding bushmasters, caimans, tarantulas, and Indians would turn her right around before she could finish unpacking.

Panting slightly, Eulalie Pritchard halted at the foot of the veranda steps and straightened her hat. She attempted to smooth the wrinkles from her jacket, then stamped her boots in an effort to dislodge the clumps of mud.

She hadn't noticed March standing in the shade. After doing what she could to straighten her attire, and believing herself to be unobserved, she cast a discreet and despairing glance at the circles of perspiration ringing her arms and creating dark shadows beneath her breasts and around her waist. A sigh of resignation lifted her lovely bosom before she withdrew a lace handkerchief from her cuff and blotted her face and throat.

March watched Miss Pritchard's hasty toilette with a glint of amusement. By now her fashionable leather boots must feel like marble weights. He knew from experience that she was walking in a quarter inch of sweat. The petticoats beneath her wool skirt were likely to be as drenched with perspiration as were her blouse and wool jacket. Trickles of sweat ran down her face, and loose strands of coppery hair had begun to curl in the humidity. He guessed she felt as if she were standing in an oven. He knew he needed to get some liquid into her and move her out of the tropical sun quickly.

Before he stepped out of the shadows, he cheerfully revised his initial estimation. She would last a week. No longer.

"Miss Pritchard?" Tossing the stub of his cigar into the muddy street, he descended the steps. "Welcome to Brazil. I'm March Addison."

"We've met, Mr. Addison, several years ago at one of your father's garden parties."

To his astonishment, the hand she extended was encased in a proper pale leather glove; her fingers were surely afloat in perspiration. The moment March made his presence known, her demeanor changed. No longer was she the disheveled traveler struggling up a muddy incline; the woman standing before him had instantaneously transformed herself into a proper English lady. Nothing in Miss Pritchard's expression indicated she was aware of her limp appearance. They might have been meeting at a proper afternoon tea.

"We need to get you inside out of the sun. Perhaps you'd care for coffee or beer?"

"Coffee?" she repeated incredulously. "In this heat? I'd prefer water, if you please. Cold water."

After he instructed the driver of the donkey cart to wait, March took her arm and assisted her up the steps. With the exception of the whores, few women wore scent in the tropics as perfume attracted insects. Therefore it surprised him when, taking her arm, he noticed the fragrance of lilac and verbena. The scent wafted to his nostrils, evoking memories of an English spring and the green fields behind his father's manor.

"I'm afraid I can't offer anything cold. Ice is unheard of in this area. And drinking the water would be stupid." A grimace froze her expression and immediately March understood they were destined to clash. He was not a man to mince words; she appeared to be a woman who preferred her words well minced.

He ran a hand over his stubbled jaw. God spare him from overly sensitive women. She stared at him as if he had labeled her stupid, which he certainly had not intended. Most new arrivals committed the error of believing the water was safe to drink. He had merely pointed out the mistake and spared her a session of stomach cramps.

"If coffee sounds unappealing, I'd suggest beer. It's warm, but it's liquid. And we need to get some liquid into you to replace the sweat you're losing."

The word "sweat" made him guilty of a fresh offense. If Miss Pritchard's delicate eyebrows had risen any further they would have merged with her hairline. Not for the first time, March silently cursed the foolishness of Victorian sensibilities. Was he supposed to pretend she wasn't standing in front of him drenched to the skin, smelling faintly like a dead sheep in her ridiculous wool suit?

In silence they entered his office. Once inside, Miss Pritchard hastily withdrew her hand from his sleeve and gazed around her.

At this time of day his brokerage was virtually deserted. Only two sleepy-eyed clerks remained on their stools. One of his secretaries was upriver on company business; the other, if he wasn't stealing a nap somewhere, was at the warehouse overseeing the loading of a rubber shipment destined for New Orleans. March's partner, Robert Beal, was taking coffee with their banker this afternoon.

The heat inside his office was scarcely less intense than that outside. Not a murmur of complaint passed Miss Pritchard's pale lips, but March noticed she swayed slightly on her feet. Taking her arm again despite a tug of resistance, he led her through his private office and out to the back veranda, which overlooked a muddy ditch. After settling her in a chair beneath the shade of a mahogany tree, he rang for his maid and instructed her to bring beer for Miss Pritchard and *cafezinho,* the strong sugared coffee that slipped down the throat like liquid fire, for himself.

As March had expected, Miss Pritchard gulped the beer thirstily. She shuddered in distaste, then gave him an embarrassed look and extended her glass for more.

"It's cooler here," she said eventually, nodding toward the branches overhead. "Is it always this hot?"

"Actually," he said, watching her as she tried not to

drink too fast. "Today is rather mild. I'd say it's usually hotter."

Although he noticed her pointed disapproval of his attire, he did not apologize for his rumpled jacket or his plaited sandals. Nor did he admit he had donned the tie and waistcoat only on the chance that she would appear. Looking at Miss Pritchard intently, he decided she definitely had the makings of a grand martyr. If by some quirk of circumstance she remained in the tropics, he could readily envision her striving mightily to maintain the worst English traditions amid conditions wildly unsuited to them and making everyone around her miserable in the attempt.

"Is something amiss?" she inquired. A frown appeared between her startling blue-green eyes. He couldn't recall ever observing eyes quite that color before. And if she had not been Frederick Pritchard's daughter, he would have wondered if her thick, long lashes were stage lashes.

Only then did March realize he was staring at her, wondering what the Amazon sun would do to skin that pale and fair. He pictured sizzling pork and dark leather.

"I was thinking you must be sweltering in that wool ensemble," he said instead. It impressed him as foolhardy that she had not removed her felt hat or wool jacket.

"Not at all," she said tartly, raising the glass of warm beer to her lips. It was a brave and foolish lie. Heat pulsed in her cheeks and at her throat. Fresh rivulets of perspiration trickled from her temples, and her cuffs were wet. But God forbid she should remove her hat or her jacket in front of a man she had met only minutes ago. What would people think?

"Nevertheless," he said, irritated by her pretense, "I hope you brought some lightweight clothing and open shoes in all those trunks and boxes."

"All those trunks and boxes?" she repeated, turning toward the veranda railing where he stood. She studied his expression. "Is that a criticism, Mr. Addison?"

Her directness surprised him. Perhaps she was not quite the fragile creature he imagined. "Since you raise the issue," he answered levelly, "it does strike me that you're traveling heavy. You do realize, don't you, that the journey to Hiberalta is long and difficult. Part of the trip will be overland by donkey. We'll need four extra donkeys just to transport your belongings."

"Then please hire them, Mr. Addison." Wearily, she lifted a gloved hand to her temple as if exploring the beginning of a headache. "As I can't think of a tactful way to state this, I shall speak frankly. Your responsibility is to see that I reach Hiberalta. It is not your obligation to pass judgment on what items I chose to take with me." Having delivered this dictum, she turned her head toward the ditch and lifted her glass of beer.

March straightened abruptly and his dark eyes glittered. His original impression of Miss Pritchard underwent a swift reevaluation. This English rose had thorns.

"Let's set something straight, Miss Pritchard. I am not your employee. You don't instruct me to hire donkeys or anything else. If—and I say if—I decide to allow you to accompany me upriver, it will be solely as a favor to your father. And *if* you accompany me, you will do exactly as I say exactly when I say it. That is a condition of your passage. Is that clear? Because if you disagree, then you and I will part company right now!"

A flash of anxiety widened her gaze for an instant. Then it disappeared, but her irritation remained.

"Really, Mr. Addison, you needn't threaten me. If you find yourself incapable of coping with a few trunks and boxes, I shall secure transport elsewhere."

"Excellent, Miss Pritchard, you do that." Incapable? Who the hell did she think she was speaking to? "But a three-thousand-mile journey is a bloody expensive undertaking and alternative transport won't come cheap." He stared at her. "Which brings us to the first of several peculiarities I noted in your letter."

"Which you did not bother to answer." She sat a little straighter and it was clear to March they had gotten off to a very poor beginning. It couldn't be helped. He and this type of woman were destined to raise each other's hackles.

"Had I responded to your letter the day I received it, my response would have reached London about the time you were crossing the equator. I suspect you dispatched your letter only a month or so before you dispatched yourself."

Her chin lifted. "A letter from Brazil takes more than two months to reach London? I didn't know."

"While I'm willing to transport you to Hiberalta, it impresses me as unlike Frederick Pritchard to request such a favor. It seems more likely your father would have contacted me directly, that he would have arranged a bank credit to cover your expenses, and that he would have accompanied you or insisted on providing a companion."

A flush of discomfort tinted her cheeks and she stood abruptly. "Whatever expense you incur on my behalf will be reimbursed when we reach Hiberalta." She hugged her reticule against her body. "I have my own money for incidental expenses."

"Miss Pritchard—why do you wish to go to Hiberalta?" March demanded. "Hiberalta is a rubber settlement. It's a muddy, unpleasant little town—if a collection of offices and shacks can be called a town—clinging to the edge of the river with nothing whatsoever to recommend it. I assure you that description makes Hiberalta sound far more appealing than it is."

The pink deepened in her cheeks and she tugged at her gloves. "I'm not accustomed to people prying into my personal affairs, Mr. Addison. Perhaps the custom is different in Brazil, but in England such questions are considered very rude." Her icy stare was clearly intended to remind him that he was an Englishman and as such was displaying an offensive lapse of manners.

March was on the verge of explaining to her that her

destination was as much his affair as hers and had become so the moment she had sent him her letter requesting that he transport her halfway up the Amazon. But before he could utter a sound she reached inside her reticule and withdrew a packet of letters. "These arrived for you on the *Victoria,"* she said.

The packet smelled faintly of lilac and verbena. A quick glance through the bundle markedly improved March's spirits. There was a statement from his bank in London, three letters from his British brokers, several from friends, and a long-awaited packet from Malaya. Mail was infrequent and therefore of consuming interest when it arrived. "We have many things to discuss, Miss Pritchard. But I'm sure you're exhausted from your voyage and would prefer to rest," he said, more interested in his mail than in continuing an annoying conversation. "If you're ready, I'll escort you to your hotel."

"I supposed we would discuss the journey."

He glanced up with a distracted expression. "We will. But not now." It had not escaped his notice that the mail packet contained no letter from her father. More important at the moment, however, were the letters from his British brokers and the packet from Malaya. Only a supreme exercise of will prevented him from tearing open the thick envelopes at once. "We'll continue this discussion over dinner. At the moment I imagine you're eager to get settled, begin unpacking, and have a bath."

Her eyebrows took flight again and her full lips compressed into a line. Her small shoulders stiffened.

"Oh for God's sake." His irritation returned full force. "You are no longer in England, Miss Pritchard. In Brazil we have the sense to recognize that people bathe. Mentioning the fact does not tip anyone into a case of the vapors."

"Surely even Brazilians possess a sense of decency," she murmured, her voice thin with offense.

"It appears the Brazilian view of decency is more

realistic than your own. Here in Brazil we have body parts and refer to them by name. We bathe. We itch and scratch. We blow our noses and occasionally make rude noises. Does that shock you, Miss Pritchard? If you intend to remain in the Amazon for any length of time, I'd advise a more sensible attitude about what is shocking or you'll spend most of your days irritating everyone by falling into near constant swoons."

It was a rude speech born of annoyance and lack of patience. Predictably, Miss Pritchard reacted as if March had doused her with ice water. Shock drained the color from her face. She began to speak, thought better of it and clenched her teeth instead. Eulalie Pritchard glared at him, then turned on her muddy heels and marched toward the door.

"I'm capable of finding my way to the Hotel Central without assistance, Mr. Addison. You need not trouble yourself to escort me," she said without looking at him.

"As you wish," he responded tightly. He had no patience for people who took offense at the truth. If she preferred to walk in the heat rather than share a carriage with him, if she chose to indulge a fit of sulks, that was agreeable to him. Speaking loudly enough for her to overhear, he instructed one of the clerks to run to the stables on the corner and unhitch his carriage. She stopped in the doorway and he thought he noticed a satisfactory drop of her shoulders. Then she straightened, squared her chin, and stepped outside to the front veranda.

He followed at a leisurely pace, pausing on the top step to lean against the vine-tangled post. "We are agreed to dinner, Miss Pritchard?"

"Yes," she answered through clenched teeth and with enormous reluctance.

"I shall call at your hotel at six."

"I shall expect you at precisely eight o'clock, Mr. Addison, the proper dinner hour." Her tone indicated an enthusiasm equal to that she would have felt at the prospect of dining with Attila the Hun.

"I shall expect you to answer a great many questions, Miss Pritchard."

"I shall expect you to appear in proper dinner attire, Mr. Addison."

Ah yes, he thought, smiling. Definitely a martyr type. If there were not sufficient inconveniences wherever she was, Miss Pritchard would construct her own. Grinning, he watched her signal to the driver of the donkey cart to follow her, then set off up the street at a brisk pace. During the few minutes they had been inside, the sun had dried the mud and baked the street into a clay ribbon. A haze of powdery gray and red dust overhung the rutted lane. He waited on the veranda, expecting her to turn back, choking and wheezing, to beg the use of his carriage.

When she continued walking, he shook his head and smiled. The sooner he put her on a ship bound for home the better. Miss Eulalie Pritchard might be lovely to look at, but he strongly suspected that if she actually attempted the journey upriver to Hiberalta, she would drive him crazy before they lost sight of Pará.

The town square came into sight before Lalie slowed her steps and calmed enough to realize she was gasping for breath. Black dots speckled her vision. Staggering, holding her side, she veered toward a bench beneath a spreading cedar tree and collapsed onto it to await the donkey cart, which progressed at a more prudent pace.

Pulling off her hat, she fanned her flushed face furiously. March Addison was a rude, crude, insufferable bore. She could hardly believe this was the same man she had met ten years ago. Granted, she had been only fourteen and not as discerning then as now. But neither had she been the only young lady at the Earl of Aden's garden party to think his son, the Honorable March Addison, elegant, charming, and dashingly handsome.

She found it nearly impossible to reconcile that earlier image of March Addison with the man she had just left. He was still handsome enough, even unshaven, with longish hair and dressed in crumpled clothing. She conceded that much. He was tall and sun-bronzed, his dark eyes hypnotically intense, his mouth wide and sensual. But he lacked the barest hint of charm and clearly possessed not a sliver of regard for propriety. The prospect of spending weeks in his company sent a shudder of distaste down Lalie's spine.

"Good heavens!" she said, frowning.

She was embarked on the greatest adventure of her life, in a strange and exotic country, surrounded by unique sights, sounds, and smells, and what was she doing? She was wasting time fuming over March Addison. After making a face, Lalie firmly pushed him out of her thoughts. She adjusted her parasol then drew a breath and looked around with eager interest.

Once away from the wharf, she decided, Pará was a pretty town. Shade trees lined the main thoroughfares. The streets were unpaved but broad enough to accommodate carriages and horse trolleys. The architecture was Portuguese colonial, a colorful display of tiled façades against dark wooden frames and shutters. Most of the shops and residences were encircled by wide verandas.

Brightly colored birds chattered in the trees along the street. Even the trees themselves seemed exotic, foreign, and wonderfully beautiful.

When the donkey cart caught up to her, she stood a little unsteadily and set off toward the town square. Immediately the oppressive heat descended. Aside from herself, no people of quality appeared on the dusty streets. Either no one walked in Pará, or the gentry were tucked away out of the dust and heat. For the first time it occurred to her that it might appear a trifle unseemly to arrive at her hotel on foot.

By the time she limped into the lobby of the Hotel Central, she was dizzy from the heat and her feet had swollen inside her boots. Her corset felt as if it had shrunk two sizes. She was too exhausted to care that several of the black and white tiles were missing from the hotel's lobby floor or that strips of wallpaper peeled from the walls like graying ribbons.

Pausing in front of a cloudy mirror to smooth down her skirts, she peered at her reflection then gasped in dismay. Dried mud ringed her hem and caked her boots. She was soaked through with perspiration. When she removed her hat, a ball of auburn fuzz exploded around her feverish cheeks. Good Lord. And she had looked askance at that insufferable March Addison for wearing a wilted collar? What on earth had he thought of her? Suddenly she became aware that she smelled of perspiration and hot wet wool. As March Addison had so rudely predicted, what she longed for most was a cool bath.

Thanking heaven there was no one in the hotel lobby to witness that she had arrived on foot, disheveled and alone, Lalie mustered her flagging spirits and walked to the registration desk.

"I am Miss Eulalie Pritchard from London," she announced. "I'll need someone to bring my things inside. I want a large pitcher of ice water brought to my suite at once, and I want . . ." How should she state this? "I want a tub."

The man behind the tall counter smiled at her uncomprehendingly. He wore a soiled shirt that might once have been white. If Lalie had met him in the street, she would have shied away in fear, thinking him a cutpurse.

"Do you speak English?"

"No speek Englaise," he answered cheerfully. After a moment during which Lalie stared at him in alarm, he turned to leave the counter.

"Wait!" she shouted at him, hoping volume would somehow aid comprehension. "I am Miss Pritchard." She pointed a gloved finger at herself then tapped the yellowing registration ledger on the counter. She felt giddy with heat, exhaustion, and the effort to make herself understood. It was nearly as stifling in the lobby as it was outside. "I wrote ahead. You are expecting me."

"Eek spect."

"Yes." Lalie had dreamed of adventure but she was beginning to suspect she might lack the talent for the actual practicalities. Gesturing toward the doors leading to the street, she shouted, "Please bring in my things."

The man smiled broadly, shrugged, and wandered through a door behind the counter leaving her alone, ready to collapse where she stood. Standing in her wool traveling ensemble was like baking inside an oven. She made squishing sounds when she walked. Heat pounded in her cheeks and her hair was wet with perspiration.

Not knowing what else to do, she dragged herself across the lobby then outside and waved her hands to instruct the driver of the donkey cart to unload her belongings. While she stood on the street watching, she could feel the sun piercing her parasol, her hat, and pounding onto her head. Perspiration ran down her face like wax melting down the sides of a candle.

Before the cart driver had unloaded all her luggage, a small filthy boy darted across the dirt street, scooped up one of her hat boxes and ran off with it. A choked protest caught in Lalie's throat. Worse, she could see others studying the situation, judging their chances for success. Gathering her strength, she stepped forward and snapped down her parasol. Using it like a club, she struck out at a small dodging thief who still managed to make off with a box of reading material.

Tears of frustration stung her eyes. What kind of barbaric country was this? The men were rude, the climate hideous, the people didn't speak English, and her luggage was not safe. Already, she herself was running after small boys and striking them across the shoulders. The wasted effort and the suspicion that her romantic adventure was beginning very badly was enough to do her in. Defeated, she stood defenseless as the young thieves encircled her.

A rattle of Portuguese sounded over her shoulder, the sharp words firing like bullets. The small boys scattered, and the driver of the donkey cart looked up then applied himself to unloading the cart with alacrity.

"Thank—" The words died in Lalie's throat as she turned to her benefactor.

The woman standing before her wore rouge and paint, and the skimpiest dress Lalie had ever seen. The dress was sewn of a gauzy material that ended scandalously high above the woman's ankles and, to Lalie's horror, the material was so sheer one could see the woman wore nothing underneath except a pair of knee-length knickers. Before Lalie averted her flaming face, she noticed the brown tips of the woman's breasts through the bodice of the dress. Shock stiffened her body. Hastily spinning aside, she stared at nothing, too stunned to speak or move.

"The little bastards will steal anything," the woman said in accented English, her full vermilion lips scowling. "Now then, do you need help inside?"

"No!" The woman was a soiled dove, of course. Who else would appear in public wearing paint and a gauze dress, her hair undressed and hanging loose? The horror of it sent tiny shudders through Lalie's body. But she couldn't help sliding another fascinated look toward the woman. She had imagined nothing. The woman was still painted like a tart, still wore a dress that was one thin layer better than being naked, and she still smelled of strong, cheap perfume.

"Suit yourself." With a shrug, the woman stepped past her.

"Wait." Biting her lip, Lalie watched the woman swing around and look at her curiously. The sun hammered on Lalie's head, dots swam in front of her eyes. "I . . . I do need assistance." Raising her eyes, steadfastly holding her gaze above the woman's chin, she drew a breath and made herself speak. "I would be deeply grateful if you would speak to the registration clerk on my behalf. I can't make him understand that I wrote ahead for accommodations."

If a respectable person chanced to drive past at this moment and observe her engaged in conversation with such a woman, her reputation would be ruined before she had passed a full day in Pará. Crimson flared on her cheeks and she pressed her gloves together. She averted her gaze from the horse trolley laboring up the center of the street. And she didn't glance at the carriages circling the town square, hoping if she didn't notice them, the occupants would not notice her standing head to head with a ruined woman. Someone stepped out of the hotel door, and Lalie swiftly ducked her head, holding her breath in anguished embarrassment until the man had passed behind her.

"My name is Clea Paralta," the woman said as if an introduction was wanted or necessary. Then she shouted and waved at the donkey cart and the driver hastened to carry Lalie's luggage inside while Clea Paralta's scowl held the gang of small thieves at bay.

To Lalie's vast relief the lobby was still deserted as she and her new benefactor crossed to the desk. The desk clerk grinned broadly and said something that made Clea toss back her black hair and laugh. Lalie wished the floor would open and swallow her. She prayed no one would enter the lobby. Averting her eyes, she waited in an agony of impatience until Clea Paralta tugged her sleeve. She had to force herself not to shrink from the woman's touch.

"Everything is arranged," the woman announced.

"Would you inquire if a letter has arrived for me?" Lalie asked in a whisper. Please, she prayed silently, let there be a letter from Sir Percival Sterling.

Clea exchanged a word with the desk clerk then looked back at Lalie with an expression of interest. "There is no letter, Senhorita Pritchard."

The soiled dove knew her name. Worse, Lalie not only knew the name of a woman of the streets but was indebted to her. The realization made her feel light-headed. "Did you mention I wanted a tub?" she murmured weakly.

"A tub and water will be delivered to your room within the hour." Clea Paralta raised a painted eyebrow. "You should have mentioned March Addison's name. Eladio would have fetched someone at once who spoke English."

Lalie glanced up from smoothing her damp wool skirts and her eyes widened in surprise. "How on earth did you know I'm acquainted with Mr. Addison?"

Clea Paralta smiled and her black eyes sparkled. Suddenly Lalie realized she was a striking woman. "You stopped by March's office before coming here. There are no secrets on the river, Senhorita Pritchard." Her laugh was low and throaty. "In the future if you encounter a problem, just mention March's name. Everyone in the Amazon recognizes March Addison's name because everyone along the river owes March a favor."

Lalie's stare deepened. The soiled dove called March Addison by his given name? The implication horrified her. Addison was a worse degenerate than she had dared imagine.

Desperate to escape the woman's presence as well as her overpowering perfume before someone entered the lobby, Lalie dug in her reticule and emerged with a few shillings. She did her best to avoid touching Clea Paralta's palm with her gloved hand when she pushed the money at her.

"You may go now," Lalie said stiffly.

Clea Paralta looked at the money, her smile fading. Her black eyes stared at Lalie. Then she smiled again, shrugged, and said something in Portuguese to the desk clerk who looked at Lalie and grinned.

"We do not pay for kindness along the river," Clea Paralta explained in a level voice. Her black eyes twinkled with impish amusement when she spoke again. "We repay a favor with a favor. The next time I need help, I will come to you, do you see?"

"Oh my heaven," Lalie breathed. Wide-eyed and horrified, she watched Clea Paralta swing her hips as she strode across the lobby. The instant the door swung shut, she lifted her hem and dashed after the men carrying her luggage up a flight of narrow stairs. Clea Paralta would seek her out? She fervently hoped not.

Chapter 2

Lalie almost failed to recognize March Addison when he entered the deserted hotel lobby. He had shaved since she had seen him last and trimmed his dark mustache. The light from the lobby's dim overhead chandelier shone on the stylish pomade with which he had dressed his hair. His collar appeared a bit limp but was dazzlingly white against his tanned skin, and she was pleased to notice his tie was fashionably knotted. He wore a proper dinner jacket and trousers. For a long moment Lalie stared at him then drew a deep breath that strained the lacings on her French corset. This was the elegantly handsome man she remembered from years before, the man who could take a woman's breath away, who could make female stomachs behave in strange, fluttery ways.

Then she saw his feet. He still wore plaited sandals.

The moment he crossed the lobby, she snapped, "Really, Mr. Addison. You can't appear in public wearing sandals!"

One dark eyebrow lifted. "Look around you, Miss Pritchard. Who is to observe and disapprove?" He indicated the empty lobby. "You'll discover a quarter of Brazil's population wears sandals. The remaining three quarters go barefoot. Only a glutton for punishment would wear closed leather shoes in this climate."

Not for one moment did Lalie believe this. But he had raised a point that did puzzle her. She had expected the lobby to be crowded with guests waiting before the large shuttered doors to the hotel dining room.

As inconspicuously as she could manage, she brushed her glove across her high lace collar, hoping to dislodge a mosquito she heard buzzing there. "Where is everyone? Are we early?"

"We're late, Miss Pritchard. I imagine the other guests have dined and retired to their rooms to seek refuge beneath their mosquito netting."

"They've dined already?" she asked, frowning up at him. "Before eight?"

"In the tropics people dine early, before the mosquitoes make life unbearable." Clasping his hands behind his back, Addison rocked back on his heels and inspected the faded frescoes on the ceiling.

"Shocking!" she murmured, her tone heavy with disapproval. Immediately she felt an invasion of insects crawling on her exposed skin and tried to assure herself it was only her imagination. But it wasn't: she saw mosquitoes everywhere now, collecting around the candle sconces, swarming toward her and surrounding Addison.

"Everything seems to shock you, Miss Pritchard."

"Why didn't you explain this custom?" She glared up at him.

"I tried. But you insisted on having it your way." Taking her gloved hand, he tucked it around his arm. "Shall we go in before they stop serving for the evening?"

The small egret plume that had cost her a fortune at Miss Fannie's in Bond Street quivered atop her auburn curls as he led her forward into the hotel dining room. She had hoped it might be cooler on the ground floor, but she had been mistaken.

Candles glowed on every table though the dining room

was now deserted. The smell of women's scent and powder, and the pungent odor of cigar smoke lingered in the room. Lalie accepted a seat by the window overlooking the town square and felt her light muslin gown beginning to stick to her shoulders and arms. Not a breath of air flowed through the opened window, just a steady flow of insects.

"The lady will have champagne, and I'll have *cachaça,*" Addison said, waving aside a limp menu.

"Champagne?" she asked. Even though he had ordered in Portuguese, Lalie had managed to recognize the word. Before he could respond, she noticed a mosquito settle on Addison's neck. She imagined a hundred crawling on her own.

"Brazil is a country of extremes, Miss Pritchard. People suffer an appalling lack of necessities and enjoy a surplus of nonessentials. This year the most abundant nonessential is champagne. In shacks where there is no food to be had, you can find several bottles of excellent champagne." He lifted a hand and smiled. "Before you ask, *cachaça* is considered the national drink. It's cane liquor, very strong. I don't recommend it until you've been in the Amazon long enough to acclimatize yourself."

Something in his voice suggested he doubted she would remain long in Brazil. "Why is there no food?" she asked, frowning. Giving in, she rubbed her hand across her neck, squashing a squadron of mosquitoes.

He stared at her, a look of displeasure in his eyes. "You don't know? Miss Pritchard, why on earth are you here? Why aren't you sitting before a comfortable hearth in London reading travel books? I suspect you're far better at reading than traveling. I assure you, the Amazon is no place for ignorant young women seeking adventure. My advice to you: go home."

Color blazed in her cheeks as fiercely as the anger blazed in her eyes. Leaning forward, she abandoned any effort to treat this offensive man with politeness. Courtesy was wasted on March Addison and only served to place her at a disadvantage. She spoke in a furious whisper. "You are a rude, unpleasant man, Mr. Addison. I've spent perhaps a total of one hour in your company during which time you have labeled me stupid and ignorant. I believe I am entitled to an apology at once!"

"Miss Pritchard, are you listening to what I'm saying?" He seemed as angry as she, although Lalie couldn't think why he should be. "We're not discussing a cruise down the Thames. We're talking about the most treacherous river in the world. People have gotten lost a few feet from shore and have died, Miss Pritchard. There are man-eating fish in the river. And the most venomous snakes in existence. If the mosquitoes bother you now—and obviously they do—imagine black flies whose bite feels like the sting of a scorpion. There are bands of Indians hidden in the jungle who would not think twice about using you as a target for their blowguns. A man can die in a dozen different ways out here, and none of them are pleasant. This is no place for a woman. Most particularly not a woman as ill prepared as you." His eyes narrowed. "Your bicycle was delivered to my office shortly after you departed, Miss Pritchard. A bicycle, for God's sake! What on earth were you thinking?"

"The purser found it? Thank goodness. I was told they'd lost it." Her bicycle was a Rudge Whitworth, advertised as the smartest and best. She had spent many determined hours pedaling over the bumpy streets of Hackney, establishing herself as a progressive woman, an image that pleased her enormously.

Addison stared at her, then lifted his hands and let them fall. "Miss Pritchard, you haven't the faintest notion what's happening in Brazil. Upriver, people are shooting each other to settle disputes over who owns which trees. Bolivia, Colombia, and Brazil are fighting over borders. Bandits frequently kill an entire ship's crew to steal a single ball of rubber or a sack of sugar. This is one of the poorest, most dangerous countries on earth. And here you come with your proper little gloves and your shiny bicycle ready for a lovely bit of sightseeing. I say again, Miss Pritchard—you've had a nice little adventure already. Now go home."

"I am not as stupid as you choose to believe, Mr. Addison." Her eyes had darkened to a stormy navy color. In her lap, her hands balled into fists. "And you won't scare me if that's what you're attempting to do. I've heard all about the excitements and the dangers. I've heard about the horrid big spiders and the savages and the alligators—"

"Caimans, Miss Pritchard. Not the same thing. May I inquire who informed you of these excitements as you refer to them?"

"My father went on at length, and I've heard dozens of exciting tales from my fiancé!" She hadn't intended to reveal her wedding plans until she obtained confirmation from Sir Percival that he had received her letter promising to join him at Hiberalta. It annoyed her that Addison had forced her hand.

"I see," he said after a moment. "And who, may I inquire, is your fiancé?"

In for a penny, in for a pound. Now she'd have to confide everything. Well, perhaps not everything. Lifting her chin, Lalie announced with pride, "I have accepted Sir Percival Sterling's offer of marriage." Sir Percival's name would put Mr. March Addison firmly in his place.

Addison's dark eyes narrowed. His mouth thinned to a line so tight it disappeared into his mustache. "Son of a bitch," he said softly. "Of course. I should have guessed. That's why you want to go to Hiberalta."

"Mr. Addison!" She half rose from her seat. "I absolutely will not tolerate profanity!"

"Sit down!" His voice roared across the deserted dining room. He looked as if he wished to throttle her. Embarrassed by the scene he was making even though there was no one to see, Lalie sat. In stiff silence they watched the waiter relight the candle in the center of their table. Addison's shout had extinguished the flame.

"Are you ready to order, Senhor Addison?" the waiter murmured.

"We'll both have *pato no tucupi,"* he snapped.

The waiter hesitated, glancing uncertainly at Lalie before he bowed and withdrew. She noticed the man's speculation and bit her lip. Whatever Addison had ordered, she would swallow every bite if it killed her. Whatever he could eat, by heaven so could she. She drained her champagne glass in a gulp.

"What do you know about Percy Sterling?" Addison asked after the waiter had gone. He refilled her glass.

"I beg your pardon?" She abandoned her heroic effort to ignore the persistent multitude of mosquitoes. Swatting desperately at the cloud before her face, she attempted to inform him with her expression that his prying was objectionable.

"Let's not go through that business about your affairs being none of mine." He stared at her. "This is important, Miss Pritchard."

He was hopeless. Good manners were not part of his repertoire. "I know everything I need to know about Sir Percival," she said with a sigh of resignation. "I intend to marry him. He isn't a stranger, for heaven's sake."

March Addison's steady gaze unnerved her. She was glad when he finally spoke. "Aside from Sterling's wealth and title, what else do you really know about him?"

Exasperation heated her cheeks. "Sir Percival is charming and witty. He has exquisite manners, a quality which apparently has no meaning to you. And . . ." She scowled at him. "I don't have to justify anything to you!" A lengthy silence began. Lalie drank more champagne. She smoothed her muslin skirts. She peered out the window. She slapped at mosquitoes. When she couldn't tolerate another moment of silence, she snapped, "Will you please stop staring at me as if I've suddenly sprouted horns?"

"I assume you know Sir Percy squandered the fortune he inherited. I assume you also know he is rebuilding that fortune at Hiberalta. But do you know how Sir Percy harvests his rubber?"

"Of course not. Sir Percival is too much the gentleman to discuss business with ladies. However, I do hope to learn more about rubber farming before we arrive at the plantation."

"Farming? Plantation?" March Addison rubbed a hand over his eyes. "Miss Pritchard . . . you are . . . you are simply hopeless." Leaning back in his chair, he studied the angry color flooding her cheeks. "Would it make any difference to you if I explained that rubber is one of the dirtiest businesses in the world? That slavery is involved, and torture? That—"

"Stop! I don't believe any of that!" She leaned forward, her fists clenched beside her plate. "If rubber is as 'dirty' as you claim, Mr. Addison, then why does your firm broker rubber all over the world? If I understand my father's comments, you too have made a fortune in the rubber trade!"

For several minutes he regarded her thoughtfully. "Yes," he conceded finally. "I'm as guilty as anyone. I've profited handsomely. And by helping to create a market I've contributed to the atrocities. But no more, Miss Pritchard." He met her blazing eyes. "I can't look away any longer. This will be my last trip upriver. My partner is buying my interest in the firm. I won't be part of this any longer."

"Part of what, Mr. Addison? Part of supplying the world with the rubber it's clamoring for? We can't turn back the clock. Rubber is part of our lives now. The world needs rubber for hundreds of items. Rubber is the wave of the future, Mr. Addison. And—"

"Spare me Sir Percy's rhetoric, Miss Pritchard. You don't know what you're talking about. There is no point in continuing this discussion."

Their dinner arrived and Lalie welcomed the interruption as an opportunity to regain her composure. Her strident behavior astonished and unnerved her. Never in her life had she met anyone like March Addison. One moment she was thinking how handsome he was, the next moment she was shaking with anger. One thing was certain—he brought out the worst in her. Her voice had become shrill; her fingers trembled; all semblance of tact, charm, and courtesy had fled. Family and friends would not have recognized her.

After a moment she realized she was staring at her plate without recognizing a thing on it. "Excuse me, but—what is this?"

Whatever it was, Addison appeared to relish every bite. "It's stewed duck and greens, highly spiced." Amusement sparkled in his dark eyes. "The river people claim *pato no tucupi* makes the heat seem less intense. Some say it's intoxicating. You may order something else if you prefer."

She watched him enjoy another bite before she sampled the dish. The first bite had an exotic taste, spicy as Addison had warned, but not unendurable. The second bite brought abrupt involuntary tears to her eyes, and she had to gulp some champagne before she could go on. By the fourth bite she could no longer feel her mouth. Champagne dribbled down her chin when she tried to drink because she couldn't feel the glass against her lips. Her tongue seemed to have vanished, it was simply not there anymore.

Quickly Lalie raised her napkin to blot the champagne from her chin. As she did so, a giggle escaped her. The idea of her mouth being dead seemed suddenly to be wildly funny. The giggle was followed by a burst of laughter. The laughter built on itself. It seemed hilarious that she was laughing, that anything seemed funny. But everything seemed funny.

Addison smiled at her. "This dish occasionally causes

newcomers to feel as if they've drunk a bottle or two of spirits. I must say, this is a welcome change, Miss Pritchard."

That too struck her as comical and she laughed until tears spilled down her cheeks. Remarkably, unbelievably, she didn't suffer from the heat anymore. The sweltering candlelit room seemed pleasant now. Her corset no longer made her feel as if it were squeezing the life out of her.

Most remarkable of all, she thought, swallowing another bite, March Addison had undergone a startling transformation. She couldn't guess how this had happened and didn't want to think about it, but a moment ago he had impressed her as an ogre and a scoundrel. Now he was so handsome he stole her breath away and she couldn't stop staring at him.

"No more champagne for the lady," he murmured to the waiter. His voice sent a shiver of pleasure down her spine. Why hadn't she noticed before what a lovely deep voice he had? Rich in timbre, baritone in pitch, an altogether seductive voice.

"Miss Pritchard, your ignorance of the Amazon is so profound that I have to wonder if you thought to bring quinine?"

She was vaguely aware he had offered an insult, but his reference to her ignorance seemed humorous. Gales of uncontrollable laughter shook her body and she thanked heaven they were alone in the large, dark dining room. The Voice of Propriety that lived in her head sternly announced she was making a spectacle of herself but she couldn't stop laughing. She wiped her eyes and tried to get hold of herself.

Addison nodded, then reached into his waistcoat pocket and withdrew a tin box that he pushed across the table linen. "Take two of these every day, Miss Pritchard. Every day without fail. To protect yourself against malaria."

Lit by the candle glow, his face was a fierce golden bronze. The pomade made his dark brown hair look as black as his eyes, eyes like ebony whirlpools. And his mouth—Lalie contemplated his wide, sensual mouth, wondering if March Addison's mouth was as numb as hers. If he kissed her would either of them feel it? Would his mustache tickle? She had no idea where this shameless image sprang from, but it sent her into gales of embarrassed laughter.

"If you only knew what I was thinking," she murmured weakly. Having lost the use of her tongue, the words came out, "If oo ony oo wash I's sinking."

When she recovered from a fresh convulsion of laughter, she pushed at the egret feather, which had sagged over her ear. A long auburn curl dropped to her breast, a mishap that would have mortified her an hour ago. Now she lifted the curl off her breast and flipped it over her shoulder. "What happened to my champagne?" The words emerged slurred and almost unintelligible. "Oh. Oh my," she gasped, wiping at her eyes.

March Addison smiled then laughed. He removed a cigar from his inside pocket and lit it without requesting her permission. "And what are you thinking, Miss Pritchard?"

It was the champagne and the crazy light-headedness caused by the *pato no tucupi* that made her say it. She cast a quick look around the deserted dining room then leaned forward and whispered in a conspiratorial tone.

"I met a soiled dove, Mr. Addison." A thrill of daring coursed through her body. She could hardly believe she was admitting to such a thing. "And she claims she knows *you!*"

"Yes, I know."

When he smiled and said nothing more, she tossed back another fallen curl and stared at him. "Well? Aren't you going to defend yourself?"

"From what, Miss Pritchard? Clea Paralta is a friend of mine. I've known her for years. Clea's a generous, warm-hearted woman. You were fortunate to run into her."

"You admit knowing her? And you . . . you think I was *fortunate* to encounter her?" Incredulity sent her voice into a spiral. "Miss Paralta is a woman of the streets! A . . . a . . ." She threw out her hands. "It was the most embarrassing, the most awkward moment of my life!" She wasn't laughing now. "I pray no one in a passing carriage observed me speaking to a woman of that sort."

"Really?" Addison examined the glowing tip of his cigar, then raised an expressionless gaze. "How many of those people in passing carriages stopped to assist you? Did any of the hotel guests rush to lend a hand? Did someone from the square run to offer assistance?"

"No. I had no choice. I had to—"

"My point, Miss Pritchard, is that Clea Paralta is the one person who troubled herself to offer assistance. You might ponder that point."

"I've thought of hardly anything else! I keep wondering if anyone noticed—"

"We won't speak of Clea anymore." He tasted the cup of *cafezinho* that had appeared in front of him without Lalie having noticed. "Miss Pritchard, does your father know where you are?"

She waved a hand at the revolting smoke curling from his cigar, then tossed back another dripping curl and smashed a mosquito against the tablecloth. "Well, of course he knows."

"Then you have Dr. Pritchard's permission to marry Sir Percy? You are in Brazil with your father's blessings?"

She pushed up from the table, swaying giddily. She blotted her lips then dropped her napkin on the floor. As it seemed about a mile to the floor, she ignored the fallen napkin. She didn't see Addison move, but he materialized at her side, his arm steadying her. He guided her toward the door and suddenly all Lalie could think about was falling into her bed and diving beneath the mosquito netting. She had an idea she would be asleep before her head hit the pillow.

"Why would my father object to Sir Percival?" she asked, tossing her head. Hairpins showered across the lobby tiles. "Of course Papa approves. You have no right to ask these personal questions. I regret the necessity of pointing this out, Mr. Addison, but you really are an odious man."

"How kind of you to mention it, Miss Pritchard," he said, smiling.

"I'll rest better knowing I've drawn your attention to your failings. Now you may begin to mend your ways." Nearly all her curls had fallen to her waist. The egret feather had disappeared. She caught his hand and gave it a solemn shake. "Thank you for dinner."

The instant Lalie grasped his hand a jolt shot through her body, leaving her shaken and feeling uncomfortably hot again. Lifting wide eyes, she stared into March Addison's hard, tanned face and she swallowed a quick breath. Why did a man this handsome, this dangerously exciting, have to be so infuriating? For a long moment, they stared at each other, standing much too close.

Then, flushing with confusion and embarrassment, Lalie jerked her hand away and wrenched her gaze from his mouth. Wobbling, she set a course for the staircase and pulled herself up the stairs. At the first landing, she turned and waved at March Addison, who stood at the bottom of the stairs, smoking and watching her thoughtfully.

"White lies don't count," she whispered, secure in the knowledge that he couldn't hear. She wasn't speaking to him anyway. In fact, she was doing her best not to think of him. She addressed the remark to the Voice of Propriety.

* * *

"You're keeping an eye on her, of course," Robert Beal said, shifting his bulk in a wrought-iron chair. Robert Beal was built like an egg with a smaller mustachioed egg on top. Unlike March, who dressed for comfort, Beal wore a white linen suit that strained at the seams. As financial manager of the firm he felt it wasn't enough to be successful, one had to look prosperous as well. One never knew if one's banker employed spies.

March nodded and lifted his face to the sun shining through a tear in the awning. "Rafael and Cadiz stay with Miss Pritchard during the day. I have one man stationed outside her door and two in the hotel lobby at night."

"Any trouble?"

"No end of trouble." March lifted a straw hat and pushed a hand through his hair. "The tally so far is two broken arms, three broken noses, a couple of knife wounds . . . it seems every man in Pará wants to steal Eulalie Pritchard's belongings or her virtue."

March and his business partner sat beneath the faded awning in front of the café named Prizini's. They sipped scalding cups of sugared *cafezinho* and watched the morning activities in the square. In particular they watched Miss Eulalie Pritchard, who strolled from market stall to stall, blissfully unaware of the two Brazilian men who followed a few steps behind. March considered it entirely possible Eulalie Pritchard was the sole person in Pará still unaware of her constant guard.

As if to prove him wrong, she emerged from a straw market and stepped up to Rafael with a bright smile. Her clear musical voice floated across the square. "As long as you seem to be following me, you might as well make yourself useful," she announced, filling Rafael's arms with her shopping parcels.

"Good God," March marveled. "She thinks they're admirers."

Robert Beal laughed. "You think they're not? Good

heavens, man, look at their faces. God help the bloke who tries to harm her. They'll rip his heart out." Beal leaned back in his chair and lit a cigar, watching as Rafael and Cadiz followed Miss Pritchard to the next stall. "How long are you going to keep her under wraps, March? Sarah is pestering me. She'd like to invite your Miss Pritchard to tea."

"She is not *my* Miss Pritchard." He beckoned to the waiter for more *cafezinho*. "If Sarah wishes to extend an invitation, by all means permit her to do so."

His idea had been to isolate Miss Pritchard and ignore her for several days in the hope she would become bored and go home. Also he knew the Hotel Central came alive at mealtimes. He felt confident Miss Pritchard was learning a great deal of dismaying and possibly frightening information over her dinners. Enough, he hoped, to discourage her from accompanying him to Hiberalta. He had relied on the probability that the tales she heard would be grim enough to persuade her to return to England immediately.

It appeared his plan had failed.

Unlike the other hotel residents, who bolted their meals then retired in lassitude to their rooms to await their departure, Eulalie Pritchard emerged each morning looking as crisp as a new pound note. She hadn't worn wool again. In one of her many trunks it appeared she had found a collection of light cotton dresses. One of her first purchases at the stalls had been several straw hats. On her second shopping venture, she had bought three pairs of open leather sandals. She was adapting.

Certainly she didn't appear to be languishing of boredom. In the mornings before the heat made walking inadvisable, she went exploring. Her little pink parasol had been observed circling the Teatro do Paz, one of the largest theaters in the region and Pará's pride and joy. She had left a card at the British Consulate expressing her disappointment that the consul was visiting England and thus unavailable. She had sketched the brilliantly colored Portuguese tiles facing the Gridley mansion. She knew several of the street urchins by name and purchased hard candy to scatter among them. She had even returned to the wharf to learn the names of various tropical fruits and watch the crates of rubber being loaded into the trading vessels.

"I think, my friend," Robert Beal remarked with a grin, "you had best reconcile yourself to company on the river. Miss Pritchard seems a determined sort."

"Something isn't right about all this," March said, watching her. As the sun climbed in the sky, heat rose and shimmered in the square. But if Miss Pritchard was sweating, and he didn't see how she could not be, the wet patches did not show on her white dress. She seemed impervious to the dust kicked up by horses and carriage wheels, shielding herself for a moment behind her parasol, then calmly going about her business. In some inexplicable way, she had tamed her hair. The unruly curls he noticed that first day had vanished. Despite the continuing humidity her magnificent coppery hair lay in a smooth coil on her neck, not a strand out of place.

"She says she has her father's permission to be here. She says she is expected upriver. Why do you doubt her?" Beal inclined his balding head toward the stalls. "Can you really imagine that woman—*that* woman—would deceive her family, hop a ship, and run off halfway around the world? Can you honestly think she's an adventuress, March?"

"No—I don't." He didn't know what to make of Eulalie Pritchard. But Dr. Pritchard's silence on the subject troubled him deeply. He couldn't imagine such a man sending his daughter to the tropics without a supply of quinine or other medical remedies. It had been reported to him that Miss Pritchard had purchased ointment for insect bites, a fungus powder, and tonic water. From the look of things, he would have sworn she had seen to her own packing and had done so with only the dimmest notion of what would be required in the Amazon.

Finally, why wasn't Sir Percival Sterling here to meet her and carry her upriver himself? Sterling had been in Pará as short a time as six weeks ago. Why hadn't he waited for Miss Pritchard? March's own history with Sir Percival Sterling was not a happy one and he could not imagine Sterling entrusting him with his fiancée. Yet it appeared he had.

Unless, that is, there was more to Miss Pritchard's story than she chose to reveal. He strongly suspected that was the case. The problem was, time was running out. He couldn't delay the voyage upriver long enough to contact Dr. Pritchard then wait for a reply. And he sure as hell was not going to track down Sir Percival Sterling.

He and Robert sipped their *cafezinho* in comfortable silence, watching a construction crew digging up the street. Soon Pará would have electric trolleys, reflecting the city's boom in growth and importance.

People strolled in and out of the square pausing to inspect the construction. No one hurried in the Amazon; time had less meaning here than elsewhere in the world. Heat boiled away any sense of urgency.

Of all the people crowding the square, only Eulalie Pritchard moved with purpose and briskness. March guessed she paid dearly for the show of energy. No doubt she spent the afternoons collapsed in a heap. But heaven forbid that she should display a little sense and adjust her pace to the requirements of the tropics. The tropics would have to adjust to her.

"You'll miss all this," Beal said at length. A vague wave of his hand included Prizini's, the *cafezinho,* the town, the jungle, the wharf, the river. "Nine years is a long time. You won't fit easily into society again. Whenever Sarah and I go home to London, I find myself counting the days until we can return to Pará." He smiled. "And I'm a far more patient man than you, March."

"I've made up my mind." But his partner was correct. March would miss the Amazon. The river flowed through his blood; its rhythms had become his rhythms. He knew the towns along the banks and the people and they were part of his life.

"The rubber boom has just begun. You're walking away from a fortune. Production doubled last year, and this is only the beginning. Next year we'll ship twenty-seven thousand tons through Pará. The world has developed a voracious appetite for rubber."

"I've already taken a fortune out of the river. And you're paying another fortune for my half of the firm."

They didn't discuss the atrocities that went hand in hand with producing the rubber demanded by the world, and they wouldn't. Like so many others, Robert Beal chose to ignore the stories and rumors that drifted downriver. But March had witnessed the abuses firsthand. He couldn't tell himself they didn't exist. Nor did he share Robert's conviction that the jungle Indians were savages who should be treated no better than animals.

He didn't condemn Robert for his beliefs. It was March who held the minority opinion. It was he who traveled the river and saw what was happening. And he could no longer stomach any of it. In many ways he was glad he was making his last trip up the river.

"It's Sterling, isn't it?" Beal asked in a quiet voice. "You can't stand the idea of Miss Pritchard marrying Sterling."

"Sometimes I think we know each other too well." There was no humor in March's smile.

They watched Eulalie Pritchard moving from stall to stall like a bright petaled blossom. She was so beautiful March ached inside at the sight of her. Robert was correct; it sickened him to realize she belonged to a man like Percival Sterling.

She circled the square and walked toward them holding

her parasol at a jaunty angle, her new straw hat shading her face. Rafael and Cadiz, their arms filled with parcels, trotted behind her wearing besotted expressions.

The instant she spotted March sitting at one of the tables beneath the awning, Miss Pritchard's smile turned into a scowl and she headed toward him.

With reluctance, March stood and lifted his hat. "Good morning."

"Will you join us for *cafezinho?*" Robert inquired after introductions had been made.

"Thank you," she said, taking the chair Robert pulled out for her. She bestowed a dazzling smile that left the man blinking and looking slightly dazed. But when she turned to March, it was with a look of displeasure. "I require a word with you, Mr. Addison. You have not returned my messages."

"When last we spoke, Miss Pritchard, I was given to understand my company was not welcome."

"When last we spoke you had just poisoned me with that wretched *tucupi* concoction."

Robert glanced at March. Amusement sparkled in the older man's eyes. *Pato no tucupi* was considered a rite of passage for newcomers, but women generally were exempted from the mischief.

"I can't be expected to take you sightseeing or entertain you, Miss Pritchard. I've been arranging the journey."

"I didn't wish to speak to you about arranging a sightseeing excursion. Exactly when does our journey commence, Mr. Addison? I've been waiting almost a week."

"An entire week?" He widened his eyes in a display of mock amazement. "I had no idea. Please forgive the delay, Miss Pritchard. Had I realized you were being inconvenienced in any way, naturally I would have stepped up the preparations. I can't conceive of anything more important than your convenience."

"Your apology is accepted."

March stared in astonishment. Robert Beal covered a sudden coughing fit with his cuff. The woman was utterly incredible. Either she had a hide as thick as a tapir's, or she didn't recognize sarcasm when she heard it.

"So, Mr. Addison, when will we be departing?" she inquired in a sweet voice.

"We'll depart three days from now," he said. "I'll send a list of essentials. As unlikely as it sounds, there may actually be something you forgot to pack." It continued to stagger him that she had brought a bicycle but not quinine. As if it had just occurred to him, he slapped his forehead and stared at her. "You did remember to bring a *bagunça,* didn't you? Of course you did. I can't imagine you without one."

"A *bagunça?"* she asked. A hint of uncertainty troubled her infuriatingly superior smile.

He rolled his eyes. "Really, Miss Pritchard. You don't know what a *bagunça* is?"

"Well, of course I know," she snapped. Her chin lifted. "And I have one."

From the corner of his eye March noticed Robert sucking in his cheeks and turning purple. "Excellent. Actually, I knew you would."

"I think you'll find you have underestimated me, Mr. Addison."

"I doubt that, Miss Pritchard."

Standing, she offered her hand to Robert, gave March a cold nod, then sailed back toward the stalls, undoubtedly in search of a *bagunça,* not realizing the word meant "disorder and confusion, a mess."

Robert laughed uproariously. "March, you're incorrigible. She'll hate you when she finds out."

"She hates me already," he said, grinning. "And I'm not too fond of her, either." With luck he would reach Hiberalta in record time, maybe in three months instead of five.

Three or four months on a small ship with Miss Eulalie Pritchard, the most beautiful, desirable, and aggravating woman he had ever met. Pushing aside his *cafezinho,* March ordered a *cachaça* and swallowed it neat. Still thinking about her, he ordered another.

Chapter 3

The scene at the wharves was raucous and chaotic, even along the area set aside for the smaller river vessels. Whistles blew, men shouted, horses and carriages raced along the front road. The smell of fish and rotting fruit intensified as the morning sun rose in the sky. Lalie pressed a scrap of lace to her nostrils in a vain attempt to filter the stench of burning garbage.

She stood at the foot of the wooden gangplank leading into the cargo hold of the *Addison Beal,* watching as two sweating dark-skinned men carried aboard her trunks and baggage. The moment should have been exciting, as this was the true beginning of her future. But her expression was distracted, her thoughts focused on an incident that had occurred two nights before while she waited in the hotel lobby for the dining room doors to open.

Lalie had been exchanging pleasantries with Mr. and Mrs. Griswold, new arrivals to Pará and thus more uplifting to converse with than those waiting to depart, when the hotel door burst open and Clea Paralta ran into the lobby.

Turning with the others, Lalie had stared in astonishment and dismay as Clea paused, scanning the company waiting to dine. And her heart plummeted to her toes when Clea's black eyes focused on her. In agony, she watched the woman stride directly toward her, while Mr. and Mrs. Griswold shrank away.

Indeed, everyone in the lobby melted backward, leaving her to stand alone as Clea reached her. Embarrassment as deep as any Lalie had experienced tinted her cheeks as crimson as the bow at her waist. Candles flickered in the sconces and the room began a slow spin. Lalie prayed she would crumple in a faint and escape an encounter that was certain to raise a scandal and blacken her name.

"I have to know if it's true," Clea said, stopping in front of her and peering into her anguished eyes. Clea's gaze was as wild as the tangled black hair flying around her cheeks. The dress she wore tonight was not gauze, but it was almost as revealing. The sleeves dropped off her bare shoulders, the neckline was low enough to skim the top of her nipples. If the dress failed to announce her profession, an unlikely supposition, her rouged cheeks and lips left no doubt.

"Oh, good heavens," Lalie whispered, wringing her gloved hands. Behind her the lobby had fallen absolutely silent.

"Is it true you're going to Hiberalta to marry Sir Percy?" Clea's black eyes bored into her. The woman actually gripped Lalie by the shoulders and gave her a small shake. Lalie overheard a smothered gasp behind her.

She jerked free and swallowed the cottony dryness closing her throat. "Yes. Why would you—"

Clea stumbled backward a step. Her arms fell to her sides and her breast heaved. "Damn you," she said softly, her voice choking on a sob. Then she turned and lifted her skirt nearly to her knees and ran out of the hotel lobby, leaving Lalie trembling on the black and white tiles with everyone staring at her.

With as much dignity as she could muster, Lalie lifted her head, her cheeks flaming as brightly as her hair, and she walked to the staircase, her gaze fixed straight ahead.

A low murmur began behind her, growing louder by the second. For the remainder of her sojourn at the Hotel Central Lalie took her meals in her room. And she thanked heaven that March Addison was finally ready to get under way.

Her thoughts returning to the present, she noticed him now on the upper deck of the *Addison Beal,* a cigar clamped between his strong white teeth as he strode about issuing last-minute instructions, correcting oversights no one recognized but himself. For a moment Lalie pondered the advisability of inquiring if March Addison knew why Clea Paralta had accosted her at the Hotel Central and what that peculiar exchange might have meant.

Her eyes narrowed beneath the shade of her parasol. She didn't need the Voice of Propriety to remind her that discussing a soiled dove was too scandalous to contemplate. Especially since Mr. Addison appeared to be a favored customer of the woman in question. Her mind shrank from such unpleasant thoughts. In any case she had already vowed not to speak a single unnecessary word to March Addison. March Addison was a coarse, infuriating man. Moreover, he made her feel peculiar inside. She intended to avoid his company as much as possible.

This, she realized after inspecting the *Addison Beal,* was not going to be as readily accomplished as she had supposed. The *Addison Beal,* crafted of seasoned Spanish cedar, was a midsized steamer built for utility rather than comfort or beauty. Unlike the other river vessels being loaded farther up the wharf, the *Addison Beal* was not fitted to carry immigrants to the sugar plantations, the nut fields, or the rubber settlements. The lower deck held cargo, covered by waterproof tarpaulins. Aside from herself and a small crew, there would be no passengers.

March Addison leaned over the railing above her. "Everything is stowed aboard but you, Miss Pritchard. Have you changed your mind?" He wore a battered straw hat shoved over his dark hair. His shirt collar was open almost to the waist, displaying an arrow of deeply tanned skin.

Dropping her eyes from his bare skin, Lalie scowled at her hem. He might wish she had changed her mind, but she had not. She lifted her skirts, drew a breath, then crossed the narrow gangplank. Someone led her to the upper deck where she dusted her white gloves together, shook her parasol, then gazed inquiringly about her.

"Does everything meet with your approval, Miss Pritchard?"

Sarcasm did not amuse her. "Everything appears to be in order. There seems to be no *bagunça,"* she snapped, leveling a hard stare at March Addison. She still had not forgiven him for his little joke. She had gone from stall to stall asking to buy a *bagunça,* leaving gales of laughter behind her until someone explained she was trying to purchase a confusing problem.

Addison grinned and flipped his cigar overboard. When she continued to stare at him with what she hoped was obvious contempt, he laughed out loud. Then his expression sobered. "Before we raise anchor, I'm going to offer you one last chance to tell the truth."

Lalie's spine stiffened and she bristled with indignation. "Now you're calling me a liar?"

"Let's say I believe it's possible you've been shading the truth."

"I do not lie, Mr. Addison!" At this moment she was angry enough to believe what she was saying.

"Then Dr. Pritchard is aware that you are here with me?"

"Yes!"

"And Dr. Pritchard does know and does approve of your journey to Hiberalta to marry Sir Percival Sterling. Is that also correct?"

"I told you he knows!"

Addison moved toward her. "Tell me again."

They were standing almost nose to nose. Lalie had to step back because March Addison was so close to her. He smelled of coconut oil and tobacco and faintly of perspiration. Heady male scents that made her feel slightly dizzy. But when she stepped backward, he followed, his black eyes staring intently down into hers.

"I explained this. My father wishes me to be happy!"

"That is not an answer, Miss Pritchard."

Her blue-green eyes flashed. She was not going to be bullied. "It's the only answer you are going to get, Mr. Addison. As I've told you repeatedly: my personal business is none of yours!"

"The hell it isn't. The minute you set foot on my ship, your business became mine, too. There's another thing, and I don't want any equivocating or I'll put you off this ship right now. If you were my fiancée I would have been in Pará to meet the *Victoria,* and I'd be taking you upriver myself. Why isn't Sterling here? From the look of it, he's abandoned you and left you to reach Hiberalta or not however you can. Is that the situation, Miss Pritchard?"

"Absolutely not!" Shock widened her eyes and she gasped. "Is that what you think? That I've been jilted?"

"It doesn't look as if this is a grand passion, not when the bastard can't even meet you or arrange your passage."

An incomprehensible sputter burbled on her lips. Groping behind her, she found the railing and leaned against it. "Once Sir Percival learns of these insults, he will thrash you soundly, sir! There is a perfectly honorable explanation why my fiancé isn't here to greet me and accompany me upriver."

"This ship isn't moving an inch until I hear it," Addison said, looming over her.

"I didn't understand it myself," Lalie conceded, sliding along the rail to escape him. "Not until I discovered how long it requires for mail to arrive." She resented his threatening manner and was disgusted with herself for cowering before it. "Sir Percival and I decided to marry when he visited London last autumn." At this point the truth veered one direction and Lalie went the other. She excused this division by reminding herself that March Addison had no right to know her personal business. It outraged her that he seemed to believe he did.

"Go on."

"Before Percival returned to Brazil, we decided I would follow as quickly as possible and we would marry here. I am solely to blame that Percival was not waiting to greet me."

"That doesn't surprise me, Miss Pritchard."

She glared at him and paused to compose herself. "I posted the letter to Sir Percival announcing my arrival at the same time I posted my letter to you."

Addison swore under his breath. "I see." After a moment he looked at her again. "Sterling is on the river six weeks ahead of us. It would be a miracle if your letter has caught up to him. It may never catch up, Miss Pritchard. The farther upriver one goes, the less chance there is of receiving mail. Sterling probably has no idea you're in the Amazon." He swore again.

She bit her lip and frowned, ignoring his profanity. Addison had just voiced her own fears. "That may be the case, Mr. Addison," she said slowly. "Which would explain why no letter from him was waiting at my hotel." She drew a breath and looked up at him. "Did I understand you to say Sir Percival was in Pará?"

"Six weeks ago."

Lalie sighed. Nothing about her grand romance seemed destined to flow smoothly.

"If that concludes your inquisition, Mr. Addison, may we please get under way?" Now that she knew Percival was just ahead, she was eager to depart.

"This explains a great deal," he said, still watching her. "It doesn't explain everything, but it will do for the moment."

Stepping away from the railing, she followed him to the wheelhouse. "Mr. Addison, is there any possibility we'll catch up with Sir Percival?"

He turned around so swiftly that she bumped into him and would have lost her balance if his powerful hands had not caught her shoulders. His touch unnerved and disturbed her. Gasping, she pulled free of his grasp.

"Understand this, Miss Pritchard. This journey is a business trip, it is not a race to catch your fiancé. The only reason you are aboard my ship is because of my high regard for your father. Your presence has nothing to do with Sterling." He ignored her gasp. "Our journey will not be leisurely, but we will be stopping along the way. If those stops frustrate you, that's just too damned bad. My primary concern is business. Not you. I expect you to stay out of the way and to make no trouble. I also expect to hear a minimum of complaints from you. Is that understood?"

White-lipped and furious, Lalie spun on her heel and marched to the railing. Behind her, she overheard Addison call to someone named Fredo. For a moment she considered disembarking and waiting in Pará until Percival could fetch her.

But the anchor broke from the murky water at that moment, and the *Addison Beal* drifted out of her slip. Black smoke belched from the stack as the engines caught, coughed, then settled into a vibrating chunk-a-chunk. Lurching forward, Lalie caught the railing, then covered her ears as the ships in the harbor gave three whistle blasts, the traditional bon voyage on the river. She glanced toward the wheelhouse in time to see Addison grin, then tug the whistle on the *Addison Beal,* deafening her.

They were finally and truly under way.

For a moment Lalie stood paralyzed with disbelief. This was the real beginning of her great adventure. Not Pará, not electric trolleys and feather beds. This—the river.

Rushing back to the railing, she leaned out as far as she safely could, peering ahead to glimpse Marajó, an island bigger than Switzerland if she had been informed correctly. The breeze caught her new hat, twirled it in the air then sent it diving into the brown water.

"Oh no!"

"The river, she always takes something, Missy." A smiling woman appeared at Lalie's side and gave her a glass of champagne. The heavy glass was inelegant, but the champagne was almost cool and seemed appropriate for the moment. "I am Maria, Fredo's *esposa.* Fredo, he is the pilot," she added proudly.

Like Fredo whom Lalie had briefly glimpsed, Maria was short and sturdily built; her skin was the color of burnished mahogany. Unlike Fredo, black eyes sparkled and the lines around her wide mouth suggested her smile was habitual. She wore a flowered cotton dress that ended at mid-calf and her bare feet gripped the deck more securely than did Lalie's smart leather sandals. Her glossy black hair was cropped short, and pockmarks speckled her cheeks. Maria was a plain woman until she smiled, then one forgot the flat nose and pocked cheeks and saw only kindness and a cheerful disposition.

"Perhaps you would show me to my cabin, Maria," Lalie said, returning the woman's smile. "I should find my brush and comb, and lay out my tea dress."

"Cabin, Missy?" Maria's broad smile wavered. "You mean the wheelhouse?"

"No, the sleeping cabin," she said. Assuming Maria didn't understand much English, Lalie folded her hands as if she were praying and laid her cheek against them. "Where we sleep."

"We sleep here, Missy." Maria waved to indicate the deck, which was empty but for a desktop bolted between supports, a few stools and chairs, and boxes of cargo covered by a tarpaulin. Now Lalie noticed an area near the entrance to the wheelhouse where baskets of fruit and crates of food supplies were scattered about. A small earthen stove sat on a square of bricks. A chicken and two sausages hung from the roof alongside a string of peppers.

"That's our kitchen?" Lalie inquired in a faint voice.

"Sim," Maria confirmed. She glanced toward the small stove with a proprietary air.

Lalie nodded. "I . . . I must speak to Mr. Addison." Holding her arms out for balance, she crossed the rocking deck to the wheelhouse door.

Fredo stood at the wheel, squinting at the river. Lalie could not have guessed his age if her life depended upon it. Weather had seamed his skin and darkened his face to a walnut shade. He didn't even look up when she entered his domain.

Addison had tilted his hat back on his head. He propped one leg on a shelf beneath the opened glass window, his forearm resting there. He looked more relaxed than Lalie had seen him until he turned to face her.

"I seem to have a misunderstanding with Maria, Mr. Addison."

Oddly, his longish hair and mustache did not appear out of place here. Nor did his casual dress. In a flash of insight, Lalie understood she was seeing March Addison in his natural element. He was no longer the elegant social creature she had met ten years ago. Time and geography had wrought a transformation. March Addison was a river man. Muscle swelled his shoulders and upper arms. Vibrant color glowed on his skin. If he noticed the heat and rising humidity, he gave no sign of discomfort. He belonged here. Suddenly, Lalie could not picture March Addison anywhere but on the river, somehow a part of it.

"Already? What sort of misunderstanding?"

His impatience broke the spell.

"I wish to go to my cabin now. I can't seem to make Maria understand."

He laughed. "That's because there are no passenger cabins."

"I beg your pardon?" She stared at him, feeling herself go weak in the knees.

Amused, he spoke to her as he might have spoken to a spoiled child. "Every available space is loaded with cargo. This isn't and never has been a passenger steamer. The *Addison Beal* is a small trader. As such, every inch of space is valuable."

Gripping his arm, Lalie pulled him out of the wheelhouse and waved a trembling hand at the empty deck. "Where, may I ask, am I going to sleep?"

"Here. In a hammock like everyone else." Her mouth fell open and she stared at him uncomprehendingly. "When we drop anchor for the night, Joao will string our hammocks between these supports." He pointed to the posts supporting the roofed section.

She closed her eyes, unable to believe what she was hearing. Then a worse thought occurred to her. Scarlet lit her face. She wet her lips then made herself whisper, "Is there . . . ah, is there a water closet?" Having to ask this hideously embarrassing question of a man caused her to die a thousand deaths in the span of a single moment.

"On a trading vessel?" He gave her an incredulous look, not because she had violated propriety and decency by mentioning a water closet, but because he seemed to think the answer should be obvious. Then comprehension dawned in his dark eyes and he frowned. "Ah, yes. I see the problem. Joao, come here!"

A short, dark boy, perhaps eighteen years of age, emerged from the staircase leading to the lower deck. *"Si, Cabo?"*

"Over here, on the side of the wheelhouse away from the kitchen . . ." Addison pointed to the roof and the railing. "String a tarpaulin across here. And build a wall here." He indicated the railing. "Enclose the railing to about this height." After squinting at Lalie, he raised his hand to mid-chest. "Build a hinged box and nail it to the wall. About this size." His hands described a box large enough to hold grooming articles and a few necessities. He glanced at Lalie, then said, "And furnish the area with a bucket."

A bucket. Good God.

"I apologize, Miss Pritchard. Of course you require a private space. One can't expect an Englishwoman to dress herself in public. The oversight is entirely mine and inexcusable."

Suspiciously she examined his face for any hint of sarcasm. There was none. "I never thought to hear an apology from your lips, Mr. Addison," she said, not entirely persuaded of his sincerity.

He looked surprised. "When I'm wrong I admit it, Miss Pritchard. I would never decline to offer an apology when one was warranted." Then he grinned broadly, destroying whatever gratitude Lalie had begun to feel. "Thankfully, I am seldom in the wrong."

A sigh lifted her bosom. "Where are my things?" she asked wearily.

He pointed to the tarpaulin-covered mass at the rear of the upper deck. "Whenever you want something, call Joao."

"I'll want my embroidery now, my tea gown at three, and a dinner gown at five."

It was his turn to release an exaggerated sigh. "Miss Pritchard. We don't stop for tea, and we don't dress for dinner."

"Perhaps you're willing to abandon civilized standards, Mr. Addison," she said, her eyes as hard as bright buttons. "But I am not. I shall have a proper tea at three-thirty, and I shall dress for dinner. I expect you to do the same."

"Then you shall be disappointed, Miss Pritchard." He

covered the deck in a few impatient strides and slammed the wheelhouse door behind him.

By teatime, Joao had assembled her private space and had dragged out several trunks from which she extracted the clothing she required to finish the day.

At exactly three-thirty, Lalie emerged from the cramped space behind the tarpaulin wearing a sprigged muslin tea gown, a shady straw hat, spotless white gloves, and a pink and white brooch that had belonged to her mother.

Beaming, Maria padded across the deck to place a crockery mug of strong, dark tea in her hand.

"No, no, this won't do at all," Lalie said, frowning. She would have to instruct Maria on how to serve a proper tea. Following a cursory inspection of the kitchen supplies, she sighed. "Joao? Come here, please."

After pulling out one trunk then another, she located a damask tablecloth, a tiny vase, a setting of silver, a bone-china plate, and cup and saucer. More digging produced a matching sugar bowl, a pitcher, a teapot, and a cozy, though she didn't think she needed a cozy. Still, there was a right and a wrong way to do things. She explained the function of the cozy to Maria and instructed her to place the pot in the center of the table, with the sugar to the right. There could be no milk for the tea, she realized. It was impossible to keep milk in the hot Brazilian climate. Lalie frowned and then decided she would just have to do her best without it.

Finally, overheated and out of sorts, she sat down to a proper tea, ignoring Maria's fascinated hovering. After a time, she felt herself relaxing. The tension drained out of her neck and shoulders, though she kept her spine straight against the back of her chair.

The steady sound of the engines was lulling and rather nice, Lalie decided. Discreetly, she covered a yawn. She was more tired than she had realized. Letting her mind drift, she drowsily watched the verdant bank slipping past on the right. The steamer stayed within sight of the shore as the powerful current in the center of the river ran against them toward the Atlantic.

There were few houses along the banks. The trees rose like vine-draped giants on the shore. She counted every shade of green imaginable. The heat and humidity drained her energy, but the breeze on the river kept the insects at bay. Whatever small fears and doubts she had harbored disappeared with the steam wafting above her teacup. The trip would undoubtedly be tolerable after all.

After stifling another yawn, she instructed Maria to take a cup of tea to Addison. After all, he had apologized. "Use the crockery mug," she added as an afterthought. He didn't merit a china cup and saucer and wouldn't appreciate them anyway.

They put into a small cove for the night, dropping anchor shortly before the sun blazed orange and red and purple above the horizon. Pleased, March clapped Fredo on the back and poured two beers. "Tomorrow the narrows," he said.

"Sim." Fredo stretched his neck against his hand and flexed his shoulders. "You want to navigate them or you want me to?"

"I'll take the wheel tomorrow." The beer, cooled by dragging the keg in the river behind the ship, tasted strong and fine.

"You gon' miss the river, boss," Fredo said.

March wiped the sweat from his forehead with the back of his hand and swallowed his beer. He leaned back, watching the sunset paint the river gold. A line of turtles plodded across the beach. Monkeys argued in the trees. Caimans, gilded by the sunset, dozed in the last rays of light. He tried to remember London at sunset, and couldn't. Maybe he didn't want to.

"Whatever Maria's cooking, it smells good."

He stopped short when he stepped outside the wheelhouse. Miss Eulalie Pritchard sat at a damask-draped table, dressed as formally as she had been the evening he took her to dinner at the Hotel Central. She wore a pale blue dinner gown, elbow-length gloves, and had dressed her fiery hair in a mass of curls at the crown, weaving the curls around two white egret feathers. She had draped a fringed silk shawl around her shoulders as protection against the hordes of mosquitoes that attacked the instant they cut the motor. Apparently the shawl was an afterthought as even from a distance he could see red welts rising on her face, her throat, and the lovely sweep of bosom.

"As soon as you have bathed and dressed, we shall dine, Mr. Addison," she said brightly.

He walked to the table and inspected the china and silver with astonishment and amusement. Then he noticed the two place settings. "We'll need three more settings."

She understood immediately and gave him a look of sharp disapproval. "You've been away from civilization too long, Mr. Addison," she said quietly. "Surely you aren't suggesting we dine with the servants."

"Of course we'll dine together. If the ship were sinking, we'd sink together. We're going to sleep together. We'll face any problems together. We're making this trip together, Miss Pritchard. There are no distinctions here. We depend on each other. I think we can damned well eat together, don't you?"

"Hardly, Mr. Addison. One doesn't dine with menials. You may have forgotten who you are, but I'll thank you to remember who I am."

"Ah yes. I see now. Sir Percival Sterling's intended bride is too exalted a personage to break bread with the hired help."

A slight flush of color painted her cheeks. She waved at a cloud of gnats and mosquitoes. "It simply isn't done. You know that, Mr. Addison."

"If I trust a man enough to place my life in his hands, I sure as hell regard him highly enough to share a meal with him." Turning on his heel, he went to the pail of water beside Maria's stove and washed his face and hands, ignoring Miss Pritchard's silent censure. "Miss Pritchard will dine alone, Maria. You may serve her whenever you're ready."

He ate his rice and stewed chicken sitting on a stool with his back to Her Majesty.

At night the river hummed with a hundred different species of insects, most of which viewed mankind as the meal of choice. Prudent voyagers retired beneath dense netting as swiftly after twilight as feasible and escaped to the river breezes at the first hint of sunrise.

While Maria washed the plates and pots, Fredo and March enjoyed a cigar and *cafezinho*, watching as Joao strung heavy cotton hammocks between the supports. Miss Pritchard strolled the deck, swatting at mosquitoes. She turned and stopped beside March, her palm fan moving in a blur of movement that stirred her auburn curls. In the light of the kerosene lantern swinging above, March saw that some of the welts on her cheeks and throat had swelled to the size of a shilling.

She looked at him, her lovely eyes wide and battling misery. "I never saw so many mosquitoes in my life. Some are huge, absolutely huge."

Without a word, he pushed from the railing and entered the wheelhouse, emerging a moment later with cotton and ammonia. "Hold still. And try not to scratch, it makes the itch worse."

It was a measure of her affliction and discomfort that she didn't protest when he smoothed ammonia across the red welts. She submitted to his ministrations like a grateful child, closing her eyes and standing still. Her thick lashes reminded him of dark silky fringe. Her cheek was as soft as pale satin beneath his fingertips. Pausing, he stared down at her for a few seconds. Abruptly he pushed the cotton and ammonia into her hands and took a step backward. "Wet down your arms and throat. The ammonia will ease the sting and itching. You're taking your quinine, aren't you?"

"Yes." Closing her eyes again, she tilted her head and drew the ammonia-soaked cotton over her throat. March stared at the slender arch leading to a swell of bosom, then he turned away and leaned on the railing, watching the forest swallow the moonlight.

"The hammocks are up, Miss Pritchard," he said over his shoulder. "I'd suggest you go to bed. Get under the netting."

He turned back to her in time to see her bite her lip and study the row of hammocks with a wary expression. When she noticed him watching, her lips came together in a line he had begun to recognize.

"Yes, Miss Pritchard, I uttered the shocking word 'bed' in your august presence. Do try not to faint. And yes, we'll be sleeping in a row, peasants alongside royalty." He placed a hand on his chest and shook his head. "I can only pray no one ever discovers you slept on the same deck as a mere cook."

"If I were the kind of woman to whom you are accustomed, Mr. Addison, I would put you in your place with a few well-chosen vile words. As I am above such crudities, I have no option but to ignore you."

Chin in the air, she turned toward the hammocks just as Joao stripped to his undershorts and slipped beneath the netting of the hammock nearest the end of the deck. Eulalie Pritchard gasped, and spun to face the wheelhouse. A tiny panicked noise bubbled in her throat.

March strove for patience. "He isn't naked, Miss Pritchard. In honor of your tender sensibilities he's wearing his undershorts. For God's sake, surely you've seen legs and a male chest before."

"Do you intend . . . that is, will you . . . oh my heavens!" She stood facing the dark river. Her fan moved at frantic speed.

He sighed. "Until we reach Hiberalta, Miss Pritchard, I'll sleep in my trousers." In an odd way he almost pitied her. Eulalie Pritchard had not chosen the world into which she was born. Until now she'd had no reason to wonder if Victorian modesty and propriety had passed the bounds of reason. Brazil and England were two very different and incompatible worlds. But true to form, Miss Pritchard could not accept that. She expected the Amazon to conform to the standards that had been ingrained in her since childhood.

Though the expression on her face elicited from March an unexpected spurt of understanding, even sympathy, she was still the most irritating woman he had encountered in years, making it impossible for him to resist saying something he knew she would find annoying. "And I would greatly appreciate it if you too would agree not to sleep naked," he said, smiling at the way she instantly stiffened and gasped. Her shoulders quivered. "I'd suggest you bundle up tight. A nightdress and your wrapper, I think. You might be uncomfortably warm, but you won't offend anyone's sense of modesty."

"You think you're so amusing, don't you? Well, you're not. You are a horrible man, Mr. Addison!"

After skewering him with a poisonous glance she marched stiffly to her private corner. Eventually, after what seemed an eternity, she emerged wearing a wrapper that covered her body from throat to toe. A long glowing braid hung down her back. Ignoring March, she walked briskly to the hammock nearest her corner and studied it.

"Do you require assistance?" he asked, after flipping his cigar into the river. Once he got her settled, they could all go to sleep. It would be a long, strenuous day tomorrow.

"No!" she snapped.

"Have you slept in a hammock before?"

She squinted toward Joao's hammock, swaying with the movement of the ship. "I shall manage, Mr. Addison. I believe we agreed that you will tend to your affairs and I will tend to mine."

No minced words there. Smiling, he leaned against the railing and waited. Maria and Fredo also found tasks to keep them in the line of sight.

Miss Pritchard dismissed them with a glance then studied the situation. Gingerly, she raised her hem and placed one knee in the center of the hammock. No one spoke. She eased her full weight onto the stretched cotton and sucked in a breath when it moved beneath her. Then she caught her balance and cast them a triumphant look. Finally, she swung her feet off the deck.

The hammock twisted, Miss Pritchard screamed and grabbed the material with both arms. In two seconds she lay sprawled on the deck, tangled in the wrapper, nightdress, and the netting, which she had pulled down with her.

March raised his eyes and sucked in his cheeks. No one spoke or dared to laugh aloud. Water lapped the sides of the ship. Something snorted and rooted in the jungle growth along the shore.

Face flaming, Miss Pritchard picked herself up and hastily arranged her attire. She didn't look at anyone. She glared at the hammock and muttered, then she tried again. Once more the hammock tipped her onto the deck where she landed with a thump.

"At what point do your affairs become my affairs, Miss Pritchard? Or are you going to keep this up until the mosquitoes have eaten us all alive?"

"You're enjoying this, aren't you, you . . . you degenerate!" Furious, her eyes flashing, her clothing in disarray, she placed a hand on the hammock and steadied it. She moved so slowly it was painful to watch, and again she did it wrong. This time she stayed on the deck, lying flat on her back, staring up at the mosquitoes swarming above her.

"All right. Are you going to help me, or are you just going to stand there laughing?"

"I'm not laughing," he lied. "Watch me. Slip under the netting and sit first," he said, moving forward. "Like this. When you feel solid, swing your legs up and lie back." He gazed up at her from the folds of the hammock, remembering the shapely curve of her calves.

"Get out of there and let me do it."

Yes indeed, they were making remarkable progress on the minced-words front, March thought. It was just possible there was a real person inside that unyielding corset and insect-bitten skin. He slid out of the hammock and stood by her side, smiling.

"Slowly," he cautioned. "Don't rush it."

This time she was successful. He couldn't see her through the thick netting, but he heard her tiny cry of relief and triumph.

After several seconds, March said, "Relax, Miss Pritchard. You're lying there as stiff as a dried hide. You can move, just do it slowly."

"Good night, Mr. Addison. You may go now."

Grinning, he extinguished the lantern, waved at Fredo and Maria who, hand in hand, scampered down the stairs for a brief sojourn below deck, then he slipped into his own hammock an arm's length from Miss Pritchard and listened to the exotic night sounds of the rain forest.

Just as he was dozing off, Miss Pritchard called to him in an urgent whisper. "Mr. Addison? Are you still awake?"

"What is it?"

"Do you hear that?"

"Hear what?"

"That thumping noise. And voices. I'm sure I hear people whispering and maybe even laughing." Her voice was strained and anxious. "The whole boat's rocking, don't you feel it? Do you think bandits are creeping aboard?"

He opened one eye, saw she had raised the netting to hear better.

"Go to sleep. Maria and Fredo went downstairs for a few minutes, that's all."

"Maria and Fredo? What do they have to do with anything?"

"You're a grown woman, Miss Pritchard, and a doctor's daughter. I think you can figure it out." He rolled over and closed his eyes. It wasn't going to be easy to sleep with a beautiful and desirable woman only a few feet away.

After a moment he heard a strangled gasp. "Oh!" Then, after a minute, "That's horrible!"

Horrible? March grinned broadly, imagining Sir Percy's wedding night.

On the Amazon River
January 1897

I fear I shall forget too much if I don't begin this journal at once. I intended to begin writing in Pará, and regret my procrastination.

Today is our fourth day on the river. This section of the Amazon is called the River Sea because the character is more that of sea than river. We still feel the tide, and gulls and terns fly overhead. Two days ago Mr. Addison piloted us through the narrows. At some points the channel was so restricted that forest growth scraped the sides of the ship. I saw several monkeys and more parrots than I could count.

The ship is small and not as commodious as one could hope, but I am taking all inconveniences in stride. I'm writing on a desktop on the upper deck. If the ink is smeared it is because the engine is beneath me and the deck constantly vibrates. I have to tie my hat with a scarf or the breeze would snatch it away.

But I'm happy for the breeze as it blows away the insects that swarm around us almost constantly.

Maria is the wife of our pilot. They are an unusually affectionate couple. Fredo stays in the wheelhouse all day, but Maria chatters away like one of the monkeys in the forest. She talks constantly about babies and I have heard about all the children in her large family. Joao is the boy who does odd jobs as we need them done.

Unfortunately, I am surrounded by people who have no understanding of proper behavior and no interest in the things that most concern me. I often think of my dear father and wonder if he is still angry with me. I hope there will be letters waiting in Santarém. I long to hear from home.

This morning I awoke to mist on the river. It looked as if the world were steaming. The heat seems to grow more intense the farther upriver we go. Sometimes I feel so very far from home. Then I think of my dear Percival and my mind settles. I know I'm doing the right thing and I long to see his dear face again.

I have coffee in the morning but not with cream. One can't drink the milk or cream here. Then plain tea in the afternoon. From then it is champagne for me, beer or cachaça *for the others.*

March Addison continues to be rude and odious. I fear he has been too long without the benefit of civilization or society. He smokes cigars without first requesting my permission. He says the smoke keeps mosquitoes away. He is wrong. Nothing keeps the mosquitoes away. I do what I can to remind Mr. Addison of the respectable life, but I fear his faults are too numerous to repair in the short time we shall have together.

There is something rather menacing about the

rain forest. At first I found it interesting, then tedious in its sameness. But recently, after listening to the unnerving sounds that come from within it, I've begun to think of it as a dark and mysterious presence.

No time to write more. Joao says a storm is brewing and I must stow away my writing implements. The way Joao and Addison are fussing one would think they were afraid of a little rain. They are rushing about tying things down and telling me to hurry as if I too should be frightened of a raindrop. Pish. It rains almost every afternoon. A little storm doesn't frighten me.

Chapter 4

Lalie had never been so frightened in her life. Water poured down the wheelhouse windows as if the ship were stalled beneath a waterfall. Only occasionally could she see outside and what she saw terrified her. The sky had turned as black as tar; rain lashed the glass and thundered on the roof. The shoreline had vanished. The *Addison Beal* pitched and slid through giant troughs of water that flung the ship forward and to the side with bone-wrenching strength.

"Oh my heavens," she whispered, staring through the glass. She pressed white knuckles to her lips, felt her fingernails cutting into her palms.

"Floating island to your left!" Addison shouted. He stood next to Fredo, his legs wide apart and braced, a dead cigar clamped between his teeth. "Tree on the right." The *Addison Beal* shuddered then began the long climb up the rolling brown wall of the next trough.

Straining forward, Lalie spotted an uprooted tree almost as thick as the *Addison Beal* whirling toward them in the water. Her heart stopped as the tree spun sharply and one of its giant roots struck the ship. The *Addison Beal* lurched, and Lalie pitched forward against Fredo. It was like bouncing off a rock. His shoulders and back were tense and hard. He didn't seem to notice she had slammed into him. But March Addison did.

Before Lalie understood what he was doing, Addison had lashed a rope around her waist and tethered the other end to himself. "You're going below," he shouted. "You'll get wetter, but we'll all be safer."

"What?"

The wind tore the word from her mouth as Addison opened the wheelhouse door and pushed her outside then leaned his weight on the door to close it again. In one smooth motion, he leaned down and scooped her shoes off her feet. They rolled across the deck and disappeared. Instantly Lalie's stockings were as soaked as the rest of her, but she found she could maintain her balance much more easily. The steps at the far end of the deck seemed a mile away, only a distant shadow in the black rain. Ducking his head, fighting the driving rain and wind, Addison made it to the first post. Slipping and sliding, her heart beating a wild tattoo against her rib cage, Lalie tried to follow.

Half a dozen times she fell to her knees when the ship pitched violently to one side then the other. Repeatedly, she fought her way to her feet, breaking her fingernails against the unyielding deck. She felt as if she might be swept away at any moment and lost forever. But the rope at her waist held and Addison helped her, shouting words she could not hear. Her soaked clothing clung to her body like a second skin; her wet hair flew around her face in the maelstrom, stinging her cheeks like nettles.

The stairs were the worst. Addison's powerful arm circled her waist, his muscles rising like thick cords. When he was certain of his grip, they leapt into the stairwell as a mountain of water rose above them then smashed down on their heads. For a terrifying moment, Lalie couldn't breathe. The water flooded her eyes, her mouth, her lungs. Then it rushed away, leaving her shaking in Addison's arms, struggling for air.

When she could see again, she saw an aisle between the mounds of cargo. "Quickly," Addison shouted, pushing her forward. At the end of the aisle, she glimpsed a shadow and recognized Maria reaching a hand toward her.

Bouncing from cargo mound to cargo mound, they struggled up the aisle, were knocked to their knees when the ship quivered then crashed down to the bottom of a trough. Squinting, his teeth clenched, Addison untied his end of the rope and knotted it to a ring in the wall. Lalie saw that Maria was similarly tethered. Making a slashing motion with his hand, Addison shouted to Maria. "Knife?" Maria pointed to the blade tied to her ankle. Addison nodded, gave them a thumb's-up sign, then began the slow return trip to the wheelhouse.

Lalie stared at the knife. She understood its meaning. If the *Addison Beal* capsized, Maria would cut their ropes so they wouldn't be dragged down with the ship. Terrified, she slid down the bulkhead and sat in the sloshing water, covering her eyes with shaking hands.

She should have kept her eyes covered. When she lifted her head a wall of brown water soared past the railing on her left, reaching the upper deck. She screamed as the wall fell with a thunderous crash and slammed over her. It happened again and again and each time was more terrifying than the one before. Each time she believed the ship would capsize and she and Maria would be dragged beneath the raging waters.

One nightmarish hour passed then another. Lalie clung to Maria, her voice hoarse from the screams that tore from her throat as the ship bucked and pitched and labored to remain upright. Water poured over the railing, drenching them before it drained away in a hissing rush. Once she looked up in horror at the underside of a grass island tossed above them in a violent swell. Another time she opened her eyes, gasping for breath and wiping water from her face, in time to see two snakes and a rain of fishes flooding the aisle. When she looked again, they were gone.

She thought it would never end, but finally it did. One minute rain and wind roared in her ears and hammered the *Addison Beal;* seemingly the next moment the air was calm and Lalie heard only the hiss and rush of the river. Hot bright sunlight burst over the end of the deck, transforming the churning black river into a rich caramel color. Until then Lalie hadn't realized how sharply the temperature had dropped or how chilled she was. The waves were still high, the river still angry and disturbed, but thank God the storm had ended.

When she stood on wobbling legs, she glimpsed the forest on the shore, glistening like a band of wet emeralds. A brilliant rainbow arched toward the sunset. To Lalie's immense relief, she noticed the *Addison Beal* was chugging toward a sheltered lagoon. When the anchor dropped and she was near enough to the high forested bluff that she could almost reach out and touch land with her fingertips, she covered her face in her hands and sobbed.

Maria held her and smoothed strands of wet hair away from her face, making soothing noises deep in her throat. When Lalie's tears finally abated, Maria picked the knots at their waists until they were free, then they made their way to the upper deck.

Addison came to her at once. Before she could utter a syllable of protest, he ran his hands over her body, beginning at her throat, down her arms, along her rib cage, then followed the curve of her legs to her ankles. The hot shock of his hands on her body paralyzed Lalie. She couldn't breathe, couldn't think. Finally, he stood and tilted her flaming face, scowled, then rubbed something stinging on her forehead and tied a cloth around her head. He wiped her face and, to Lalie's astonishment, his handkerchief came away spotted with blood.

"One small cut, that's all." His voice was as hoarse as her own. He looked exhausted. Nothing in his expression indicated he knew he had touched her as no man had before. "We lost your tarpaulin, but Joao is hanging another. You need to get into some dry clothing."

Lalie stood like a rag doll, struggling to keep her balance on legs that had turned to taffy the moment his hands began to shape her chilled body.

Finally, she moved to lean against the railing, and dulled by fatigue, she watched Joao string her tarpaulin. She could hear Fredo moving about in the wheelhouse, restoring order; Addison left the upper deck to check the cargo lashings below. Maria began the process of reassembling her kitchen. At last, so sore and battered she could hardly move, Lalie followed Joao to the mound of cargo that was hers and removed a towel and a dry nightgown and wrapper from the first trunk he uncovered.

For the first time in her life Eulalie Pritchard ate supper, tinned beef and cold rice, in her night clothes. She was too exhausted to observe propriety, too confused by the memory of Addison's hands on her body. Sitting on a stool near Maria's stove and eating with the others, her wet hair hanging like a curtain around her pale face, she steadfastly resisted looking at Addison, afraid she would turn scarlet if she met his eyes.

"You saved the ship," Addison said quietly, looking at Fredo. "It was a superlative performance."

"You had the wheel as often as I did." Fredo shrugged, but he looked pleased.

After that no one spoke. Only the roars of the howler monkeys chasing through the forest and the water slapping the sides of the ship broke the silence. They were too tired to converse.

After supper Lalie stood by the railing away from Addison's cigar, watching Joao hang the hammocks and silently urging him to hurry. She could hardly keep her eyes open.

"How did you know this would be such a horrible storm and not just the usual afternoon rain?" she asked Addison, needing conversation to stay awake. Now she could feel the cut above her eye. A dull throbbing pain built toward a headache. She had no memory to explain how she had been injured. But the rest, the terror and the wind and the rain and the walls of foaming water were alive in her mind like a waking nightmare.

"Nine years on the river. After a while one develops a sixth sense," Addison said, releasing a puff of smoke. The smoke hung on the still air, a pale ghost against the dark night.

"Must you smoke that vile thing?"

"Yes, Miss Pritchard, I must. And I'm in no mood for a lecture."

"I'm in no mood to deliver one," she said with a sigh. She gazed at the hammocks with longing. The instant Joao finished securing hers, she moved toward it and climbed inside, settling into her cocoon with a sigh of relief and pleasure. To her great surprise she had discovered hammocks could be as comfortable as a bed.

But as tired as she was, Lalie didn't immediately fall asleep. She swayed gently in her hammock, remembering the events of the day. The storm in all its fury raced through her mind, but what was clearest in her memory, what remained in her thoughts in the greatest detail was March Addison's strong hands running over her body.

She understood his exploration had not been purposely provocative or seductive. She knew that he had been checking for injuries and nothing more. But still the memory of his touch was upsetting and confusing.

March Addison was the first man to touch her in so intimate a fashion and her face flamed at the memory. Lalie had supposed the man who would first touch her like that would be her husband. Guilt preyed on her mind. She wondered if she had betrayed Sir Percival in some obscure way.

After a while, listening to March Addison turn in his

sleep not an arm's length away, she decided not to be offended but she was embarrassed. Remembering his touch, her face grew hot in the darkness. Because it disturbed her to think about Addison's hands molding her body, she forced her thoughts back to the storm.

Until today her courage had never been tested. Oh, she had thought it had, but she was wrong. No real courage was required to pedal a bicycle around rural Hackney. Courage wasn't needed to refuse half a dozen suitors she didn't care about anyway. It hadn't even required a great deal of courage to leave home and sail to Brazil. Every step of the way she had been looked after by someone. Until today. Even with Maria beside her, Lalie had been alone in her terror, alone with her half-formed plans of what she would do if the ship capsized.

Now, in her hammock with no place to hide from the truth, Lalie wondered if she had acquitted herself well or if she had failed her first real trial. An uncomfortable suspicion arose that she had failed. Certainly she had not behaved with any dignity or notable bravery.

Without warning or expectation a vivid memory whirled out of the past.

Lalie recalled standing beside her father at her mother's gravesite. Again she heard her father's whisper. "Poor Rose, she never really lived."

The words had surprised Lalie; she didn't understand them. Of course her mother had lived. Later, puzzled, she asked her father what he meant, but he had forgotten what he had said.

It took Lalie years to fully comprehend the meaning of her father's statement. Rose Pritchard had not really lived because Rose Pritchard was a woman and women lived a pale half-life compared to men.

Rose Pritchard had passed from father to husband without ever residing alone, without sampling the revelations of solitude. She had never made an important decision, not even the decision of whom she would marry.

She had never earned a shilling through her own efforts. She didn't understand business or politics nor did she consider it important that she should. She had not dreamed of traveling alone and had in fact begged off when Lalie's father traveled to the Amazon and later to Sumatra, claiming it didn't seem ladylike to visit the tropics.

Rose Pritchard's excitements had been small, her adventures confined to kitchen and garden. What triumphs she counted were unknown beyond the perimeters of her family. Rose Pritchard had been loved and cherished, but she had passed calmly through life without leaving a ripple behind her.

Lalie lay in her hammock, staring into the darkness with moist eyes. How sad it was. "Poor Rose, she never really lived." A shudder passed through Lalie's body. She didn't want anyone ever to say: "Poor Eulalie, she never really lived."

Was that the true reason she had come to Brazil? Because she had glimpsed an opportunity to taste a bit more of life than was ordinarily permitted? Was it possible she didn't love Sir Percival after all, but loved instead the idea that Sir Percival maintained a home high on the Amazon?

The thought horrified her. She did love Sir Percival *and* she loved it that he had a home on the Amazon. The two thoughts were not exclusive of each other. Relaxing, feeling better, she eased back into her hammock and closed her eyes.

She had made the right decision to follow her fiancé to the Amazon. And clinging to Maria in the wind and rain, drenched to the skin and terrified, she had felt more vibrantly alive than ever before, even if she hadn't comported herself with much courage. At least she could assure herself on one important point. After this journey no one could ever say that poor Eulalie Pritchard had never really lived.

* * *

Milky drifts of mist overhung the river until late afternoon the next day. The *Addison Beal* hugged the shore so as not to miss the harbor and the sea wall announcing Quantos. Trees rising one hundred feet into the mist slipped past like ghostly silver shadows. Once or twice March noticed movement in the brush along the shore and instructed Fredo to put in at one of the tributaries emptying into the river. He left a sack of sugar and one of salt beneath an improvised shelter but he didn't linger to greet the Indians who would take his gifts. The Indians along this stretch of river were accustomed to March's donations, but he had not made contact with them. Now he knew he never would.

He put the thought firmly out of mind and concentrated on piloting the *Addison Beal* into the Quantos harbor. Already Joao had assembled the goods March was bringing his friend Father Emil, kerosene, salt, mail, and a box of books. Ordinarily March would have dropped off the books on his way upriver and would have stopped on his way back to discuss them with Father Emil. This time he would not be stopping on the return voyage to Pará.

"Will we drop anchor soon?"

"Miss Pritchard, I've asked you twenty times not to come into the wheelhouse." He turned to glare at her and felt his stomach tighten at her beauty. Today she wore a broad-brimmed straw hat and a light dress trimmed with green ribbons. The cut on her forehead was scarcely noticeable, unlike the excitement dancing in her beautiful eyes. "Be patient. You'll be standing on land in forty minutes," he said, turning back to the wheel.

He knew why she was excited. She hoped she would find word from Sir Percival waiting in Quantos. Unfortunately that was doubtful. The best chance for Miss Pritchard's letter to catch up to Sir Percival was in Manaus, seven hundred miles upriver. It was March's fervent hope that one of Sir Percy's henchmen would be waiting in Manaus to take Miss Pritchard off his hands.

Exactly as he had predicted, her presence on the *Addison Beal* was proving an unending irritation. She insisted on changing her clothes several times each day and taking her meals alone at a table set with silver and china; she pestered everyone with thousands of questions; she contributed nothing to the journey; and she had altered the routine of his crew.

For nine years his crew had relieved themselves in the river. Now, to prevent Miss Pritchard from sinking into a faint, Joao and Fredo relieved themselves in a bucket behind a screen. They slept in their trousers. No one had enjoyed a bath because no one could figure how to have a bath without offending Miss Pritchard. And Maria was actually serving tea each afternoon and badgering Fredo not to eat with his fingers as he had done all his life.

As for March, Miss Pritchard detested his cigars, hated his language, hated his dress, hated his habit of sharing his meals with his crew, hated everything about him.

March had not grown any fonder of her, either. Her prissy, proper ways set his teeth on edge. He loathed her damned raised eyebrows, her excessive modesty, her determined tight-jawed cheerfulness. Her throat and arms were covered with mosquito bites and a raw sunburn peeled her nose, yet she hadn't murmured a word of complaint. He had expected her to complain constantly. It annoyed hell out of him that she didn't. He did not want to discover anything laudable about Her Majesty, Miss Eulalie Pritchard.

Frowning, he guided the *Addison Beal* into the Quantos harbor before relinquishing the wheel to Fredo to ease the ship into a docking slip. His concentration hadn't been worth a tinker's damn since the aftermath of the storm when he had run his hands over Miss Pritchard's lush body searching for cuts or broken bones.

Since that moment he had been unable to glance at her without remembering the curve of her waist, the provocative flare of her hips, the softness of her thighs and calves. In his mind he saw her standing before him, her wet dress molded against her magnificent body, her hair hanging to her waist, her face so pale that her mouth resembled a rosebud in cream.

Trying to sleep was pure hell. Last night he had lain in his hammock and stared up at nothing, acutely aware that a beautiful, desirable woman lay not three feet away. Every time she sighed in her sleep, he twitched and clenched his teeth.

The situation was ludicrous. March did not like Eulalie Pritchard, nor did he enjoy her company. She was contrary to everything he found attractive in a woman. Yet each time he glimpsed that splendid mass of auburn hair or recalled her tiny corseted waist beneath his hands a wave of desire seemed to flow through him.

"Miss Pritchard?" he called, leaning out of the wheelhouse door. She turned from her position at the rail, her expression cautious. "You will sleep on shore tonight. My friend Father Emil has a small guest house, and I'm sure he will be happy to offer you the use of it." Because he felt an idiotic need to punish her for his own disturbing thoughts, he stared at her for a moment then committed a deliberate offense. "Father Emil will offer you a real bath. I'm sure you feel sweaty and in need of a thorough wash."

True to form she turned scarlet, then shot a venomous glance at him before she raised her chin and turned her back. Grinning and feeling as if he had scratched an irritating itch, March returned to the wheelhouse and released the anchor chain.

Quantos was not an actual town but it was the nearest thing to one along this stretch of river. A tree-lined promenade paralleled the seawall, leafy palms swayed above a small dusty plaza. A dozen or so thatched-roof huts surrounded one of the oldest churches in the Amazon, a huge redbrick building erected in the eighteenth century. Everyone in Quantos had collected along the seawall to watch the *Addison Beal* drop anchor. Father Emil stepped forward as March and Eulalie climbed the stone steps to the top of the wall.

"March!" Father Emil gripped his hand. "It's good to see you again!"

Father Emil, a tall, thin, handsome man in his fifties, wore his immaculate white cassock with the panache of a warrior devoted to fighting God's battles. A dozen years on the Amazon had not diminished his zest for life or for his calling. Though it surprised March that a man of Father Emil's intelligence and vibrancy had been abandoned to this insignificant parish, no word of complaint passed Emil's lips. Once or twice he had alluded to an unfortunate indiscretion that had resulted in his current assignment, but he referred to it without bitterness.

"Father Emil, this is Miss Pritchard. She's traveling to Hiberalta."

Her displeasure at the casual introduction was only too obvious to March. But by the time Miss Pritchard turned to the priest, her grimace had dissolved into a charming smile.

"Hiberalta?" Father Emil said, a note of surprise in his voice. He took Miss Pritchard's gloved hand and tucked it around his arm, then led her through the crowd of curious onlookers toward the rectory, all the while exchanging polite repartee that Miss Pritchard drank in like nectar from the gods.

March followed at a slower pace, pausing to greet familiar faces. He arrived at the rectory in time to observe Miss Pritchard clapping her gloves together at the sight of Father Emil's piano.

Sinking into a comfortable chair, he accepted *cafezinho* from Emil's manservant and listened to Emil and Miss

Pritchard engage in a conversation that was as annoying as it was predictable.

First Miss Pritchard made an elaborate production of noticing the piano and mentioning how much she loved to play. Taking his cue, Father Emil entreated Miss Pritchard to honor them with a selection. Naturally, before Miss Pritchard would touch the keys, it was necessary to demonstrate she was well bred and modest. Therefore she demurred prettily, casting down her eyes and managing a charming blush.

"I'm afraid I haven't played in ages," she announced.

As expected, Father Emil coaxed her toward the piano and positioned the stool. "We'll be enchanted by whatever you decide to play, Miss Pritchard."

"I really shouldn't . . ."

"But you must. It's been so long since Quantos has been visited by an accomplished young lady. And much too long since this poor piano has been graced by a gentle hand."

Miss Pritchard trailed her fingertips across the keys in a graceful, indecisive manner. "If you really insist . . ."

"For God's sake! Will you sit down and play the damned thing?" March scowled when Miss Pritchard and Father Emil turned to stare at him. They had been enjoying the ritual exchange to the extent they had almost forgotten his presence. "Either play it, or come over here and drink your lemonade."

Miss Pritchard's blue-green eyes glittered. "You don't believe I can play, do you?" she demanded.

"That is not the issue, Miss Pritchard. I'm confident you've memorized two or three set pieces for occasions such as this. So get on with it if you please." He cast a look of longing toward the chess set waiting on the table between his chair and the priest's.

Father Emil smiled. "I notice your patience has not improved, March."

"Nor his manners," Miss Pritchard muttered. She settled herself on the piano stool, arranged her skirts to fall in a charming drape, then removed her gloves and flexed her fingers. Mozart himself couldn't have made a greater production of preparing.

March sighed and steeled himself for the parlor piece that she did indeed play and play well. At the finish, while Father Emil gushed with praise, Miss Pritchard tossed March a triumphant glance.

He regarded her over the rim of his cup of *cafezinho.* "Do you actually read music, Miss Pritchard? Or have you merely practiced a couple of pieces until you can play those selections without error?"

Her Majesty accepted the challenge. Grim-faced, she lifted the pile of music sheets from the top of the piano, fanned out the pages, and silently offered March his choice. He selected one at random, also without speaking, glanced at the sheets then handed them back to her.

After studying the pages for a moment, she placed them in front of her and music rolled across Father Emil's comfortable living room.

But it was not the piece March had selected. He did read music and knew at once she wasn't playing his selection. He was about to expose her deception but suddenly found himself incapable of doing so. It impressed him as preposterous and a little touching that she could not admit she was only comfortable performing her set pieces. Was this annoying, insulting, judgmental woman really so unsure of herself that she couldn't even admit she didn't read music very well?

She struck the final chord with a flourish then spun on the stool to face him. "Well, Mr. Addison?" she asked, a trifle uncertainly.

He hesitated then decided to grant the deception as it seemed terribly important to her while it meant very little to him. "I stand corrected, Miss Pritchard."

"I should think so," she said, her arrogance returning so quickly that March instantly regretted his decision. "I believe I'll have that lemonade now, if I might," she murmured to Father Emil, accepting the priest's praise and his hospitality with a modest smile.

March listened to as much polite repartee as he could endure before he excused himself and left the rectory after promising to return for dinner and chess. It galled him that he had allowed her to believe she had bested him again.

Lalie couldn't recall when she had enjoyed an afternoon more. By the time Father Emil suggested a walk before dinner, she felt as if she had known him for years.

But it wasn't until now that she realized how skillfully Father Emil had drawn her out. She had talked far too much about herself. She had told him about her mother's death, about helping in her father's surgery, about managing the large residence in Hackney, among other things. "I owe you an apology," she murmured. "All I've done is talk about myself."

"I've enjoyed every moment," he said, patting the glove wrapped around his thin arm. "I hope you'll pardon my flock." A crowd had gathered in the plaza to stare in curiosity and fascination at Lalie's pale face and fiery hair. "It isn't often an English lady passes this way, particularly so charming and pretty a lady."

"I'm flattered, indeed," she murmured, appreciating his compliments and lovely manners. So unlike the crudity of some people she could name.

In truth it was a pleasant novelty to be the object of such rapt attention. Father Emil's flock thronged the plaza for a glimpse of her lacy parasol and shining green ribbons. Most of the crowd were Indians and mulattos, Lalie noticed. Only a few European faces were visible among the spectators.

Tilting her parasol back, Lalie leaned close to Father Emil's ear. "Are those . . . are they savages?" she whispered, studying an Indian woman as they waited for a mule cart to pass.

Father Emil smiled and pressed her arm. "Don't let March hear you refer to the Indians as savages," he advised. "You'll receive a tongue-lashing if you do."

"Mr. Addison is a . . . an unusual man," she finished tactfully, altering what she had intended to say.

Father Emil's smile broadened. "Indeed he is." He glanced down at her. "Do you know March well?"

She made a face. "Not well at all. I believe I prefer it that way."

They completed a turn around the plaza before Father Emil spoke again. "When I arrived in Quantos—a dozen years ago—I discovered the clapper was missing from the steeple bell. The bell had not pealed in nearly a quarter of a century." He tilted his head to admire the sunset. "Quantos is a very long way from Rome, Miss Pritchard. Year after year I dispatched petitions requesting a new clapper, but such a thing was not important to anyone but me. Then one day the *Addison Beal* delivered not a clapper, mind you, but an entire, wonderful new bell." His gaze shifted to the steeple. "A year later I discovered Rome had not authorized my bell. March Addison bought it. Not that March would accept a word of thanks. The closest he came to admitting his generosity was not to deny it. Do you know where he is now, Miss Pritchard?"

She hadn't thought about March Addison's absence except to feel grateful for it. "At the ship, I suppose."

Father Emil nodded toward the jungle encroaching on the thatched huts. "March is in the brush with Cao and Jesus Maria delivering medicine to Mother Amity, who doctors Quantos as best she can. March will give her thirty pounds sterling worth of remedies, which will save at least eight lives, and Mother Amity will give March a few shillings worth of Brazil nuts in exchange. He has struck similar bad bargains all the way upriver for years."

Surprise widened Lalie's eyes and she paused to consider this information. Then she lifted a hand. "If you're attempting to persuade me that March Addison is a saint—"

"A saint?" Father Emil's burst of laughter startled her. "No, indeed, Miss Pritchard. In fact, many is the time I have despaired for March Addison's immortal soul. He's killed two men that I know of, has engaged in at least one duel, and is considered by many to be a pirate because of the hard bargains he drives with the rubber men. You'll hear that he's a womanizer and that he can outdrink any man in the Amazon. You'll be informed that March is considered something of a legend as a result of a jaguar hunt five years ago. And it's true he's acted with foolhardy bravery on more than one occasion. You'll hear it stated that March is a dangerous man to cross. All of this is true to a greater or lesser degree."

Halting, Lalie frowned and turned to face the priest. "Then . . . ?"

"March is also a genuinely courageous and good man, Miss Pritchard. The Indians have no better friend than March Addison. No one has labored harder to improve the working conditions on the sugar and nut plantations. You'll be hard-pressed to find a town or a family along the river that doesn't owe March a debt of gratitude. There are many—and I count myself among their number—who believe March's decision to leave the Amazon is the worst calamity to befall the area in decades. He'll be sorely missed."

At that moment the object of their conversation came into view. Lalie turned with Father Emil in time to see March emerge from the jungle, a cigar clamped between his teeth, a machete swinging in his hand. His hat was pushed back from his sweat-damp curls. He wore knee-high jungle boots and dun-colored pants, but no shirt. His naked chest gleamed in the sunset rays like sculpted bronze.

Lalie sucked in a hard breath and stared. "Those scars! I . . . What on earth happened?"

March's bared chest was taut and heavily muscled. Perspiration gleamed on his skin like oil. But what riveted Lalie's shocked attention were the scars. Three jagged scars slashed through the thicket of dark hair covering his chest, ugly, painful-looking scars that glowed pale against his dark tan.

Father Emil patted the fist she had unknowingly made. "One of the scars resulted from a knife wound. One was made by a poisoned dart. I'm not sure about the last."

"Good heavens," Lalie whispered, staring at March's hard, lean body. Suddenly she remembered his powerful arms holding her during the storm and her cheeks flushed bright pink.

March smiled and raised his machete in greeting but continued past them toward the wharf.

"Supper in half an hour," Father Emil called. "Don't let those rascals delay you." He referred to the entourage who followed at March's heels. A dozen people chased after him, carrying gifts of Brazil nuts, woven cloth, palm mats. One even had a chicken.

"Give me twenty minutes to wash." A laugh trailed after him. "I intend to win the match tonight. We're playing for your church and your rosary, aren't we?"

Father Emil laughed. "I thought we were playing for the *Addison Beal.*"

March shouted something they didn't hear, then Father Emil gently turned Lalie back toward the rectory. "If we don't go inside soon, the insects will eat us alive. That reminds me of the time March and I—"

But Lalie had heard all the tales about March Addison

that she wished to. Now she preferred to hear wonderful stories about her fiancé. Murmuring an apology, she interrupted to inquire if Father Emil knew Sir Percival.

"Yes."

"Sir Percival and I plan to marry," Lalie confided with pride. Then she waited, gazing up at the priest expectantly, but he said nothing more. Surprised, she waited another moment then tried again. "Do you know Sir Percival well?"

"Well enough. Ah, here we are. Do come inside. We'll have a glass of champagne, plentiful this year, then you must share all the news from London."

Pausing in the doorway, Lalie regarded him with a curious frown. The Amazon was indeed a peculiar and exotic place if a man like March Addison was lauded whereas Sir Percival's name evoked only silence. Or, she thought uneasily, not really believing it, perhaps Father Emil had been in Quantos too long. Perhaps the constant heat and the jungle had altered his values.

Nevertheless when March appeared half an hour later, darkly handsome and smelling of soap, Lalie couldn't help regarding him in a slightly different manner. He had purchased the bell for Quantos. She would never have suspected him capable of doing such a thing. This was not the simple, uncomplicated man she had considered him to be.

Shortly before she retired to the rectory guest house and the bath she eagerly anticipated, leaving March and Father Emil to their chess game, Lalie found herself standing before the window, alone with March. She hated to admit it, even to herself, but she had been seeking just such an opportunity.

"There's something I have to say to you," she said in a low voice. Reluctant to continue, she gazed out at the thick foliage brushed silver by a crescent moon. She remembered the scars zigzagging across his naked chest, an image that made her feel inexplicably warm and peculiar inside.

"I intend to finish my cigar, Miss Pritchard," he said calmly, exhaling a stream of blue smoke into the night. "You may save your breath and spare me your complaints."

She clenched her teeth and forced herself to follow through on the decision she had taken. "I didn't play the piano selection you chose. I played one of my set pieces."

There, she had admitted it. A rush of embarrassed pink flooded her cheeks. Lalie hadn't a notion why it seemed important to confide the truth. It just did. Her decision had something to do with March's scars, with his hands touching her body after the storm, and with the bell for Quantos. Her thoughts twisted in a tangle of confusion that she didn't wish to examine too closely.

"I know."

"You *know?*"

"I read music, Miss Pritchard." His dark eyes twinkled. "Once upon a time I played the violin. Young gentlemen are also expected to have accomplishments to trot out for guests. Once upon a time in another life I was a young gentleman."

She stared up at him, trying to understand. "You made a fool out of me," she said finally. "You let me believe I'd deceived you."

"You didn't need me to make you feel foolish, Miss Pritchard. You managed it all by yourself."

Her gaze narrowed in embarrassment and anger. "How could I possibly have guessed that you—you!—read music?" He had trimmed his mustache and exposed the sensual curve of his lips. Lalie gazed at his mouth and her breath caught in her throat.

It made no sense to her that she could be so angry and still manage to notice his mouth. It made even less sense that there could be something attractive about that mouth.

March Addison was the most confusing man she had ever met.

Suddenly she realized they stood entirely too close to one another. She could feel the heat of his body mingling with the heat of the night. Silver shadows teased through his hair and glowed in his dark, intent eyes. He had removed his jacket and his shoulders seemed wide and strong to her. His white linen shirt made his deeply tanned skin seem even darker.

"I'm not the barbarian you imagine, Miss Pritchard." He smiled, laughing at her. "Almost, but not quite."

She stumbled backward a step. "Tell me," she whispered. "Exactly how far is it to Hiberalta?" Suddenly it seemed imperative that she reach Sir Percival as swiftly as possible. Sir Percival, whose features had inexplicably begun to blur in her memory.

"On the river we measure distance in days, not miles. I hope to deliver you to Hiberalta within four months."

"Four months." Shock darkened her eyes to a slate color. The next words were blurted out and appalling in their rudeness. "I don't believe I can endure your company for four months, Mr. Addison."

His gaze lingered an instant at her lips then returned to her eyes. "I find you tedious as well, Miss Pritchard. Your self-righteousness would try the patience of a saint."

They glared at one another, intensely aware of flashing anger and tense bodies, of beckoning moonlight and clashing values.

"Here we are," Father Emil said cheerfully from behind them. Bending, he placed a silver tray on the table holding the chess set. "Brandy and—"

"No thank you," Lalie snapped, turning on her heel. Recovering her composure, she offered her hand to Father Emil then fled to the guest house.

March watched the swirl of her skirts as she left. The candlelight flickering in the foyer gleamed like flame in her hair. He guessed he could span her waist between his hands.

The priest seated himself before the chess board, tented his long fingers beneath his chin, and studied the board. "When Percival Sterling learns Miss Pritchard is aboard the *Addison Beal,* there's going to be trouble. You know that, March."

"I know." He continued to regard the staircase. An elusive scent of lilacs and verbena lingered behind her.

"But there's trouble already, isn't there?" Father Emil inquired softly, looking up at him.

Frowning, March turned from the staircase and took the chair across from the priest. "Are you going to spoil the game by preaching?"

Father Emil smiled. He looked pointedly at March's shaven cheeks and trimmed mustache, the spotless shirt and stylishly knotted tie. "It's your move."

Although he didn't want another cigar March lit one, hoping to overwhelm the traces of Lalie's perfume. A scowl of resentment darkened his expression. This was possibly the last time he would sit over a chess board with Father Emil, his friend of many years. He had anticipated an evening of quiet talk and shared remembrances.

Instead his thoughts strayed to Eulalie Pritchard. He imagined her easing her dress over her head then pulling the pins from her hair to free a silken cascade. He could envision her unhooking her corset and removing her undergarments to reveal her soft, pale skin, skin that had never been touched by the Amazon sun. He imagined her easing herself into the tub, the warm, scented water lapping the tender underswell of her breasts.

Emil captured his rook and chuckled when March stared incredulously at the board.

"No, don't apologize for being an easy mark tonight," Father Emil said, freshening their brandy snifters. "I'm delighted. I couldn't be happier for you."

"I don't know what you're talking about." He was

genuinely puzzled by the remark. But he didn't request enlightenment because he sensed he would dislike the priest's reply.

"No, I don't believe you do." Sympathy softened Father Emil's gaze. He glanced toward the door with a thoughtful look. "But you will." He returned his gaze to March. "I have an idea you underestimate Miss Pritchard. And you shouldn't, March. She isn't what she seems. There's much more to her than meets the eye."

March stared. "You've been out in the sun too long. Miss Pritchard is a frivolous piece of fluff held together by rigid convention and a lunatic devotion to etiquette."

"You're wrong. Miss Pritchard wants to be a woman of her time, and I believe she is capable of a good deal more than you suspect."

"I cannot imagine why you would form such an astonishing opinion," March said, turning his queen in his hand. He wondered what on earth Miss Pritchard and Father Emil had discussed in his absence. And he wondered why she had confessed her deception at the piano. Would he ever understand this woman? She was a mass of confusing contradictions.

He released an unconscious sigh. "I wonder how long I'll last before I toss Her Majesty overboard, shout good riddance, and sail off without her." When Emil laughed, he frowned. "You know damned well I hate that holier-than-thou knowing look. Will you just play chess?"

The priest grinned. "I'd be happy to oblige. But it's your move."

It was. March looked at the queen in his hand, rolled his eyes toward the ceiling, released another enormous sigh, then made an absolutely idiotic move. He blamed Miss Pritchard. The woman was driving him crazy.

Chapter 5

After departing Quantos the journey upriver settled into a steady, monotonous routine. The days blurred in Lalie's mind, one melting seamlessly into the next. The heat, the river, even the scenery seemed identical every day. To the south a broad expanse of brown water opened toward the horizon, interrupted here and there by small islands. An unchanging picture stretched along the near shore, an expanse of glistening caramel water, a band of feathery green, and overhead the hot blue sky.

Occasionally they dropped anchor near one of the rare stilt houses along the riverbanks to trade kerosene or champagne for fresh fruit and a scrawny chicken. From time to time the day was enlivened by a dash for shore to seek shelter from a sudden storm. And once in a while Addison navigated the *Addison Beal* up one of the many small tributaries emptying into the river. There he and Fredo would load the dugout with supplies. Then the two men would paddle away to trade with forest tribes, leaving Lalie and Maria to broil beneath the scorching afternoon sun. Occasionally, like today, it was necessary to drop anchor so Joao could forage in the forest for wood to feed the steamer's boiler.

Leaning on the rail, welcoming the diversion but fretting over the delay, Lalie stared at the thick explosion of green overhanging the nearby riverbanks, trying to catch a glimpse of Joao. The dense jungle foliage had swallowed him immediately and she spied no sign of movement.

Removing a handkerchief from her cuff, she mopped her throat and temples, and she thought of Joao enjoying the cool shadows within the forest. Right now Lalie would have traded her prized book of etiquette for a five-minute escape from the shimmering heat and pervasive insects.

Pulling off her straw hat, she fanned her face and listened to the silence, gradually realizing that it wasn't silent at all. Insects hummed near her face. Brightly colored fish leapt above the water for an instant. On occasion she heard growling in the nearby undergrowth, followed by the screams of parrots and monkeys. The screeching emphasized the silence that followed. Without the sound of the engine the ship seemed unnaturally quiet. She could hear Fredo and Addison murmuring inside the wheelhouse, while Maria prepared the midday meal.

Lalie finally turned away from the railing and shoved a limp strand of hair back from her cheek. Without much enthusiasm she stepped behind her tarpaulin and removed her morning dress, standing for a moment in her corset and petticoat, longing for a cooling breeze. Sighing, she glanced over the top of her privacy wall at the hot sunlight reflecting off the surface of the water.

Would it really be so terrible to cast aside her corset? For an instant she contemplated the deep breaths that would be possible without the garment. She tried to imagine the pleasure of stray breezes unimpeded by a barrier of steel and thick layers of cloth. The thoughts exerted a seductive appeal.

Suddenly she started and placed a hand over her mouth. What was she thinking of? She couldn't possibly go without her corset. It wouldn't be proper; it was almost uncivilized. The future bride of Sir Percival Sterling could not be seen without proper and decent undergarments.

Lalie sighed again and put the thought out of her mind. She smoothed ammonia over the red welts dotting her throat and shoulders before she dropped a flowered muslin afternoon dress over her head and pressed down her skirts. After tying a taffeta sash around her ever-so-properly corseted waist, she added a necklace and earrings made of tiny pink shells, then she drew on lace gloves and covered her coppery hair with a wide-brimmed hat.

Before she stepped out on deck, she paused to examine herself in the silver-framed mirror her father had given her on her twentieth birthday. And she asked why she bothered to change her clothing three times a day. For whom did she maintain the standards that seemed so crucial at home?

For March Addison? She almost laughed. Whatever manners and standards Addison might once have held dear had vanished years ago. No, Lalie maintained her standards solely out of pride and because she knew Sir Percival would expect no less from his future wife. A gentleman such as Percival would not squander his affection on a corsetless hussy.

Fortified by these thoughts, Lalie pulled back the tarpaulin flap then paused to regard the forest towering above the stacks of the *Addison Beal.* A frown wrinkled her sunburned brow. Whenever the ship dropped anchor, the rain forest dominated her thoughts, rising before her like a menacing challenge. It was impossible to ignore the forest, much as Lalie tried.

And she tried because the forest frightened her. It was a mysterious presence filled with strange sounds and sometimes bizarre foliage. At times she felt certain that unseen eyes peered out of the jungle undergrowth, watching her.

At the same time the towering swell exerted a fascination. These two forces, fear and attraction, tugged at Lalie's mind. She wanted to explore the rain forest, to see its mysteries for herself. At the same time, the thought of setting foot within that seemingly impenetrable darkness sent shudders of apprehension through her.

Now, staring at the wall of green, she imagined faceless voices. "Poor Eulalie. She traveled all that distance but never set foot in the forest. All she saw, poor thing, was the river."

Poor Eulalie, she never really lived.

Lalie's spine stiffened and her eyes narrowed on the thick stand of Brazil-nut trees along the shore. Eventually she would have to marshal whatever courage she possessed and explore within. She wouldn't be able to live with herself if she didn't conquer her fear. After all, she intended to make her life in the Amazon. Pride demanded that she overcome her conviction that the forest teemed with a multitude of creeping, crawling, and growling creatures that sought nothing more than to dine on the succulent flesh of Englishwomen.

The farther up the Amazon she'd traveled, the more she'd questioned her courage. And today it seemed that if she did not take some action soon, she never would.

Frowning in dismay, she stared at the forest. It occurred to her that while she sought romance and adventure, it was just possible she lacked the courage to follow through when she found them. This thought was so objectionable that Lalie tried to push it to the farthest corner of her mind—a place it stubbornly refused to go.

She must do something if only to prove to herself she was not a complete coward, and she must do it now before she changed her mind.

Biting her lip in dread, Lalie returned to her cubicle and changed from her afternoon dress to a plain dark skirt, a crisp white blouse, sensible shoes, and a hat.

Today would be the day.

"You are an Englishwoman," she reminded her mirror. "You march forward undaunted. Nature is your friend."

So why did she stand with her back to the shore?

"Missy asks Cabo to take his food at her table," Maria said, leaning into the wheelhouse.

Ordinarily March would have refused. Today, however, he hesitated before offering a reply. Although the windows were propped open within the wheelhouse, it was stifling inside and would be until Joao returned with the wood enabling them to again get under way. His charts and logbook were updated. Fredo dozed in the heat, preferring a nap to conversation. March felt restless and in need of diversion, even as unsatisfactory a diversion as Miss Pritchard was likely to be.

"I'll join Miss Pritchard in fifteen minutes." Her Majesty would require a moment or two to scramble up an additional place setting, he knew. Not for an instant did he believe she would be content to set a place with the scarred crockery used by his crew.

Shaking his head, March turned to look at the river opening like a wide tunnel before him. Within the week they would steam into the crystal-blue waters of the Tapajos River and soon afterward they would dock at Santarém. For several miles below Santarém, the blue waters of the Tapajos ran side by side with the Amazon's brown flow. He didn't anticipate any trouble along this stretch of river.

Drawing on his cigar, he glanced through the door and watched Eulalie Pritchard arranging the table to her precise specifications. As always when first he glimpsed her, his stomach tightened and unconsciously he clenched his jaw. Her beauty continually took him by surprise as did her obvious unawareness of her physical appeal. Although she constantly fussed with her appearance, changing her clothing several times a day, it had not taken March long to understand she responded to habit and the dictates of etiquette, not to the demands of vanity.

In fact Miss Pritchard was one of the least vain women March had ever encountered. Even Clea Paralta, who impressed him as a sensible woman, would have bewailed the multitude of swollen and disfiguring insect bites. But Miss Pritchard appeared more concerned that her gloves were spotless than with the fact that her cheeks were swollen and blotchy.

And certainly she was no flirt. Although he was beginning to consider her a very seductive woman, Eulalie Pritchard's seductiveness was unconscious, without awareness or guile. It was a result of the way she moved, the way she walked, a certain hypnotic quality in her eyes.

She wove a spell with her curious vulnerability, with the distance she maintained from others, with the small sighs she made in her sleep. She beguiled when she arched her throat to stroke ammonia along its creamy length. She enchanted when she strolled the deck in the warm moonlight. And she bewitched when she emerged from behind her tarpaulin wearing a frothy white nightgown beneath an enveloping wrapper, a glowing braid draped over her shoulder.

The rest of the time she irritated the hell out of him.

There had been numerous women in March Addison's life, too many, some said. At times he had been accused of being a womanizer and probably he had been. Once or twice he had considered marriage but had come to his senses before he framed the actual proposal. But never before had he wanted a woman in quite the same way as he wanted Eulalie Pritchard. And never before had he understood his desire so little.

He stared at her profile across the deck, trying to understand how he could possibly desire her and dislike her at the same time. Her rigidity was absolutely abhorrent to him. Even sitting down she was ramrod straight, held in beautifully erect posture by her steel-ribbed corset. His gaze was drawn to her coppery hair, her rounded breast. And he wished to Christ she was engaged to marry anyone but Percival Sterling. He couldn't tolerate the thought of that bastard touching her.

"I suppose it would be too much to ask that you don a proper jacket," she said as he approached her table. One of her eyebrows arched in disapproval. He had never encountered another human being with such mobile eyebrows or with eyebrows capable of expressing condemnation so eloquently. He frowned at her.

"It's one hundred degrees in the shade, Miss Pritchard, and humid as well. You'll simply have to adopt a humane attitude and overlook shirtsleeves and an open collar." What was God thinking to waste this much beauty on so superficial a woman?

"Would you at least remove that beastly hat?"

"You dislike my hat?" he asked in surprise. After three years he had finally gotten it broken in just right. But the Amazon had not diminished his manners to the extent that he would have dined with a woman while wearing his hat. He turned the straw in his hands, then placed it on the deck.

"If you'll forgive me for saying so, that—hat—should have been replaced long ago. It's a disgrace."

"If you'll forgive me for saying so, a woman should never attack a man's hat, dog, horse, or prowess. These items are sacred." She didn't react, her thoughts were clearly focused on other matters.

Sunlight glinted on delicate china cups ornamented with tiny pink roses and gold rims. "I requested something light today," Miss Pritchard murmured as Maria served baked bananas in rum sauce.

"So I see."

Miss Pritchard stared straight ahead for a moment as if deciding the direction the conversation would take. At length she released a breath and affected a dazzling hostess's smile.

"Sugar, Mr. Addison?" With graceful, practiced movements she poured tea from a china pot.

"Thank you." He would have preferred *cafezinho,* but refrained from saying so.

"The heat is tiresome, isn't it?"

"Worse than yesterday, I believe."

"Will it be snowing at home by now do you think?"

Without thought he fell into habits learned in his youth. Follow the hostess's lead. Introduce no controversial topics. Still, he sensed there was a purpose behind his presence at her table. Eventually she would reveal the reason behind her invitation. He could wait.

Meanwhile he conceded that Miss Pritchard played her role well. She leaned slightly forward as if eagerly awaiting his reply, as if the fate of the world depended on March Addison's opinion. Without difficulty he pictured her sitting in a London drawing room, presiding over a tea cart, supreme in her gifts as a hostess, able to charm without effort.

"The Amazon is home to me," he said, watching her. She smiled and gazed at him as if giving great consideration to his statement. March didn't deceive himself that Eulalie Pritchard had suddenly developed a burning desire to learn his opinions. She wanted something.

"Come now, Mr. Addison, don't you ever think of England, of Putnam Hall, your father's lovely estate? I especially remember the gardens, and the lovely oak trees there." She drew a breath, held it a second, then continued. "I haven't noticed any oak trees along the river. Do oaks grow in the Amazon?"

By now he recognized that feigned look of innocence. Finally they were approaching the reason she had invited him to share her table.

"You didn't have to stage this luncheon, Miss Pritchard. If there's something you want, all you need do is say so."

"I beg your pardon?"

"Directness, Miss Pritchard. What do you want? I doubt

you conceived a sudden passion for my company. So why did you invite me to share your table?"

A flush tinted her cheeks. "Truly, Mr. Addison, you have the manners of a peasant. You lack any talent for pleasantries."

"The point, Miss Pritchard. May we skip to the point?"

She frowned, uncertain now what to do. After a few seconds she began. "Actually there is something I wish to discuss." The admission emerged with difficulty and seemed to annoy her. "I had hoped we could ease into the subject . . ."

"You're longing to discuss horticulture? Gardens and oaks? Am I supposed to guess the topic you wish to discuss?"

She pressed her lips together and, unless he imagined it, her face paled beneath her peeling sunburn. "As a matter of fact you aren't far wrong. I was thinking . . ." She drew another breath, gasping slightly as if the air had thinned. "I believe I would like to explore the rain forest. I've never seen one."

March couldn't understand her obvious distress, but he did understand her request. In fact, he had anticipated her curiosity would have led her inland before now. On those rare occasions when he permitted passengers to accompany him upriver, they generally succumbed to the lure of the forest long before the *Addison Beal* reached Quantos.

However, after thinking about it a moment, he realized her reticence did seem to make sense. He couldn't picture Miss Pritchard striding through the undergrowth swinging a machete.

Belatedly he recognized that she was not wearing one of her frilly afternoon dresses. She wore a plain skirt and shirtwaist, a sturdy hat, and no adornment. He assumed she considered this her visit-the-forest ensemble.

"Are you saying you wish to explore the forest? Now?"

She wet her lips and nodded. "Unless you forbid it."

He tilted his head and studied her expression. She said

she wanted to see the forest, but her expression and attitude did not match her words. She appeared almost ill at the prospect, and he had the absurd impression that she hoped he would refuse her. He didn't begin to understand. But then, there wasn't much about Miss Pritchard that he did understand.

"Why on earth would I forbid you to visit the forest?" He shrugged. "Sooner or later everyone wants to view it. And they should. The rain forest is as much the Amazon as the river." Pushing back from the table, he stood. "Now seems as good a time as any. We'll be anchored here until Joao returns with the wood." After retrieving his hat, he glanced at her attire. "Would you consider donning a pair of Joao's trousers?"

Instead of looking appalled by his suggestion as he half expected, she appeared vastly relieved. "Well, that's it, then. If trousers are a condition of visiting the forest, I'm afraid I must decline. No one could blame me for refusing to dress like a man. It's a scandalous suggestion."

"Miss Pritchard, you try my patience." Dropping his head back, he examined the deck roofing before he looked at her again. "I did not say wearing Joao's trousers was a requisite for visiting the rain forest. I meant only to suggest you would be more comfortable without all those skirts. If you wish to wear skirts, then wear skirts. I don't give a damn."

When she slowly stood to face the forest edge, her face had bleached to the color of paste. Even her eyes appeared a lighter shade. "I see," she whispered. "Then we can go?"

Suddenly it dawned on him. "You're afraid." The truth lay in her chalky face, in the tremble she tried to hide by thrusting her hands within the folds of her skirt.

"I am *not* afraid!"

"There's reason for caution, but not fear," he said finally.

She whirled on him, her pale eyes flashing with pride. "I

don't require a nursemaid, Mr. Addison. I'm not one of those fragile creatures who need constant coddling."

The look in his eyes clearly suggested otherwise.

The color flooded back into her face and she leaned forward. "I am weary to death of your condescending manner, Mr. Addison."

"And I am weary of your prickly sensibilities, Miss Pritchard. Do you wish to visit the rain forest or not?"

The indecision returned and embarrassed her. She pressed her lips into a line and twisted her hands together. She shifted her weight from one foot to the other. "You said everyone visits the forest . . ."

"Miss Pritchard—"

"Yes, I intend to go," she stated so quickly it seemed almost one long word.

Striving for patience, March exhaled slowly. "You don't have to do this. I knew a Frenchman who steamed upriver, lived in Manaus three years, and never once entered the rain forest."

"Are you suggesting I'm a coward?"

"No one said anything about—"

"I'm quite ready." Her head lifted and her gaze turned cold. "Shall we go to the rainforest, Mr. Addison?"

Addison rowed them from the ship to the shore, where he helped her out of the dugout and onto a strip of pebbles and sand. Quickly Lalie scanned the beach, looking for dozing caimans while Addison secured the boat. She jumped when a parrot screamed and a cloud of blue and red macaws rose from the surrounding foliage and fluttered to higher perches.

Addison noted her startled movement. "It's not too late to change your mind," he said.

"Don't patronize me. I am *not* afraid," she insisted stiffly, but even as she spoke she was certain thousands of eyes watched, hungry stomachs growled, and stalking predators crept toward her, licking their fangs.

Driven by pride and the infuriating amusement twinkling in Addison's eyes, Lalie braced herself then stepped to the edge of the forest. Lifting his machete, Addison hacked an opening into the jungle and Lalie followed him, her heart thumping against her corset.

Stepping into the rain forest was like moving instantly from the dog days of summer into a cool, almost chill, autumn evening. The difference in temperature was marked and lovely, Lalie thought with surprise, waiting a moment for her eyes to adjust to the interior gloom. Here and there shafts of light penetrated the vaulted ceiling, reminding her of sunlight filtering through the windows of a medieval abbey, but for the most part the forest was dim and shadowy.

Tier upon tier of vegetation rose up and up and up, the highest tier lost to sight. Lianas hung like thick cobwebs from the upper reaches or wrapped about the tree trunks. Giant ferns carpeted the floor of the forest. Every imaginable shade of green was present, unrelieved by any other color.

"Are there no flowers here?" Somehow it would have seemed wrong to speak above a whisper even if Lalie could have found her full voice.

"Not many, frankly," Addison said from directly behind her. "It's a treat to discover a blossom. Flowers aren't rare, but they aren't common, either."

To Lalie's amazement the undergrowth thinned as they progressed farther from shore. The floor of the forest was not littered with dead and fallen leaves as she had expected, but was clean, almost manicured in spots.

As if he'd read her mind, Addison smiled and pointed the barrel of his rifle. "Ants," he explained. "And termites. The lack of debris is one of the marvels of the rain forest. The insects break down the debris almost immediately." He touched a fallen log with the toe of his boot and it crumbled to dust.

"You know how to get back to the ship . . . don't you?"

They had penetrated the forest only about twenty yards but already Lalie was hopelessly lost. She couldn't have chosen the proper direction back to shore if her life depended on it. And it did, she thought uneasily, staring at the riotous undergrowth. It all looked the same to her; there were no discernible landmarks.

It occurred to her that she and Addison were utterly alone. Her gaze traveled up the swell of his shoulders to the cords along his neck and finally to the speculative look in his eye. She hated realizing her dependency on him as much as she hated the sudden awareness of being alone with him. Once that thought entered her mind, bringing with it an uncomfortable feeling, she could hardly think of anything else. Wetting her lips, she averted her face from his handsome features.

Once Addison assured her that he could indeed direct them back to the ship, Lalie tried to put her fears aside and decided to see all there was to observe, as she was sure she'd never visit the rain forest again. Once was enough. The oppressiveness disturbed her, as did being alone with Addison. After giving her head a shake, she tried to concentrate on the chaos of plants she could not name.

"Your hem," Addison called after they had walked deeper into the forest.

Stepping away from him, Lalie tilted her head to inspect the overhead canopy. No wonder there was little to observe. She had been looking in the wrong place. The life of the forest was lived in the upper reaches. Monkeys swung from liana to liana. Brilliantly colored birds chattered overhead. A blanket of butterflies covered a limb.

"Your hem, Miss Pritchard. It's covered with ants."

"What?" In horror, she glanced down and saw that her hem was alive. Hundreds of ants busily explored the bottom of her skirt. Holes were appearing where none had been before. Lalie whirled in a mad circle, slapping at her

skirt, stamping her shoes. She had never seen so many ants before, or ants so large, and they were crawling on *her.* It was the worst horror she could imagine.

Until she saw the snake.

She tried to scream but could manage only a strangled squeak, and she stumbled backward until she met an obstruction and could no longer move. She froze in place. The hair on the back of her neck stood up. Her heart thundered madly. She stood helpless and speechless, unable to breathe, staring at a mottled vision from hell. Not in her wildest, most horrifying nightmares had Lalie envisioned a snake this enormous. Its coils, wrapped around a tree trunk, were as wide as her thighs. If someone had been insane enough to unwind the snake and stretch it flat, she was positive it would be as long as the *Addison Beal.*

"Miss Pritchard? Are you coming?"

"Snake," she tried to say but only emitted a terrified wheeze.

"What?"

Again she tried to speak but couldn't.

Addison shifted the Winchester to his shoulder and came back to stand beside her. Bending and looking annoyed, he flicked the forgotten ants from her skirt.

A gigantic snake was about to leap on them. Was he blind? Sweat appeared on her brow, she was shaking from her hat to her toes. She screamed but no sound emerged. "Snake," she wheezed, but once more the sound was only a desperate gurgle. "Snake, snake!"

"If those choking sounds are supposed to be comprehensible, they aren't. Speak up, Miss Pritchard."

Perspiration flooded her temples, streamed down her sides. Her heart pounded in terrified fits and starts. "Up there," she gasped, strangling. "Up there. Snake!"

"What?"

If she had been able to move, she would have pummeled him to the ground. But all she could do was pray he hadn't drawn the snake's attention. She couldn't move. It made her dizzy with fear to look at the snake but she was too terrified to glance away in case it seized upon her lapse of vigilance to slither down and jump on her. Whimpering, bubbling squeaks constricted her throat.

"Oh, for God's sake." Addison pushed aside the ferns that enveloped her, then leaned his head near hers and followed her paralyzed stare. Straightening, he shouldered the Winchester and laughed. He laughed! If they survived this encounter, Lalie swore she would strangle March Addison with her bare hands.

She was positive the snake turned toward Addison's laugh, preparing to launch itself upon them. Addison had secured their doom. Now the snake would attack. Only Addison's fingers gripping her shaking shoulder kept her from collapsing in mortal fear.

"It's only an anaconda, Miss Pritchard. Villagers along the Amazon keep anacondas in their gardens as pets to hold down the rodent population. There's nothing to fear."

She darted a swift look toward him. The man was a lunatic. He was stark raving mad. Jerking her head, she looked back at the snake and sucked in a breath. During the time she had glanced away, the snake had come closer, she was positive of it.

"Shoot . . . it," she gasped.

Addison sighed and rolled his eyes. "No, Miss Pritchard."

Courage, she prayed, give me courage. Stop my cowardly legs from shaking. If she could just regain control of herself, she would snatch the Winchester from Addison's shoulder and save them herself. She knew how to shoot. Her father had taken her to a dozen clay matches. The forest seemed to be closing around her, the mists lowering from above, the vegetation encroaching from below until there was nothing in front of her eyes but the hideous snake.

Then she heard a growl from terrifyingly nearby followed by Addison's shout of delight. But Lalie paid attention only to the roar. Her knees collapsed and she fell onto the moving carpet of ants. Chaos erupted overhead. Suddenly the branches were filled with fleeing monkeys, a few of which paused to hurl fruit pits down at them. Seeds and pods pelted Lalie's hat. Birds screamed. A shower of twigs and leaves fell from above.

Lalie saw a glow of yellow eyes then a tawny body that loomed out of the shadows, flashed in front of her and vanished before she could decide what she had seen. But she recalled ivory-colored fangs and claws as long as the tines on a pitchfork.

"Well, I'll be damned," Addison said softly, looking in the direction the creature had gone. "It isn't everyone who gets to see a jaguar their first time in the forest. A daylight sighting is considered a sign of good luck."

"You are a madman," she whispered. The anaconda was about to attack, a jaguar stalked them, she was being devoured by ants. And March Addison stood there as if he were in the middle of Hyde Park with an umbrella on his shoulder instead of a rifle. "You idiot!" she shouted, springing to her feet. "You're supposed to protect me!"

After delivering a stinging slap across his face, she whirled in the opposite direction from that which the jaguar had chosen. Terror drove her. All she could think of was escaping the anaconda before it shot forward and grabbed her. Screaming, she crashed through the ferns and tangled vines, her only thought to reach safety. Behind her, she heard Addison shouting, but his shouts didn't matter. Fear pounded in her heart and narrowed her windpipe. She couldn't breathe.

Gasping, blinded by tears of fright, she struggled forward. By sheer happenstance she burst through a wall of thorny brush and emerged on the beach. "Thank God. Oh thank God." She could see the *Addison Beal* fifty yards down the beach.

Then she saw the caimans dozing along the shore, their

leathery snouts almost at her feet. One of them yawned, exposing rows of glistening daggerlike teeth.

"Oh my God!" Heart in her throat, she spun and crashed into the brush, thrashing back the way she had come. Her pulse thundered in her ears, she was shaking so badly she could not breathe. If she survived this nightmare, Lalie swore she would hurl all her corsets overboard.

When she ran full tilt into Addison, she screamed then burrowed into his arms seeking safety and shelter. She held him as tightly as she was able, and she pressed her face into his collar. But Addison pried her hands loose and held her away from him. He gave her a hard shake and glared into her eyes.

"Don't you *ever* do that again!" A red hand print flamed on his cheek. "You stay with me! You do *not* run off on your own. Ever! Do you understand me? What in God's name were you thinking of? You could have been—"

Lalie stared over his shoulder, saw a gray furry creature gripping a tree limb with claws as sharp and long as talons. She gasped.

"It's only a sloth, Miss Pritchard. Miss Pritchard?"

The sloth lifted a front leg and a shaft of sunlight struck his claws. A shuddering sob convulsed Lalie's body. Then her eyes closed and she pitched forward into March Addison's arms.

Chapter 6

After lighting his after-dinner cigar, March tossed the spent match into the river then leaned back against the railing. He listened to Maria humming as she worked, anticipating the time below deck with Fredo. Fredo was a lucky man, March thought.

"You want play cards, Cabo?" Joao asked, removing a worn deck from his pocket and passing it to Fredo. Fredo clamped his teeth around a cigar stub and fanned the cards beneath the light of a kerosene lantern.

"Not tonight, but thank you, gentlemen."

A huge lemon-colored moon emerged from behind a wisp of cloud to illuminate the evening and shower golden streamers across the river. A symphony rose from the forest, night voices singing songs of love and battle.

March drew on his cigar and shifted against the rail to idly watch Eulalie Pritchard pacing the width of the far end of the deck. Moonlight gleamed in her coppery hair and caressed her throat and shoulders. As her head was down, he couldn't observe her expression.

She hadn't spoken a word since he carried her back to the *Addison Beal.* Maria had treated the ant bites on her ankles and calves while Miss Pritchard sat rigidly upright, her dulled eyes fixed on a point in space. Afterward, she sought refuge behind her tarpaulin, emerging only to dine alone at her table. Now she paced, head down, moving rapidly back and forth as if the devil nipped her heels.

Releasing a sigh, March pushed away from the rail. Earlier her expression had warned him not to approach. But perhaps he should. Miss Pritchard was his passenger and as captain he bore a responsibility for her welfare. Although he didn't have the slightest notion what he would say to her, he strolled toward her.

"Pleasant night," he commented, placing a boot on the pile of cargo and gazing at the moon-dappled river. Out of the corner of his eye he watched her pause at the railing, then pace behind him leaving a whisper of lilac and verbena on the moist night air. Her beauty took his breath away.

"Anyone would have been frightened!" She halted at the far railing and glared at him, daring him to contradict her. When March didn't speak she resumed pacing, trailing perfume and frustration in her wake.

March didn't utter a word. He puffed on his cigar and studied a cluster of mosquitoes. He began to wish he'd had the good sense to remain at the front of the ship with the others. Waves of anger and defensiveness emanated from her small body. She threw out her hands.

"Perhaps snakes can't launch themselves off trees. I didn't know that this afternoon. But you can't tell me that jaguars aren't dangerous! And that sloth thing!" A shudder convulsed her shoulders.

"Jaguars can be dangerous," he agreed. He tried to hide a smile. "Sloths—well, sloths are not as dangerous."

"Don't patronize me, Mr. Addison." She spun around at the railing and her gloved hands clenched into fists. "I am sick of being patronized as if you were an all-knowing adult and I were an idiot child!"

"I'm not patronizing you. I agreed with you. Jaguars can indeed be dangerous."

"There you are. Did you hear the tone of your voice? I *know* jaguars are dangerous. I don't need you to inform me of that fact!"

He straightened, examined the glowing tip of his cigar, then studied her furious, beautiful face. "Miss Pritchard. I regret that you were frightened today and made a fool of yourself. But let's attempt to be reasonable, shall we? The first time one sees an anaconda can be . . . unnerving. And a jaguar appearing unexpectedly can be frightening. As for the sloth, a snail can outrun a sloth, but you didn't know that."

"You're being patronizing again, don't claim you aren't!"

"No, damn it, I'm not." He moved closer to her and bent to scowl into her eyes. "Fear is an asset in the jungle. Fear prevents one from becoming careless. I'm not ridiculing your fear nor am I patronizing you. There's nothing to be ashamed of in being frightened. Where you erred was in running off by yourself. *That* was the most dangerous thing that happened to you today. And *that* is an act worthy of condemnation. Don't ever do it again."

For a long moment she returned his angry stare, then her shoulders sagged, her head dropped, and her arms fell to her sides. The fight seemed to drain out of her before his eyes. His instinct was to reach for her, but she stepped back.

"I was so frightened," she whispered, her lashes closing against her cheekbones. "So damned terrified."

March coughed on the smoke from his cigar. It would be easier for him to believe in generous bankers than to believe he had overheard a swear word emerge from Miss Pritchard's prim, inviting lips.

"You aren't the first," he managed to say. Suddenly he remembered her small, yielding body pressed against him as he carried her out of the forest. She weighed scarcely more than a child and was much more fragile than he had realized.

"You don't understand," she said, biting her lip. Moisture glistened in her eyes. "I've always believed I had courage." Self-disgust fueled her words. March guessed she would be furious with herself tomorrow for having revealed these confidences to him. "Now I know I'm a coward. And I hate that."

Pacing again, she moved away from him, swatting distractedly at the mosquitoes. "I used to assist my father in his dispensary. I helped set broken bones, mopped up blood, saw horrid things I can't bear to describe, and I never fainted. Not once. And I was the first person in Hackney to ride a bicycle—the first woman anyway. I fell again and again but I always picked myself up and tried once more. And I made the journey from London to Brazil alone. I planned the trip myself and I saw it through."

She halted in front of him. "I thought that meant I had courage. I *believed* it. I believed I could cope with any situation in which I found myself. I believed I was a sensible and worthy woman Sir Percival Sterling would be proud to wed."

Oh yes. She was going to regret this conversation in the morning. But it interested March that she actually considered herself sensible.

"Now I discover I'm a spineless wretch with no more courage than a flea. How did you get those scars on your chest?" she asked abruptly, peering at March through the shadows.

March smiled. "Someone who looked a lot like you once informed me that prying questions are indescribably rude."

Her eyes widened like bright jewels in the moonlight and her hands flew to her mouth. "Oh good heavens. I apologize. I don't know what came over me, I just . . . You're correct, of course. I can't imagine what I was thinking of, this is so embarrassing, I—"

Though it was tempting to let her run on, March

laughed and raised a hand. "Stop." Even in the shadows he could see that her face had turned as fiery red as her hair. "Not everyone considers such questions offensive. Some might be flattered by an expression of interest."

Expressing interest in March Addison didn't sit well with her, either. He smiled as her blush intensified.

"If you'll excuse me," she said stiffly. She looked toward the front of the ship where Joao was stringing the hammocks and Fredo yawned and winked suggestively at Maria. "Suddenly I'm very tired . . ."

"One final remark, Miss Pritchard . . . I don't know if you're a coward or not. Frankly, you don't know, either. In my view, you haven't experienced a genuine test."

"I don't know why you're being agreeable tonight but I deeply appreciate the gesture." She spoke in a low voice and without glancing at him. "But you're wrong. I've been tested and I failed."

March watched her lift her head and walk toward her tarpaulin. Turning to the river, he leaned on the railing and studied the trail of a silvery piranha flashing through the water and he thought about the conversation that had just ended.

It interested him that Miss Pritchard condemned her own behavior in the rain forest. Her fear had not surprised him. He had fully expected her to swoon and gasp and start and jump. In his opinion her only cause for censure had been her headlong flight away from him. But she viewed her reaction to the anaconda and the jaguar as cowardice. Hell, he had seen grown men collapse in fear at the unexpected sight of a jaguar. Would Miss Pritchard have labeled them cowards? Perhaps he had labeled them so himself. But they were men.

It had not occurred to him that women might wish to be admired as courageous. Most of the women he had known in England considered themselves to be fragile flowers and willingly left all acts of bravery to men. Had society changed so radically in nine years? Or was it possible that Miss Eulalie Pritchard was unique in this regard? That possibility troubled him.

Long after Maria and Fredo returned upstairs, March lay in his hammock, arms behind his head, thinking about Miss Pritchard. He would have sworn her only goal in life was to live by *Mrs. Wilkie's Rules of Etiquette,* the accepted standard for proper behavior in British society. Now he discovered she wanted to test her courage. He could not reconcile two aims he viewed as contradictory.

"Mr. Addison? Are you still awake?"

"I thought you were sleeping." Shifting, he turned his head toward her hammock. Silvery shadows draped her netting, but he could see a pale oval blur within. She had lifted on one elbow and was looking at him.

"I intend to return to the rain forest. I won't be conquered by it." She drew a long breath. "I wish to accompany you the next time you and Fredo visit the savages."

"Indians, Miss Pritchard. Not savages, Indians," he replied in a pained voice. "And you don't have to do that."

"Yes. I do." The finality in her tone warned against argument.

"I'll consider your request," he said at length, speaking with reluctance.

Putting up with her would be an enormous inconvenience. Her intolerance for customs other than her own held endless possibilities for offense. If Miss Pritchard believed dining at six o'clock was shocking . . . It gave him a headache to speculate on her reaction to naked Indians.

On the other hand, it might be beneficial for her to observe a tribe in their natural environment. Too often, otherwise intelligent people believed that the Indians were subhuman, fit objects for the slavery that was becoming their destiny. Certainly Miss Pritchard would observe enslaved Indians at Hiberalta. With no experience to counterbalance Sir Percy's self-serving practices, she might believe her future husband's claim that Indians did not feel beatings. That caging an Indian was no worse than restraining a dog. That torture was an apt punishment for subhuman beings.

"Mr. Addison?"

"Go to sleep, Miss Pritchard."

"How *did* you get those scars?"

He grinned at the netting over his head. When Miss Pritchard ignored etiquette and allowed herself to be human, he could almost like her.

When he eventually answered he was no longer smiling. "Three years ago I chanced upon a man beating Clea Paralta. When I raised the point that no man worthy of the name raised his hand against a woman, a fight ensued. During the fracas I was slashed across the chest."

"I hope the brute did not emerge unscathed," she sputtered. "Did you thrash him?"

"I tried to slice off his balls, Miss Pritchard, but I failed." He smiled at her gasp. "But the gentleman did not emerge unscathed. I managed to inflict a four-inch wound on his groin. For a time it appeared he might bleed to death, but the son of a bitch survived."

"I see." She dropped back into her hammock and he watched the hammock conform to the provocative curve of her buttocks and legs. "Good night, Mr. Addison."

She would see that four-inch groin scar on her wedding night, he thought. The bastard beating Clea had been Sir Percival Sterling.

Below Santarém the Tapajos had flooded. At high tide the trunks of the smaller trees were almost completely submerged and their leafy tops emerged from the water like giant green mushrooms. In a nerve-wracking excursion, Fredo navigated the *Addison Beal* through the flooded area along a tributary channel. When the rain forest narrowed around them, Addison dropped anchor and they spent the night.

Now, in the hot morning sunshine, Joao loaded the dugout with the supplies Addison and Fredo would take upriver to an isolated village populated by the Mundurukú Indians.

Lalie squared her shoulders, inhaled deeply, and descended to the lower deck. "Well?" she asked in a voice that didn't sound quite like her own. "May I accompany you and Fredo?"

She cast an uneasy glance at the foliage encroaching on the shores. Holding her breath, she awaited Addison's reply, hoping he would refuse her request.

Addison straightened above the dugout to inspect her dark skirt and rose-colored shirtwaist. "Would you consider wearing a pair of Joao's trousers?"

"Certainly not."

After glancing at the morning sky, he shrugged. "You may accompany us. But only if you agree to follow my instructions without question or hesitation." He lowered his head and his dark eyes told her he meant what he said.

"I agree."

"Our lives could depend on your obedience."

"I said I agree." Fredo helped her into the dugout, his fingers like bands of rock around her hand. He settled her in the center of the little boat and packed boxes around her. She was shocked to discover how narrow the dugout was and how low it rode in the water.

"The Mundurukú have never heard of etiquette or propriety, Miss Pritchard." She glared at him. Didn't he ever button his shirt? His tanned chest glistened with perspiration. "The customs of the Mundurukú are different from those you are used to, but let me assure you the customs of the Mundurukú are every bit as rigid as anything the most proper English lady or gentleman ever thought of. Therefore, no matter how silly or senseless you might think an act may be, do it, Miss Pritchard, when I tell you to."

"What sort of acts are you referring to, Mr. Addison?" she asked uneasily, glancing up at the towering treetops. Already she regretted this decision. If she could have lived with herself after acting the coward in front of him—again—she would have climbed out of the dugout at once.

"Avert your eyes when you address an Indian." Stepping backward, Addison checked off the last item on his list and handed the papers to Joao, who would remain behind with Maria. "If you gaze into the eyes of an Indian male, he'll believe you're flirting with him. Eye contact between sexes is courtship behavior. Eye contact between members of the same sex is considered a hostile act. For me to look into the eyes of a male or for you to look into the eyes of a female before we have been officially welcomed to the village will be interpreted as a challenge. Don't do it." He met her unblinking gaze. "Don't forget, Miss Pritchard. Or your shrunken head may end up decorating some warrior's hammock."

"The Mundurukú are head hunters?" she gasped.

"They used to be. Or so it's said. Let's not find out." After checking the lashings, he stepped into the dugout and took his place in the bow, picking up an oar. "The tribe will be naked. Only Europeans are idiotic enough to wear numerous layers of clothing in tropical heat."

"Naked!" She hadn't thought about that. Biting her lip, she looked back at the *Addison Beal,* trying to think of a reasonable excuse to remain behind.

"The men wear a coarse string around their waists," Addison said over his shoulder before Fredo pushed off and Addison dug his paddle into the blue water of the tributary. "The string is used to tie up their penises. A dangling penis is considered the height of impropriety. I suspect even Mrs. Wilkie would agree."

Scarlet exploded on Lalie's cheeks. Even her scalp felt hot with embarrassment and affront. Moreover, she knew his words had been said partly because he delighted in shocking her. She did appreciate the advance warning. It gave her time to prepare herself for the distress of observing what he described. But why did he have to state things so crudely? She frantically put the issue to the Voice of Propriety. Should she be offended, or should she act as if he had said nothing upsetting at all?

Eventually she decided it was best to know in advance what to expect. She said nothing about Addison's rude remarks. Scarlet heat pulsed in her cheeks for a full fifteen minutes as she tried to visualize the string article Addison had described. When she realized what she was doing, she hastily thrust the images from her mind. She would discover the truth all too soon.

They didn't speak throughout most of the journey up the tributary. It was easy to forget Fredo, who sat behind her. But it was impossible to overlook Addison. As she sat facing him, Lalie couldn't help watching the smooth, muscled flow of his shoulders as he leaned into the paddle, straightened, flexed, then pushed down again. She lifted her gaze to the dark hair showing beneath his hat brim, curling over the collar of his shirt. When she discovered herself wondering about the texture of his hair, if it was silky to the touch or thick, she bit her lip and shifted her glance to the forest that closed in on them. When that proved unnerving—she was certain she felt eyes observing them—she turned back helplessly to Addison, watching a damp spot widen and lengthen down the back of his white shirt.

An hour later Fredo guided them into a small cove to rest, and Lalie let her hands fall into the water, hoping the water on her wrists would cool her strangely turbulent thoughts.

When she saw the snake slipping along the surface of the water her first instinct was to scream and snatch her hand back into the boat. But she didn't. This time she would not make a fool of herself. Tiny beads of sweat appeared on her brow. And she clamped her teeth together to hold back the scream building in her throat. Her entire body tensed and went rigid, and she felt light-headed with the effort to appear brave and at ease.

"Miss Pritchard." Addison spoke in a low, terse voice. "Take your hand out of the water. Now!"

She wriggled her fingers, sending little waves toward the snake that floated perhaps a hand's length away. Every nerve in her body screamed for rescue. Sweat rolled down her face. With supreme effort she unclamped her jaws.

"It's just a snake, Mr. Addison," she wheezed. A strangled sound came out of her mouth. If a dying person could laugh, it would have sounded like that.

Sweat appeared in Addison's mustache. His black eyes were narrow and unblinking, focused on the snake. "Don't move, Miss Pritchard. Not a twitch."

The last syllable was hardly out of his mouth before Fredo's machete whistled past her shoulder and sliced through the water and the snake. Lalie stared in disbelief. She hadn't heard or felt Fredo moving up behind her.

A long sigh of relief escaped Addison and he looked up at Fredo then back at Lalie. "That was a bushmaster. One of the most venomous snakes in the world. Take a good look at the pieces, you little fool, so you'll recognize a bushmaster the next time you see one." Fury blazed in his eyes. "And the next time I tell you to do something *now,* you do it. Or I promise you, Miss Pritchard, you'll live to regret it." His black eyes narrowed to furious cold slits.

"Bushmaster," Lalie whispered, gripping the sides of the dugout as Fredo returned to the stern and sat down. "Most venomous . . . in the world. Oh my God. I could have died."

"Yes, Miss Pritchard. You could have died. In agony."

Pitching to one side, she vomited into the water.

March and Fredo vaulted into the water and pushed the dugout up onto the shore. A row of turtles plodded over the sand. Clouds of white and yellow butterflies fluttered upward at the approach of the dugout. Otherwise the forest was ominously silent.

Still furious, March extended his hand and assisted her out of the dugout. "You swore you would obey on the instant, Miss Pritchard."

"I said I was sorry." She pressed down her skirts and straightened her straw hat. Her face was still the color of whey. "It was a foolish thing to do. I just . . . I wanted to prove I'm not a coward."

"Miss Pritchard," he said, mopping his brow. "I don't *care* if you're a coward. I would in fact prefer that you be a coward. It would be safer for all of us." He settled his hat back on his head and stared at her.

"I didn't say I wished to prove anything to you. I need to prove something to myself."

"Courage is an instinct. Your instinct was undoubtedly to pull your hand inside the boat away from the bushmaster. As I *told* you to do. Trust your instinct, Miss Pritchard. If you err on the side of cowardice, you can apologize for it later. At least you'll be alive."

She met his eyes. "I don't believe courage is a sometime event, Mr. Addison. It's a character trait, one that can be developed."

"Believe whatever you like, but kindly reserve further character development until such time as you are Sir Percy's responsibility and not mine." He spoke in a blunt, harsh tone. "Do we understand each other? For the next few hours, you will do exactly as I tell you. Or so help me—"

She glared at him furiously, as if ready to do battle, and March realized she responded to threats as to a challenge.

She focused squarely on his raised voice and not on what he was saying. Turning away from him, she squared her shoulders then followed Fredo, who had entered the forest.

"We've forgotten the supplies," she called, looking back over her shoulder.

"The Indians will strip the dugout before we've walked ten yards into the forest." When she looked at him questioningly, he explained. "The Indians have no concept of personal property. What belongs to one belongs to all. If they see something they want, they take it. I hope you didn't bring anything you would mind losing." She looked down at herself, patted her reticule. "It would be the height of impropriety to refuse the Indians any item they wish to have. And you may take anything of theirs that you would like."

She bit her lip and blinked uneasily at the forest undergrowth. "If the Indians will strip the dugout the minute we walk into the forest, that means . . ."

"Yes, Miss Pritchard." He moved up beside her. "They're here now, all around us." A sound broke from her lips and her blue-green eyes widened. She stared at the foliage and edged nearer to him. "You won't glimpse them until they choose to show themselves."

She wet her lips and whispered. "How do you know they're here?"

"The silence. Don't you hear it?" Bending, he pulled back the fronds of a giant fern and gestured for her to precede him. "They've been tracking our dugout for several miles. We're expected."

The trail inside the forest seemed so obvious to March that he had to remind himself to be patient with Miss Pritchard's confusion. London eyes did not see Amazon trails. But she heard the sounds. At every noise her shoulders contracted and her hat brim quivered. Watching her, he smiled in exasperation. No doubt she was practicing her courage.

When he spotted the first outlying manioc garden he

moved closer to her. "Remember—no eye contact with the men. No eye contact with the women until after we've been welcomed. Eat whatever they offer you; to refuse will be an insult. After the welcome you'll be free to wander about the village as you like, but not before. All the tribes hold children in high regard. If you wish to make a good impression, treat the children with the same courtesy as you would an adult."

"Do they speak English?" she whispered, darting nervous glances all around her.

"Of course not." He rolled his eyes toward the forest canopy. "They speak a variant of Tupi. Mawe, the headman, spent a year at the mission in Santarém. He speaks some English. Fredo and I speak some Tupi."

"Then we'll—" In mid-sentence she froze.

Ahead of Fredo, a warrior had appeared on the path. One moment there was nothing but ferns and manioc plants overhanging the faint trail, the next moment a man stood there, his arms crossed on his naked chest, his legs planted wide apart. A six-foot blowgun was strapped to his shoulder, and he held one of the darts between his brown fingers.

"He's wearing war paint!" Miss Pritchard gasped. She trembled from head to foot. "He's going to kill us!"

"Don't be an idiot, Miss Pritchard. And remember—no eye contact. He's painted because he's a warrior. Part of his decoration is a tattoo, part is paint."

She swayed and touched the back of her hand to her forehead. "Where *do* I look, Mr. Addison?" Her face pulsed with hot color. "He's so . . . naked!"

"Look at his chin, his mouth, his chest. Look at his feet, his knees. Look at the forest or the ground. I think you can work this out, Miss Pritchard."

"You don't have to sound so bloody annoyed," she snapped. Then her voice quavered. "What will he do to us?"

"He will escort us into the village. Stand quietly while I

greet him." Moving past her, he walked forward until he was near enough to recognize the man. He smiled at the red feather piercing the Indian's left ear. "Greetings, Mawe. I've brought the things you requested."

"Your gifts are already in the village, Addison Cabo." Mawe glanced toward Miss Pritchard. "You bring Mawe a wife, Addison Cabo?"

"No, this woman is my wife." Behind him he heard Miss Pritchard's sputter, then Fredo's low voice explaining if a woman was not a wife, she was a gift.

"The people no see white woman before. Many believe whites have no women of their own." He peered curiously at Miss Pritchard, who, March was relieved to see, kept her eyes focused steadily on a manioc plant. "Is your wife good at—" He mentioned the Tupi word for intercourse, a topic of abiding interest.

"A disappointment actually," March answered with a shrug. Momentarily he had a vision of Miss Pritchard orchestrating a bedroom scene. This knee here, that hand there, no unpleasant heavy breathing if you please, no unnecessary touching or probing. The procedure must unfold according to Mrs. Wilkie's etiquette for proper bedroom obligations. March was glad Miss Pritchard didn't understand the focus of Mawe's interest. It would have required the rest of his life to convince her this was a common expression of tribal interest and was not a sign of crudity or disrespect.

"I offer condolences, Addison Cabo. You share this wife with friends?"

"No."

A flicker of relief passed like a shadow across Mawe's expression. According to custom, host and guest established at the outset which courtesies would be observed. Had March wished to trade wives for the duration of his visit to the village, Mawe would have been obliged to agree.

"You sleep in village, Addison Cabo?"

"We thank the people for their hospitality, but we will not be sleeping in your village."

"The people thank Addison Cabo for his gifts."

March followed Mawe past the manioc gardens and into the village. Behind him, Fredo led a wide-eyed and shaking Miss Pritchard.

The clearing was large enough to contain the central building or *maloca* and the half-dozen thatched enclosures that surrounded it. Sunlight streamed on the cleared ground, the heat welcome after the chill of the forest. Mawe led them into the *maloca.* With a grand gesture he offered March and Fredo his own hammock and indicated a banana leaf at their feet for Miss Pritchard.

As she slowly sank to her knees then sat on the leaf, a murmur of surprise rose from the women's end of the *maloca.* They edged forward to stare at Lalie.

"Mawe has told them you're a woman," March explained, smiling at her. "They didn't know. To them I imagine we all look alike. Plus, they haven't seen a white woman until today."

"Oh dear. They look so . . . so *naked*!" she whispered. Her face continued to burn violent pink, deeper in color than her rose shirtwaist. "I never dreamed people could look so . . . well, so *naked*! It's all one sees really, the, ah, nakedness. And they look so fierce!"

Years ago March had ceased to notice the Indians' nakedness. He saw them as adapted to their environment. Clumsy Europeans required clothing to protect them from the scrapes and scratches of travel in the forest, but the Indians slipped gracefully through the underbrush, avoiding thorns and sharp branches.

To one unaccustomed to them, he conceded the Mundurukú did look fierce. Years ago, the Mundurukú had been a warrior tribe, feared by their neighbors. When provoked they were still capable of ferocious attacks. They maintained their fighting skills. But those like Mawe, who had witnessed the white man's influence firsthand, knew that the ways of the Indians had forever been altered. All the tribes along the river were helpless against the advance of something incomprehensible called civilization.

Civilization had invaded even the depths of the forest. The Mundurukú women wore red and white beads on their wrists, ankles, and around their throats. One of the warriors cradled a scarred Winchester in his tattooed arms. In the boxes March had brought were fishhooks, penknives, hatchets, beads, and two machetes. In his pockets were peppermints for the children. Eventually the tribes would die out or learn the ways of European civilization. Their Stone Age culture would be lost forever.

"Oh dear, oh dear, oh dear."

"Miss Pritchard, stop making those sounds." He frowned at her. She was wringing her hands and staring here and there with glazed eyes. "You're in no danger. The people are coming to welcome us, not to take our heads."

"They have guns and machetes and blowguns!"

"And bows and arrows," he added pleasantly. "Which they won't use if you conduct yourself in a quiet, calm manner."

Each man in the village filed past March and Fredo and each asked the same questions in Tupi. "Where do you come from? Where are you going? How are you?" Pará and Hiberalta were names that meant nothing to them, but they listened and nodded as if they had visited Pará only yesterday. They ignored Miss Pritchard, who in turn did not lift her gaze above the bare feet that passed in front of her.

Then came the women. First the mothers of families brought food for the visitors. They placed baskets of manioc cakes on the ground in front of the hammock, and offered *bia,* the inevitable hot chili sauce. March and Fredo sampled the cakes and murmured approval before March passed a cake to Miss Pritchard.

"One bite will be sufficient. Look pleased." Before he

could warn her not to sample the part of the cake spread with the chili sauce, she had done it.

"Oh my Lord!" Tears sprang to her eyes and she fanned her lips with her fingertips. "Oh. Oh!"

"Remain seated," March murmured grimly.

"Water . . . must find water."

He clamped a hand on her shoulder and held her in place. She was gagging and gasping and making spitting noises, trying to jerk away to find water. March gave Mawe a weak grin of apology, then he examined a sloth hanging from the thatched roofing while the village's unmarried girls filed past, setting jugs of manioc beer before him and Fredo. Miss Pritchard fell on one of the jugs with admirable enthusiasm and tilted it to her lips. She swished the beer around her tongue and cheeks, trying to rinse away the stinging scorch of the chili sauce.

"Don't spit," he warned from the corner of his lips. "Swallow."

"Arghhh." The strangling sound informed him what she thought of manioc beer. When Miss Pritchard eventually learned that Indian women chewed the manioc then spit it back into the pot as part of the process of making the beer, he suspected she would make worse sounds than she was making now. "More," she gasped, holding a hand to her throat.

"We're almost finished," he said, giving her another jug of manioc beer. He smiled at the children and young adults who passed before them. "Once you've eaten and refreshed yourself with beer, the welcome is complete."

She coughed into her hand and tried to clear her throat, then asked in a high, choked voice, "My throat is on fire. What happens next?"

He smiled. "You are at home. You're free to wander at will. I imagine the women will want to inspect you."

"I beg your pardon?"

"They appear timid now," he said, glancing at the cluster of Indian women who were staring at Miss Pritchard and chattering with excitement. "But these are curious people."

The words were no sooner out of his mouth than the welcome concluded. Mawe stepped forward with a broad smile and clasped his hand. "Welcome, Addison Cabo. We haven't seen you for long time. Is it true you soon leaving the river?"

"Stay with Miss Pritchard, Fredo," March said before he joined the men across the clearing.

Annoyed that Addison had abandoned her, Lalie slowly raised her eyes. "Can I look at the women now?" she whispered to Fredo.

"Si, Missy."

She didn't do so at once. First she tried to glimpse them from the corner of her eye, saw their small, very naked, cinnamon-brown bodies and swiftly looked away, swallowing hard. Sir Percival had hinted at the decadence of the Indians, but she hadn't believed him. And when Addison warned her of their indecency, she had assumed he meant they were naked except for a covering over their private parts. But these people were totally *naked* except for a few beads, which covered nothing.

Feeling the color pulsing in her cheeks, she glanced outside the *maloca* at the men drinking manioc beer in a circle that included March Addison. Addison, the only person wearing clothing, was watching her, his dark eyes twinkling with amusement. She glared at him then swiftly looked away in agonizing embarrassment when the man next to him adjusted the string holding his penis upright. Scarlet pounded in her cheeks. Not knowing where to look or what to do, she slowly rose to her feet.

One of the women darted forward, and Lalie sucked in a breath, certain the woman was running forward to stab and maim her. Before she could scream, the Indian woman jerked Lalie's straw hat from her head and gave her hair a stinging tug.

"Say nothing, Missy," Fredo warned in a low voice. He stood at the entrance to the *maloca,* watching.

The Indian woman frowned, then gave Lalie's hair another yank. Hairpins rained around her then her hair fell in a tumble to her waist. Tears of pain glittered in Lalie's eyes but she could see across the compound. The men no longer pretended not to watch what the women were doing. Even Addison stared at the red cascade that spilled over her shoulders.

"Please don't hurt me," Lalie whispered, her heart thudding painfully against her corset restraints. The Indian woman lifted a lock of red hair and rubbed it hard against her palm then inspected her hand, which she raised to show the others.

"She surprised no color rub off, Missy," Fredo offered.

Next, as Lalie stood still as a stone, her pulse banging, the woman dug her fingers into Lalie's scalp, looking to see if dye stained her skin. She shouted at the other women who edged nearer. Finally, she peered into Lalie's eyes, hesitated, then pointed to her own breasts before she pointed to Lalie's chest.

"I . . . I don't understand." Lalie couldn't bring herself to glance at the woman's breasts, but whatever the woman wanted had something to do with that area. Frowning, Lalie looked back at Fredo. From the corner of her eye, she watched March Addison's grin broaden. "What does she want?"

Fredo sucked in his cheeks and studied the parrots strutting across the dirt floor of the *maloca.* "She isn't convinced you're a woman. She wants to know if you have, well, if you have . . ." He tugged uncomfortably at his collar and looked away.

Impatient with curiosity and urged on by the other women who had now surrounded Lalie, the woman stepped up and cupped Lalie's breasts in her hands. The shock of being touched so intimately jolted Lalie and her face went blank with offense then a furious blush fired her cheeks and throat.

Without thinking she slapped at the woman's hands and tried to back away, but instantly all the women were on her, each trying to discover for herself whether she had breasts. One of them ran a hand up under her skirts and probed beneath her knickers before Lalie could stop her. The worst of it, the hideous worst of it, was knowing this intimate inspection took place before everyone in the village. Including March Addison.

Tears of shock and helplessness gathered in Lalie's eyes. A multitude of emotions flowed through her; humiliation, resentment, violation, and embarrassment deeper than any she had known. She couldn't have looked at Addison if her life depended upon it. But she didn't need to. Suddenly, he was standing beside her.

"Listen to me, Miss Pritchard," he said, his low voice directly above her head, his steadying hand on her arm. "I know this must be absolutely terrifying for you, but believe me, these people mean you no harm." She stood unmoving, too mortified to speak. She wished the earth would open and swallow her. "Their concept of modesty is drastically different from yours. They have no notion that they have offended you or caused you discomfort. It would shame them to understand they have discomfited a guest."

She wished he would go away. She wished she were home in London where people wore clothing and behaved predictably and did not carry blowguns. Surrounded by nakedness, she was acutely aware of March Addison's hand on her arm.

The women had fallen back in confusion at the sight of her tears. Now they pushed forward an old woman with white hair and breasts that hung to her waist. Lalie backed up until she pressed flat against Addison's solid body.

"Don't be frightened," he said in a soothing voice. "They saw your tears and they think you're injured or ill.

They won't be satisfied until the healing woman assures them you are well."

Further indignity followed. While Addison held her trembling body, the old woman methodically checked Lalie for injury. Two fingers slipped into her mouth and pulled back her cheek. Wide-eyed and feeling faint, Lalie rolled her eyes down to watch the old woman peer into her mouth. Next came her eyes and her ears, then gentle hands moved over her limbs. When the old woman dropped to her knees and poked her head under Lalie's skirt, Addison laughed.

"I hate you," Lalie said, closing her eyes. Beneath her skirts, the old woman poked and probed at her legs and stomach. When she emerged, she said something to Addison. "What did she say?" Lalie demanded in a low, outraged voice.

"She says you're in good health but you aren't pregnant. She offered her commiseration to me. She has officially announced that you are indeed a woman."

Giggling, eyes bright, the women again surrounded Lalie, separating her from March Addison. They caught her hands and pulled her deeper into the *maloca,* taking turns stroking her long hair, so different from their own short, straight black hair.

Looking over her shoulder, Lalie turned wide, frantic eyes to Addison. "Where are they taking me?"

"They wish to show you the women's quarters." He smiled and lit a cigar. "Except for husbands, men are forbidden in the women's area."

"You're enjoying this, aren't you?" She knew her voice was shrill but she couldn't help it. He looked so smug, so damned sure of himself. He also looked tall, at ease, and familiar when nothing else was. Confusion swirled through her thoughts. Never had she known such an infuriating man. At least he had come to her aid when the women were examining her. She halted, resisting the tugs on her hands, and she met his dark eyes across the *maloca.* "I don't understand you," she said quietly.

"It isn't necessary that we understand each other, is it, Miss Pritchard?"

"I suppose it isn't, Mr. Addison," she murmured.

The tugs on her hands grew more insistent, and reluctantly she allowed the women to pull her toward a small fire surrounded by utensils fashioned out of bone and turtle shells.

March returned to the men and passed cigars to those who wanted them. All were intensely curious about Miss Pritchard and he answered a dozen questions about his "wife." Yes, the color of her hair was genuine. No, it did not mean she was a shaman. Yes, she had breasts beneath her clothes. No, she would not show them her breasts. He explained that white men did not routinely share their women, and this was not selfish or insulting, but a time-honored custom. Eventually the conversation drifted to hunting and fishing.

When the manioc beer had been consumed, Mawe drew March aside and they stood smoking in silence while Mawe composed his thoughts.

"Where do you go when you leave the river, Addison Cabo?"

"To England first, then to Malaya on the other side of the world." Neither England nor Malaya would mean anything to Mawe, but March spoke as if Mawe were as familiar with the sites as he.

"It's no good that you leave, Addison Cabo. The tribes need friends." Mawe waved his cigar at the crates in the center of the compound, emptied now of their treasures, then he met March's eyes. "What you give from the heart costs dear from others." His voice hardened. "Last month Teclati give his sister for a white man's gun. A machete costs a girl child." Disgust darkened his face.

"In time . . ." But March knew this was not true. Time

would not diminish the white man's conviction of his own supremacy. Time would not reduce the plantation lords' need for cheap, expendable labor. The tribes were doomed. They had no future. When he gazed into Mawe's sad eyes, he understood his friend knew it, too. "I'm sorry," he said quietly.

Mawe ground his cigar beneath the sole of his bare foot. If he felt pain there was no sign. "The rubber men have been here, Addison Cabo."

"This far downriver?"

"Si. They don't steal my people this time. But we move deeper in the forest."

There was more to say, much more. But discussing the problem was pointless. March could offer the tribe no words of encouragement or hope. He clasped Mawe's hand and Mawe returned his grip. "I wish you luck, good hunting, and many sons, my friend."

"And you, Addison Cabo."

Miss Pritchard emerged from the *maloca* then. March stared at her then laughed aloud. The women had painted red crescent moons on her cheeks. They had braided blue and green feathers in her hair. Most startling of all, March imagined he could see Miss Pritchard's nipples outlined beneath her hastily assembled shirtwaist. It looked for all the world as if she were not wearing her corset. Her figure was fuller, more lush than he had noticed earlier.

His suspicion was confirmed an instant later when one of the women emerged from the *maloca* giggling madly and wearing a satin Paris corset festooned with pink and blue ribbons. Another, equally hysterical with laughter, wore a white linen chemise and a muslin petticoat. Another kicked out her legs to display Miss Pritchard's pale cotton stockings and elastic garters. Someone else wore her straw hat and carried her reticule.

Miss Pritchard gave him a weak, dazed smile. She tried to speak but no words came out of her mouth. When she realized she was making no sound, she shrugged and gave him that peculiar smile again.

Fredo plucked Miss Pritchard's hat from the head of the Indian girl who wore it and pushed it on Miss Pritchard's head, then he scooped her into his arms. She blinked at him and mouthed his name, still making no sound.

March knew at once what had happened. The *bia,* the hot chili sauce, had seared her voice. And she was drunk on manioc beer.

"Well, Miss Pritchard," he said, bending to look into her unfocused blue-green eyes. She smiled at some unseen horizon. "You do have a way of creating memorable occasions. In case you're concerned"—she didn't look as if she were concerned about anything, but he continued anyway—"your voice will return sometime tomorrow. You probably won't care because you'll be thinking about your hangover. Or, knowing you, you'll be mortified that you've left behind three quarters of your clothing."

Her dreamy, unfocused eyes gazed at a point somewhere between his mustache and his chin. Then she hit him in the jaw with her fist.

"What the hell?" Stepping backward, he rubbed his jaw and stared at her. Before she closed her eyes and passed out, she gave him a happy smile.

March stared at her unconscious figure a moment then apologized to Mawe for his wife's unseemly exit and expressed his gratitude for the tribe's hospitality.

"You wife big trouble," Mawe said, grinning. "No sleep for husband of such a one." The other men nodded and laughed.

Fredo carried her back to the dugout and they stretched her out on the bottom of the boat. She opened one eye then fell back asleep. Before March climbed into the dugout, he studied her for a long moment. With her flaming hair spread around her like a halo and her lush figure finally unrestrained, she reminded him of a beautiful

Viking princess. Somewhere he had read about sleeping Vikings drifting in the currents.

Where on earth did that absurd thought spring from? Shaking his head, he stepped over her and took his place in the bow. For a moment he wasn't sure whether he was relieved or disappointed that he wouldn't be in the stern, where he'd have a perfect view of her full breasts all the way back to the *Addison Beal.*

"What happened?" Maria cried when March carried a still unconscious Miss Pritchard on board and held her while he waited for Joao to string her hammock. Hovering, Maria stared at the bright red moons on Miss Pritchard's cheeks and the feathers woven through her hair.

"Little Missy drink too much beer," Fredo explained, smiling.

"Little Missy?" Maria stared in disbelief. Then she leaned closer as March placed Miss Pritchard in the hammock. "Where her clothes?" After March explained, Maria frowned and wrung her hands. "Little Missy not going to like this. She not like it at all, Cabo."

March dropped the insect netting over Miss Pritchard's sprawled figure. He imagined he could still feel her silky hair and soft skin. He rubbed his jaw and strode toward the wheelhouse.

"Give her a cup of *guaraná* with her breakfast." The drink was a mild narcotic made by roasting then grinding the *guaraná* nut and stirring it into a tumbler of warm water. The Indians used it to treat fever, headache, and cramps. And Miss Pritchard was going to have one hell of a headache in the morning.

When Fredo came into the wheelhouse, March touched his jaw again and said in disbelief, "She hit me!"

Fredo slid a look at him and grinned.

"I'll be damned." March laughed out loud.

Chapter 7

Lalie finished writing her latest journal entry, put down her pen, and took another sip from the cup of *guaraná*. Despite smelling like old rhubarb and looking like mud, the brown sludge had wrought a miracle. The worst headache of Lalie's life had nearly vanished.

She felt recovered enough to experience an agony of humiliation regarding the previous day's events, none of which appeared in her journal in their true form. She had recorded observing a bushmaster, but had not mentioned her stupidity, the memory of which made her feel ill. Nor had she admitted that she'd arrived at the Indian village shaking with fear and departed in a drunken stupor. She would rather have died than commit to paper that she had struck March Addison.

A disheartened sigh lifted her bosom and Lalie stared at the verdant foliage slipping past along the shoreline. The problem with private journals was the writer's fear that someone else would peruse the pages. Thus one censored and bettered the very experiences one wished to record for later recollection.

Lalie sighed again and pushed her journal aside. The person she hoped would glimpse her private journal was Sir Percival Sterling. In her daydream he noticed the journal and read a few pages. After he was done, he gazed at her with unabashed admiration. He swore a lesser woman could not have endured the hardships Lalie dismissed with equanimity. Then he gathered her in his arms and kissed her until she swooned like the heroine in Mrs. Theodora White's romance, *The Adventures of Miss Braithwaite.*

Looking toward the wheelhouse door, Lalie pondered what it would be like to swoon in a man's arms. To feel so overwhelmed with—yes, passion—that one actually felt faint of mind and limb.

Though it concerned her a little to admit it, she had not felt faint of mind and limb when Sir Percival kissed her the night before he returned to the Amazon. Thrilled, yes. The instant Percival's lips touched hers, a bolt of electricity had shot through her body. But that was the thrill of a new experience, the guilty thrill one felt at the taste of forbidden fruit. And of course the thrill of finally being in Sir Percival's arms. But Lalie did not believe she had actually succumbed to passion.

Passion, as she understood the concept, meant standing in the grip of an emotion so powerful that all else fled the mind. One could think of nothing but surrender. Passion was a delicious madness, a euphoric blending of urgency and burning desire. Without passion marriage played on a dark stage.

At least that appeared to be the view of Mrs. Theodora White, whose novels had done much to shape Lalie's ideas of romance, adventure, and the ideal marriage.

She believed she conformed to Mrs. Theodora White's image of the spirited young woman who thought nothing of throwing a few items into a portmanteau before setting off on a journey to adventure. But she was falling far short on passion and swooning.

However, according to *Mrs. Wilkie's Rules of Etiquette,* passion and swooning were condemned as having no place in a proper young woman's life.

After countless hours of anxious contemplation, Lalie had concluded the views of Mrs. White and Mrs. Wilkie could not be reconciled. To follow one was to repudiate the other, thus creating a troubling dilemma for one such as herself who longed to experience passion but who also valued propriety and desired to do the right thing at all times.

"You want more *guaraná,* Missy?" Maria asked, appearing at her table. Behind Maria, freshly washed laundry flapped on ropes strung between the support posts.

At home respectable folk did not hang men and women's clothing on the same line to dry. Lalie glanced at a pair of her knickers pinned next to March Addison's deck britches and hastily averted her eyes. Sometime before the next laundry she would have to instruct Maria how to properly handle the wash.

"I'm feeling much better. Are you having *guaraná,* too?"

"No, Missy. I grind powder from the leg bone of a fox and stir with manioc beer. Drink every day to make baby." Maria smiled sadly. "No baby yet. Fredo and me, we try and try, but no baby come."

Lalie thought of Maria and Fredo's nightly trysts below deck and a pink bloom spread across her cheeks. Mrs. White would have found the subject romantically intriguing. Mrs. Wilkie would have been appalled.

After closing her journal, Lalie handed two creamy envelopes to Maria. "Will you take these to Mr. Addison, please? This one, with the writing, is for Mr. Addison. Ask him to address and post the other envelope to Mawe."

The prospect of changing clothes for luncheon seemed pointless and daunting as the heat and the *guaraná* had sapped her energy, but Lalie forced herself to do so anyway.

When Lalie emerged from behind her tarpaulin, dressed rather less elaborately than usual for luncheon, Addison was standing at the end of the upper deck waiting for her.

"What the hell is this?" he asked without preamble, waving the envelope she intended for Mawe.

"It's a thank-you note, of course. And an apology."

"A thank-you note?" He stared at her, then he raised his hands toward heaven. "Miss Pritchard, you leave me speechless." After a moment he looked at her again and summoned what patience he could muster. "First, no mail packet visits the tribes. Second, no one in the village can read. Third, a thank-you note is not only pointless but is absurd. And fourth, you have no cause to apologize."

Clutching her parasol in both hands, Lalie turned her back to him. "The issue is not open for discussion, Mr. Addison. Please address the envelope to Mawe and post it when we reach Santarém."

"Did you hear anything I said? All right, Miss Pritchard, you had to be carried home from the party." Lalie closed her eyes and felt a burst of loathing. He could have stated the circumstance more tactfully. "It was your first experience with manioc beer, you couldn't guess how potent it is. But, all in all you comported yourself well. Miss Pritchard, turn around and look at me." She refused. "You accepted the people's hospitality and you repaid it with gifts of your own. There is no need to apologize."

Lalie closed her eyes tightly and felt her cheeks flush. She had arrived dressed like a proper lady and had departed wearing only her shirtwaist, skirt, and shoes. Disgraceful. And the Indian women had played with her as they might have played with a doll. They had plaited feathers in her hair and painted her cheeks.

Though she had scrubbed her cheeks until they were raw and stinging, she had been unable to remove all of the dye. Beneath a liberal dusting of rice powder, one could still discern faint traces of the red moons.

Suddenly angry, she swung around and faced Addison. "I don't care if Mawe can read my note. I don't even care much if he receives it! But I want you to post it. Just do as I ask, Mr. Addison, if you please!"

He studied her expression and she had an impression he was trying not to laugh at the powder-coated moons. "I see," he said finally. "The letter is for your sake rather than Mawe's." When she wouldn't answer, he lifted the note she had addressed to him. "As for this, I accept your apology, Miss Pritchard. And I will rely on your promise to follow instructions on future excursions. But didn't you omit something?"

She glanced at his jaw and she was disappointed to notice no bruise. "Mr. Addison, please," she said in a low, angry voice. "I've apologized for my behavior. Must we discuss specifics?"

A drop of rain landed on the deck between them and they both scanned the afternoon clouds then moved under the roof. Addison paused to frown at her then continued walking toward the wheelhouse. Lalie watched him go with an expression of relief.

The afternoon rain cooled the air, and when Fredo dropped anchor for the night, the evening was pleasant and not as hot as usual. For once there didn't appear to be many insects. As usual Lalie dined alone, watching and listening to the others who gathered around Maria's stove. They spoke of the flooding along the shore, discussed a steamer that had passed them earlier in the day returning to Pará, spoke of other voyages and other times.

Lalie listened to the rise and fall of Addison's voice, to his occasional laughter. Dining by herself every day was becoming a lonely experience, but she still couldn't bring herself to join the others.

To her surprise Addison brought her after-dinner coffee to her table. "May I join you?" he asked, sitting down with his *cafezinho* before she officially granted permission.

Flustered, Lalie called to Maria. "Remove these dishes, please, and turn up the lantern, and—"

Addison waved Maria back to her stool. "Finish your supper." To Lalie, he said, "Don't fuss on my account." Certainly it didn't appear that he intended to offer any concessions on her behalf. Leaning back in his chair, he lit a cigar and exhaled a stream of fragrant smoke. He crossed an ankle over his knee and studied her until Lalie frowned, wondering if he could still see the moons on her cheeks in the dim light.

"We'll dock in Santarém early tomorrow afternoon," Addison said when she scowled at him. "We'll stay overnight."

"Is that necessary?" Sometimes she thought they would never reach Hiberalta. She would spend her life sailing on the *Addison Beal* trying to endure March Addison and her maddening attraction to him.

"We're delivering cargo and taking on more. Maria needs to replenish her kitchen supplies. These things take time." He leaned forward to sip his *cafezinho*. "You will stay on shore with Mrs. Capuchin. Emily is a widow. I think you'll enjoy her company. You'll endear yourself to her immediately if you offer to exchange volumes of Mrs. Theodora White's novels with her."

Lalie blushed. "I read other authors as well," she said defensively, listing travel journals, biographies, and fashion magazines.

"If you're interested in travel journals I have several volumes about Malaya that you might find diverting."

Lalie had noticed him reading in the wheelhouse occasionally and knew his appetite for the printed word to be voracious. "May I inquire as to the purpose of your interest in Malaya?" she asked.

His teeth looked very white when he smiled. "I plan to make my home there, Miss Pritchard. Years ago I visited Malaya briefly and, as I remember, there are numerous similarities to this country." A wave of his cigar indicated the river, the night sky, and the singing rain forest.

"I see," she said untruthfully. If Addison sought an area like the Amazon, why didn't he simply remain in the Amazon?

"Miss Pritchard, why did you strike me?"

The blunt question took her by surprise. Lowering her head, she frowned and plucked at her napkin. "I thought we agreed to avoid further discussion of yesterday's events."

"I don't recall such an understanding. I'd like to know why you hit me." Leaning back, he drew on his cigar, and she understood that he wouldn't depart until she had satisfied his curiosity.

Lalie released a sigh. "You won't be content until you hear me admit to being . . . inebriated, will you?" Anger tinted her cheeks. "Very well, Mr. Addison. I was inebriated. For the first—and last—time in my life, I drank too much. I was—drunk. There. I've said it, are you happy?" Furious, she started to rise, but there was no place to go.

"That isn't what I asked. Why did you hit me?"

"Because I wanted to!" His constant questioning was angering her. "You insist on an explanation? Then you shall have one! I hit you because you infuriate me. Because you're rude and crude and offensive. Because you laugh at me. Because you scorn your background and everything civilized. Because you force those around you to sink to your level and become as frank and rude as you are yourself. Because you make me feel confused and angry and I don't like it. Because you make me doubt myself and I like that even less! That's why I hit you, Mr. Addison, that and being drunk on manioc beer. I do not apologize nor do I regret my action. I only wish I had injured you dreadfully and taught you a lasting lesson!"

At the end of her speech, her eyes were blazing and her heart had quickened with emotion. Never had she attacked another person or made such an appallingly rude speech. Doing so was both exhilarating and dismaying.

"Well done," Addison said softly. A glint of approval lit his gaze. "Now let me tell you something. London is stuffed with people who brush past each other on the streets, who dine at one another's tables, who conduct business together or pay one another calls and they do so without ever causing a ripple of doubt or stirring any emotion. If I cause you to question yourself, if you cause me to question myself—then we have genuinely met. And we have both benefited from the encounter."

Lalie blinked. "I cause you to doubt yourself?"

"Yes, indeed. You remind me that patience is a virtue I lack. You remind me of a world I have chosen to leave behind and you reinforce that choice. You are a constant reminder of a fascinating and aggravating force that no male fully comprehends. You remind me that I have no heir and must one day remedy that circumstance. Your presence compels me to evaluate the past nine years and to ponder the future. And each of these reminders raises doubt."

"What are you saying, Mr. Addison?" she asked, staring at his face in the mellow light falling from the kerosene lantern.

He smiled. "I'm saying you make me as confused and angry as I apparently make you, Miss Pritchard. I would never strike you, but I would dearly love to throw you overboard and proceed upriver in peace."

For a moment neither of them spoke then Lalie surprised them both by breaking into laughter. When she recovered enough to catch her breath, she smiled.

"One day when I was small, I came upon our gardener who was arguing with his wife, our cook. Mrs. Culpepper stormed back to the kitchen, leaving Mr. Culpepper standing over his shovel looking after her. He threw his shovel and his hat into the flower bed and shouted, 'I'd like to pound her into the ground.' To which I said, 'Oh no, please, you mustn't.' And he looked at me as if I were mad and replied, 'Well, of course I aren't goring ter do it. I love her like me own heart.'"

When Addison laughed and claimed perfect understanding, Lalie hid her face above her coffee cup, suddenly realizing the story wasn't appropriate at all. Hastily she murmured, "Our situation is vastly different, of course, but we are bound together for a time yet." She risked a glance at him and made an attempt to turn the story to advantage. "I wonder . . . perhaps we should set aside our shovels, Mr. Addison."

"If you're proposing a truce, Miss Pritchard, the idea has a certain appeal."

Standing, Addison surprised her by offering his arm. If he could be conciliatory to the extent of minding his manners, Lalie could repay the gesture by accepting. After the briefest of hesitations, she slipped her arm around his sleeve. They strolled the deck, passing out from under the roof into the starlight glowing softly across the lower deck. A warm night breeze caught the smoke from Addison's cigar and floated it toward the forest edge.

"What terms do you propose, Miss Pritchard?"

She considered. "On future excursions I shall obey your instructions at once."

"Very clever. You offer a concession thereby obliging me to make one also."

Arm in arm they paused at the railing to admire streamers of moonlight rippling across the river. Addison's arm felt strong and firm to Lalie. It occurred to her that some women might view March Addison as a man to lean on, a man with whom they could feel safe and protected.

"I should like you to refrain from making crude remarks deliberately intended to offend or shock me."

He raised his cigar and inspected the growing ash. "That concession presents difficulties as everything seems to offend your tender sensibilities. While I am sure it seems that I deliberately offend, it may surprise you to learn that I seldom set out to do so, though I concede I have occasionally been guilty of that charge." They strolled past the wheel casing and turned down the stairs to the lower deck. "Nine years of frank speaking cannot be overcome in a moment. How do you suggest I cultivate artificiality and avoid offense? Without, that is, entirely altering my character?"

"Altering your character might prove to your benefit, Mr. Addison," she murmured.

"No more so than altering yours. The benefit lies in one's point of view, does it not? But we're negotiating a truce, not a conquest. I can agree to cease any deliberate affronts, but I can't promise not to offend inadvertently." He patted her hand. "I'm afraid that is the best I can manage. On your side, I would appreciate a cessation of your constant efforts to reform me. I am well acquainted with the rules of polite society and find I can live happily without them."

They walked between the rows of tarpaulin-covered cargo into the darkness near the engine room. Beyond the railing, moonlight bathed the water in golden tints. Here the shadows were warm and thick and smelled of the vanilla beans packed in the crates beneath the nearest tarpaulin. Belatedly Lalie realized this was where Maria and Fredo came every night to make the baby Maria longed for. She wondered if they shared their passion here beside the vanilla beans. Heat rose in her cheeks.

Addison paused and she felt him turn toward her in the darkness. "We can sketch a summary of this truce by stating we will try our best not to annoy one another. Is that your understanding?" There was amusement in his voice, but something else too, an odd tension she hadn't felt from him before.

Lalie wet her lips and lifted her head, uneasy that she couldn't see his face through the shadows. She too felt a peculiar tightening and pleasant discomfort. "Yes." Her voice was hardly more than a whisper. A dark wedge opened down the front of his white shirt. She could smell the lemony tang of soap and the scent of the champagne he had enjoyed with his dinner. The strange tension seemed to mount as they stood together in the shadows.

"Miss Pritchard—are you very certain you wish to marry Sir Percy?" His voice was low and intense, surrounding her in the darkness.

Any other time his prying would have offended her. But at this moment Lalie had the distinct and surprising impression that his question was prompted solely by concern for her welfare.

"I love Sir Percival," she whispered, speaking the words aloud for the first time. As if in proof of her statement a weakness stole over her limbs and she noticed her breath came a little faster. She wished March Addison were Sir Percival, wished that now, right now, she could step into his strong arms and discover passion in the vanilla-scented darkness.

Shameless images of moon-drenched kisses and starlit passion flooded her mind, making her feel warm and strange inside.

When Addison touched her shoulder Lalie smothered a gasp and wondered if the night heat had addled her nerves and brain. For an instant she believed her own fancy and reacted to Addison's touch as she would have to Sir Percival's, with a shiver of excitement and expectation.

Addison's fingertips remained on her shoulder, and he looked down at her in the darkness. "I'll say this once then never again." He spoke quietly but in that same tension-filled voice, standing so close that Lalie felt his body heat, felt his warm breath on her cheek. Dizzily she wondered if her sleeve had melted and his fingertips rested upon her bare arm.

"I won't attempt to dissuade you from marrying Sir Percy. I have no right to speak to that issue. But if ever he mistreats you, go to the nearest settlement and mention my name. Inform the mayor, if there is one, that March Addison guarantees your expenses back to London. Then swallow your pride and go home."

His words broke the spell woven by shadow and starlight and the perfumed night. Lalie jerked away from his hand and stumbled backward. "How dare you, sir!" Anger washed over her like a flood tide. Even her voice trembled. "How dare you presume that Sir Percival would mistreat me! Sir Percival Sterling is a gentleman! He would never—never!—mistreat a woman!"

"Listen to me, Eulalie. For once in your life just listen!" Addison gripped her shoulders and he gave her a shake. "The man you met in London is not the man you will wed in Hiberalta! When you met Sir Percy in London, he was wearing his best manners. It's clear you're not capable of distinguishing between manners and character. By the time you discover there's a vast difference, you're going to be isolated in a rubber settlement four thousand miles from civilization. Listen to me! Percival Sterling owns Hiberalta. No one defies him there. If you need assistance, no one will dare offer it."

Lalie clapped her hands over her ears and twisted away from him. "I won't listen to this slander. You don't know Sir Percival."

"Damn it, Eulalie. It's you who doesn't know Percival Sterling." Addison pulled her hands from her ears and held them tightly. "I've known Percy for nine years." He leaned over her, his face inches from hers. "Percival Sterling is a despot, a tyrant, and a thief. He murders his laborers by working them to death or by flogging them to death. He beat his last mistress so brutally she nearly died. Do you think he won't raise his fist to you? Is that what you think, Eulalie? Because if you do—you're wrong. Dead wrong."

"A mistress? A murderer? None of this is true!" Tears sprang to her eyes. "How can you be so cruel? What kind of monster are you? Does it satisfy some wicked perverseness to wound me with your lies?"

"I'm trying to prevent your making a terrible mistake, for God's sake. You're throwing yourself away on a man who isn't worthy of you. A man who will introduce you to more misery than you ever dreamed of!"

Lalie struggled to escape his hold and staggered backward against a cargo pack when he released her. "Can you really believe I traveled halfway around the world to marry a man I don't know?"

"That's exactly what you've done." Anger thickened his voice. "The mystery is why Dr. Pritchard provided his consent. Frederick surely would not accept Sir Percy without first conducting an inquiry into his character and background. Even a cursory investigation would reveal an unsavory taint."

"Percival Sterling would never commit the crimes you accuse him of committing! He isn't like that. I don't understand why you're saying these terrible things. But I know I was a fool to think you could ever act like a decent man. You delight in inflicting offense, Mr. Addison. You are reprehensible!"

"No, Miss Pritchard." Resignation eased the anger from his tone. "My intention was to spare you great injury." He ran a hand through his hair and watched her gather her skirts then run toward the stairs.

When March returned to the upper deck, she was already in her hammock. After Joao retired and Fredo and Maria disappeared below deck, March leaned against the railing smoking and thinking about his conversation with Eulalie Pritchard.

He should have known she wouldn't listen. Women in love were deaf to reason and loyal to the point of self-destruction. What had he imagined she would do? Politely thank him for his insight then depart the *Addison Beal* in Santarém and sail home to London?

He flipped his cigar into the dark night currents and swore under his breath. He was as great a fool as she was.

The Santarém mud flats and the wooden steps leading down to them were submerged beneath the flood waters so Fredo was able to navigate the *Addison Beal* close to the town.

Lalie waited at the railing, a tapestry overnight bag near her feet, moodily watching a bullock-drawn cart plodding along the bank toward a large open-air market. What she could see of the town was disappointing.

Santarém was four times the size of Quantos, but only a fraction the size of Pará. The wharf area stank of decaying fish and piles of mangoes and papayas rotting in the sun. Buzzards picked through the debris littering dusty streets. A dozen rubber steamers bobbed at anchor among the fishing vessels and scattered dugouts, and the distinctive pungency of raw rubber permeated everything.

March Addison leaned his elbows on the railing beside her. "Ordinarily the water is cleaner," he commented, indicating the garbage and refuse floating against the sides of the ship. "When the tide comes in the Amazon pushes back the Tapajos and holds the refuse near the shore. In the morning you'll see clear blue water from here to the horizon."

"Don't speak to me," Lalie snapped.

"There's Mrs. Capuchin," he said, as if she hadn't uttered a sound. Lifting a hand, he waved as a small pretty woman stepped out of a carriage.

Joao positioned a plank between the lower deck and the dock, and Addison hoisted Lalie's overnighter to his shoulder then followed her across.

Mrs. Capuchin had eyes only for Addison. Raising her hem, she hurried forward, her eyes bright and her full mouth curved in a smile of delight. "March! I came the moment I heard the *Addison Beal* was coming in."

To Lalie's astonishment, Addison dropped the overnighter then caught Mrs. Capuchin by the waist and swung her in a circle before he placed her on her feet and returned her embrace. "I swear, Emily, you're more beautiful every time I see you. Age doesn't touch you."

Mrs. Capuchin laughed and her lovely eyes sparkled. "March Addison, you'll turn my head and earn yourself a thrashing from Thomas. You will come to supper, won't you? Only last night Thomas was complaining that it's been far too long since we've enjoyed your company." She placed her gloved hand on his cheek and smiled with affection. "We'll have roast *tucunaré* and *pítanga* pie afterward. All your favorites."

"Homemade biscuits?"

She laughed again, the sound as enchanting as chiming bells. "And a fresh pot of turtle butter to go with them. Did you bring the jars of honey?"

"Now Emily, would I forget you?"

Lalie cleared her throat. It appeared Addison was too bewitched to recall his passenger.

After she cleared her throat a second time, Addison touched her elbow and guided her forward. "Mrs. Capuchin, may I present Miss Pritchard recently of London?"

Lalie turned and stared at him in amazement. Even the inflection of the introduction was correct. And he had removed his hat upon seeing Mrs. Capuchin. Still puzzled, she looked away from him as Mrs. Capuchin took her hand and clasped it warmly.

"How do you do? I hope March invited you to stay with Mr. Capuchin and myself. Yes, of course he did. I do hope you'll agree to accept our hospitality. Surely you must be eager to sleep in something other than a hammock and I am equally eager for company." She spotted Lalie's overnighter and clapped her hands together in delight. "Excellent. We'll have you settled in no time." Mrs. Capuchin linked arms with Lalie as if they were acquaintances of long standing and guided her toward the carriage. "Supper at six, March," she called back to him, smiling. "Don't be late. Oh," she said, stopping. "Did you bring books?"

He made a flourish with his hat and leaned into a bow. Lalie stared as he straightened and grinned. "I've brought you a crate of the latest novels. Three are by Mrs. Theodora White, a taste you share in common with Miss Pritchard, by the way."

"How lovely." Mrs. Capuchin entered the carriage first and took the seat facing the driver. Lalie followed, accepting the backward-facing seat. "That scoundrel, March. He might have sent word that he was bringing us a lovely young guest. I could have aired the guest linens and arranged a soiree."

"I'm sure the accommodations will be admirable, Mrs. Capuchin," Lalie murmured. "And a soiree isn't necessary."

While Mrs. Capuchin pointed out the plaza and the chemist shop and the dry-goods emporium, Lalie studied her hostess.

Mrs. Capuchin was perhaps thirty, dressed in cool, pretty muslin styled in the latest fashion, which she had adapted for the heat by removing the collar and shortening the sleeves. A leghorn straw shaded a luxuriant mass of dark curls, and she carried a tiny striped silk parasol.

Her eyes were a warm melting shade of brown, lively and vivacious. A habitual smile lingered on her mouth. The sun had tinted her complexion a lovely golden shade that enhanced the natural rose of her lips and cheeks. She was small and slender and altogether beautiful.

"Here we are," Mrs. Capuchin said, directing a smile toward a graceful two-story house built in the Portuguese colonial style. A small Indian boy darted forward to open the carriage door. "My dear Miss Pritchard, I hope you won't think me too forward if I urge you to call me Emily on such short acquaintance. Along the river one lacks the time to permit a gradual ripening of friendship. Either one forgos the pleasures of intimacy or one jumps headfirst into friendship. I prefer the latter. If it would not discomfort you too greatly, I hope you will permit an instant friendship before the river takes you away again."

It was impossible to resist Emily Capuchin's warmth and guileless smile. "Please call me Lalie," she said. "I am fairly dying to discuss *The Adventures of Miss Braithwaite.*"

"Oh my dear, so am I! I can see we shall be great friends."

They climbed from the carriage and, arm in arm, proceeded into a charmingly decorated home the likes of which Lalie had not glimpsed since leaving Hackney. A wave of homesickness overwhelmed her as she gazed into a crowded parlor replete with knickknacks, fringed scarves, bibelots, upholstered furnishings, and tasseled lamps. She paused before a standing embroidery hoop and blinked rapidly.

Seeing her distress, Mrs. Capuchin bent to the hoop, tactfully diverting her gaze from Lalie's damp eyes. "I must apologize for my rose loops." An elaborate sigh lifted her exquisite small bosom. "Perhaps you could demonstrate the newest stitches before I lose you to the river."

"I'm sorry." Lalie dabbed at her lashes. "Suddenly I just . . . your parlor is so like our parlor at home, I . . ."

Mrs. Capuchin led her toward the maid waiting in the foyer. "Come. Let's give over our hats, gloves, and parasols. Then you must accompany me to the kitchen and tell me all the news while I make March's *pitanga* pie. Cook is wonderful with fish and will perform marvelously with the *tucunaré,* but I always make March's pies myself. We'll have lemonade and gossip about Mrs. White's heroines."

The Capuchin kitchen was large and airy and the cook, Mrs. Clouseau, seemed accustomed to Mrs. Capuchin invading her territory. While Emily Capuchin assembled the items she would require to make March's pie, Mrs. Clouseau showed Lalie a heavy nickel-plated stove, a double iron sink, and other assorted utensils that were demonstrated with pride.

After accepting a lemonade, Lalie settled herself on a stool to watch as Emily pinned on an apron then sprinkled flour over a rolling pin.

It suddenly occurred to Lalie that only days ago she had sat on a lower stool and watched two Indian women mix manioc cakes after they had proudly displayed their clay pots and turtle-shell bowls. Following the demonstration of their cooking skills, one of them had exhibited her needlework on a barkcloth cape. Then the women had taken Lalie behind the village to inspect their manioc gardens.

"When we finish here, I must show you my courtyard," Emily said happily. "I'm having wonderful success with my geraniums, but not such good fortune with the roses from England. Gardening is so different in the Amazon."

Chapter 8

March Addison arrived promptly at six, and to Lalie's surprise he looked stylish and immaculate. He was freshly barbered and shaved, his mustache trimmed to perfection. A pale panama suit emphasized his broad shoulders. He wore a silver vest and perfectly knotted tie. Dark evening slippers gleamed with polish, and he carried an ivory-handled walking stick. Tonight he had tamed his dark curls with pomade and he smelled slightly of expensive English cologne.

Too taken aback to utter a word, Lalie gaped at him while Emily Capuchin offered champagne then insisted Addison accept the place of honor in a mauve wing chair. Within minutes Emily had coaxed him into relating wonderfully amusing stories about life on the river.

Lalie seated herself and sipped her champagne, unable to believe her eyes and ears. Emily's skills as a hostess drew her into the conversation despite her intention to maintain her reserve, and Lalie found herself participating with questions and laughing at Addison's outrageous tales.

This was a side to March Addison that Lalie hadn't imagined existed. This, then, was a rare glimpse of the Earl of Aden's son. Addison charmed, he amused, he offered lavish compliments to Emily and Lalie, he anticipated their every wish, he dazzled with his drawing-room performance.

"Madam?" A butler in green and mauve livery appeared in the parlor doorway. "Mr. Capuchin sends his apologies to you and to his guests. He will be unable to join you for dinner."

A look of concern crossed Emily's features. "I'm afraid Thomas has been under the weather of late." She turned to Lalie. "My dear husband will be distraught at not meeting you." Then she smiled brightly. "But we won't allow this disappointment to spoil our evening. Thomas will want us to enjoy ourselves."

Emily insisted that Addison occupy the head of her table, and throughout a superb supper he continued to regale them with tales of the Amazon. Lalie learned that Joao had been abandoned outside an Indian mission and Addison had raised him from the age of nine. She learned of Fredo's impassioned courtship of Maria, how it had been necessary for Fredo to charm, threaten, and bribe Maria's multitude of brothers, cousins, grandparents, and parents before he finally won her. She heard a thrilling account of a tapir hunt. She learned of El Dorado and the men who had died searching for its mythical treasure. She laughed and smiled, and once she almost wept as Addison wove his stories. Through it all she peered at him as if she had never met him before.

Conceding the point reluctantly, she decided Addison looked especially handsome tonight. The panama suit imparted a careless elegance that suited him admirably. His collar was stiffly starched and starkly white against his sun-bronzed skin. And when he gazed at Emily Capuchin, his dark eyes sparkled and danced with affection.

After dinner he held Emily's chair and Lalie's then escorted them to the parlor before he returned to the dining room to enjoy a cigar and brandy.

Lalie accepted the *cafezinho* Emily offered and watched as Emily shuffled through a sheaf of sheet music before making her selections. Unless Lalie imagined it, she noticed that Emily's eyes were brighter than before and a charming pink now bloomed on her cheeks.

As if aware of these telltale subtleties, Emily cast Lalie a shy smile. "It's such a treat to see March. He's been a wonderful friend to us." She looked toward the parlor door and a lovely smile illuminated her expression. "There you are, March. Were your ears burning? We were chattering about you."

Addison crossed the parlor and took Emily's hands in his. "Will you show me your garden? The evening is warm and lovely, and a short stroll will settle that excellent dinner. Did I mention that no one makes *pitanga* pie as well as you?"

The invitation so obviously excluded Lalie that she felt a sting of rejection. Emily too seemed to forget she was present. They departed by the French doors and left Lalie sitting in the parlor alone, apparently forgotten.

The snub was out of keeping with the evening and Lalie keenly felt her exclusion. Further, her resentment bordered on jealousy. Certainly March Addison had never treated Eulalie Pritchard with the courtesies he bestowed so lavishly on Emily Capuchin. Prior to this evening, he had never hastened to hold Lalie's chair, or made any attempt to entertain her with charming and amusing stories. Until tonight he had never complimented her on her gown or remarked on the arrangement of her coiffure.

When Lalie realized that she felt slighted and piqued by March Addison's attentions to another woman, she gasped with shock. Embarrassed, she hastily looked about to discover if anyone had been watching, as if her thoughts could be read in the blush that crept upward from her collar.

What possible difference did it make if Addison and

Emily Capuchin harbored an affection for one another? The warmth between them had nothing to do with herself. Lalie had no claim on March Addison.

This thought also shocked her. Why would such a fancy even enter her mind. Frowning, Lalie concentrated on recalling Sir Percival Sterling. An image flickered in her mind: shining gold hair, pale intriguing eyes, a sensual mouth. Bond Street clothing, exquisitely tailored, exquisitely worn. The image wavered and blurred and fluttered away. Try as she might, Lalie could not hold Sir Percival's portrait before her. The gleaming gold hair became tousled dark curls beneath a battered river man's hat. Sir Percival's pale eyes deepened to vibrant brown. His elegant figure lengthened and broadened to accommodate sun-browned muscle. The image she had inadvertently conjured was that of March Addison.

Biting her lip, disturbed and confused, Lalie glanced up as the French doors opened and Emily and Addison returned.

Emily's eyes were moist and reddened; she pressed a lace handkerchief to her lips. "Forgive me, dear Lalie. I've just learned the dreadful news that March is leaving the river." For a moment she leaned her head against Addison's shoulder. "Such upsetting tidings. If you'll excuse me a moment, I must inform Thomas immediately. He'll be as distraught as I."

Lalie and Addison watched her run from the parlor and turn up the staircase, then Addison poured a snifter of brandy from the decanter on the serving cart.

"She cares for you," Lalie said softly.

"I know." Addison swallowed his brandy in one gulp.

When he said nothing more, Lalie cleared her throat then also fell silent. A dozen tactless and improper questions burned on her tongue. Finally Addison turned away from the serving cart.

"You understand that I had to speak to her alone."

"I . . . yes, I believe I understand that now." After a

moment, Lalie frowned up at him. "There's something—I'm certain you mentioned Emily was a widow, yet . . ."

Addison examined the depths of his brandy snifter. "Three years ago Thomas died of yellow fever while on a survey expedition along the Mosquito River."

Lalie stared. "Oh my God," she whispered.

"Ordinarily Emily would have accompanied him, but she was pregnant with their first child. The pregnancy was difficult. Eventually she lost the child."

The information was so stunning that Lalie didn't think to object to his phrasing or blunt presentation. All she could think about was Emily, upstairs speaking to her dead husband.

A moment later Emily bustled into the room, smiling gaily. She had splashed water on her face and applied a fresh dusting of rice powder to her cheeks. "What must you think of me, running off like that?" she apologized to Lalie before turning sorrowful eyes to Addison. "Thomas is as saddened as I to lose our dearest friend. He begs that you write as soon as you're settled in Malaya so we may learn of your wonderful new life." After Addison promised to correspond, she bent beside the piano and lifted a violin case. "I can't let you escape without favoring us with a selection."

When Addison protested, Lalie cast him a wicked smile. Her eyes sparkled. "Surely you have a set piece or two that you might perform for us."

Wonderfully discomfited, he glared at her, then managed a tight smile for Emily. "I'll play but only if you accompany me."

Lalie assured herself she was not disappointed that he had chosen Emily as his accompanist and not her.

After pouring more *cafezinho,* Lalie settled on the horsehair sofa to listen, prepared to uncover a dozen points to criticize. But the evening ended as astonishingly as it had begun. Addison maneuvered the violin as masterfully and confidently as he handled the *Addison Beal.*

Clearly Addison and Emily had performed duets before. They harmonized flawlessly, jesting with each other through the music, teasing, laughing, and finally, in a piece aching with sweet melancholy, saying good-bye.

When the final chord died, Emily looked up from the piano keys and tears glistened like diamonds on her dark lashes. "Dear March, I shall miss you dreadfully."

Addison lowered the violin and touched her cheek. "If ever you tire of that dullard, Thomas, and find yourself longing for adventure with one who has admired you for years—send for me at once."

Laughter sparkled through Emily's tears. "What a rogue you are, March Addison." She pressed his hand to her cheek. "If Thomas were well enough to join us, truly I think he would have to challenge your impertinence."

Addison's wink included Lalie. "Tell Thomas I see through his game. He's hiding upstairs for fear I'll best him and carry off the prize."

Laughing, Emily followed him to the door. "Have a care what you say. You know I tell Thomas everything." The laughter died on her lips when Addison opened his arms. With a tremulous sigh she moved forward and pressed her face against his chest. Cheeks flaming, Lalie leaned to examine a foyer painting as Addison and Emily embraced. "Will you stop at Santarém on your return to Pará?" Emily asked hopefully.

"I'll be traveling light and fast." He smoothed back her hair then brushed his lips across her temple. "Tell Thomas good-bye for me. I shall expect letters from you both."

After Emily closed the door, she lowered her head and raised her cuff to her eyes. "Forgive me," she murmured to Lalie. "But I couldn't think more of March if he were my brother."

"Thank you for a lovely evening." Lalie touched her forehead, feigning drowsiness. "I believe I have a small headache. Would you be terribly offended if I retired early?"

Emily Capuchin was too well bred to display relief. If Lalie hadn't witnessed her distress of a moment ago, she would have believed Emily's concern on her behalf was the sole thought on the woman's mind. But she sensed her hostess longed to be alone.

Earlier Lalie had looked forward to sleeping in a feather bed between lavender-scented linen sheets. But sleep didn't come. Long after the household had quieted, she lay awake, watching the shadows of palm fronds brush the back wall, and thinking about the evening and her strange, confused feelings.

She didn't know how to regard March Addison's conduct tonight. Nor did she know how to interpret Emily Capuchin's demeanor toward her dead husband. Particularly she could not sort out her confusion regarding Addison's affection for Emily.

In the hibiscus- and lavender-scented darkness, with no one to know, she could however admit to a tiny inexplicable sting of jealousy. It disturbed and confused her. She was well aware it was an unforgivable lapse given her status as bride-to-be.

Dawn had lightened the sky before Lalie finally slept. And then she dreamed of a dark-eyed man in a panama suit.

The flooded river broadened above Santarém, and the southern shore could be glimpsed only as a thin green band above the watery horizon. Oddly melancholy, Lalie found herself contemplating the remote horizon and thinking of home and faraway friends. There would be snow in London now, and ice skaters on Griffith Pond. Old Mr. Everley would feed the fire in her father's office every few hours and her father's patients would warm their palms at the hearth as they listed their ailments. Lalie put aside her embroidery and sighed. Did her father ever spare a thought for her? Had he forgiven her?

Too restless to summon the patience required for

stitchery, Lalie blotted the perspiration shining on her brow then wandered to Maria's kitchen. "You're making farinha?" she asked after seating herself on a nearby stool.

"Si, Missy." Maria smiled. She was grinding a lumpy powder out of toasted manioc. "Bean stew tonight. Farinha, rice, beans, and bits of chicken."

No meal along the Amazon was complete without generous helpings of the ubiquitous farinha. As Maria made it, farinha had a delicious nutty flavor for which Lalie was beginning to acquire a taste.

She chatted with Maria for a while. Then, too fidgety to remain seated for very long, Lalie opened her parasol and strolled the deck, turning her face into the breeze created by the movement of the ship. Eventually she noticed the *Addison Beal* followed the shoreline into a tributary.

Entering the tributary meant Addison intended to visit another Indian village. And it meant another delay impeding their progress upriver. Lalie released another sigh. Not for the first time she wondered if waiting in Pará for Sir Percival to receive her letter and to fetch her might have proved quicker in the long run. As it was, her future seemed no nearer than it had when first she sailed from London. Each day on the river brought renewed frustration.

Turning at the end of the deck, Lalie kicked at her hem, twirled her parasol between her fingers, and glanced toward the closed door to the wheelhouse. She hadn't seen much of Addison during the two days since they had left Santarém behind. He spent his days inside the wheelhouse, ate his supper with the others, then read beneath a lantern until Joao strung the hammocks.

Lalie told herself she wasn't lonely. Certainly she did not need March Addison to occupy her. During the day she read or sketched or composed letters or wrote in her journal or worked her embroidery. Sometimes she daydreamed about the home she would make in Hiberalta and the genteel life she would enjoy with Sir Percival.

Sometimes she chatted with Maria and surprised herself by enjoying the anecdotes about Maria's large family.

But occasionally it would have been welcome, she thought, looking at the wheelhouse door, to share the company of her peers. To have a companion at dinner, someone who could converse well when he chose and who had amusing tales to relate about life on the Amazon.

Lalie sighed then tossed her auburn head. Addison was not rejecting her, for heaven's sake. He was the captain of the *Addison Beal* and she was his passenger. That's all they were to each other.

The tributary narrowed so tightly that Lalie could have touched the banks on either side if she had wished to reach her arms outside the dugout. Holding her straw hat, she ducked her head beneath overhanging branches and remained low until the dugout emerged again into a wide span of clear water. For the hundredth time that day Lalie questioned her decision to come ashore again and visit another village. Her first two expeditions into the rain forest had both ended in unmitigated disaster, and she had no desire to be humiliated once more. Still, she would be proving herself to be a coward if she refused to set foot into the jungle again, and Fredo, Maria, and Joao had all assured her repeatedly that she would have no problems this time. In fact, they had all seemed strangely eager that she should go. Lalie prayed she had made the right decision. They paused to rest in a place where lily pads covered the surface of the water, some as large as tea trays.

Fredo plucked one of the water blossoms and presented it to her before he passed a canteen of fresh water to Addison.

Lalie watched Addison pour water into his palm then rub it over his face and throat. He offered her the canteen but she shook her head no, holding the blossom to her nose.

"I . . . there's something I wish to ask you," she said when he still didn't speak.

"If I recall correctly, your last instruction was that I avoid speaking to you."

She blushed. "That's correct," she admitted with reluctance. "But you spoke to me at Mrs. Capuchin's home. I assumed you chose to disregard that wish."

"It would have distressed Emily if her guests refused to converse. It was my assumption that you and I shared an agreement to set aside our differences for that one evening." He saluted her with the canteen then scanned the riverbank. "Now that we've restored the status quo, I cede to your wishes."

"Mr. Addison, wait," she said when he returned to his oar. Suddenly she regretted this conversation. She had no idea how to broach the issue that troubled her. He lifted his hat, pushed back his hair, then settled the battered straw again before he looked at her impatiently. "Mr. Addison . . . that evening at Mrs. Capuchin's your manners were faultless. You didn't insist on dining with servants, didn't swear, you didn't use offensive or objectionable terms, you requested permission to smoke, you . . ." She raised her hands. "Why did you act the gentleman with Mrs. Capuchin, but you don't behave in that manner with—" Coloring, she broke off in embarrassment and bit her lower lip.

Addison leaned forward in the dugout, resting his elbows on his knees, and studied her face. "In the nine years I have known Emily Capuchin, I have never known her to cause anyone a moment's discomfort by imposing her standards upon them. Far from it. I've seen Emily use the wrong fork rather than draw attention to a guest's error. I've watched as she listened to abrasive gutter talk without flinching. I have observed her in camp with Thomas, eating from a tin plate in front of an outdoor fire, laughing at the rude jokes of the machete men. I've seen her straddle a horse like a man, wear breeches when it was sensible to do so, and I've never known a guest to depart her hospitality without feeling better about himself than when he arrived."

Lalie frowned at her hands and felt the color burn on her cheeks.

"I'd wager the *Addison Beal* that Emily knows Mrs. Wilkie's rules of etiquette as well or better than you. And when it's prudent and reasonable to do so, Emily lives by those rules. *She* lives by them, Miss Pritchard, she does not intrude her choice on others. If those around her choose a less restrictive or artificial course, Emily does not condemn them but accepts them without censure. Because I respect and admire Emily Capuchin, I conduct myself by her standards when in her presence. That is my gift to her. I offer that gift as a token of appreciation for the gift she gives to me. Which is the knowledge that she accepts me and holds me in esteem whether or not I position her chair or request her permission to enjoy a cigar."

"If you're saying that I—"

"I was not criticizing you by praising Emily Capuchin, Miss Pritchard. If you choose to find relevance to yourself in anything I've said, excellent. Whether you do or not is of no concern to me. As to why I don't permit Mrs. Wilkie to dictate my behavior—it is because I reject having Mrs. Wilkie imposed on me. I think it ludicrous to insist on grape scissors or a tea cozy or to change one's clothing three or four times a day in the middle of the Amazon. I find it laughable that anyone would insist that I request permission to smoke aboard my own ship. It passes belief that rules for drying laundry exist or that you would attempt to impose such foolishness on Maria. Your inflated sense of modesty has everyone on this voyage sleeping in layers of hot and uncomfortable clothing. My crew snatches baths as they can. You are visiting the Indians today solely so that Joao and Maria may bathe. Tomorrow you will remain on the ship so that Fredo and I may bathe. Your stubborn insistence on playing the lady has inconvenienced my crew, myself, and even you. I will not contribute to your charade." He stared at her. "Does that answer your questions, Miss Pritchard?"

"It wasn't necessary to deliver an oration," she said in a low, angry voice, understanding at last why the crew of the *Addison Beal* had been so eager to see her go ashore.

He nodded over her head at Fredo. "Are you ready to proceed?"

Tight-lipped, her face burning, Lalie watched him turn then dig his oar into the water to make the dugout shoot through the lily pads. Regardless of his protest to the contrary, Lalie was certain his speech professing his admiration for Emily Capuchin was also a stinging criticism of Eulalie Pritchard.

Thinking about it, Lalie wondered how much of what he had said about Emily was true. She absolutely could not imagine Mrs. Capuchin wearing breeches, eating from a tin plate, laughing at coarse jests. To embrace these improprieties required an adaptability Lalie could not grasp.

Which, she thought, narrowing angry eyes on Addison's back, was obviously the point he wished to score.

Well, he was not entirely correct, she decided. She too could be adaptable when the occasion warranted. In a feat of daring she prayed no one ever learned of, she had not worn her corset on this journey to the Indian village. She didn't have so many corsets that she could afford to lose another. If that wasn't a stunning act of adaptability, she didn't know what would be.

And oh heaven, the lack of hot, binding restraint felt wonderful.

Of course March had noticed she wasn't wearing her corset. He had no idea what that omission meant. Maybe all her corsets were in the laundry. Perhaps she feared losing another to the Indian women's curiosity. She hadn't cast off the garment as a concession to her whereabouts, of that he could be certain.

Frowning and out of sorts, he pulled on the oar, taking grim pleasure in the physical labor. It annoyed hell out of him that he was thinking about the fullness of Miss Pritchard's shirtwaist instead of concentrating on the job at hand. Although Fredo would say nothing, it was inconceivable that he had failed to notice March's jerky, inefficient movements today.

He also resented Miss Pritchard's questions about Emily. It seemed Miss Pritchard felt no compunction about prying when it suited her to do so. Or had he read subtleties into her questions that weren't present? He supposed it didn't matter. Dear, sad, sweet Emily. His relationship with her had always been flirtatious, protective, close, even when Thomas was alive.

One thing was certain. Emily Capuchin had never disturbed him in the same way as the idiotic Miss Pritchard did. He had never occupied hours of his time fantasizing about hurling Emily overboard for the sheer pleasure of seeing her dignity shattered.

And he had never tossed and turned through a tropical night unable to sleep because he burned with desire for Emily Capuchin.

"Cabo?"

When Fredo interrupted his reverie, March glanced up to discover he was guiding the dugout past the point at which they should put to shore. Swearing under his breath, he pulled the boat back around and nosed the dugout up on the pebbled shore.

After Fredo assisted Miss Pritchard out of the boat, March checked that the supplies he had brought were easily accessible, then he straightened and looked over Miss Pritchard's head toward the forest foliage. Nothing moved in the mid-morning heat. The absence of bird calls and monkey chatter informed him that the Indians were nearby.

"This visit will be much like the last," he said to Miss Pritchard. He kept his gaze on her sunburned face and resisted the impulse to glance at her breasts. "The tribe we're visiting is Mundurukú, but not the same branch of the tribe as we visited below Santarém."

She nodded nervously and adjusted her hat.

"The warriors in this village wear geometric tattoos. They can be startling at first glance. Most of the tribe blackens their skin with *genipapo,* a fruit from the coffee family. Despite their fearsome appearance, you'll find them as curious and friendly as were the other Mundurukú."

"I won't bring disgrace on our party, Mr. Addison," she said grimly, meeting his eyes.

Looking into those gemlike blue-green depths, aware of her full bosom and flaring hips, he was amazed that the Indians could mistake her for a male.

Before they entered the forest, she placed her hand on his sleeve, removing it almost at once. "There's something I feel I should say to you, Mr. Addison."

"What now?"

She drew a breath, squared her shoulders, then stepped past him to follow Fredo into the forest. "You play the violin beautifully," she stated.

He stared after her and shook his head in exasperation. She was the most confounding, annoying, and frustrating woman he had encountered in years. Perhaps ever.

"Thank you," he snapped, and followed her onto the trail.

Knowing what to expect made all the difference. Lalie knew not to taste the hot chili-pepper sauce on the manioc cakes, or to do more than sip the manioc beer. When the official welcome ended and the women advanced on her, curiosity replacing their timidity, she maneuvered them into the *maloca,* away from the gaze of the men, before she submitted to the examination that proved her womanhood. The probing inspection was still an affront, still demeaning, but at least the process was not conducted in front of March Addison.

The Indians' black-dyed skin and the tattooed lines made them fierce looking, but they acted very friendly. Their nakedness would never be comfortable to observe, but she wasn't as wide-eyed with shock as she had been at her first exposure to total nudity. Further, she could now observe the village life taking place around her.

The children racing through the clearing were not idly playing games as she had first supposed, they were enacting a hunt, using miniature bows and arrows. Employing a tree limb as a target, some practiced with blowguns and darts, others experimented with the penknives Addison had brought them.

Inside the *maloca,* a cluster of women cleaned a basket of fish while others plaited liana fibers to make new hammocks. They seemed excited and upset, continually casting frowns out the women's door to the manioc gardens behind the *maloca,* then shaking their dark heads and muttering.

Curious, Lalie lifted her skirts and wandered out to the gardens, even though she experienced a distinct impression that the women did not wish her to go there.

She hadn't progressed far before she heard moaning and weeping. Following the sound through a stretch of forest, she came upon a young tattooed warrior, an older woman, and a young pregnant woman in the center of a manioc garden. For a moment Lalie observed them in puzzled silence, not understanding what they were doing.

The pregnant woman squatted on a large banana leaf in the center of the garden, her arms hanging over a crossbar. The older woman worked behind her, pushing her hands down on the young woman's swollen belly. The older woman was sweating and anxious; the young pregnant woman looked half-dead with pain and exhaustion; the warrior sat on the ground holding his head in his hands. Although Lalie took care not to look into the eyes he raised to her, his distress was obvious.

"Fredo?" she called softly, knowing he had followed her. "What is happening here?"

Speaking in Tupi, Fredo stepped forward and addressed the warrior. The man pointed to the half-conscious pregnant woman, then to the sun. His arm moved across the sky in a circle.

Fredo nodded then spoke to Lalie. "This warrior's wife has come to her garden to have her baby. Her mother has been trying to push the baby out for one and a quarter days, but no baby come," Fredo said. "The wife is very weak."

"Ask him if I may approach."

After the warrior shrugged and turned aside, Lalie lifted her hem and stepped over the rows of manioc plants then knelt beside the young woman who did not stir at her approach. The older woman, sagging with weariness, rocked back on her heels and closed her eyes.

Carefully and gently, Lalie examined the young woman then straightened abruptly. Lifting her skirts to her knees, she ran back the way she had come, Fredo hurrying after her. She burst into the central clearing, looked around her, then ran toward a gathering of men. It seemed that she overheard Sir Percival Sterling's name as she approached, but this seemed so unlikely she put the possibility out of her mind.

"Mr. Addison," she gasped, fighting to catch her breath. "There's a young woman behind the *maloca* in one of the manioc gardens, and she's dying!"

"What are you talking about?" he demanded.

"She's been in labor longer than twenty-four hours. I'm certain it's a breach presentation. Unless the baby is turned, both mother and child will die. It must be done and soon. Didn't you tell me the Indians have some form of doctor? Why isn't the doctor attending her?"

At once Addison turned to the group of men staring at Lalie's fiery hair. From the inflection in his voice, Lalie understood he was questioning them. When he turned back to her, a variety of emotions sped across his face: anger, frustration, resignation.

"The healing woman was recently captured in a slaving raid. Her apprentice is currently in the forest undergoing a *paricá* dream. *Paricá* is a hallucinogenic snuff, and dreaming is part of the apprentice's training." Sympathy softened his glance. "Nothing can be done for Irikina."

"Wake the apprentice!" Lalie practically screamed. Knowing the young woman's name made her plight worse somehow.

"Waking her suddenly could kill her, Miss Pritchard. These people have already lost their healing woman. To lose the apprentice would leave them defenseless. They have made the decision to abandon Irikina and her baby to fate rather than risk the life of the apprentice." He touched her shoulders. "There's little the apprentice could have done anyway. She would place her lips on Irikina's belly and attempt to suck out the evil spirits that are preventing the baby from emerging."

"But that's . . . barbaric!" She stared at him.

"No, Miss Pritchard. That's ignorance. This is a primitive culture. They live very like our own ancestors must have lived at the dawn of time."

"We can't just stand aside and let that woman die!" Wringing her hands, Lalie looked toward the forest and the drama unfolding in the manioc garden. She turned back to Addison and drew a deep breath. "Once I assisted my father at a breach presentation."

Addison gave her a disbelieving look. "I can guess what you're thinking, Miss Pritchard, and I urge you to put such thoughts out of your mind. If you were to interfere and Irikina died . . ." He cast a pointed glance at the bows and arrows, the blowguns, and machetes behind him. "We'd never get out of here alive."

Lalie bit her lower lip. "What are we supposed to do? Sip our manioc beer and take our ease while that girl is dying in the garden? We can't do that."

Addison stared down at her. "Can you save the mother and child?" he asked bluntly.

"I don't know," Lalie admitted, anxiety thinning her voice. "It may be too late. I may not be skilled enough, but I have to try." She was a doctor's daughter. Everything in her background made her believe it was her duty to relieve the young woman's distress. To do otherwise was unthinkable.

"You're absolutely certain you must do this? And you understand the consequences if you fail?"

Her heart pounded but her gaze did not waver. "Yes," she whispered.

Slowly he nodded. "Miss Pritchard," he said, "you are a confoundingly difficult woman to understand." Then he turned again to the men waiting behind him. It seemed that he spoke to them a very long time and Lalie shifted from one foot to the other in a frenzy of impatience. Every minute that passed made the task ahead that much more perilous.

Finally Addison returned to her, his expression sober. "I've told them you are a healing woman, very powerful because of your red hair. I've told them you can save Irikina." For a moment he didn't speak. Then he said, "They will permit you to minister to her. If you succeed, they will honor you with a feast."

"And if I fail?" she asked, meeting his gaze.

"They will kill us."

Lalie spoke rapidly and frankly. "Irikina has lost a lot of blood. She's barely conscious. I believe the problem is a breach presentation, but it could be something else that I can't repair. I don't know that I'll be successful if it *is* a breach. Irikina could die regardless of what I do." Her gaze met his. "It's your life too, March. You and Fredo face the same consequences as I. We must agree on this."

"What course would you choose if the decision were solely yours?"

Lalie glanced back toward the manioc garden. "I . . . I would try to help that young woman," she answered finally. She spread her hands in a helpless gesture. "It's the only thing to do."

Addison glanced at Fredo who had joined them and Fredo nodded. He turned back and met Lalie's eyes, amazed at her strength and determination. "Then do it."

Chapter 9

Everyone in the village came to the young mother's manioc garden to scrutinize the red-haired healing woman and the magic she would use to save Irikina and the child. Once Irikina's mother understood she was to be displaced by a stranger, she screamed and wept and had to be dragged away. Comforted by friends, she sat at the edge of the field, rocking back and forth and keening the tribal wail for the dead.

Pausing for an instant, Lalie studied the warrior's weapons and shuddered. Then she drew a long breath and, using Addison as an interpreter, she called for a cloth soaked in honey and water that she inserted between Irikina's lips for the young woman to suck and bite on. Next she shouted for fresh banana leaves and pulled forward four women to hold the leaves as a screen to protect the young woman's privacy and her own. There was no time to erect a sun shade, though Lalie longed for one as the sun blazing overhead baked the field and those standing in it.

Lalie kicked aside the bloody banana leaf and arranged fresh leaves on the ground between the rows of manioc plants, then she gently guided Irikina off the crossbar and helped her lie down. Only half-conscious, Irikina lacked the energy to protest. Dangerously weak, she blindly did as she was told.

Aware that Addison watched above the screen of banana leaves, Lalie straightened her shoulders and rolled up the sleeves of her shirtwaist. As she did so she raised her head and looked into March Addison's eyes, as if trying to draw strength from him. He smiled back at her reassuringly. She focused her concentration and commanded her hands to stop trembling. Then she touched Irikina's swollen belly. A flutter of weak movement indicated the baby was still alive. Lalie breathed a sigh of relief. What happened next, she realized, would be a violation the tribe would not understand.

As she guided Irikina's legs apart, Lalie called over her shoulder to Addison. "Keep everyone away from the screen. Order those holding the leaves to turn their faces away. Tell them they must not watch or . . . or the magic won't work."

As Addison repeated her instructions in Tupi, Lalie whispered a prayer and sternly told herself this was no time to think about modesty, her own or the young mother's. Modesty was a social concept, she told herself; it had no relevance when a life was at stake. And this was no time to turn squeamish. Placing one hand on Irikina's stomach and inserting her other hand between the young woman's legs, Lalie made herself think of nothing but turning the baby.

The blistering sun battered her back and pounded the top of her head. Perspiration dampened her hair and plastered her shirtwaist to her shoulders and breasts. Once someone wiped the sweat from her brow. It must have been Addison, but she didn't glance up. Another time her heart almost stopped as she thought Irikina had died.

She looked at the woman's face in horror and shouted Irikina's name. "You can't die! Breathe! Please breathe,

Irikina!" The girl's naked breasts shuddered, and her chest convulsed then slowly lifted in a fluttering breath followed by a pause then another uncertain gasp.

At last, when Lalie had begun to despair of success, she felt the baby's head between her slippery fingers. Blinking rapidly, she leaned her arm on the mother's stomach and guided the baby down the canal. Finally, a tiny, perfectly formed infant emerged and Lalie gently wiped his face, then wrapped him in a clean banana leaf.

"A knife," she called to Addison, hardly daring to look away from the infant or Irikina.

Then finally, finally it was over. Smiling, exhausted, more exhilarated than she had ever felt before, Lalie stepped from behind the banana leaves, holding an infant boy in her bloody arms, cradled against her breast. For a moment no sound disturbed the motionless hot air. Then the infant cried and a cheer broke from every throat.

Stepping forward, smiling, Lalie placed the infant in his father's arms. To her astonishment tears ran down the warrior's tattooed face. He wiped his eyes then peered behind her with an anxious expression, not looking at the child until Lalie nodded and assured him as best she could that his young wife would survive. Irikina would need weeks of recovery, but she would live. A woman hurried past her, carrying manioc beer to the new mother; another woman brought a gourd bowl filled with fish broth. The chief strode to the center of the field and blew a reed trumpet to announce the birth of a new warrior.

Lalie moved aside, no longer needed. She lifted radiant tired eyes to Addison. "What is the father's name?"

"Buti."

"Buti wept," she whispered, tears filling her own eyes. "He wept."

Only now as the tension drained from her body did she realize the terrible strain of the last hour and a half. A tremble started at her toes and swept upward. Her vision blurred. Heedless of the blood on her hands, Lalie covered her face and sobbed with joy and relief.

When she recovered, she accepted the handkerchief Addison pressed into her fingers. She felt his hand on her elbow as he led her into the cool forest, out of the sun. Finally they came to a waterfall that spilled into a lily-strewn pool below.

Gratefully, Lalie sank to her knees and bent over the pool. She scooped water to her face, throat, and temples, and washed her arms, shivering as the cool water touched her hot skin. When she lifted her face to the sun, she felt Addison's gaze and opened her eyes, suddenly aware the water had sculpted her shirtwaist to her breasts.

He was staring at her with a hard, intent expression, his face so still it seemed carved of stone, his body tight as if her tension had passed to him. "You were magnificent," he said quietly.

For a moment Lalie was unable to respond. The intense concentration in his eyes and the rough timbre of his voice conspired to dry her throat, to send her pulse racing. When she realized she held his stare far longer than she had intended, she swallowed with difficulty and looked away. Flustered, she attempted to make light of his compliment.

"I never expected to hear such praise from your lips, Mr. Addison." Against her will, her gaze dropped helplessly to his mouth.

"Nor did I," he said, still watching her. Extending a hand, he assisted her to her feet then cupped her chin and lifted her face. "What you did was courageous and splendid."

His unexpected touch paralyzed her and she was unable to step back. They stood so close that Lalie could feel his breath on her cheek, could see the fan of lines radiating outward from the corners of his eyes. Behind her the waterfall splashed into the pool. The air was thick with the scent of water lilies. For one moment time lost all relevance. They stood together in a primitive paradise, surrounded by water and sunlight and leafy forest. Expectancy tingled in the scented air.

"It could just as easily have gone awry," she said in a whisper. With an effort she pulled her gaze up from his wide mouth. Her heart was thudding crazily and she couldn't breathe. "Irikina and the baby could both have died."

She hadn't realized how thick and long his dark eyelashes were, or that intriguing green triangles flecked the brown of his eyes. She hadn't noticed before how luxuriant his mustache was or how it shaped the sensual curve of his lips. She had never even really noticed how tall he was. She could have walked beneath his chin.

Later Lalie couldn't guess how long they stood immobile. His fingertips caressed her cheek gently while they studied one another's faces as if they were seeing each other for the first time. It might have been a lifetime; it might have been mere seconds that they stood transfixed, but during that span of time, a transformation occurred. Sentiments altered; a new and disturbing awareness emerged.

When the *turé* reed trumpeted the beginning of the celebration feast, Lalie turned toward the sound with an air of self-consciousness and shy reluctance. The spell that shimmered around them slowly evaporated.

Addison cleared his throat, then extended his arm. "May I have the pleasure of escorting the guest of honor?"

"Lead on, Mr. Addison," Lalie murmured. She gazed up into his strangely intent expression and a light shudder rippled through her. Arm in arm, and acutely aware of each other, they silently followed the trail back to the village.

The feast enabled Lalie to think about something other than those unsettling moments beside the waterfall. The women had prepared numerous dishes of meats and exotic vegetables. Great clay jugs of manioc beer waited to be poured, and one of the men produced a bottle of *cachaça,* which he presented to Buti, the new father.

Irikina had been moved into the central *maloca* where she lay receiving visitors with gratitude. When Lalie called on her after eating, Irikina offered a shy smile, then to Lalie's embarrassment, the woman caught her hand and kissed her fingers. Solemnly, she removed a bracelet of red and white beads and pressed it into Lalie's palm then closed Lalie's fingers around it. With tears in her eyes, Lalie nodded acceptance, then she pushed her lace handkerchief into Irikina's hand.

After the exchange Tilwe, the chief, appeared before her. He wore a woven bark cape and a crown of brilliant red and yellow toucan feathers. To Lalie's relief he had also covered his nakedness with a shieldlike affair made from the tough skin of forest lizards. After indicating she should follow, he led her to a stool positioned in the midst of scattered toucan feathers. It was clearly a place of honor.

After glancing at Addison, who smiled encouragement, Lalie seated herself. Each person in the village passed before her and each made a speech in Tupi, which Addison loosely translated, expressing his or her gratitude that Irikina and her child had been saved. Some placed small gifts of food or beer or beads at Lalie's feet. Last to come before her was Irikina's mother. The old woman made an impassioned speech during which she tore at her hair, beat her sagging breasts, hammered her thighs and knees. She swayed, she moaned, she raised her palms to the forest canopy. After ten minutes of wailing and shouting, she placed a large, beautifully polished turtle-shell bowl at Lalie's feet and prostrated herself on the ground.

Lalie glanced uneasily at Addison. "What did she say?"

"She said thank you."

"All that meant thank you?" Lalie asked, looking up at him.

"That was the gist of it," Addison said, smiling. "If you wish to forgive her earlier doubts, you may help her to her feet."

After Lalie did so, Tilwe signaled the entertainment could begin. First came a demonstration of the warriors' skills. Contests with bow and arrow commenced, followed by demonstrations of skill with blowguns. Lalie watched with uneasy interest. The warriors were deadly accurate.

It wasn't until the dancing had ended, the fires had burned low, and Lalie noticed several young couples slipping into the forest that she realized how late it was. A pale crescent moon glimmered through the treetops, the temperature had dropped.

Stifling a yawn, she turned a drowsy smile to Addison. "Shouldn't we be leaving?"

Addison scanned the nearly empty clearing, stubbed out his cigar. "We'll stay here tonight. It would be too dangerous to attempt the river in the darkness."

The day had been long and eventful; Lalie didn't argue. When Tilwe led her toward the women's quarters in his thatched hut, she followed willingly, believing she would be asleep in two minutes. Even the discovery that she was expected to sleep on a wooden platform with a log for her pillow didn't daunt her.

Stifling another yawn, whispering so as not to disturb the people dimly seen on the other platforms, she asked Addison, "Why wasn't I given a hammock?"

The sudden realization that March Addison had accompanied her into the women's section of the hut puzzled her, and she peered at him over the embers of the fire at the foot of the platform.

"Single people sleep in hammocks. Married couples use the platforms." His eyes twinkled. "You recall our subterfuge? As a married couple, Tilwe expects us to sleep together."

All thoughts of slumber fled Lalie's mind. "We can't

actually . . ." She waved a hand over the sleeping platform; her voice emerged in sputtering sounds. "Mr. Addison, surely you aren't suggesting . . . Oh my heavens." Raising a hand, she pressed it to her forehead. Suddenly the platform looked appallingly narrow.

"Now, Miss Pritchard, let's not turn difficult, shall we?" Sitting on the edge of the platform, Addison pulled off his boots with a sigh of pleasure. "Think of it this way. For two months you and I have been sleeping approximately three feet apart. Tonight, out of necessity, we're forced to close that distance just a little." When she gasped and clapped a hand to her breast, he smiled but didn't look at her. "My dear Miss Pritchard, you may sleep without fear for your virtue. I promise not to molest you, touch you, brush against you, or even to breathe in your direction. You have my oath as a gentleman."

"But you're not a gentleman!" The accusation emerged in a strangled whisper. She stared at him in horror as he stretched out on the platform and settled his dark head against the log.

Addison laced his fingers across his chest and opened one eye. "I take offense at that statement, Miss Pritchard. May I remind you that I am a gentleman by birth and occasionally by inclination. Moreover, I have never yet dishonored an oath."

Spinning on her heel, Lalie scanned the darkness in search of another empty platform. All the platforms were occupied. And the occupants were unmistakably making love.

"Oh dear." Closing her eyes, Lalie hastily sat on the edge of the platform and stared at her shoes. "Those people," she whispered. "They . . . they're . . ."

"Stop being silly, Miss Pritchard, and come to bed."

She imagined his grin and his pleasure at her embarrassment. "You promised not to deliberately use terms you know will offend," she snapped.

"So I did; my apologies. Very well, stop being silly, Miss Pritchard, and come to slumber. Better?"

"You're ridiculing me." And she had been foolish enough to believe something had changed for the better beside the waterfall.

"Good night, Miss Pritchard."

Glaring over her shoulder, she studied his face by the dim light of the glowing embers. She didn't believe for a moment that he could possibly be comfortable, laid out like a corpse at a wake. What looked suspiciously like a smile hovered at his lips. When her eyes dropped to his opened collar and the dark hair curling from the edges, she jerked her head around.

After a while Lalie abandoned the notion of sitting on the side of the platform all night. She cast Addison a hard, suspicious glance then cautiously stretched out on the boards. Holding rigidly to her side of the platform, she placed her head on the log, clasped her hands over her breast, and stared up at the smoke-blackened rafters beneath the thatch. A monkey stared back at her. She sat up and made certain that her skirt covered her ankles, then arranged herself again on the very edge of the platform.

All around her she heard the embarrassing enthusiasm of the Indians making love, the rustle of moving bodies, the whisper of quickened breath. Apparently the presence of others didn't inhibit Tilwe or his wife or his family in the least. But being an unwilling eavesdropper was agony for Lalie. Acutely aware that she and Addison were the only clothed people within miles, possibly the only couple in the village not making love, Lalie lay as rigid as the log beneath her head, staring blindly upward, feeling the heat pulsing in her face, throat, and breast. Strange, peculiar feelings tightened her skin and caught at her breath.

"Stop thinking about it and go to sleep."

She jumped at the sound of Addison's voice and raised up on one elbow to scowl at him. She hated the amusement in his tone, hated it that he had guessed what she was thinking.

"If you ever tell anyone about this night," she said in a low, urgent whisper, "I promise I . . . I'll do something terrible to you!"

Before he rolled over, Addison opened his eyes and smiled at her. "Threats, Miss Pritchard? I wonder how Mrs. Wilkie views threatening one's bed partner? Somehow I feel she would disapprove."

Lalie gasped and stared at him with murder in her eyes, too furious at the satisfaction in his expression to utter a word.

Sometime during the night March awoke to find his arms around Eulalie Pritchard. As the temperature had dropped and the embers died, she had moved across the platform and now slept with her small head pillowed on his shoulder, her body curved into the warm hollow made by his.

Instantly he felt the hard force of his response and eased his hips away from her buttocks. Closing his eyes, he turned his face against her hair, inhaled the faint scent of her perfume, and clenched his jaw. Not daring to move lest he wake her, he permitted himself to become aware of her back against his chest, of her silky hair on his throat. Her warm fragrance inflamed his senses and he became agonizingly aware that his arm rested in the curve of her waist and that her soft, full breast lay cupped in his palm.

He tried desperately to think of something—anything else. But the image that rose before him was Lalie beside the pool, her face raised to the sunshine, her lashes and throat glistening with droplets, her wet shirtwaist molded to her body so perfectly he could see her nipples thrusting against the cloth.

That image coupled with the reality of holding her in his arms made his groin tighten painfully. Desire mounted.

Never had honor required so great a strength.

Slowly, cautiously, he moved her bright head away from his shoulder then he inched off the platform, easing himself away from her. For a moment he stood looking down at her slumbering beauty, fixing the image in his mind. Then, swearing softly, furious for no discernible reason, he picked up his boots and stumbled outside the hut into the cold, starry dawn.

A soft, warm rain fell on the river and spread a blanket of mist over the forest treetops. Each time it rained, Lalie expected the air to cool but it seldom did. Putting down her teacup, she tilted back her head and blotted her throat and face.

Since returning from the Indian village, she hadn't worn a corset, and she no longer changed clothing except for dinner. She told herself she had not abandoned her standards; she had simply altered her habits in consideration of the climate and of Maria. Fewer changes of clothing meant less laundry. Eschewing her corsets meant she could breathe easier and the heat didn't trouble her as greatly.

This last proved not to be true. The heat was a never-ending discomfort. Lalie had assumed she would grow accustomed to the tropical blaze and she had assumed it could get no worse. She had assumed incorrectly on both counts.

Recently the sun itself seemed to have entered her body. Now she felt heat radiating from within as well as from without. The vibrations of the engine beneath her feet sent bursts of heat pulsing through her body. Her blood felt hot beneath the surface of her skin. An undefinable fever burned within her.

Evening brought no relief. In the privacy of her hammock, concealed by the drape of netting, Lalie shed her wrapper and pulled open the collar of her nightdress, but still she felt a fire in the pit of her stomach. She found herself thinking of Addison, wondering if he too noticed the nights had turned unbearably hot. But she didn't inquire. It became a test of character, desiring to speak to him as they lay side by side in their hammocks, but not permitting herself to do so.

Instead she lay in hot, sleepless silence, listening as Addison turned and moved in his hammock. Occasionally she remembered awakening in the Indian village, horrified to discover herself on Addison's side of the platform. The memory made her blush furiously. Thankfully, Addison had risen early and was gone when she awakened, so he didn't know what she had done.

Remembering that strange, unsettling night now made her feel restless and overheated. For a moment she listened to the rain caressing the deck roof, then she stood abruptly and carried her tea things to Maria.

"Tell again about Irikina and the baby, Missy," Maria begged. She couldn't hear the story often enough, though by now she knew every word of it by heart.

Lalie enjoyed telling of the experience. It had been a turning point for her. Never again would Lalie err by referring to the Indians as savages. Not while she retained the memory of Buti's tears or the joy in Irikina's eyes when she first held her newborn son. As she told the story again, Lalie turned Irikina's beaded bracelet on her wrist.

After Lalie finished the story, Maria sighed heavily and leaned to stir a fish stew bubbling atop her earthenware stove. "Sometime I think me and Fredo we never have a baby," she confided in a low voice. She lifted a hopeful face to Lalie. "You know how to make a baby, Missy? Tell Maria what to do."

Scarlet flooded Lalie's cheeks. "I'm sorry, but . . . I'm an unmarried woman. I don't know about such things." Even as she spoke the words, Lalie knew they weren't entirely true. She had secretly read enough of her father's anatomy tomes to know that a woman's most fertile period fell midway between her terms of menstruation. But she could think of no decent way to explain this to Maria.

Maria's dark eyes pleaded. "If you know anything, Missy . . . anything at all."

"Oh dear." The color deepened on her cheeks. Then she remembered Maria drinking powdered fox bones and manioc beer. "Well. Ah, let's see now. Do you . . ." She drew a breath. "Do you have a regular onset of the curse?"

"The curse?" Maria asked, frowning. She clutched her throat in alarm. "I'm cursed? That is why we no make a baby?"

"No, no. That isn't what I meant." Lalie bit her lip then plucked at her skirt. She wished to heaven this conversation had never begun. "I meant, you know, that time of month when you are indisposed."

"What is 'indisposed'?"

A long sigh lifted Lalie's breast. She searched for words that would be delicate yet would explain exactly what she meant. Her face flamed. She looked despairingly at an uncomprehending Maria. Finally she drew a breath, pushed the Voice of Propriety firmly into a corner, then explained in very blunt terms, indeed.

Frankly she didn't believe the information would prove serviceable as Maria and Fredo attempted to make a baby every night, thus indulging during the fertile period without success. But she couldn't bring herself to dash Maria's longing by raising the possibility that the couple might be forever childless.

Afterward, Lalie wandered to stand beside the railing, watching as the rain diminished and the afternoon sun reemerged. The steaming mist lifted and tall rust-colored bluffs reappeared along the near shore. As Lalie watched, a huge section of earth broke away and crashed into the turbulent river. As the *Addison Beal* chugged past, Lalie studied the altered shoreline.

It occurred to her that the river was altering her, too.

Some of the changes she recognized. Others she only sensed.

Turning from the shoreline, she frowned at the wheelhouse door and felt the feverish heat rising inside her body.

A three-quarter moon hung in the dark sky like a paper cutout surrounded by millions of tiny spangled lights. It seemed there were fewer insects tonight and what there were congregated around the lanterns above Maria's stove and tubs.

As had become his habit recently, March carried his after-dinner *cafezinho* to Miss Pritchard's table. And, as had become her habit, she invited him to join her.

"Do you mind if I smoke?" he inquired, surprising them both.

A wry smile touched her lips. "A man should not have to request permission to smoke aboard his own vessel. Or so someone recently informed me."

"Touché, Miss Pritchard," he said, laughing. He touched a flame to his cigar then tossed the spent match past the railing.

"But thank you for inquiring," she added in a soft voice. As she had leaned away from the candle, March couldn't see her expression. But he could see the milky swell of her breasts revealed by the low cut of her dinner gown. Her sunburn had faded, leaving behind a charming golden tint on her face, throat, and arms. But untouched by the sun, her breasts were so white he could glimpse the faint blue tracing of her veins.

"It doesn't seem as hot tonight," he said, making himself look away from her breasts. The forest glowed silver in the moonlight. The *Addison Beal* was anchored close to the shore and the earthy scent of ferns and night-blooming jasmine pervaded every breeze.

"Do you think so?" She sounded genuinely surprised by

his comment. "It's seemed much hotter since we returned from the village." While he tried to make sense of that, she asked, "Will we be visiting another village soon?"

"There's a village above Parintins, but we won't stop. We'll leave supplies on the shore."

"Will we stay over in Parintins?"

"Only a few hours. Not overnight."

They lapsed into silence, enjoying their coffee and the warm, fragrant night. Since the moment beside the waterfall their silences had been comfortable, the wariness and hostility they had felt toward each other had temporarily abated. Content with the day's progress, having dined on Maria's excellent stew, March drew on his cigar and leaned back in his chair. There was no better way to end a day than in the company of a beautiful woman and enjoying the pleasure of a fine Cuban cigar.

"There's something I've been meaning to ask, Mr. Addison." Leaning forward, Miss Pritchard tasted her coffee then added a spoonful of brown sugar. "When I ran up to tell you about Irikina, you were conversing with Tilwe and some of the warriors. I know this doesn't sound credible—in fact I feel foolish even mentioning it—but I had the distinct impression that I overheard Sir Percival's name. Is that possible?"

March's contentment vanished in a stroke. Straightening in his chair, he tipped his cigar into the ashtray he suddenly noticed she had provided.

"Yes," he admitted reluctantly.

Candlelight illuminated her puzzled expression. She folded her gloved arms on the table and raised an eyebrow. "I confess I'm surprised to learn Tilwe knows of Sir Percival. That Sir Percival would be the object of a discussion in an Indian village astounds me. May I inquire as to the nature of that conversation?"

"I'm willing to relate the discussion, Miss Pritchard, in fact I had intended to from the beginning, but I would prefer to do so at a later date. Let's not spoil a pleasant evening by raising a topic that is certain to upset you."

She frowned and looked at him intently. "I fear you've piqued my curiosity, Mr. Addison. As you're willing to discuss the subject, whatever it is, I insist that you do so now." When he protested, she added, "I've found conjecture is often more worrisome than fact. If you don't tell me now, I shall very likely imagine something worse than you have to tell. Besides, isn't it possible you're overestimating my response to this mysterious conversation?"

"I doubt that very much, Miss Pritchard." He recognized her determination and understood she would pester him from this moment forward if he did not tell her. "Very well, let the consequences be on your head." After lighting a fresh cigar, he began speaking. "Do you recall I mentioned the village's healing woman had been captured in a slaving raid?"

"Yes, I do." Her frown intensified. "How does that incident relate to Sir Percival? Please come to the point, Mr. Addison."

"That is the point. Sir Percy's men raided the village and captured the healing woman and three men."

She stared at him. "That is an outrageous slander!"

"No, Miss Pritchard, it is not. Sir Percival Sterling's men and his slave ships are well known to the Indians along the Amazon. Tilwe and his warriors tracked the slavers' dugouts back to the main river and recognized Sterling's crest on the ship's bow."

Pushing her coffee cup and saucer aside, Miss Pritchard leaned forward, until her breasts were illuminated by the candlelight. "You forget that I witnessed a demonstration of Tilwe's warriors' skills. Do you expect me to believe a group of unscrupulous men strolled into the village, snatched up some people, and walked away unscathed? No one protested?"

"Unfortunately, bows and arrows are no match for

Winchesters. The Indians tried to protect themselves, but their efforts were futile. Four people were kidnapped—three warriors died trying to rescue them. One of the slavers was hit with a poisoned dart, the rest escaped without injury." He touched his chest. "Speaking from personal experience, I can assure you the slaver will be damned lucky if he survives."

She stared at him in silence. "You can't prove those men were connected to Sir Percival."

Reaching into his trouser pocket, March withdrew a small pocket book and opened it to the page he had drawn for Tilwe. He laid it beneath the candlelight and pointed to rough drawings of various crests. "Everyone on the river is familiar with these crests. You've seen several of them yourself. Can you guess which of these crests Tilwe identified?"

Her flashing eyes settled on the crest bearing a rose and a stag, and he nodded. "That proves nothing, Mr. Addison! Tilwe could be mistaken. Or maybe those men stole Sir Percival's ship. Or maybe they acted without Sir Percival's knowledge."

"Those men were exactly what they seemed to be. Slavers seeking labor to work Sir Percival's rubber trees. That's how most of the rubber barons amass their fortune, Miss Pritchard. Slave labor cuts the cost of doing business. If you don't have to pay your labor force, profits increase at a wonderfully rapid pace."

"That is a shocking and a reprehensible accusation! Sir Percival Sterling would never degrade himself by stooping to slave labor. He is not the monster you make him out to be. He is thoughtful, caring, and generous to those less fortunate than he!"

"The wealth that funds his generosity was gained by slave labor. Like it or not, Miss Pritchard, that is a fact."

"I don't believe a word of this! The authorities would never permit such atrocities as slavery and, and . . . whatever else you're suggesting."

March's laugh was harsh. "The law? Hiberalta is two hundred miles from the nearest official. Percival Sterling is the law in Hiberalta. If a government official were cunning enough or suicidal enough to challenge Sir Percy's business practices, he would find himself richer through bribes, or very dead. The only surprise in Tilwe's story is that Sir Percival's men are working this far downriver. My guess is the rubber barons have decimated the villages upriver or have driven the tribes into hiding deeper in the forest. It appears they're forced to range farther afield to find cheap labor."

Miss Pritchard sprang to her feet. Her eyes blazed like sapphires. "There may be rubber men who commit the egregious crimes you mention. But Sir Percival Sterling is certainly not one of them. For reasons known only to yourself, you chose to lump Sir Percival with such criminals in an attempt to blacken his name. Speak what slander you will to others, Mr. Addison, but I know better than you what kind of man Sir Percival Sterling is!"

"You don't know anything, Miss Pritchard. And your mind is closed as tightly as a banker's heart." Summoning patience, he paused before he continued. "I believe I understand your obstinacy. It must be frightening to find yourself halfway around the world from home and then discover the man you intend to marry is not the honorable fellow you believed he was. But shutting your mind to the truth will not resolve your dilemma, Miss Pritchard. Either you accept Sir Percival's practices, or you rethink your future and sail home to London."

"You could not be more mistaken! I haven't experienced a moment's doubt about Sir Percival or my intention to marry him!"

Something in her expression suggested otherwise and March wondered if a small crack had appeared in her determination to believe Sir Percy a blameless gentleman. Possibly Miss Pritchard hadn't yet recognized this herself. Certainly she was not prepared to admit it.

"It seems we are not going to agree on your fiancé's character, Miss Pritchard. You view him as a dashing, romantic figure; I see him as a cruel and unscrupulous man. I'm certain you have your reasons; just as I have mine. Let's leave it at that, shall we?"

She looked doubtful, and clearly she burned to say more. In the end prudence proved victorious. After reseating herself, Miss Pritchard made an elaborate production of smoothing her skirts, patting her hair and rearranging the articles on the table.

"Are the healing woman and those three warriors lost forever?" she asked after a time. "Can anything be done?"

Addison turned away from the candlelight. He flipped his cigar into the dark river. "I've changed my mind about Hiberalta, Miss Pritchard. I'm as eager to arrive there as you are. That is why we won't be stopping over at Parintins. And that is why we'll stay in Manaus only as long as it takes to provision for the next leg of the journey."

Now he turned to meet her eyes. "I'm going to search Hiberalta until I find the healing woman and Tilwe's warriors, then I'm going to take them home. If they're still alive."

"You won't find any slaves at Hiberalta, Mr. Addison," she said after a lengthy silence. Tilting her head, she studied his face. "Aren't you concerned that I'll inform Sir Percival of your accusations?"

His smile was grim. "I don't give a damn if you do. If that's where your loyalties lie, then do whatever you must."

Chapter 10

Above Parintins
March 1897

We stopped in Parintins long enough for Maria to visit the market and purchase fresh provisions. There were no vegetables. Apparently such things are in short supply along the river. Parintins was small and dirty, populated by rough, hard-eyed people with ancient faces and ragged clothing. I was relieved to get under way again.

We're making better time now and my spirits have improved despite the heat. Although we pause to leave supplies for the Indians and for Joao to cut wood for the boiler, Mr. Addison and Fredo have not visited any more villages. We don't drop anchor until well past twilight.

Pausing, Lalie blotted the perspiration from her forehead then dipped her pen into the ink pot. Sunlight reflected from the water into her eyes, making it difficult to concentrate.

The heat is so dreadful it saps one's energy and inspires lassitude. I haven't sketched or picked up my stitchery for weeks. When we anchor I occasionally follow Joao a few yards into the forest to enjoy the cooler temperature. To pass the time I read aloud to Maria. I've read Mr. Addison's volumes about Malaya, and yesterday, thinking I should prepare for my future, I started to read Dr. Glazer's Advice to Maidens, Wives, and Widows.

Dr. Glazer seems a trifle confused. He advises maidens to suppress their fleshly desires, then advises wives to perform their duty no matter how distasteful, as if wives lack any fleshly desires.

Marital duty has been much on my mind of late. I have resolved to be sensible and straightforward. I shall endeavor to perform my duty in a cordial manner without burdening Percival or myself with an excess of modest disclaimers. I would not admit this to any soul but you, dear journal, but I think my marital duty shall not be a duty at all. However, in the event I turn squeamish or frightened, I trust dearest Percival to proceed with tenderness and gentle regard for my sensibilities as Dr. Glazer reports considerate husbands are wont to do.

The peculiar interior heat pulsed behind her forehead and in the center of her stomach. Lalie nibbled the tip of her pen, sighed, and continued writing, bumping her thoughts away from heated contemplation of her marital duty.

As we draw nearer to Manaus and the possibility that Percival may be waiting there, I have naturally devoted much thought to my future.

At age twenty-four, I am two years beyond my prime. Fully half of the young ladies in Miss Cheltenham's form are now married, and three have children. It is time that I too married.

Sir Percival Sterling is a brilliant man.

Sir Percival is titled, wealthy, and well connected.

I shall have a fully staffed home in Hiberalta, another in London, lovely clothing, and an exciting life.

No one will be able to say: Eulalie Pritchard did not live her life to the fullest.

Sir Percival offers all a woman could wish toward the attainment of mortal happiness.

Lalie reread the words she had written. Suddenly she realized that in listing her reasons for marrying Sir Percival she had penned nothing about love. But of course she loved him. Hadn't she dared all for his sake? Frowning, she capped her pen and ink pot and absently waved her palm fan before her face.

Suppose, she thought, idly watching ripples of caramel water lap the shore, just suppose March Addison was correct. Suppose Sir Percival did indeed employ enslaved Indians to work his rubber plantation . . . how would she feel about that discovery?

An image of Irikina and Buti rose in her mind. What if Buti had been one of the captured warriors? In that event he would never have experienced the joy of seeing or holding his newborn son. Irikina would have returned to her parents' hut, bowed with grief and sorrow. The infant would never know his father.

Lalie's frown deepened. Surely Sir Percival could not be involved in slaving. Addison must be in error. Yet Tilwe had identified the Sterling crest. Troubled, Lalie raised her parasol, got to her feet, and paced the deck, too restless to remain seated.

That evening when Addison carried his *cafezinho* to her table he looked at her questioningly. She waved him to a chair. As the night seemed especially sultry, Lalie had dressed simply, choosing a light, plain muslin, not an evening gown at all, but one of her afternoon dresses. She wore her hair unadorned, plaited around her small head like a crown. Her only jewelry was Irikina's bead bracelet. She assured herself that she had not relaxed her standards; she had merely adapted to circumstance.

Addison lit a cigar then pushed back in his chair and crossed one sandaled foot over his knee. He wore britches and an open-collared white shirt, the sleeves rolled to his sun-darkened elbows. His hair was still damp from washing, drying in tight dark curls around his face, and he still smelled of strong soap. Lalie bit her lip and transferred her gaze to her champagne glass in front of her.

"I've been thinking I should prepare myself for Hiberalta," she murmured. "Would you be good enough to relate what you know of it?"

The pleasure drained out of Addison's expression. "Hiberalta is a *barracão*. That's a rubber depot, not a real town," he said finally. Clearly he would have preferred another topic. "You'll find an office, three or four warehouses, a barracks for the *matteiros*—those are machete men—a company store, a few assorted outbuildings, housing for the estate manager, and the main house."

The smile of expectancy slowly faded from Lalie's lips. She glanced at the arrow of sunburned skin leading from Addison's throat to his chest then looked away. "Are there neighbors?"

"None that you'll see often. The last I heard, Sir Percival and the Sanchez brothers were still involved in a border dispute." No humor animated his smile. "If the Sanchez brothers come to call, they'll be carrying Winchesters and wearing nasty expressions."

"I see." She tried to contain her disappointment. Thus far Hiberalta sounded isolated and not at all appealing. "What is the manor house like?"

"One can hardly call it a manor house, Miss Pritchard. The accommodations are not as lavish as a London townhouse, or as commodious as a home in Manaus, however I think you'll find it satisfactory. As I remember, the house is two-storied with a heavy thatched roof. It's surrounded by verandas. The interior is airy and stuffed with enough superfluous furnishings to delight any woman's heart."

"It has a thatched roof?" she inquired in a faint voice.

He smiled. "You'll recall that every item must be carried upriver then overland. If native materials are available, they must suffice. Actually thatch makes a solid, cool roof."

"Things live in thatched roofs, Mr. Addison," she said, staring at him.

"Things also live beneath them, Miss Pritchard."

She sipped her champagne and thought about Addison's dismaying description. There would be no social calls to pay or to receive. No place to wear the lovely gowns filling her trunks. Suddenly Lalie brightened. Hiberalta would not form the sum total of their lives. And she hadn't chosen Sir Percival as a vehicle to launch her socially, had she? She had chosen him because he had swept her off her feet with his golden good looks and his exotic background, because of her affection for him. She would be content to spend several months each year in Hiberalta, having her husband all to herself.

An uneasy thought occurred to her. She had no idea if Sir Percival enjoyed reading or what he might like to talk about in the evenings. In London he had related exciting stories of the Amazon. When he was in the Amazon did he relate stories about London? As she was familiar with London, these stories wouldn't be half as interesting. What would they talk about?

Pushing these unsettling thoughts from her mind, she accepted more champagne and leaned toward the candlelight. "Can one see the plantation from the main house?"

Addison stared at her then sighed. "Miss Pritchard, a rubber holding is termed a plantation only for ease of reference. If you're assuming neat rows of hevea trees, you're mistaken. The hevea trees are scattered far and wide throughout the forest. A few planters have attempted to grow them close together, but in crowded circumstances the trees develop a leaf disease and die. In the forest they may be separated by as much as a mile."

Lalie frowned. "I distinctly recall from the books you leant me that rubber trees can be grown on a plantation."

"The plantation format is successful in Malaya because Malaya is free of the diseases found here. In the Amazon one must find the hevea trees where one may."

"Very well. And how is that done, Mr. Addison?"

"A *matteiro* opens each new *seringal.*"

Lalie sighed. "Speak in terms I can understand, if you please."

"An expert machete man, the *matteiro,* explores new tracts of forest and cuts paths through the undergrowth from one hevea tree to the next. This course is termed a *seringal* or a rubber estate, and it can cover several miles. Several *seringais* comprise an overall estate. The *matteiro* defines the perimeters of a *seringal,* then supervises the *seringueiro* who will work it. A *seringueiro* is a rubber tapper, usually an Indian, usually present against his will. The *seringueiro* buys his tapping equipment from the company store at ridiculously high prices and on credit, thereby beginning his new career deeply in debt. He never escapes that bondage, Miss Pritchard."

She narrowed her eyes and drew a breath. "Let us hold to the topic at hand, which is making rubber."

"The *seringueiro* lives in a thatch lean-to at the end of one of the trails. For six months, he rises at dawn and taps his trees. He scores a spiral cut around the trunk of the tree and attaches a tin cup to catch the latex that drains out of the cut. Each day he empties the tin cups early, before the latex coagulates in the heat. On a good day he'll collect perhaps nine liters of latex."

"What happens to the latex?" Leaning forward, she poured more *cafezinho* into his cup.

"Before the *seringueiro* goes to sleep, he'll smoke the gum he's collected over a palm fire that creates a dense white creosotic smoke. He turns the gum on the end of a pole over the palm fire. The rubber hardens around the pole, condensing as he adds more latex each day, until it forms a dark ball weighing about fifty kilos. Those are the balls you've seen in the harbors being loaded for shipment."

"I see."

"No, Miss Pritchard, you don't see," Addison said angrily. "You don't begin to grasp what brutal backbreaking work rubber gathering is. You can't comprehend how difficult it is to turn fifty kilos above a choking fire when you're so malnourished and exhausted that tears run down your cheeks and your arms shake with the effort. And you're riddled with insect bites and open sores. You can't imagine what it means to eat rotting meat or manioc flour infested with insects. You don't have the faintest notion of the fear a man experiences when he can't get his four or five kilos of rubber a day and knows he won't be able to reduce his debt at the company store or that he's destined to be flogged. You don't know what it is to live in a flimsy lean-to in the middle of the jungle with only insects for company for six months. You can't begin to comprehend the pain of carrying heavy buckets on a shoulder yoke through overgrown paths. You—"

"Stop." Lowering her head, Lalie touched her fingertips to her temples.

"When it's all said and done," Addison said, frowning at the dark shore, "the *seringueiro* is paid less than a thirtieth of what his rubber is worth. This pittance won't be sufficient to clear his credit at the company store for such items as matches or candles or his food. There won't be any money to send to his family or to visit them. Assuming he isn't a slave. And assuming he survives his six months in the forest."

"You have to emphasize the ugliness, don't you, Mr. Addison?" Lalie asked in a quiet voice.

Now he met her eyes. "There's nothing pretty about a

rubber tapper's life, Miss Pritchard. You wanted to know how rubber is harvested? That's how it's done in the Amazon."

They stood at the same moment and looked into each other's eyes over the candlelight. Then Lalie turned toward the stern of the ship where moonlight gleamed across the deck.

"Do you really think conditions will be different in Malaya, Mr. Addison?"

He followed her, leaned his elbows on the railing, and looked out at the shimmering water. "Rubber is in its infancy in Malaya. The growers have an opportunity to avoid the inequities found here." He glanced up at her. "Malayan growers can choose to pay the *seringueiros* a living wage for their labors, thus avoiding dependency on slave labor. They have an opportunity to expand a profitable industry and do it in a humane way."

Lalie paused beside him and watched a family of swamp deer emerge from the dark underbrush to drink at the river's edge.

"Considering your opinions, I find it astonishing that you would even consider growing rubber."

"I'm not against rubber, Miss Pritchard. I'm opposed to the practices employed by the rubber barons here in the Amazon. I believe growing rubber can be done with greater efficiency and without cruelty. No one agrees with me, but I predict the Amazon rubber boom will collapse as soon as Malaya establishes itself and enters the rubber market. Here the rubber must be shipped four thousand miles downriver. In Malaya, the rubber can be grown near the coast. Malaya can grow rubber cheaper and ship it faster than the Amazon can. It offers a marvelous opportunity for the right man."

Lalie stood beside the railing, so near Addison that she felt his body heat. A strange weakness spread through her body, sapping the strength in her knees and arms.

"It's true then," she said, touching a handkerchief to her throat. "I didn't believe it, but you honestly don't miss Putnam Hall, or London, or the English countryside."

Straightening from the rail, Addison looked down into her eyes. "Do you, Miss Pritchard? Have you left anything behind that you truly cannot manage without?" When she didn't answer, but pretended interest in her handkerchief, he added, "You of all people should agree that I no longer fit into polite society. Hypocrisy was never my long suit. I enjoy the comforts of society, Miss Pritchard, but without the burden of society itself. There's nothing in England to draw me back. I've finished with London."

"But Putnam Hall . . ."

"My brother Edwin will inherit Putnam Hall. Edwin is well suited to his destiny," Addison said, smiling at the river. "He revels in playing the country squire, dabbles in politics, frequents his club. Curiosity does not trouble him. Wanderlust is not part of my brother's character, Miss Pritchard. He no more understands or envies my life than I understand or envy his. Because of this, we are friends."

Lalie leaned her back against the railing and looked up at the velvet sky. "My father is a wonderfully skilled doctor, but I believe he once had a touch of the wanderlust you speak of. He traveled to the Amazon and to Sumatra." She smiled, but without humor. "My mother was more like your brother, I think. She stayed behind. Travel made her nervous." Poor Rose, Lalie thought sadly, she never really lived.

"Your mother is dead if I recall . . ."

She gave him a pained look. " 'Passed on,' Mr. Addison. The proper term is 'passed on.' She passed on ten years ago." Ducking her head, she plucked at her sleeve. After ten years the loss still felt fresh.

"Are there other brothers or sisters?"

"Just myself."

Addison blew a curl of smoke toward the shore. Something tawny glided into view among the trees, perhaps an ocelot. It was gone almost before the eye registered movement.

"Many young women in your circumstance find themselves on the shelf, caring for a widowed father instead of managing their own households."

Lalie's burst of laughter was genuine. "You don't know my father." Suddenly she missed Frederick Pritchard so strongly it was almost a physical ache. "Each time I rejected an offer, Father grew anxious that I did so on his account." She looked at the moon, feeling a sudden pang of homesickness. "He would summon me into his library where we would have sherry and cakes while he fumbled about trying to assure me that he would hate to lose me but he would also never forgive himself if I should be denied a full life on his account."

"Were there many offers?" Addison inquired, gazing out at the water. A peculiar gruffness roughened his tone.

"It may surprise you to learn I had my share of suitors," Lalie replied with a touch of defensiveness.

"I'm not at all surprised."

"There was one I almost . . ." She stopped speaking when she realized what Addison had said. Turning, she stared at his profile, amazed.

"Go on."

Hesitating, Lalie shifted position to watch Joao stringing their hammocks between the support posts. "Well, there was one man, his name was James Worthington. And I . . . but Mr. Worthington's character was much like that of your brother Edwin." Frowning, she turned to find Addison watching her with expressionless eyes. "I didn't think of it until you made mention, but curiosity is indeed an important quality, isn't it? Mr. Worthington lacked curiosity. He purchased books by the pound weight to furnish his library. So far as I know, he never glanced at them again. He lived according to an unvarying routine—from the City to his town home, to his club, to his house in the country then back again. It seemed so"—a blush colored her cheeks—"so dull and tiresome."

"Why Miss Pritchard, you're an adventuress after all!" Addison said, smiling.

She stared at him, appalled. "Indeed not, Mr. Addison! It's just that—that I wanted something more interesting from life than Mr. Worthington's routine would ever provide."

Addison gazed into her upturned face. The look in his eyes, his closeness, his alluring male scent all conspired to overwhelm her. She stumbled backward a step, waving her handkerchief in front of her throat.

Suddenly Lalie wondered about the symptoms of the fleshly desire Dr. Glazer's book of advice warned against, those fleshly desires that could overcome the most diligent maiden. Nowhere did Dr. Glazer list the characteristics of these desires. How was she to guess if she might be succumbing to them when she didn't know the symptoms? Might they include an internal warmth, a shortness of breath, weakness in the limbs, a heightened awareness of the senses? Did fleshly desire shatter concentration, set one's blood aflame, and cause one to fixate on a man's mouth, eyes, and hard, sun-bronzed flesh?

Swallowing with difficulty, Lalie tried to look away from March Addison but found she could not. Instead she discovered herself caught in the grip of a velvet trap that left her powerless and feeling distinctly peculiar.

"You prefer the life you believe Percy will offer?"

"I . . . yes." It appalled Lalie to realize that if she had indeed identified the symptoms of fleshly desire, she was experiencing them all, but with the wrong man. Lifting a hand, she clenched her teeth and made herself step backward, trying to concentrate on Sir Percival. "And of course, I felt an attachment for Sir Percival." Before she could trouble herself with the realization that she spoke in the past tense, she continued talking, placing her hand on Addison's arm. She felt an immediate involuntary tightening, as if his muscles were hardening beneath her palm. "Please. I beg you not to seize this opportunity to further assassinate Sir Percival's character. You've made your dislike abundantly clear, Mr. Addison."

The look of indecision in Addison's dark eyes indicated he found it difficult to honor her request. Finally, he patted her hand and nodded. Only then did Lalie realize that she had allowed her hand to remain on his arm. She was, in fact, powerless to remove it. Truly she was in the throes of some debilitating malady. She must remain on guard at all times to resist embarrassing and improper impulses.

Later, as she lay sweltering in her hammock, listening to the sounds singing through the forest, trying not to overhear Maria and Fredo's enthusiastic exertions on the deck below, Lalie pulled open the collar of her nightdress. Her fingers on her skin felt hot. Her skin itself was burning and covered with a light sheen of perspiration. Her nightdress shaped itself to her damp form in a manner that was partly pleasurable, partly uncomfortable. After checking to see that her netting was in place and that she was hidden beneath it, she kicked her legs free of her hem, shamelessly exposing her limbs to the night air.

"Mr. Addison?" she whispered. "Are you asleep?"

"No, Miss Pritchard. It's difficult to sleep when someone keeps talking."

"I've been wondering . . . there's something . . . ah, what exactly is the nature of your acquaintance with Clea Paralta?"

His shout of laughter mortified her and Lalie shrank into her hammock, her cheeks hot with embarrassment. How could she have asked such a thing? It wasn't at all what she had intended. The question had come out of nowhere.

"Are you inquiring if I've slept with Clea?" Addison asked bluntly. She didn't answer, couldn't answer, but lay rigid with shame in her hammock. He laughed again. "It's none of your business, Miss Pritchard, but no. I haven't slept with Clea. I met her years ago when I undertook

Joao's support. It was Clea who brought him to my attention. We've been friends since."

"You don't condemn her, ah, her profession?" Lalie whispered.

"It saddens me that some women must take to prostitution simply in order to survive," Addison said at length. "I've wondered what kind of woman Clea might have been if she'd had the advantages you've enjoyed. But Clea is uneducated. Her father was a Spanish sailor whose name her mother did not even remember. Her mother died giving birth to her tenth child. For several years Clea was the family's sole support. On occasion you demonstrate glimmerings of compassion and sense, Miss Pritchard. Can you honestly condemn Clea for taking to the streets rather than watching her family starve to death?"

Lalie didn't want to ponder that question. She knew prostitution was a horrible thing, yet if what Addison said was true, perhaps Clea had had no alternative. It was simply too confusing to think about. "Have you ever considered marriage, Mr. Addison?"

Helplessly, she bit her tongue. She had no idea where these unforgivably prying questions sprang from or where she found the courage to ask them. She had only wanted to change the topic of conversation, but it was as if a devil had seized her tongue, making her ask one embarrassing question after another.

She heard the humor in his voice. "I've had my share of admirers, Miss Pritchard, hard as that may be for you to believe. Like you, I considered marriage at one time."

"Can you speak of her?" Lord, lord. She couldn't stop herself. And she wanted to. Lalie absolutely did not want to learn about March Addison's private life. She knew entirely too much about him as it was.

She had observed his laundry flapping off the stern of the ship and knew he wore no knickers beneath his trousers. She knew he read voraciously. She knew he was a card shark and Fredo and Joao played with him at their peril. She knew he felt a passion for chess and chose his opponents with as much care as some men spent choosing a wife. She knew how he looked in the morning with his dark curls tousled, his expression ferocious until Maria placed a cup of strong Brazilian coffee in his hand. She knew he sometimes snored and occasionally muttered in his sleep. She knew far more about March Addison than it was proper for a young lady to know about a man who was not her brother, father, or husband.

"Her name was Amelia Humphrey," he said, startling her. "She was a lovely little thing, not much taller than you. This was ten years ago, when I was twenty and green and unable to see beyond a pretty face. Amelia was nineteen, eager to wed and eager to make her way in society."

"What happened?" Lalie asked, lifting up on an elbow to peer across the darkness.

"Her father objected, of course." A chuckle floated from Addison's hammock. "He felt she could do better than a second son with limited prospects who had gained something of a reputation for rough and ready ways. At the time he was quite right. My world was centered around fast horses and fast company. It wouldn't have been much of a life for an ambitious young lady." Lalie heard a rustle that might have been a shrug. "For a time we exchanged clandestine letters, formulated agitated plans to elope, but in the end, Amelia could not defy her father. Amelia wept; I swore. But I suspect Amelia was as relieved as I. Six months later she married a cabinet minister's son."

Lalie fell back in her hammock and gazed at the netting overhead. "She obeyed her father's wishes."

"Of course. I suspect I owe the old gentleman a large debt of gratitude. Had he offered us his blessing, I would now be trapped in a conventional, lackluster life, as would Amelia. She would have missed her cabinet minister's son, and I would have missed a fortune and a life on the river.

Mr. Humphrey, may God give him grace, knew us better than we knew ourselves."

"Are there any more questions, Miss Pritchard?" he asked, after a moment's silence. "Tomorrow will be a long day." He stifled a yawn.

"I apologize for prying. Good night, Mr. Addison."

After a time she heard Maria and Fredo tiptoe back to the upper deck and slip into their hammocks. Two howler monkeys quarreled in the forest canopy until something growled and they fell abruptly silent. Insects batted against her netting.

Lalie folded her arms behind her heat-damp hair and thought about these nightly chats with March Addison. They had recently developed the habit of conversing a while before falling asleep.

Ordinarily they spoke of the small events that made up their day. Sometimes they discussed the books they were reading. Occasionally Addison told her anecdotes about people he knew along the river. Lalie remembered friends in London, put into words her impressions of what she had observed since coming to Brazil, and asked questions about the Indian villages and tribes.

Occasionally the conversation took a serious turn and Lalie used the darkness to discuss topics she could not have discussed in the light of day. One evening they explored their feelings about God, and Lalie confessed what she had never confided to another living soul: she just didn't know whether God existed or not. Addison had not condemned or ridiculed her confession. In fact, he professed similar doubts. They decided they hoped there was a God. Another night they discussed science and Mr. Darwin's stunning theories.

On rare occasions, like tonight, their conversation strayed into private areas. Oddly it was Lalie who tended to instigate personal conversations and not March Addison. Always she was mortified by her lapses, and always she wondered what aberration had impelled her to cast convention aside.

Troubled by the heat and unable to sleep, she rolled onto her stomach and lifted up on her elbows, peering through the netting toward the moon-washed foliage on shore. The exquisite scent of forest jasmine haunted the evening air. For no reason at all, the sweet fragrance made Lalie's throat tighten and brought tears to her eyes. Not understanding her own reaction, she closed her eyes as Addison turned toward her in his hammock.

By now she had conquered her initial embarrassment and aversion to sleeping near him. His presence was, in fact, a comfort. So much had changed since the beginning of their journey, she thought. The night predators prowling the forest no longer disturbed her thoughts. It no longer discomfited her that Addison, Fredo, and Joao had observed her in her nightdress with her hair braided for sleep. It seemed natural and welcome to end her day quietly conversing with March Addison and to awaken to the cries of toucans announcing the dawn.

It occurred to Lalie that she would miss these nightly conversations when she left Addison at Hiberalta. Lowering her head, she gazed at his hammock and experienced an uncanny impression that Addison was also awake and watching her. After a while she decided the shadows and moonlight played tricks with her thoughts.

Dropping back on her hammock, she closed her eyes. With all her troubled heart she wished she could remember what it was about Sir Percival Sterling that had brought her halfway around the world to share his life. It frightened her that his memory became more elusive with every passing day.

Straw-colored houses appeared on the shore with increasing frequency after the *Addison Beal* entered the black humus-laden water of the Negro River that ran side by side with the Amazon below Manaus. Old people or young women with babies appeared in doorways of the stilt houses and waved as the ship steamed past. Lalie saw their candles or lanterns after dark, burning in the doorways to protect them from the terrors of the night.

Here the river widened, as much as seven miles across in some places, rimmed even in flood season by steep high banks that shimmered in the steaming morning mist like the walls of a red fortress. And every tree that slipped past along the shore, every puff of smoke that belched out of the stacks, brought Lalie closer to Manaus and closer to word from Sir Percival. She told herself over and over that she badly needed to see him and be with him again.

Tense with nervous excitement, she accosted Addison when he appeared at Maria's stove for his midday meal.

"How much longer until we reach Manaus?" she asked, stepping back as he poured water over his hair then shook out the droplets.

"Be patient, Miss Pritchard. A few more—"

An odd series of sounds interrupted his reply. Lalie heard the engine cough, sputter, then grind to a stop with a clanking sound. She pitched forward, nearly falling to the deck. Addison straightened and waved aside a platter of cold rice and assorted fruits, frowning as Fredo stuck his head out of the wheelhouse door.

"We got a *bagunça,* Cabo," Fredo called. Frustration lined his face.

"What's the problem?"

"Can't say yet." Fredo shook his head. "Need to look."

Addison nodded. "We passed a lagoon a short time ago. Let her catch the east current and drift back. We'll put in at the lagoon and see what we've got." He finished toweling his hair then smiled at Lalie without humor. "Don't make such a long face, this won't be as unpleasant as you imagine. There aren't any mosquitoes on the Negro."

Sighing, Lalie unfurled her parasol and leaned over the railing beside Maria's kitchen to watch Addison and Fredo maneuver the *Addison Beal* into the lagoon. With the ship becalmed, the breeze died and the heat escalated. Feeling a sense of envy, Lalie watched Joao dive over the side of the ship then take up a position on the shore with his spear. Within fifteen minutes he had caught a fish and brought it to Maria to roast for dinner.

Maria sliced the fish into thick steaks and removed the bones, handing Lalie a clean, perfectly round bone to examine.

"This is good luck," Maria explained happily. "This fish, a *boto,* he is big magic. On hot moonlit nights the *boto,* he take the form of a handsome man dressed in white. He go to the river towns and there he seduces the virgin girls."

Smiling, Lalie lifted the round bone to her eye and peered through it as if it were a spyglass. When Addison walked through the wheelhouse door, she watched him through it.

Addison blinked and gave her a startled look, then he laughed aloud and winked.

Still watching him through the round bone, Lalie frowned. "What was that all about?"

Maria's black eyes twinkled. "The legend say if a man look at a woman he desire through the eye of a *boto,* the woman be attracted to him plenty much. She give in to him."

"What?" Hastily, Lalie lowered the round bone, feeling a blush set fire to her cheeks. "What utter nonsense."

"No nonsense, Missy. Missy be in a soup now. You and Cabo look each other through the eye of the *boto.* Now Missy belong to Cabo."

As Maria spoke, Lalie chanced to glance across the deck and discovered Addison standing beside the rail. He turned an engine part between his hands, but he was not looking at it. He was watching her. The amusement had faded from his eyes, leaving them hard, almost black and very intense. He pushed back his straw hat and slowly his gaze moved from the flare of Lalie's hips along the curve of her waist, up across her unfettered breasts to her parted lips.

When his gaze reached and held hers, Lalie's throat went dry and a tremor shook her body. She could not look away. Her heartbeat quickened and a wave of hot weakness washed over her. When Addison finally released her gaze and disappeared over the side of the ship, Lalie sat abruptly on the kitchen stool.

Bewildered and still trembling, she tried to sort out what had happened.

Maria smiled. "The eye of the *boto,* Missy. Now you belong to Cabo. And he belong to you."

Chapter 11

The sun rose in the tropical sky. A hot breeze blew ripples of dark water against the shore. Scarlet ibises posed in the shallows; a half-dozen pacas, animals that reminded Lalie of giant mice, rooted in the shoreline foliage.

Strange clankings and explosive curses emanated from below deck while Maria napped beside her stove.

Lalie tried to write in her journal, but the intense heat muddled her concentration. The same affliction discouraged reading. Finally, she abandoned anything that required movement and relaxed, idly fanning her face and throat and sipping glass after glass of tepid champagne.

The afternoon passed. A peccary chased the paca into the underbrush and a flock of gaudy curl-crested toucans set up a raucous cry. As the engine coughed into life, the sun exploded into twilight flares of orange and violet and gold.

Tired but pleased with themselves, Addison, Fredo, and Joao came upstairs to the upper deck and toasted success with a bottle of *cachaça*. They were streaked with oil and grease; sweat plastered their shirts to their bodies.

"The *bagunça* is repaired?" Lalie asked. Addison's wet shirt was nearly transparent. She could see curls of dark hair matted beneath the damp material.

"All fixed," Fredo said, grinning happily.

Addison wiped his forehead with the back of his hand and swallowed half his cup of *cachaça.* "She'll hold together until we reach Manaus." He pulled his collar open, leaving a smear of grease across his chest. "God, it was hot down there."

Fredo and Joao nodded. Maria fanned her legs with the hem of her skirt. "It hot up here, too. We all plenty cooked. Drink three bottle champagne but no help pretty much."

Joao hung over the rail looking longingly into the sparkling lagoon waters, but it was Fredo who stood suddenly, walked to the ladder, and stripped off his oily clothing. In a moment he was naked. As Lalie's mouth dropped, Fredo dived off the upper deck into the water.

With an exuberant shout Joao ripped off his clothes and followed. Lalie blinked and gasped as a flash of naked skin sailed over the railing and splashed into the water below.

"Yes." Grinning, his eyes on the railing, Addison tossed back the rest of his *cachaça,* then stood and threw off his shirt. He reached for the buttons on his trousers.

Lalie's hands flew to her mouth and her eyes widened. "Mr. Addison? Mr. Addison!"

She covered her eyes as his trousers dropped to the deck, then his sandals. She heard the sound of running feet and peeked through her fingers in time to see him dive gracefully over the side.

Eyes round, her heart pounding, Lalie turned toward Maria's delighted laugh. "Maria, no! You can't," she whispered as Maria pulled her sweat-damp dress away from her body then up over her head. In an instant Maria stood before her, naked, her black eyes sparkling with anticipation, then she ran across the deck, climbed the railing, and jumped. A cheer sounded from below.

Lalie stood as if rooted to the deck, listening to the sounds of joyful play. *Cool* joyful play. Wet splashing play. She glanced down at the sweat-soaked muslin sticking to her body, feeling trickles of scalding perspiration run down her sides. If it was possible, she felt hotter than before, knowing the others enjoyed the pleasure of relief.

Knowing she shouldn't, telling herself she wouldn't, Lalie slowly walked toward the railing, irresistibly drawn by the delighted shouts and laughter, by the delicious cool sounds of splashing. Light-headed from the heat and too much champagne, numbed by the shock of seeing naked bodies, she drew a scorching breath and gazed down into the twilight waters of the lagoon.

They were playing like happy children, innocent of their nakedness, caught up in the pleasure of the cool water. Maria's sleek dark head surfaced, then she shrieked with laughter as Fredo dived beneath the water, caught her and pulled her under.

Lalie touched her fingertips to the wet hair at her temples, felt her gown sticking to her body. Then her fingers fumbled with the row of buttons down the front of her dress. She thought of nothing, saw nothing, except the cool mesmerizing water. A longing to immerse herself in it overwhelmed her. She yearned for the water; craved it. She could no more have stopped herself than she could have held back the sunlight.

Once her buttons were opened, she peeled the muslin away from her arms and pushed the bodice to her waist then stepped out of her dress and petticoats. Though she longed to be as naked as the others, even in her trancelike state she could not take that final step.

Clad in her chemise and lace-trimmed knickers, she kicked her sandals away and climbed over the railing. Not pausing to contemplate the distance between the upper deck and the water, not allowing herself to think about what she was doing, she simply stepped into space. Dimly she heard a shout of surprise then a chorus of cheers before she entered the water and a blissful wave of coolness closed over her head.

The bracing water rushing against her heated skin was

an exhilarating shock. A gentle current loosened her hairpins and freed her hair. When she surfaced and raised her face to the dying sun, an auburn cape spread over her shoulders.

"Splendid!" she cried, closing her eyes against the mellow golden rays. A rapturous smile curved her lips. "If I live to be a hundred, there will be no finer pleasure than this moment!"

Addison's laugh sounded from nearby. When she opened her eyes, he was standing a few yards from her, grinning. "I owe you an apology, Miss Pritchard."

Cautiously she extended her legs and discovered she could touch the sandy bottom if she stood on tiptoe. Assured, Lalie laid her head back in the water, luxuriating in the cool, sensual ebb and flow of the currents. Through a haze of champagne and joy, she laughed aloud at the orange and violet sky.

"There are few events I enjoy more than hearing you apologize, Mr. Addison." Spreading her arms, she let her body drift up and float on the surface. This must be how heaven felt, weightless, without care.

"I would have wagered the *Addison Beal* that Miss Eulalie Pritchard would melt to a puddle before jumping into the midst of a group of naked swimmers."

A dreamlike smile curved her mouth. "You would have been right. Five minutes ago I would have backed the same wager."

March stared at her, his smile fading. The flimsy chemise and knickers were far less protection than she dreamed. He gasped as her pink nipples appeared through the thin material. A coppery triangle was visible between her legs. He drew a sharp, involuntary breath. Lingering twilight gilded her skin; sparkling droplets hung on her lashes like honied dew. With her hair floating around her face, her arms outflung, the wet cloth as transparent as light, she was breathtakingly, nakedly beautiful, a nymph risen from the depths of the sea.

His response was immediate and painfully intense. He wanted her. He wanted her with a passionate, single-minded intensity that began in the pit of his stomach and ached through mind and hard body. He wanted the soft curve of those full breasts beneath his palms, wanted to feel her golden legs tighten around his waist. He wanted to cup her hips and guide her onto him, wanted to taste and lick and awaken those dreaming lips.

Tipping his head back, March closed his eyes and suppressed a groan. This woman, this strange, confusing woman, had crawled into his mind and into his body. His blood rushed and sang of her. Muscle and tendon tightened at the nearness of her. His flesh responded to the sight and scent of her. He thought about her; he dreamed of her. The instant he believed he understood her, she shimmered and altered and another dimension opened to dazzle him. She had been magnificent in the manioc garden with Irikina; she was magnificent now.

As if she were alone, she rolled languorously in the water, blissfully cooling her sun-heated skin, innocently unaware of her ripe sensuality. Sunlight caressed the curve of her inner arm and gleamed on her wet shoulders and cheekbones. Dark auburn hair floated back from her head revealing a perfectly oval face.

Her eyes closed, a euphoric smile on her full lips, she floated on the surface of the water, arching throat and breasts to the shimmering light, unaware that her body lay revealed to March's hungering gaze as if she were naked.

The others forgotten, he stood unmoving, aware only of her body and his own hard need as the gentle current brought her closer to him. Beneath the water his thighs tightened and his taut muscles rippled. At this moment he would have bargained ten years of his life to have this woman.

As he watched, she opened her eyes and smiled dazzlingly up at him. Then she smacked the water with her palm, splashing his face.

"What? You . . . !" Wiping the water from his eyes, he scowled as she laughed and swam away from him. In a minute he was after her, his powerful strokes driving through the water like pistons. When he caught her, he tumbled her then placed his hand on her bright head and dunked her beneath the surface. Laughing, he swam away.

She emerged, sputtering and grinning, splashing Fredo and Maria, a beautiful woman-child at play. Maria's bare buttocks gleamed in the light as she swam away from Fredo, knowing he would follow. The crew of the *Addison Beal* played and frolicked like children.

Eventually, tired and happy, Maria pulled herself up the side ladder to prepare their dinner, and a few moments later Fredo and Joao followed.

Loath to shatter the spell, Lalie lingered at the foot of the ladder, tilting her face toward the first stars that appeared along the final fringes of gold and violet. Lifting her arms, she slicked back her hair and smiled. The tops of her breasts broke from the surface of the water.

"This was wonderful," she said softly. Crystal droplets clung to her eyelashes. "I'll never forget it."

"Nor will I," March said. He stood so near that he observed the exact instant when she became aware of his naked chest and shoulders, knew the moment she realized they were alone together. Her eyes widened, like aquamarines in the dimming twilight, and nervously she wet her lips with the tip of her tongue.

"Lalie," he said, the sound like a groan.

As if she were in the grip of something greater than herself, she slowly reached out her hand and one trembling finger touched then traced the jagged scar on his chest. Her touch was a pinpoint of fire on his skin. His body flamed to immediate urgent life and the breath rushed out of his lungs. When he opened his eyes, he saw the creamy tops of her breasts, and felt he would certainly lose control of his own actions.

"Oh God. Lalie . . ."

Her face had paled. Her breath came in short gasps. When she raised her eyes from his naked chest, her expression mirrored her confusion and desire. "March, I . . ." Her whisper died. Her lips parted and she stared up at him helplessly. Then, as if she were too weak to support herself, she gasped for breath and placed her palms on his shoulders to steady herself.

Unable to stop himself, March reached for her beneath the water. She sucked in a sharp breath at his touch, but she didn't pull away. Her fingers tightened on his shoulders; she gazed longingly at his mouth, then slowly, her eyes rose to meet his hard gaze.

His hands on her hips, he guided her against his body, holding her there, feeling her soft legs and thighs tangling with his beneath the water. And he groaned when she pressed her hips against his in response, knowing she felt the hot urgency of his erection and his need for her.

A moaning sound came from her parted lips. Her breasts were thrust against his chest as her head fell backward and her eyes closed. Her fingers dug into his shoulders and her legs wrapped around his, pulling him more tightly against her until his erection throbbed between them, a rigid strength pressing against her soft, yielding body.

March's hands sculpted her hips and her waist. They curved up her rib cage and paused beneath her breasts. A sound like a sob tore from her throat, but she didn't pull away. A sudden ragged breath lifted her breasts above his hands and he stared down at the hard rosy tips thrusting above the surface of the water.

"Lalie," he whispered. He slid one hand to the small of her back and held her pressed against him, his other hand moved slowly to cup her breast, teasing the hard nipple. Her breath was as rapid and choked as his when she met his eyes with a look filled with helpless urgency.

Still holding her tightly, shaking with the sweet ache of restraint, he slowly lowered his head and pressed his lips to her throat. He heard and felt her sharp, agonized intake of breath, felt her hips move against him in involuntary response. Moving his tongue on her throat, he tasted her, licked her and found she tasted of the river and sunshine.

With tormenting slowness, exercising a patience and tenderness he had not known he possessed, he moved his mouth and tongue over her throat, teasing upward toward the swollen promise of her lips. His hand slid up from her back to cup her small head.

"Oh my God. March . . . March . . ."

Her words emerged part sob, part plea, and her body tightened around his. Beneath the water he felt her pressing against him, searching, seeking, awakening powerful needs and desires in them both. Slowly he raised her head, focused on her parted lips, on the sweetness of her breath mingling with his in quickened passion.

"Supper, she is ready," Maria called above them. She peered down from the top railing then her fingers flew to her mouth. "Oh! Sorry, sorry, very sorry!" she said then disappeared from view.

March saw the confusion and sudden look of shame in Lalie's eyes. Beneath the water, her legs released his abruptly and she jerked away from him, turning blindly to the ladder. She pressed her forehead against a ladder rung and fought to calm her breath.

"Lalie—"

"Please," she said in a low, ragged voice, refusing to look at him. "I beg you . . . say nothing, Mr. Addison."

He touched a strand of hair floating behind her. "If I've offended you, I apologize," he said in a thick voice. His blood roared with frustrated need.

Her head lifted, and anguished eyes met his. "The offense is equally mine," she whispered. "I apologize. I don't know what . . ." She bit her lip and squeezed her eyes shut. "I can only promise that such an appalling lapse will never happen again." Without looking at him, she almost ran up the ladder and disappeared over the railing.

He watched her wet knickers define the sweetly provocative curve of her buttocks, then he threw himself into the water and swam the length of the darkening lagoon. He swam until the taut ache in his body finally relaxed into exhaustion. When March pulled himself up the ladder and Maria handed him his clothing, Miss Pritchard was nowhere to be seen. She remained hidden behind her tarpaulin through supper and did not emerge on deck until the hammocks were strung. Then she hurried to her hammock without looking at anyone, swathed from throat to toe in a voluminous wrapper.

Long after everyone else had slipped into their hammocks, March stood in the darkness beside the railing, smoking and listening to the cicadas strumming their single-note symphony. He contemplated the smoke curling from his cigar, and tried to understand fully what had happened that day. In the gleam of starlight he could glimpse the shroud of netting draping her hammock. As she was a restless sleeper, he knew from her stiff, motionless form that she was awake.

After a time he extinguished his cigar, flexed his shoulders, still stinging from her fingernails, and walked through the darkness to stand beside her hammock.

"We need to talk," he said quietly. The night was too black to observe anything beyond the netting.

"Go away, Mr. Addison," she whispered. Her voice trembled. She was weeping. The realization devastated him and something ached inside his chest.

It rained constantly the following afternoon, but as usual, the rain did little to diminish the sultry heat. Lalie stood near Maria's stove, sipping papaya juice and idly watching the rain pelt the surface of the Amazon and Negro. The two rivers ran side by side, the confluence sharply defined.

Steam floated above the water, concealing the forest canopy from time to time. The humidity was so high that

Lalie occasionally felt as if she were actually breathing water. Her shirtwaist adhered to her body, clearly revealing that she had resumed wearing her corset.

The rigid bands running from breast to hip constrained her rib cage and restricted her breathing, but she felt armored, safer somehow than she would have felt without it.

But safer from whom? she thought, biting her lip and staring out at the pouring rain. March Addison—or herself?

A shudder passed through her body and she moved away from the dripping edge of the roof, walking toward a support post. Turning her back to the wheelhouse door, she leaned against the post and frowned at the turbulent wake trailing behind them.

She knew she could easily blame Addison for what happened. Undoubtedly Addison himself expected no less. Assuming a posture of deep offense and fury at him was unmistakably the course to adopt. Anything less placed Lalie in a reprehensible position.

But that was squarely where she found herself. No one had forced her to throw off her clothing and jump into the lagoon. She had known beforehand that Addison was naked. A tremor passed through her body at the memory of his glistening chest and the forest of dark hair slashed by old scars, the way the sunset rays had burnished his skin to tones of bronze and copper.

Worst of all, he had not taken her into his arms against her will. Shame burned her face and throat. She had not pushed him away, had not struggled to escape his hand on her breast, his mouth on her throat, or the heated pressure signaling his desire. She had in fact surrendered eagerly. She had thrust her hips against his; had parted her lips to receive his kiss; had wanted . . . had wanted whatever would happen next.

Her face burning, Lalie covered her eyes and thanked God that Maria had appeared at the railing when she had.

Otherwise, her betrayal of Sir Percival would have been as complete in fact as it had been in thought.

And she was as much to blame as March Addison. Confusion mingled with her feelings of disgrace. She did not understand what had come over her. Addison had not changed. He was still the same rough, rude, opinionated man who had first offended her in Pará. His language was still offensively direct, he still dined with menials, continued to slander Sir Percival, swore at will, and performed his personal ablutions without a trace of modesty.

Modesty and propriety should have risen to her rescue. But both had vanished the instant Addison's hands reached beneath the water and encircled her waist. She might at least have pretended not to understand his physical reaction. Any decent woman would have reacted with surprise and bewilderment. A decent woman would not have known what pressed against her with such throbbing, hard urgency.

But Lalie had known exactly what thrust against her beneath the water. Without thinking, she had dropped the pretense of unawareness, had abandoned all sense of modesty. In the grip of shameless passion, she had forsaken any claim to ignorance.

A tiny drop of blood appeared beneath her teeth, and she realized she'd been biting her lip. Self-disgust flowed through her like a wave. She had dared to wonder if she would ever experience fleshly desires. The memory almost made her laugh. She was certainly not immune to Dr. Glazer's fleshly desires; she was awash in them. Aflame with fleshly desire. Pulsing and burning with fleshly desire. She had stood in her underpinnings in the embrace of a naked man and trembled with desire, yearning to surrender, to fill an emptiness she had previously been unaware of.

And that man was March Addison, a man she had almost learned to tolerate but certainly not to admire. How could such a miscarriage have happened? Was she so demented, so consumed by fleshly desires that she was willing to throw herself at the nearest man, no matter how distasteful or offensive? Was she ill? Stricken by a strange, exotic tropical fever? Had the heat or the rigors of travel affected her brain? In her distress, she was even willing to offer credence to Maria's silly story about the eye of the *boto* and think herself bewitched.

Pacing the deck, Lalie flogged herself with remorse.

"Damn this heat!" Pausing at the rail, she pressed a hand to her breast and licked the sweat from her upper lip. She touched her fingertips to her throat where Addison's mouth had licked her skin. And a fever ignited in the pit of her stomach. "Damn," she whispered, tears glistening in her eyes.

When she realized she had uttered a swear word, despair caused her shoulders to sag. She wrapped her arms around the support post and pressed her forehead against the damp wood. Slowly, bit by bit, the river and this journey were stripping away all she had believed herself to be. Would there be anything left of the old Eulalie Pritchard when she finally met Sir Percival? She could no longer be certain and that thought terrified her.

After dinner March carried his *cafezinho* to Miss Pritchard's table, but she didn't invite him to join her and he noticed she had not set out the saucer she usually designated as his ashtray. He seated himself anyway, watching without expression as she scowled then reached forward and pinched the flame on her candle. When she leaned back in her chair, her posture was rigid and unnatural. At once he realized she was wearing her corset again.

"We'll dock in Manaus sometime tomorrow, probably before midday," he said after he lit his cigar.

After a short silence, March spoke again, addressing

her profile. "I estimate we'll need five days in Manaus to find the parts we need and make permanent repairs to the ship." He waited for her to comment, but she said nothing. She looked at her lap, at her napkin, at her cup, toward the stern. Anywhere but at him. "I have friends in Manaus with whom you can stay, or, if you prefer, there are several good hotels."

Finally she spoke, but still without raising her head in his direction. "I posted a letter in Parintins to some friends of Sir Percival's and announced my forthcoming arrival. I don't presume to anticipate an invitation, but if one arrives it will be welcome. Otherwise, I'll stop at a hotel."

"May I inquire the identity of Sir Percival's friends?"

She hesitated then said, "Mr. and Mrs. Gunter Rivaldi."

"Rivaldi." For several minutes he said nothing more. Rivaldi was one of the wealthiest rubber barons in the Amazon. And one of the most ruthless. When smaller growers refused to sell Rivaldi their *seringais* for a pittance, Rivaldi seized the *seringais* and the owners vanished. It was rumored that Rivaldi maintained a harem of young Indian girls to satisfy his pleasures and that of a favored clique. He ruled Manaus in all but name.

On the other hand, March thought, frowning at his cigar, Rivaldi was no more unsavory than the other rubber barons. Rivaldi and his wife would install Lalie in their lavish mansion and honor her with a series of fetes. They would pamper her and enfold her within the gilded trappings of Brazilian society.

She had suffered the sun, a peeling burn, a multitude of insect bites. She had existed on simple river food, had slept in an open-air hammock for three months. She'd endured an almost constant lack of privacy. She had stood on deck in the pouring rain; had survived the indignities of the Indian women's examinations. She had ridden in dugouts; had tramped through forest and jungle.

Even if she might have listened, did he have the right to ask her to choose a hotel rather than accept the luxury the Rivaldis would offer solely because he disliked Gunter Rivaldi? March realized he very much wanted Eulalie Pritchard to dislike the people and things he disliked and care for the things and people he cared for.

This last insight surprised him. He could think of no reason why Lalie Pritchard should share his opinions, his biases. They were as different as oil and water. He had no claim on her. The incident in the lagoon had changed nothing. It had only created a larger distance between them. That, he did regret. However uneasy their truce had been, he had enjoyed their nightly conversations, the exchange of small confidences.

"Miss Pritchard, are we going to make an issue of what happened in the lagoon?" he asked suddenly.

March saw her stiffen and instantly regretted his words. The Amazon had not eroded his instincts to the point that he had forgotten what decency demanded. Any gentleman worthy of the description would accept full blame in this instance. And he was willing to do so. While his claim to be a gentleman was somewhat dubious, he certainly understood the proper response in this situation. He was willing to apologize profusely for taking advantage of her and for forcing his attentions on her. He was willing to forget that Miss Pritchard had reached for him and submitted to his embrace. He was willing to act against truth and logic because he understood she would consider herself ruined if he did not. In fact, he was willing to do anything to put her at her ease once again.

"We are not going to make an issue of . . . of anything, Mr. Addison." She bit her lips and twisted her hands in her lap. "I could explain that I drank too much champagne or that I was overcome with heat, or that I was strangely ill and out of my senses." Her jaw clenched then released with effort. "Those explanations may even be true. But they excuse nothing. Mr. Addison, I beg you to forgive my behavior. Far from making an issue of the incident, I am desperate to forget it ever occurred."

A moment elapsed before March grasped the implications of what she was saying. Miss Pritchard was not blaming him; she had accepted all blame herself. His gaze narrowed and he stared at her in astonishment. This was very out of character. Any proper English lady would have blamed the man in an incident like this one.

Perhaps Father Emil had been right about her after all. Perhaps there was more to Eulalie Pritchard than he'd ever suspected.

"My dear Miss Pritchard," he said after a few moments of silent contemplation. "I'm beginning to understand. I wonder if you realize what a fraud you are."

No wonder she studied Mrs. Wilkie so diligently. She did so because she feared that left to her own inclinations, she would disgrace herself. The Miss Pritchard who could profess shock that Amazonians dined indecently early was not the real Miss Eulalie Pritchard, she was a creation.

Looking backward March sensed that he had committed a serious misjudgment. He had accepted the image Miss Pritchard intended him to see and he had looked no deeper. Now he recalled a dozen examples where she had spoken as directly as he could wish and without mincing words. And he realized she more often reacted to an offense as if she *should* be shocked, rather than as if she genuinely were shocked.

"A fraud," she whispered sadly. "Yes, perhaps I am."

Curiosity and sympathy overwhelmed him. He hadn't a notion what she thought she admitted to, but she had certainly misunderstood his meaning. She didn't even comprehend that she labored to present a image that was not her own. He doubted she had an inkling of understanding that the woman she struggled to hide was far superior to the woman she labored to create.

He smoked in silence, studying her stiff profile, reviewing his conclusions and trying to decide on the best course of action.

"Miss Pritchard," he said finally, "I earnestly beg your forgiveness for my inexcusable offense against you. I acted selfishly and without regard for common decency or for your wishes. I have no excuse to offer in defense and can't think why a woman of your breeding and impeccable reputation would accept this poor and inadequate apology, but I pray that you will. You have my word of honor as a river captain that no living mortal shall ever learn of this incident from my lips and I hope that you can find it in your heart never to mention my abominable behavior. I am as eager as you that my offense be forgotten, and I praise your generosity for suggesting it."

Suspicion darkened her eyes. "Why are you saying these things?" she demanded in a low voice.

"Surely a devotee of Mrs. Wilkie need not ask such a question," he answered with a gentle smile. "I genuinely regret causing you a moment's discomfort."

"That was a generous gesture, Mr. Addison. But I don't understand you," she whispered. "Just when I think I do, you do something that . . ."

Standing, he held her chair, something he had not done throughout her sojourn on the *Addison Beal.* If someone had pressed him to explain why he did so now, March could not have been able to answer. It was just that she seemed so miserable, so vulnerable.

They circled the deck while Joao strung the hammocks, not speaking, not touching. He told himself that he didn't smoke because he did not wish to dilute the whiffs of lilac and verbena that floated his way.

Although neither of them fell asleep immediately that night, they did not converse as they ordinarily did. Despite his apology and his willingness to absolve Miss Pritchard of any culpability in the lagoon incident, March lay in his hammock and thought distinctly ungentlemanly thoughts. He remembered the feel of her body and the sound of her voice breathing his name. He remembered the smooth curve of her skin, the warm fullness of her breasts. Sweat broke over his brow and his body tensed.

She spoke only once in a despairing whisper, and he wasn't certain she even realized she had spoken aloud.

"I must get to Hiberalta soon. Soon . . ."

Chapter 12

As with all river settlements, a heavy stench signaled Manaus before the self-styled Paris of the Amazon came into view. The reek of civilization assaulted Lalie as the *Addison Beal* maneuvered toward the town's famous floating docks. The ship had to vie for space with ocean-going liners from Paris, London, and Lisbon, with trading steamers, barges, fishing vessels, and boats. A hundred dugouts and rafts bobbed among the larger vessels. These comprised a floating market selling bread, limes, jaguar skins, *barbasco* roots, and malodorous, hastily cured tapir hides.

Ranged along the harbor walls, adding to the stink of sewage and smoldering garbage, were tin-roofed stalls offering dried boa skins, tanned caiman hides, piranha teeth, skulls, and monkey testicles. But it was the pungent sulfurous smell of smoked wild rubber that dominated the yellow haze overhanging the city.

Most of the trading vessels rode low in the water, piled high with black balls of smoked rubber. Men worked the docks, loading the heavy oblong balls and leaving piles of mangoes, papayas, and bananas to rot under the sun. Other commodities could wait. Rubber was gold in the Amazon, and the men who controlled it were kings.

Before the *Addison Beal* dropped anchor and Joao

threw out the ropes, a half-dozen men congregated before the bow, grinning and shouting good-natured obscenities at March Addison, who grinned and shouted back. Offended by the coarse humor, Lalie frowned with disapproval. She noticed the men wore captain's caps bearing the insignia of March Addison and Robert Beal's brokerage firm.

To explain the men's presence March tilted his head toward the forest of ship's stacks sprouting along the docks. "Several of the trading steamers are ours," he announced. Lalie looked in the direction in which he pointed, taking care not to accidentally brush against him. "It appears our captains have secured the lion's share of the consignments going downriver," Addison said with pride.

Responding to the chaotic bustle along the docks, Lalie glanced at him. How could he choose to leave all this behind? She watched Addison exchange his battered straw hat for the cap with the firm's insignia, which Fredo also donned with pride, then Lalie recalled her own reason for wishing to reach Manaus and a surge of nervous excitement shivered down her spine.

After smoothing her sprigged muslin, adjusting her hat, and shaking out her parasol, she hurried to the rail and eagerly scanned the faces and vehicles jamming the wharves. Her gaze jumped from one head to another. She sought out immaculate panama hats and stared briefly at the men in white suits who stood smoking and leaning on gold- and silver-headed walking sticks as they watched sweating stevedores carry balls of rubber aboard the trading vessels.

Once she thought she saw Sir Percival, and her heart banged painfully against her corseted ribs. But eventually she accepted that her fiancé was not among the hundreds of people on the wharves. Deeply disappointed, Lalie glanced toward Addison and bit her lip. It seemed they were destined to continue upriver together.

Once the boarding plank was down and in place, a man stepped out of the throng and requested permission to board the *Addison Beal.* It was impossible to overlook him as he wore a footman's full livery, including a gray wig that had fuzzed in the heat and humidity. His green worsted jacket was soaked with perspiration. Lalie stared in disbelief and suddenly saw herself as Addison must have seen her the day she arrived in Pará. Dressed with ludicrous inappropriateness and miserably uncomfortable.

But surely no one this far upriver could be as ignorant of the tropics as Lalie had been the day she arrived in Pará. She stared at the man and pondered his sanity. Perhaps he punished himself for some unknown reason.

Neither conjecture was accurate. Lalie suddenly realized the truth: the man wore the miserably hot clothing because he was forced to, because he was what he looked to be, one of Mrs. Gunter Rivaldi's footmen come to fetch Miss Eulalie Pritchard.

Appalled that an employer would insist on such a torturous costume, Lalie raised her eyes and spotted a black brougham bearing the same crest as the footman wore on his breast. Even at a distance Lalie could see that the woman inside was beautifully gowned and wore a hat that would not have shamed its wearer in any of the world's capitals.

Addison appeared at her side and he too studied the lavishly attired woman. After directing the footman to Lalie's luggage, he turned to Lalie, not bothering to lower his voice. "Truda Rivaldi amuses herself at the expense of others. Verbal daggers are her forte. Just remember—you're worth a dozen like her." His dark eyes narrowed as if he might have revealed more about the Rivaldis, but when he spoke again he merely said, "I'll collect our mail and deliver yours this evening."

Before Lalie could respond, Joao had guided her across the plank and through the crush of people. The footman hurried ahead to open the brougham door, snap down the step, and hand her into the cool interior. Lalie stepped inside and waited for her eyes to adjust to the absence of burning sunlight.

"We were delighted to receive your correspondence, Miss Pritchard," said a husky voice as Lalie settled herself on richly upholstered cushions. "A friend of Percy's is, of course, a friend of ours and a welcome guest."

"Thank you for extending your hospitality, Mrs. Rivaldi. Sir Percival spoke in the highest terms regarding you and your husband. I pray you don't think it presumptuous of me to have written, but—"

"Not at all," Truda Rivaldi protested, waving a lace glove drenched in expensive French perfume. "Conventions are necessarily relaxed in this dreadful place. You acted quite properly, I assure you." She tugged a velvet cord to signal the driver to proceed, then tilted her head and studied Lalie openly, as if completely unaware that her direct inspection might be unsettling or a lapse of manners on her part.

Lalie also examined her hostess but without, she hoped, such blatant scrutiny. Truda Rivaldi was perhaps thirty-five. Despite the richness of her dress and exquisite grooming, a faint insinuation of coarseness existed. There was an indefinable something underlying Mrs. Rivaldi's voice and manners that Lalie sensed would cause most men to regard her as seductively beautiful rather than merely handsome. Lalie suspected that men would be drawn to Mrs. Rivaldi like moths to a flame and that Mrs. Rivaldi subtly encouraged such interest.

"Since receiving your letter I've naturally been consumed by curiosity as to your connection to Percy. However, you can tell me about that later. In truth it hardly matters. Everyone in Manaus is bored with one another and so eager for fresh faces that you would be welcome whatever your connections."

Truda's amused glance made Lalie wish she had worn her silk-trimmed afternoon gown and a more elaborate hat. Her simple white dress and gloves seemed provincial when compared to Mrs. Rivaldi's ribbons and lace. For jewelry Lalie had chosen her mother's pink brooch, never dreaming her hostess would appear in pearls before supper. And such pearls. The string fell to Truda's corseted waist in a lustrous flow. Each gleaming bead perfectly matched the next, and all matched her ear drops. In comparison Lalie's pink brooch seemed girlish and embarrassingly meager.

Aware that she didn't quite measure up in Mrs. Rivaldi's judgment, Lalie cleared her throat self-consciously and tried to ignore the blush coming to her cheeks. "As this is my first visit to Manaus, Mrs. Rivaldi—"

"You wish to know about the city." Unlike Emily Capuchin, Truda Rivaldi did not invite immediate intimacy. There was no suggestion of exchanging first names on short acquaintance. "The place is abominable, of course," she said with an exaggerated sigh. "The heat is insufferable, the insects merciless, and try as one will one cannot eradicate the lizards. The rains are torrential, the lack of seasons depressing, and there's no place inside the city where one can escape the stench." A lazy smile curved her lips. "There are more brothels than churches, more beggars than barons, more rum and *cachaça* dens than decent dining clubs. Whatever one's vice, Miss Pritchard, one may easily indulge it in Manaus. An entire section near the wharf is given over to satisfying men's most depraved pursuits."

Lalie blinked and swallowed hard. She lacked the faintest notion of what an appropriate response might be.

"One can buy whatever one wishes in Manaus, and that, of course, is a pleasant benefit. Diamonds, silks, Italian slippers, French porcelain, Chinese art . . ." Truda shrugged. "The schools are impossibly provincial. We're forced to send the children to Paris to school, but I suppose we would have done so anyway. Naturally everything one requires for decent living must be imported. Or exported. These people have no conception of cleanliness; it's necessary to send the laundry to London."

"To *London?"* Lalie repeated, her eyes widening. The cost of such extravagance exceeded her ability to calculate.

"Indeed. As these people can't adequately launder a simple handkerchief, you can imagine the damage they inflict on one's niceties. We do, however, have some rather decent seamstresses." She glanced at Lalie's costume. "If you're stopping long enough, I can recommend a reasonably talented French modiste."

The carriage paused, caught in a traffic snarl of wagons, donkey carts, and coaches. On the cobblestone walkway beyond the carriage window, a string quartet played a Liszt selection to the patrons of a sidewalk café.

"Ah yes, we do have our amenities," Truda Rivaldi remarked, smiling at Lalie's surprise. "Manaus is not without culture. One of the entertainments I have planned for you is an evening at the opera house. La Movita—from Milan, I believe—is performing later this week."

"How lovely," Lalie said in a faint voice. She tried to envision an Italian opera singer traveling up the Amazon to perform in the jungle. The idea stupefied her as greatly as hearing Mrs. Rivaldi casually refer to brothels and depravity.

Once freed of the traffic congestion, the brougham entered a section of the city that was paved with stones imported from Portugal. Here the wide boulevards were handsomely landscaped with palm and cedar trees, beech and fragrant eucalyptus. Mounds of hibiscus and bougainvillea added splashes of brilliant color to the cooler green. Behind tiled privacy walls, beautiful colonial mansions lined the streets.

The brougham turned down a tree-shaded drive and circled before the door of a tile-roofed mansion faced with Italian marble. The foyer inside was also tiled in creamy cool marble. Carved doors opened into rooms filled to overflowing with glossy antiques and classic statuary. The illusion of being transported to a European palace was complete when Lalie noticed fireplaces in every chamber.

A laughing Truda Rivaldi preceded her up a sweeping staircase. "They've never been lit and never will be. But the house would be wrong without them, no?"

The suite into which a flurry of footmen and housemaids showed Lalie was as extravagant as everything she had observed so far. Two lace-covered poster beds occupied the bedroom and an armoire for her clothing had been built to cover one wall.

Overwhelmed, Lalie seated herself on the edge of a damask upholstered settee and withdrew the pins from her hat. Almost immediately, a maid appeared bearing crystal flutes of French champagne that, miraculously, was almost cool.

Truda handed her hat and gloves to a maid then settled cozily into a wing chair. "Now, my dear Miss Pritchard, my curiosity will be contained no longer. Do tell me of your connection to Percy." Her amber eyes studied Lalie's simple coiffure. "You are a cousin, perhaps?"

Lalie drew a breath, feeling under siege beneath the woman's scrutiny. "Sir Percival and I are to be married, Mrs. Rivaldi."

"Married?" Truda Rivaldi sat up straight and stared. "I confess I am not often surprised, Miss Pritchard, but your announcement takes my breath away. Married. How stunning." For an instant she examined a point in space, then her mouth twisted in an annoyed smile. "I wonder why Percy said nothing of this. He didn't even mention your name. How very curious."

Eagerness lit Lalie's expression. Setting down her champagne, she leaned forward. "Then you've seen Sir Percival recently?"

Truda laughed as if Lalie had said something amusing. "Oh yes. I've—seen—Percy recently. He passed through

Manaus not three weeks ago. I assure you, nothing in his words—or deeds—indicated a pledge to marriage." Her lifted eyebrow invited elucidation.

Feeling terribly uncomfortable, Lalie related her story.

Truda looked fascinated. "So. Dear Percy doesn't know yet that his fiancée is soon to arrive on his doorstep. What a delicious surprise for everyone." She laughed. "I must say, Miss Pritchard, I can think of a dozen women whose hopes you have just dashed."

A charming bloom colored Lalie's cheeks, disguising her disappointment. Mrs. Rivaldi's comments made it obvious that her letter had not reached Sir Percival. There would be no communication from him when Addison delivered her mail.

"March Addison!" Truda said with a sniff of distaste when Lalie mentioned Addison would be stopping by later to deliver any letters that might have come for her. "What an odious, rabble-rousing man. Why ever did you select March Addison to transport you upriver?"

"Mr. Addison is known to my father," Lalie answered stiffly, looking toward the palm fronds waving outside the sitting-room window. "He's a friend of the family."

"No longer, he isn't," Truda said with a husky laugh. When Lalie turned and raised an eyebrow, Mrs. Rivaldi leaned forward with an arch look. "Didn't you know? Percy and Addison are bitter enemies." Her voice dropped to a conspiratorial whisper. "I believe there was a fight some years ago over a woman . . ." When Lalie didn't speak, Truda shrugged and leaned back in her chair. "Addison has few admirers among the rubber men. He charges exorbitant transportation fees and demands a larger commission than any broker on the river."

Surprised by the defensive edge in her tone, Lalie said, "It appears Addison Beal Enterprises doesn't lack for commerce. I noticed at least half a dozen fully loaded traders at the dock."

"All too true." Truda's reply was accompanied by an

annoyed sigh. "Addison's firm is incomparably more reliable than the others. None of his shipments disappear —if you know what I mean. And his bookkeeping is scrupulous." She shrugged. "There you have it. Men like my husband are forced to pay Addison's outrageous fees to obtain swift, reliable transport and accurate accounting. You can understand why Addison is roundly loathed. He names an exorbitant price and the rubber men must pay it." Her rouged lips curved in a mirthless smile. "Gunter, my husband, will not be pleased that Addison is coming here tonight."

"I didn't realize—if you'll allow me the use of a messenger, I'll make other arrangements. I could instruct Mr. Addison to send my mail by messenger or—"

"You misunderstand, Miss Pritchard. Neither my husband nor I would dream of offending your Mr. Addison. Not without severe provocation. To do so could have unfortunate consequences for future shipments. Although the rubber men would relish breaking Addison's stranglehold on shipping, I'm confident they would prefer to choose their circumstances and timing. I shall send a messenger to Addison at once, inviting him to the reception tonight in your honor."

"A reception . . . ?"

Standing, Truda Rivaldi directed an amused gaze toward the gowns her maid had withdrawn from Lalie's baggage. "How quaint. I had no idea London lagged so far behind the fashion." She bestowed a dazzling and supercilious smile on Lalie. "But I'm sure your beauty transcends mere fashion, Miss Pritchard." She inclined her head. "If you'll excuse me, I'll leave you to rest. You've given me much to ponder, my dear." She shook her head and laughed aloud. "Fancy—Percy Sterling married."

She cast Lalie a look of amused sympathy before she gathered her skirts and left the sitting room trailing liveried servants behind her.

Lalie too had much to ponder. March Addison and Sir

Percival Sterling had fought over a woman? A sting of something very like jealousy bit into her thoughts. Who was the woman and what had been the outcome of the fight?

Then came the surprising revelation that March Addison was not as widely esteemed as Father Emil and Emily Capuchin had suggested. It appeared he was roundly disliked in Manaus.

Finally there was the disturbing elusive smile on Truda Rivaldi's lips when she agreed she had "seen" Sir Percival of late. Her look and her tone imparted a whiff of unpleasant innuendo.

No, Lalie thought, standing abruptly. She would not build mountains out of molehills. She would not upset herself with ludicrous imaginings. This was an opportunity to enjoy herself in a civilized manner and she intended to seize the chance and not allow anything to spoil it. That she found Truda Rivaldi a trifle unsettling could be attributed to the state of her own nerves.

Naturally she experienced a trace of apprehension about meeting Sir Percival's friends. As they would soon form part of her life too, she felt it crucial to make a favorable impression.

Clenching her teeth, Lalie planted her hands on her hips, a decidedly improper but determined stance, and she scowled into the armoire, trying to decide which "quaint" costume she would wear for that evening's reception.

Gunter Rivaldi presided over the dinner gathering much as a pharaoh might preside over his subjects. Dressed in sharply contrasting tones of black and white linen, he dominated the head of the table with a slightly bored, slightly menacing air. Having only just met him, Lalie could not decide if Gunter Rivaldi was indeed a menacing personality, or if his swarthy skin and hooded black eyes merely made him appear so.

It was true that the Rivaldis' dinner guests seemed to subtly seek his approval before pursuing a line of conversation, and it was true the dinner company deferred to him as if he had surrounded himself only with sycophants. It was also true that Gunter Rivaldi had complimented Lalie's gown and beauty and welcomed her to his home in a display of faultless manners. He presented her to his dinner guests as if she were visiting royalty, which appeared to amuse his wife greatly.

But he was not the sort of man with whom many women would feel comfortable, Lalie decided uneasily. Beneath the polished manners and his handsome silver hair lurked a suggestion of unpredictability and danger.

Thinking her host menacing and her hostess unsettling was not a good beginning, Lalie told herself. She wanted to like Sir Percival's friends and wanted them to like her.

In that regard, Lalie believed she acquitted herself well at dinner once she recovered from the astonishment of discovering each lady had received an uncut diamond as a favor and each gentleman had received a silver money clip.

Never before had Lalie dined in such exalted company. Every woman and some of the men wore a multitude of jewels. Diamonds and emeralds flashed and dazzled in the candlelight. Silk and satin, imported lace and rare feathers all told her these people who surrounded her possessed enormous wealth.

She might have succumbed to intimidation had not Manaus society proved hungry for news. The dinner company plied her with questions about England, fashion, and events in the outside world. They all seemed interested in her impressions of the Amazon. They made her the focus of attention and insured her success.

Gunter Rivaldi lifted his hooded gaze and regarded Lalie's flushed cheeks. "Knowing Addison's peculiarities, can we assume he exposed you to the *bichos da mata?*"

A slight frown appeared on Lalie's face as she returned

Gunter Rivaldi's mild look of curiosity. "I beg your pardon? I don't believe I'm familiar with that expression."

A gentleman dressed in the latest Paris fashion explained. "The beasts of the forest, Miss Pritchard. The savages. Everyone knows March Addison is an Indian lover. He calls on Indian villages as if the savages were people."

A woman who had been introduced to Lalie as the Contessa d'Alessio shuddered with distaste. "If anyone has discovered how to wrest a decent day's work out of a savage, I beg to be informed." Her powdered bosom rose in annoyance. "The filthy creatures behave as if they've never seen a broom before. As for soap . . ." She rolled her eyes toward the diamond dust sparkling in her dark hair. "They'll eat soap before they'll use it to good purpose."

"Flogging is the only thing a savage understands," Truda said firmly, nodding to the butler to remove the plates. Tonight she wore satin encrusted with tiny sparkling rubies. Silk flowers set with diamond centers adorned her hair. "A sloth works harder than a stupid savage."

"Flogging?" Lalie whispered, looking from face to face.

Truda laughed at her horrified expression. "It isn't like flogging a person." Perfectly coiffed heads nodded along the table. "They're animals, my dear. They don't feel a flogging any more than a mule does. To them it's like a tickle. But what else can one do? The savages are the laziest creatures on earth. If you don't watch them every minute, they steal everything shiny or edible, nap, or try to run off. If they didn't fear the lash, they wouldn't work at all."

Lalie said nothing as the conversation centered on vilifying the Indians. Each person had a story to relate. Lalie heard contempt, superiority, and a stunning disregard for the Indians as human beings. Though she was tempted to protest, to inform the company of Irikina and Buti and Tilwe, she glanced at Gunter Rivaldi and held her tongue. His expression told her emphatically that nothing she said would alter the opinions of the glittering company seated at the Rivaldis' long table. But the contemptuous, often shocking stories were difficult to hear and Lalie squirmed in her seat until Truda Rivaldi rose and led the women into the parlor, leaving the men to their cigars and brandy.

Moments after the ladies had settled over coffee cups and gossip in Truda's gilt and velvet parlor the butler appeared. Inclining his wigged head, he spoke in Mrs. Rivaldi's ear, and both glanced at Lalie. Lalie slowly put down her coffee and stood as Mrs. Rivaldi approached.

"You're wanted, Miss Pritchard. A friend requests a word." A frown of annoyance drew Truda Rivaldi's lightly penciled brows. "Your—friend—has arrived early. I believe the invitation specified ten o'clock."

"An oversight, I'm sure," Lalie murmured, her cheeks burning. Trust March Addison to muddy her budding success with the Rivaldis. Gathering her skirts, biting back her annoyance, she followed the butler to a small receiving room opening off the far side of the foyer.

March Addison paced before the window, hands clasped behind his back. When Lalie entered the room, he spun on his heel and faced her, scowling furiously.

"You lied to me," he accused the instant the butler withdrew.

The reprimand Lalie had prepared died on her lips. For an instant she stood rooted in place, staring at his white Irish linen, his freshly barbered jaw and pomaded hair. His hard eyes stared back at her, flashing anger and accusation.

"I beg your pardon?" she said faintly. But she could guess what was coming.

"Damn it, Miss Pritchard. You swore you were in the

Amazon with your father's blessing. That was a bald-faced lie." Reaching inside his jacket, Addison withdrew a thick cream-colored envelope and waved it in front of her. Lalie recognized her father's neat handwriting on the face.

"I didn't exactly say my father offered his blessing," she whispered, sinking to the nearest chair. "It's true I may have implied as much, but . . ." Her heart thudded against her corset stays as she looked at the envelope. "Precisely what did Father tell you?"

"You know damned well! He said you ran off without his permission or his knowledge. He said he refused Sir Percival Sterling's request for your hand, that he objects in the strongest terms to Sterling as a husband for his only daughter. He castigates me for conspiring in your scheme, and he demands that I place you on the next ocean-going liner bound for London."

Lalie looked down at her hands and bit her lip. "I'm sorry Father blames you. I left him a letter explaining everything. I thought it would reassure him of my safety if I mentioned you would be taking me to Hiberalta."

"What you did was imply that I concur in this lunacy, and that I'm part of it. In so doing, you impugned my honor and my standing as your father's friend. You implicated me in your disobedience, your elopement, your lack of judgment."

Her chin lifted and she met his angry eyes stubbornly. "I'm sorry. It was not my intention that my actions should reflect poorly on you." She scowled. "But what was I to do?"

"You were to listen to your father, Miss Pritchard. You were to accept his judgment. You were not to lie to me."

"I . . . I regret lying to you. But if I'd told the truth, would you have brought me upriver?"

"Hell, no!"

"Exactly. There's your answer, Mr. Addison." Standing, Lalie faced him across a lacquered table overflowing with silver bibelots. "I am twenty-four years old, quite old enough to decide for myself whom I will marry, where I will live and in what circumstances. No one has the right to make those decisions for me. I believe I know better than anyone where my happiness lies!"

"Your logic takes my breath away," Addison said angrily. "You adhere slavishly to small conventions, but sweep aside larger traditions if they displease you. Centuries of tradition and legal convention mean nothing to you. Your father's informed opinion is worthless."

"You take my breath away as well, Mr. Addison. I should think you of all people would defend the right of individual freedom of choice!"

"I do. Except in this instance your father is right and you are disastrously wrong. Marrying Percy Sterling is the worst blunder you could commit. Now get your things. I've booked passage for you on a boat that sails downriver at dawn. After you reach Pará you will take the first available ship to England." His dark eyes bored into her. "Is that understood, Miss Pritchard?"

"No, Mr. Addison, it is not!"

He clenched his hands at his sides. Even though the table was between them, he seemed to loom over her.

"You will be on your way home tomorrow morning, Miss Pritchard. Your passage is bought and paid for, courtesy of the credit established by your father. I don't know what your father said to you in his letter, but I can guess. And you deserve the verbal lashing you are sure to receive."

Lalie turned the envelope between her fingers, staring at it as if the pages within held the power to wound her as deeply as March's words had already done. He wanted to send her away forever. Somehow learning that was almost too much to bear.

However, he was offering her a way out of the confusion

that had secretly begun to plague her. The nearer she approached to Hiberalta, the more bewilderingly uncertain she became of the future she had chosen.

Biting her lip, she gazed up at him. "I am going to Hiberalta, Mr. Addison." To her own ears, her voice lacked conviction. Her tone fairly begged him to override her.

"Damn it, Lalie—"

"Is there a problem here?" A deep voice spoke from the doorway and Lalie whirled as Gunter Rivaldi entered the room. He came to her side and placed a proprietary hand on her elbow. "My wife overheard voices and suggested you might require assistance, my dear."

Addison spoke to Rivaldi, but he didn't take his eyes from Lalie's burning face. "The lady thanks you for your hospitality, Gunter, but she'll be departing now. She's sailing for Pará in the morning."

One black and silver eyebrow rose as Rivaldi glanced down at Lalie. "I believe you're mistaken. I have received a communication from Sir Percival only today requesting that I see to Miss Pritchard's journey upriver."

Lalie spun to face him. "Then Sir Percival finally received my letter! But why didn't he respond to me directly?"

Reluctantly, March reached into his coat and withdrew a long dove-gray envelope that he dropped on the table between them.

She stared at him in astonishment. "Not giving me Sir Percival's letter is unforgivable," she said through trembling lips.

"I hoped to persuade you to change your mind."

Gunter Rivaldi's black eyes narrowed. "It appears the lady will continue to accept our hospitality. You're mistaken, March. Miss Pritchard will not be sailing in the morning."

"Stay out of this, Gunter, it doesn't concern you. I am

acting at the express desire of Dr. Frederick Pritchard, at his direction and with his authority. He has instructed me to make sure his daughter returns to London as soon as possible."

"And I am acting in Sir Percival Sterling's stead at his request. I will guarantee Miss Pritchard's passage to Hiberalta and assume responsibility for her welfare. From this moment, March, you have no further interest in the affair."

The two men stared at each other, measuring, deciding how far the challenge would extend. Desperate for the scene to end, Lalie held her breath.

Finally March turned to her. "We've reached an impasse that you must resolve. If your decision is to obey your father's wishes and the dictates of good sense, I'll take you out of here right now. If, however, you're determined to throw your life away, that is also your choice. Say so and I'll depart at once."

"Oh March." Tears of helplessness and anger filled her eyes. "Don't you understand even yet? You're asking me to choose between my father's wishes and my own happiness. But I made that decision months ago. I can't . . . I won't give up now. I'm going to Hiberalta and I'm going to marry Sir Percival."

He stared at her and his fists opened and closed as if he wanted to shake her. "You little fool, is your pride so damned important that you can't admit you've made a mistake? Are appearances that important to you?"

Her chin quivered, but she met his gaze squarely. "Are you so arrogant that you believe you have the right to decide my life?"

Gunter's smile deepened and became unpleasant. "Was there anything else, March?" he inquired smoothly. "If not . . ." He moved aside, opening the way to the door.

Addison's stormy dark eyes searched her face. "You are the most stubborn, pig-headed woman I've ever met. You won't hear or see the truth. Very well. The best I can hope for you now is that you never recognize the truth. God help you if you ever take off your blinders and realize what you've done."

"That's enough," Rivaldi interrupted sharply. "I'll not have a guest insulted in my home." He tugged a bell rope. "Good evening, Mr. Addison."

"There's no call to summon aid, Rivaldi." Addison's smile turned grim. "My business is finished here." His face like stone, he inclined his head to Lalie. "Good-bye, Miss Pritchard."

Lalie thrust her shaking hands into the folds of her skirt and watched him stride toward the door. Two swarthy men appeared in the arch and she sucked in a breath. Addison taunted them in a low voice and both men turned hard, questioning eyes to Gunter Rivaldi. Rivaldi raised a hand and shook his silvery head. Addison laughed and the men stared after him angrily.

Then he was gone.

Lalie gazed at her letters. She could not endure the rest of the evening without reading them. "If I might have a few minutes alone . . ."

"Of course." Gunter brought her fingertips to his mouth, not quite touching them to his lips.

"Please accept my profuse apologies for this . . ." She waved a hand, her cheeks burning with embarrassment. "This scene. And thank you for your assistance, Mr. Rivaldi."

"It was my pleasure, Miss Pritchard." A look of speculation glittered in his black eyes. "It would please me greatly to see Percy married to so charming a lady, and settled down." The cold smile returned to his lips. "Now, if you will excuse me . . ."

Lalie stared after him. When he had gone, she slowly sank onto the nearest chair and touched her fingertips to her aching temples. The scene had given her a headache, and reading her father's furious letter was not going to make her feel better. Percival's letter she would save for last.

She placed her thumbnail under the flap of the envelope and broke the Pritchard seal. But she wasn't ready yet to face her father's anger or her own guilt regarding how she had betrayed his love and trust. Her father only wanted what was best for her. But according to his determination, not hers.

Dropping her head backward on the top of the chair, heedless of her coiffure, Lalie closed her eyes and drew a deep breath. It wasn't only the letter in her lap that upset her. The parting with Addison had occurred too abruptly, too unexpectedly. She hadn't been prepared for it. And it was so final. She knew he was out of her life forever. The thought caused a peculiar distress in the pit of her stomach.

Her turmoil was not caused by the fact that she would never again share March Addison's company, Lalie told herself sharply. What she felt was simply regret at the manner of their parting. After all these weeks together, there should have been more ceremony to their farewell. They should have reminisced a bit then wished each other well in future endeavors. Their parting should have been courteous, an expression of shared experience and mutual respect. Instead the moment had been tense and angry, the words hard and accusatory. And over it all hung an impression of loose ends, dangling threads, words not spoken.

Lalie dashed her hand across her lashes with a furious gesture, then ripped open the letter from her father.

The letter was every bit as scathing, accusing, and dictatorial as Addison had hoped and she had feared. When she finished reading the letter a second time, Lalie dropped her head in her hands and wept. She had hurt her father deeply.

Finally, she tore open Sir Percival's letter and shook out the pages with a trembling hand.

Dearest Lalie,

Your surprising and delightful letter was waiting when I returned to Hiberalta. What an amazement that you are somewhere behind me on the river.

I am confident at least one of my messages will catch up to you in Manaus. From that point, dearest Lalie, you are in my care. What matters most is that you depart Addison's company at once, if indeed you are in his company as you intended. With this post, I am sending Rivaldi instructions to arrange the next leg of your journey.

I deeply regret that I cannot be there to welcome you with a kiss, my beautiful Lalie. But a bothersome border dispute requires my presence in Hiberalta.

Please know you have made me the happiest of men. I eagerly await your arrival, my dear bride.

Your future husband,
Sir Percival Sterling

Lalie read the letter again, then drew a deep breath and closed her eyes against a tiny rush of panic. She could no longer recall Sir Percival's features with any real clarity. His romantic image as a rubber baron had blurred considerably under Addison's assault.

But now there was no longer room for doubt or confusion. She was committed. Percival was expecting her as his bride. Moreover, if she backed down now, her father's pain would have gone for nothing. She would have wounded him needlessly.

Standing, Lalie blotted the dampness from her lashes and pinched color into her cheeks before she rejoined the party.

Once she saw Percival again, everything would come right. She had to believe that. She did believe that.

But suddenly she felt shaky inside and almost ill. She had traveled nearly four thousand miles to marry a man whom she knew less well than she knew the man who had brought her here.

And instead of feeling joyful, she felt as if she had suffered a grave loss.

Chapter 13

The rainy season had ended but rain continued to fall every afternoon. Lalie could distinguish very little difference between the rainy season and what Truda Rivaldi laughingly called the "dry" season. In any case, the light afternoon sprinkles did nothing to cool the scalding air. Nor had the humidity diminished. While keeping pace with Mrs. Rivaldi's many social obligations, Lalie felt as if they dashed about through hot water, breathing it, speaking through it, swallowing it with every tea cake and every glass of tepid champagne.

Throughout the last four days Lalie had seen enough of Manaus to be awed, fascinated, and faintly depressed. The fabled city was as fabulous as she had been given to believe. The hotels were opulent, the food prepared by European chefs, the nightlife as varied and exotic as anywhere in the world. Massive warehouses crowded the wharf area, dazzling shops lined the thoroughfares. Private estates featured zoos as well as aquariums, and gleaming greenhouses.

But for all its opulence, Manaus was a walled city, oppressively bounded on three sides by the encroaching jungle. The men who listened to Liszt and Mozart in the sidewalk cafés wore the hard-eyed expressions of men not far removed from what the city's residents referred to as the "green hell." An air of dangerous expectancy vibrated through the city as if the inhabitants awaited an explosion that never came. There was something frantic in the eternal pursuit of pleasure and the search for new ways to spend new money.

"I have just the thing to improve your spirits, a surprise for you," Truda announced, sweeping into Lalie's bedroom one morning. "Today we're going to visit Percy's house. You did know Percy was building a house in Manaus, didn't you?"

"I believe he mentioned it," Lalie answered, trying to recall if he had.

"Everyone's talking about it." Truda's gaze grew speculative. "You'll be mistress of the largest mansion in Manaus, my dear. Your social success is assured." Smiling, she plucked at the Venetian lace covering her ample bosom. "Not that you wouldn't have been a success otherwise, of course."

Lalie watched a house lizard skitter across a silk-covered wall. Truda Rivaldi had a way of stating things that suggested she meant the opposite.

Sighing, Lalie pushed to her feet and reached for her hat. She wondered what Fredo, Maria, and Joao were doing. And March Addison. Where was Addison on this hot, steamy day? And did he too regret the manner of their parting?

Lalie lapsed into awed silence as the Rivaldis' carriage halted before a massive tile-roofed villa. Though still under construction, the mansion facing San Sebastian Square took her breath away.

Slowly, she descended from the carriage and followed Truda across a litter of construction debris then into the house. The sound of hammers and workmen's shouts echoed through the empty rooms. Pausing, Lalie realized her father's entire house would have fit comfortably into

Sir Percival's foyer. A huge crystal chandelier hung from the two-storied ceiling. A double staircase swept to the floors above.

"Can you see yourself floating down the staircase to welcome guests?" Truda asked, her voice hoarse with undisguised envy.

All Lalie could think of was the appalling cost of importing the double staircase from France, the tiles from Portugal, the statuary from Greece. Silently, she peeked into the rooms opening off the foyer. Here too there were beautifully appointed fireplaces in which no fire would ever blaze.

They walked through room after room of polished rare woods and Italian marble columns and lapis lazuli insets. And Lalie tried to imagine herself presiding here, tried to imagine this palace as her home.

Truda tilted her head to inspect an upper-story ceiling replete with cavorting plaster cherubs. "If I were you, I wouldn't indulge a moment's worry that all this is a trifle ostentatious even for Manaus," she murmured, planting the thought in Lalie's mind. "Percy is young and impetuous. Clearly he hasn't given a care to overstepping himself."

By building a larger house than the Rivaldis', Lalie thought, mentally finishing Truda's sentence. Raising her glove, she traced a finger along brass-framed tiles fronting the hearth of yet another useless fireplace. And suddenly she recalled Addison's description of malnourished *seringueiros* fighting fatigue, disease, and loneliness in the forests and jungles. Their labor was paying for the crystal and imported woods and marble, for the courtyard fountains and wasted fireplaces.

Abruptly it occurred to Lalie that she might have viewed Sir Percival Sterling's future home—and her own—in vastly different terms if she had not met March Addison.

Frowning, she lifted her hem, walked out onto a balcony,

and drew a deep breath of scorching air. Below and to the right she spotted an alleyway crowded with tin-roofed lean-tos. Half-naked children sat listlessly in front of the cook pots the women had set up in the street. An odor of burned beans and rotting fruit assailed her nostrils and she closed her eyes then turned in the other direction.

Here Lalie saw the gold dome of the opera house glittering against the blazing sky. The sharp contrast between the alleyway with its air of hopelessness and grinding poverty and the gold leaf garnishing the opera dome made her feel dizzy.

"Percy has thought of everything except a whipping post," Truda said, laughing at Lalie's side. "Considering the size of the staff you'll need, I should think a whipping post *de rigueur.* You must tell Percy I said so." She examined Lalie's expressionless face curiously. "Well, my dear Miss Pritchard. What do you think of your future home?"

"I don't know," Lalie answered truthfully. When Mrs. Rivaldi's eyes widened, Lalie bit her lip and attempted to explain a little of what she was feeling. Truda Rivaldi clearly didn't understand. Finally Lalie concluded, "The house is just—it's a bit overwhelming, don't you agree?"

Truda's laugh dismissed Lalie's reservations. "One grows accustomed to wealth more quickly than one might believe. In no time at all you'll be in complete command of the situation."

Biting her lip, Lalie again directed her gaze to the alleyway. "Do you ever think about the people who actually tap the rubber and make all this possible? Does it trouble you that people fight with street dogs for table scraps within a few feet of your door?"

Truda Rivaldi gazed at her as if Lalie had taken leave of her senses. "Good God, no! And you shouldn't give such matters a thought, either. Those people are animals, not even a generation removed from the jungle." Her features twisted in distaste. "They are stupid, ignorant, filthy, and uncivilized. They would slice your throat in a moment. They don't know the word gratitude!"

Lalie thought of the tears in Buti's eyes, of the feast given in her honor after she saved Irikina. But Truda offered her no opportunity to speak. As they descended the staircase, Mrs. Rivaldi related a story to prove her point. "Last year Gunter gave me an Indian girl as a pet—"

Lalie froze. Her hand gripped the banister. "As a pet?"

"I lavished attention on that girl. I let her sleep on the end of my bed, gave her sweetmeats, dressed her in lace, taught her a few simple tricks, and do you know what she did?"

Lalie stared.

"She ate dirt, handfuls of it. To punish her, I withheld her meal, thinking she would comprehend the difference and learn something. So what did she do then? She ate her dress!" Disgust twisted Truda's lips. "She ate her lace dress! Now there is gratitude for you. I had that dress specially made for her. She ate the dress, cried all the time, refused to wear her shoes, and wouldn't perform her tricks in front of company."

"How old is this child?" Lalie whispered.

"Savages don't know how old they are. She was five or six; what difference does it make?" After leaving the house, Truda entered the carriage and fanned her face. "Finally, I gave up and turned her out after she started stealing buns from the kitchen." Truda rolled her eyes. "And what do you suppose the little beast did then? She wouldn't go away. Do you believe it? She wouldn't do a thing to please me then complains when she's thrown out. She stayed by the kitchen door, setting up a racket, crying and carrying on until I had to order Mr. Clemente to drive her away."

Lalie tried to speak, but no words emerged from her mouth. Shock drained the color from her face and left her weak and shaking. She gripped the wrist where she had once worn Irikina's bead bracelet and felt ashamed of herself that she had left the bracelet aboard the *Addison Beal*.

"Ah, here we are," Truda said as the carriage rocked to a halt before the Rivaldi mansion. "We have time for a nap before we dress for the opera. Do take tea as supper will be late tonight, after the performance."

"Mrs. Rivaldi, where is the Indian child now?"

"I have no idea. Why on earth would you ask?"

Lalie closed her eyes, feeling dizzy in the relentless heat. "The thought of a six-year-old child wandering lost and penniless in this city . . ."

"Ah, I see." Genuine amusement softened Truda Rivaldi's expression. "I forget how new you are to the Amazon. You still think the savages are human." She patted Lalie's arm. "Soon enough you'll see them as everyone else does. Filthy, lazy little beasts. Like monkeys, really."

Only by reminding herself that she was a guest in Truda Rivaldi's home, did Lalie manage to bite off words of outrage. None of the Indians she had met in the forest were "filthy, lazy little beasts." No Indian village stank like the white man's cities along the river. And no Indian would ever conceive of making a pet out of a child. Nor did they dispose of children like unwanted cats or dogs.

Only in the cities had Lalie observed unhealthy Indians or Indians who found no joy in life. Only in the cities did she observe hopelessness and drunkenness or Indian women dressed like Paris whores.

"Please excuse me," she said.

Once in her suite, Lalie lay down on the four-poster and pressed a damp cloth to her forehead. For once she did not worry that the omnipresent lizard might drop from the ceiling onto her body.

She thought about Sir Percival's opulent new home. She thought about six-year-old girls eating dirt and dresses. She wondered if Sir Percival would ever give her some other woman's child as a pet. Surely not; a shudder passed through her body.

Yet Sir Percival and the Rivaldis were friends, and friends shared common opinions.

The nearer Lalie drew to seeing him again, the more she realized how troublingly little she knew about Sir Percival Sterling.

Excitement danced in Lalie's eyes; high color tinted her cheeks. The society cramming the Salão Nobre, a salon for private parties within the opera house, was garbed in dazzling Parisian gowns and the best London tailoring. Diamonds were commonplace. French champagne flowed like the Amazon itself, and two dozen waiters circulated with silver trays buried beneath tiny exquisite pastries.

It was as stunning to discover this magnificence as it was to think of opera in the jungle in the first place. But the glittering opulence existed. Everything Lalie saw wrested a gasp from her throat.

Heavy Venetian mirrors reflected Greek gods and goddesses chasing across frescoed ceilings. The room was hung with massive crystal chandeliers and imported tapestries. The champagne arrived in delicate crystal, and for those who preferred coffee or chocolate, Sèvres cups and saucers were served. Every few feet along the richly draped walls stood an Indian boy waving a palm fan against the damp heat. Their combined efforts almost created an illusion of coolness.

"Are you enjoying yourself?" asked Contessa d'Alessio. The tiny jewels pasted to her fan winked and flashed as she lazily created her own breeze.

"I'm speechless," Lalie admitted, finding it impossible to believe that a week before she had been aboard a rusting steamer, blistered by the heat. It was difficult to recall the poverty and squalor she had witnessed as little as a few hours ago. "Someone informed me the opera house cost millions to build. Can this be true? I knew Manaus was prosperous, but . . ." Words failed her.

Contessa d'Alessio laughed and her husband smiled. "The prosperity will never end, Miss Pritchard," the count said, accepting another champagne from a waiter's passing tray. "This is merely the beginning. Rubber is still in its infancy. Manaus will do nothing but grow richer and richer."

"It doesn't concern you that Malaya will soon enter the rubber market?" Lalie asked, recalling Addison's predictions.

The count smiled and dismissed her statement with a negligent wave. "Gaze around you. Can you imagine all this will fade away? Let Malaya come into the market. There's profit for everyone." He winked at her. "The Amazon will do it better."

As it would have been rude to disagree, Lalie offered no comment. But she recalled the books Addison had lent her about Malaya, the ease of transport, an available labor force, the ideal climate for rubber, and the lack of disease.

But she did accept the count's advice to gaze about her as the first bell rang and the company drifted toward the main theater, toward tiers of balconies curving around the stage front. Elaborate iron balustrades draped the private boxes like gilded lace. The stage curtain was painted with mythical creatures romping through an idealized rain forest. And over all hung the mingled scent of perfume and cigars and gaslights.

Lalie seated herself in the Rivaldis' private box and spread her white silk skirt in graceful drapes before she idly glanced across the orchestra pit toward the boxes on the facing side.

Immediately she saw March Addison and her pulse skipped a beat. A rush of startled color tinted her throat and cheeks and she hastily raised her fan to conceal her face. But her efforts to conceal herself were unnecessary.

March Addison hadn't noticed her. He was completely absorbed by the Brazilian beauty he led into his private box; any man would have been. Unable not to stare, Lalie studied the young woman who was ravishingly lovely and a natural flirt. Her dark eyes sparkled as brilliantly as the diamonds in her hair. As Lalie watched, the young beauty murmured to Addison and he threw back his head and laughed. Lalie bit her lip. She would have given everything she owned to know what the young woman had said to him.

Helplessly, she stared across the filled house. March Addison was so blindingly handsome that it astonished her that every woman in the opera house wasn't staring up at him. He wore full dress and no detail had been neglected, from his Irish linen waistcoat and white lawn tie to the dark coat and snowy handkerchief and gloves. He carried a black silk hat and an elegantly plain stick with no ornamentation. A tremble began in Lalie's fingertips and her fan dropped to her lap.

"Stunning, isn't he?" Truda Rivaldi murmured. She too was studying Addison with a narrowed predatory stare. "I wonder if March is as exciting in bed as his reputation claims . . . do you know, my dear?"

Lalie gasped. "Certainly not!" she protested, but a vivid, disturbing memory leapt into her thoughts. A flash of naked muscle and sinew. Crystal droplets glistening on a bare chest. The hard throb of exposed flesh pressing against her shaking body. Swallowing hard, Lalie raised her fan and waved it in front of her scarlet face.

"A pity." Truda tapped her fan against her palm, still watching Addison. "He's with Emanual Botega's daughter. How do you suppose he managed that coup, I wonder, when even Percy could not? They make a handsome couple, don't you agree?"

Thankfully the curtain rose and Lalie was spared a reply. But she found it impossible to concentrate on La Movita's lusty arias. Despite her best intentions Lalie continued to peek at Addison and his stunningly beautiful companion. And each time she peeked, Addison was devoting his full attention to Miss Botega instead of the opera. Their two dark heads were always bent together behind Miss Botega's jeweled fan.

Lalie felt chilled yet burning, ill and headachy. The pleasure had gone out of the evening. La Movita's high notes irritated and deepened her headache. She thought she might feel better if she moved about or had a breath of air.

At intermission, she turned to Truda Rivaldi and spoke in a falsely bright voice. "Seeing Mr. Addison reminds me—I must instruct him to transfer my luggage to the launch your husband is arranging. Perhaps I should do so now . . ." She had the most appallingly peculiar feeling that if she didn't speak to Addison immediately, right this instant, she would explode into hundreds of tiny fragments.

"Didn't Gunter tell you?" Truda examined the crimson burning Lalie's cheeks. "He sent for your luggage, but it's gone."

"Gone?" Lalie repeated incredulously. For the first time since spotting Addison, her full attention focused on something else. "I don't understand."

"It seems your Mr. Addison had your luggage sent on board a boat going to Pará. I'm sorry, I thought you knew."

Lalie blinked in shock then stared at a point over Mrs. Rivaldi's bare shoulder. "That means I have only those items I brought to your home," she said slowly. The light clothing suitable for river travel was on its way to Pará along with her sturdy shoes and her bicycle and her teapot and the rest of her china. Along with her beloved journal and Irikina's bracelet and her reading box. And her stitchery, her paint box, and the gown in which she had intended to be married.

Whirling, Lalie directed a furious scowl across the orchestra pit. This time she didn't care if March Addison noticed her staring. Folding her arms across her breast, she glared at him through the second half of the performance. If Addison had glanced at her even once, her fury would have scorched the tan right off his bronze skin. But he didn't look in her direction. And that, she realized, made her even angrier.

March was acutely aware of Miss Eulalie Pritchard. From the instant he stepped into his box and saw her, it seemed to him that Lalie Pritchard's fiery hair captured every particle of light from the chandeliers and the gaslights, leaving the rest of the house in darkness.

A halo of flame surrounded her oval face. He could have sworn the captured light shimmered around her. In the glow her lightly tanned face, shoulders, and bosom resembled ivory porcelain. And even at a distance he imagined he could see her beautiful eyes sparkling like sapphires.

Even if her beauty hadn't set her apart, her simplicity of dress would have. In a society where women felt undressed without a multiplicity of jewels, Lalie was the only unadorned female in the theater. Her beauty and simplicity drew every eye.

"She is very lovely," Graciela Botega murmured. "I am wild with jealousy."

March laughed. "I can't imagine the ravishing Miss Botega being jealous of any woman. Half the young swains in Brazil are languishing on your father's doorstep, perishing for want of a glimpse of you."

Graciela tapped her fan on his arm and formed her full lips into a pout. "When I was ten years old, you promised to marry me when I grew up. Now I'm grown but here you are staring at that woman and she is staring at you." She looked at him flirtatiously. "You are ignoring me."

"Spoiled child, hasn't anyone ever told you not to be so forward?" Grinning, he patted her hand affectionately.

"That woman—she is not right for you." Raising her

opera glasses, Graciela studied Miss Pritchard until, laughing, March pulled her arm down. "Her skin is the color of a dead fish's belly." A mock shudder constricted her bare shoulders. "She is too pale and unhealthy looking. Her eyes have no color. I have a finer bosom than she does and a smaller waist."

March choked on a burst of laughter. "Spoiled and wicked," he said, grinning at her. "When was the last time you were spanked?"

She laughed, then slowly the laughter faded from her liquid eyes. Tilting her head, she studied him seriously. "You're not going to take me with you to Malaya, are you, March?"

He touched his fingertips to her satiny skin and thought how beautiful a woman she had become. "No."

"I love you, you know," she said in a whispery voice. "I've loved you since I was a child."

"Dear little Graciela." Leaning toward her perfumed ear, he spoke in a low voice. "I'm flattered that you think you love me. Hearing you say it makes me feel ten feet tall. But darling girl, I'm too jaded, too cranky, too set in my ways, and too old for you."

"I'm nineteen and you're thirty. The difference is ideal."

"You've grown into a stunning young woman whom any man would be proud to call his own. But to me you will always be that large-eyed little ruffian whose braids I used to pull, who sat in my lap and searched my shirt pockets for peppermints."

"Oh March." Tears glittered on her lashes. "Can't you see I've grown up? That I'm a woman now?"

Gently, he tilted her face up to him. "I love you too, but not the way you wish. Very soon now, a young man will come into your life who will love you and whom you will love. He'll lavish the attention on you that you deserve. He'll make you so happy that you'll remember this moment and say: Addison was right. Thank God I didn't throw myself away on such a cad."

She smiled sadly. "I'll never say that." For an instant she let her head fall against his shoulder. "You're leaving me behind because you love someone else."

The idea was so ridiculous that he smiled. But then she lifted her glossy dark head and gazed into his eyes with the wisdom and maturity of a woman twice her age. He had the uncomfortable impression that she had penetrated a veil he himself could not see behind.

"Oh yes," she said softly, sadly. "It's in your eyes. You love her."

"Love her?" he repeated, smiling. "Love who, Miss Gypsy?"

"The fire-headed woman with the fish-belly skin," she said tartly, sounding more like herself. Then she dug the tip of her fan into his ribs. "I hope she makes you suffer and sigh. I hope she makes you thoroughly miserable."

He chuckled. "*If* I were in love with anyone, and *if* that person were the one you suggest—I would be suffering and swearing and as miserable as you could wish."

"Good!" With the resilience of youth, she turned a beaming face toward the stage. If she suffered more than a momentary heartache over March's rejection, it wasn't readily apparent.

Smiling and shaking his head, he gazed across the darkened house at Lalie. He couldn't be certain, but it appeared she was staring directly at him. Since intermission her posture had altered. She sat stiff and rigidly upright, her shoulders back, bosom forward, chin elevated.

Regret darkened his smile. Though she was breathtakingly lovely tonight, this was not how he would remember her. The image that haunted him was the memory from the lagoon. Even now, he could almost feel her in his arms, her pale throat arching away from him, her breasts lifting to his palms, her soft, yielding body pressed against his.

A stirring in his loins caused him to look away and frown at the stage.

Good God. Was it really possible that he was infatuated with another man's bride? With a woman who had lied to him and tricked him? With a woman who drove him crazy and disliked him intensely?

Impossible.

But he turned to look at her again and remembered the way her wet chemise and knickers had molded her body, remembered the taste of her skin. March touched his handkerchief to his forehead and thanked God his association with Eulalie Pritchard had ended. Eventually he would forget her. Eventually she would fade from his restless nights and from his daydreams.

Every afternoon at three o'clock, Manaus's rubber kings gathered in the plush lobby of the Hotel de Paris to await that day's quotes on the price of rubber. The powerful and the merely hopeful lounged on long sofas surrounded by servants and a haze of cigar smoke.

When March entered the lobby, the quotes had already arrived and consequently much of the tension had eased. After exchanging a few words with Emanual Botega and nodding coolly to Gunter Rivaldi, March took his usual chair, lit a cigar, and examined the commodities quote sheet. Satisfied, he relaxed and accepted a *cafezinho,* sipping the hot, sweet coffee with pleasure.

Before he finished his second cup, he noticed Fredo standing beside a potted palm, cap in hand, gesturing to catch his attention. Standing, March crossed the lobby. "What is it?"

"Big *bagunça,* Cabo," Fredo said, raising worried eyes. "Tomorrow Rivaldi sending Missy upriver with Lum Sarto."

A cold knot formed in March's stomach. Slowly he turned to stare at the back of Gunter Rivaldi's head. "Why in the name of God would Rivaldi send her out with

Sarto?" he said in a low, furious voice. "That's the same as guaranteeing that she'll arrive in Hiberalta raped and beaten—if she's still alive."

Fredo nodded. "Sarto bad customer, Cabo."

March's eyes narrowed to slits. He asked himself again why Rivaldi would send his friend's fiancée upriver with a thug who was certain to abuse her.

The answer lay in a snippet of gossip he had overheard the day before. Apparently most of Manaus knew that Percy Sterling had bedded Truda Rivaldi. It appeared Gunter also knew.

The only explanation that made sense was revenge. Gunter Rivaldi was avenging himself on Percy by sending Percy's fiancée upriver with Lum Sarto. Lalie would arrive at Hiberalta—if she survived—bleeding, beaten, and brutally deflowered.

Chapter 14

Truda Rivaldi pleaded a headache that the scorching midday sun would exacerbate, therefore she bade Lalie farewell from her marble foyer. It was Gunter Rivaldi who escorted Lalie to the docks and led her aboard the *Raider,* a sun-blistered steamer about half the size of the *Addison Beal.* A moment passed before Lalie grasped that the three slovenly Spaniards slouching on the rail were the *Raider's* crew.

"This is Miss Pritchard, Captain Sarto," Gunter Rivaldi said after directing his footman to place Lalie's pitifully small collection of luggage near the stern. "I charge you to care for her as you would care for your own daughter. She is to be shown every courtesy."

Lalie felt a rush of alarm as Captain Sarto grinned and scratched the bare belly extending below a soiled, ragged shirt. His watery black eyes, peering out of folds of brown flesh, looked speculatively over her bosom and hips.

"I look after her, all right," he said, grinning. His lips moved around a thick dead cigar. The other two men inspected Lalie with sly glances and laughed.

Wetting her lips, Lalie edged closer to Gunter Rivaldi. "How long . . ." She cleared her throat and tried again. "How long is the journey to Hiberalta?"

Lum Sarto shrugged, his gaze openly fixed on Lalie's breast. "It depends. Maybe ten days upriver, four days overland, another day on the Yaki River."

"I see," Lalie whispered. She would be fifteen days with these frightening men.

Indecision stiffened her expression. Instinct warned her to leave the *Raider* immediately. But how would she explain to Gunter Rivaldi that she intended to further impose on his hospitality because she didn't approve of the ship or the crew he had hired to take her to Hiberalta? If she insisted on such an insulting lack of gratitude, what on earth would he think of her?

And yet . . . She gazed at the grinning, dirty Spaniards and her heart sank to her toes.

"Bon voyage, Miss Pritchard." Rivaldi brought her shaking fingertips almost to his lips and inclined his head. "It has been my pleasure to be your host during your stay in Manaus."

"I can't thank you enough for all you've done," she said in a barely audible voice. The Spaniards continued to stare at her as if she were a succulent confection they could scarcely wait to sample. "But I wonder . . . perhaps I should—"

Rivaldi didn't allow her to express a desire to disembark. His hand tightened painfully around her fingers and his black eyes narrowed above a cold smile. "When you speak to Percy, you will give him this message: an eye for an eye."

"I beg your pardon?"

"What is done to mine shall be done to his—only worse, far worse." He touched the brim of his hat and nodded, his black eyes glittering. "Good day, Miss Pritchard."

For an instant Lalie didn't move a muscle. Hot sun pounded the crown of her hat. The raucous din of the wharves rang in her ears. She stared after Gunter Rivaldi's retreating figure and frantically tried to understand his message to Percival.

She didn't comprehend the meaning, but she had a muddy sense that the implications for herself were ugly. Dreading what she would see, she raised her eyes and discovered all three Spaniards watching her, grinning with obvious anticipation. The short one rubbed a hand suggestively over his genitals.

Black dots speckled Lalie's vision and her knees collapsed. She would have fallen to the deck if she hadn't caught herself against the railing. A strangling tightness choked her.

She could not remain on board the *Raider*. It didn't matter what the Rivaldis thought. She had to return to shore.

As if Sarto had read her mind, he stepped past her and pulled in the plank, shouting orders at the other two. When he grinned at her, Lalie saw he was missing a front tooth. The rest of his teeth were coated by a mossy green tint. Rough fingers lifted her chin. "Pretty thing, ain't you?"

His fetid breath made her gag and Lalie wrenched away from him, fearing she would vomit. Instead, she whirled to the rail and gripped it as the ship drifted from its slip. She ordered herself to scream.

But she saw Gunter Rivaldi standing beside his brougham, smoking, observing her distress with a smile. And Lalie's heart skipped in shock. Rivaldi knew these men. He knew what they would do to her. Now she knew, too.

She screamed, but the sound was drowned by the traditional three blasts of the steam whistle. When the whistle died the short Spaniard appeared at her side, grinning, stinking of *cachaça*. He let her see the knife in his hand before he stepped up against her and pressed the tip of the blade below her left breast. *"Silencio,"* he warned, grinding his pelvis against her hip. "You scream all you want later."

A sick-tasting bile surged in Lalie's throat as she turned

her face away from the Spaniard's breath. In frantic silence she watched the wharves recede and gradually slip behind them.

"I don't understand," she whispered, more to herself than to the man pressed against her. "What did I do to offend?"

The Spaniard brought the back of his hand up over her breast to her throat. Lalie shrank from his touch and from the sunlight glittering on the blade of his knife. "You skin is soft like an orchid." His erection ground against her hip. "You see? Ramon is romantic. Say pretty things. You gonna like Ramon."

Lum Sarto's ham-sized hand grabbed Ramon by the shoulder and pulled him away. "Later, you sum'bitch. Get you skinny arse to the boiler and throw in some wood." His other hand closed on Lalie's buttock and squeezed. His sweat dripped on her breast. "You stand here nice and quiet, *silencio* till we git 'round that bend ahead. Then maybe we have us some little fun. Them boys no gonna wait till night."

"If you touch a single hair on my head," Lalie said in a shaking whisper, "Sir Percival Sterling will thrash you!"

He laughed and gave her buttock another painful squeeze. "Is'at so? Then I already in the stew, ain't I?" Running his hand up her back, he knocked off her hat and buried his fat fingers in her hair then jerked her face close to his. "You don't unnerstand how things work. Nobody on this river cross Mr. Rivaldi. Sterling no gonna like getting used goods, but he no gonna squawk, neither. He in Mr. Rivaldi's pocket like everybody else, you unnerstand?"

When he released her, Lalie stumbled and almost fell. Hairpins scattered over the deck and a mass of fiery curls tumbled to her waist as the knot at her neck came undone.

"Jesus," Lum Sarto breathed, staring at the silky auburn spill. "Them bastards touch you 'fore I do, you hollar big." He wiped a hand across his lips. "I be back."

Shocked beyond rational thought and physically ill, Lalie

gripped the railing and leaned over it. Manaus now lay behind them. Ahead was a wide stretch of empty brown water bending into a gentle curve around a jungle promontory.

Raising a shaking hand, Lalie pressed her glove to her breast. Behind her corset stays her heart pounded in wild, erratic beats. Her breath emerged in terrified gasps.

Closing her eyes tightly and panting for breath, she tried to calm herself.

She breathed as deeply as her corset would allow, pulling the hot air into her lungs and holding it to the count of five.

Better. Now, she commanded herself—think.

Opening her eyes, she tried to gauge the distance to the nearest shore. She wasn't a strong swimmer, but she thought she might make it. The distance wasn't that far. Then she glanced into the water and noticed the silver flash of piranha. Desperation pinched her mouth. If she entered piranha-infested waters, the fish would strip the flesh from her bones within minutes.

At least it would be swift, she thought, staring down at the teeming water. Swifter than what Sarto and his men would do to her. Oddly the thought was calming. The piranha provided an option, a choice. An unthinkable choice, but it offered Lalie a tiny glimmer of control over her fate.

For the first time since the horror began tears welled in her eyes. To Lalie's surprise the tears were not due to self-pity, nor even because she might die. Her tears were tears of anger.

It made her furious that she was so close to her goal yet she would fail.

Lalie blinked away the dampness in her eyes and turned to scan the deck for anything she might use as a weapon. There were barrels of manioc flour, a crate of chickens, and another of *cachaça,* but she saw nothing that might help her.

Despairing, she looked toward the shore. The *Raider* was almost around the bend, almost out of sight of Manaus. She heard Sarto inside the engine room trading obscenities with one of his men and knew they were discussing her.

Fear must be making her hallucinate, she thought suddenly. It seemed to Lalie that a section of the jungle detached itself from the shore ahead and drifted toward her. Shielding her eyes from the sunlight bouncing off the surface of the water, she blinked hard and stared.

The hallucination was incredibly real. The section of jungle moved toward the *Raider* at a swift pace. Truly, she was losing her mind.

Confused and terrified, she slid along the stern railing into the shadow and out of the sun. Concentrate, she admonished herself, find something to use as a weapon.

Sarto lumbered out of the engine room and Lalie froze as he ripped open a crate to get a bottle of *cachaça*. Straightening, he pulled the cork with his teeth, then looked toward shore with an expression of astonishment. "What the hell is that?"

Before the words were out of his mouth, Lalie rushed forward and recognized what *that* was. Her imaginary lump of floating jungle was a ship covered by a net struck through with leaves, branches, and vines.

From that point events happened so swiftly that later she had difficulty remembering the sequence.

Grappling hooks flew out of the camouflage netting and bit into the decking of the *Raider*. Invisible hands jerked the netting away.

"River pirates!" Sarto screamed, dropping the bottle of *cachaça*.

The other two Spaniards ran out of the boiler room in time to see March Addison and Fredo appear on the lower level of the *Addison Beal*, Winchesters aimed at the men on the *Raider*. Addison puffed on his cigar and his smile was as cold as Rivaldi's had been.

"Don't move, gentlemen, and maybe you'll come out of this alive." His dark eyes shifted to Lalie, who had sagged against the stern rail in relief. "Miss Pritchard, come forward to the railing and take Joao's hand." His gaze glittered. "I don't want any argument, Lalie. You're coming with me."

"No argument," she whispered, her voice grim. "I've never been so glad to see anyone in my life." Relief sapped her strength and she wasn't certain her legs would support her weight. She fixed her eyes on Joao's outstretched hand and wobbled toward him. It seemed that an eon elapsed before she reached the boy, but finally his strong hand pulled her over the coupled railings and onto the lower deck of the *Addison Beal.*

"You makin' big mistake, Addison," Sarto shouted. Lowering his bulk, he sat on one of the crates and removed another bottle of *cachaça.* "This ship belong to Rivaldi. You hear? Rivaldi!" After spitting out the cork, he took a long pull on the bottle then wiped his lips.

Addison watched Joao pull Lalie off her knees and onto her feet. Immediately Maria rushed forward and shoved back Lalie's loose hair, inspecting her for injuries.

"Missy plenty scared and shaking, Cabo, but no hurt."

"That's good," Addison said, glaring at the crew of the *Raider.* "You gentlemen get to live a little longer. Joao?" He jerked his head toward the *Raider's* engine room. "Make sure these gentlemen stay here a while. Don't forget to disable the whistle."

Covered by Addison's and Fredo's Winchesters, Joao jumped onto the *Raider's* deck and ran toward the engine room. One of the Spaniards slid his hand toward the knife in his belt, but Sarto raised a hand and shook his head.

"No knife, you stupid bastard. Our time come 'nother day." Sarto took another long swallow from the *cachaça* bottle, then looked up and narrowed his eyes on Addison. "Rivaldi bin waiting fer a reason, Addison. You jist give him one." A shrug lifted his belly. "What goes upriver gots to come down. You know there'll be gunboats waiting. No sum'bitch hijacks Rivaldi's ship and pirates off a passenger without getting hisself killed."

"You tell Rivaldi to hire another broker. He and I don't do business anymore. He'll receive a final accounting as soon as I return to Pará."

Sarto's laugh rippled his exposed belly. "Ain't you listen? You a dead man, Addison."

Lalie sat shivering on a stool, her back pressed against Maria's knees, her heart still banging against her rib cage. With wide, dilated eyes, she watched Joao emerge from the *Raider's* engine room and move swiftly along the deck, cutting the ropes holding the grappling hooks. He vaulted the railings as the two ships began to drift apart. Addison stayed at the rail of the *Addison Beal,* the Winchester cradled in his arms as Fredo ran upstairs. In a moment the engine chugged to life and the distance increased between the *Addison Beal* and the disabled *Raider.*

When they had moved out of gunshot range, Addison lowered the Winchester and walked to Lalie. Standing over her, he scanned her tangled hair and chalky face. His eyes were expressionless.

She gazed up at his battered straw hat, at the dark wedge of skin that ran from his opened collar to his waist, at the muscles still tense and swollen on his shoulders. The only thing that prevented her from flinging herself into his arms with sobs of gratitude was the suspicion that her legs were still too wobbly to support her. She clung to the stool knowing there was a real possibility that if she relaxed her grip, she might topple onto the deck.

"Was Sarto right?" she asked in a barely audible voice. "Will gunboats be waiting for you when you come downriver?"

"That's my problem, not yours. I'll deal with it if it happens."

Releasing the edges of the stool, she gestured helplessly. Her expression pleaded for understanding. "Will you take me the rest of the way to Hiberalta?"

An explosive burst of swear words broke from his lips. He stared at her and then called to Maria. "I think everyone here could use a cup of *cachaça.*" Shouldering the Winchester, he strode toward the stairs.

"Mr. Addison?" Lalie pushed to her feet, testing legs that felt like sticks of straw as she shoved back waves of loose hair.

"What?"

"I . . . thank you," she whispered, meeting his eyes. "If you hadn't come when you did . . ." Bowing her head, she pressed her fingertips to her eyelids then drew a breath and looked at him again. "I owe you a debt I can never repay. Those men . . ."

"You're damned right you owe me! You have been one hell of a lot of trouble, Miss Pritchard."

She followed him up the staircase onto the upper deck and accepted with gratitude the cup of *cachaça* Maria pressed into her hand. The fiery liquid brought involuntary tears to her eyes. Lalie blinked them away and took another deep swallow. Maria smiled, nodded, then discreetly withdrew into the wheelhouse to talk to Fredo. Joao also disappeared.

March stared down at the silky cascade of hair falling almost to her waist. "Why the hell didn't you get off that ship the minute you saw Lum Sarto and his men? What in the name of God were you thinking of to go off with men like those?"

Lalie swallowed another draught of *cachaça,* then glanced away from Addison's angry eyes. "I was afraid Mr. Rivaldi would think I didn't appreciate his generosity if I turned my nose up at his arrangements."

"You deliberately put yourself in danger because you were worried about what Rivaldi would think?" March exploded. "That is the most idiotic, stupid, most careless, reckless—"

"You're absolutely right," Lalie said quietly, gazing into her cup.

He stared down at her. "You agree?"

"This incident has given me a great deal to think about, Mr. Addison." It was the understatement of a lifetime. Leaning her elbows on the railing, Lalie turned her face into the river breeze and closed her eyes, luxuriating in being alive—and in being with March Addison again.

She turned to face him, feeling the breeze lift her hair. "How did you know I was on the *Raider* and needed rescue? And why have you agreed to take me upriver?"

Lifting his cup of *cachaça,* Addison saluted her. "We are becoming more direct, aren't we, Miss Pritchard?"

"You don't need to rub my nose in it, Mr. Addison," she said, not raising her voice.

He studied her face then lit a fresh cigar. "All right, let's say what has to be said and get this over with. Fredo learned Rivaldi had hired Lum Sarto to take you upriver. Sarto is not a subtle man; his reputation is well known." He shrugged, then moved to stand beside her at the railing. "Whether I like it or not—and I sure as hell don't—you've involved me in your elopement. Having failed to send you back to Pará, I'm in an awkward position. Since you're so hell bent on marrying Percival, I may as well make sure you reach Hiberalta safely."

Addison stood so close Lalie could see the green flecks in his dark eyes. The proximity unnerved her. Pretending that the smoke from his cigar annoyed her, she bit her lip and eased away from him.

"You knew I'd be on the *Raider*. And you guessed I wouldn't have the sense to disembark," she said dully. Disgust at her own stupidity overwhelmed her. When she lifted her head, Addison was watching her. "I wonder if you can solve the biggest mystery of all? Why did Gunter Rivaldi choose Lum Sarto to take me upriver? I saw Gunter's face, March—he knew what those men would do." It was hard to speak the next words. They emerged in a whisper. "He wanted them to . . . to do what they intended to do."

Addison turned to the river and leaned on the rail. "All that really matters is that nothing happened. Rivaldi is a man without conscience or scruples. Let's leave it at that."

Three months ago Lalie would not have dreamed of pressing anyone to speak of matters he obviously did not wish to discuss. But she was no longer mired in the swamps of proper convention. Not now. There were moments when the Voice of Propriety fell silent and this was one of them.

"Rivaldi deliberately gave me to Sarto and his men even though he knew their character and what would happen. And I think you know why." She placed her hand on Addison's arm, feeling the rock-hard muscle beneath her palm. "I need to know."

Straightening from the rail, Addison faced her. He stared into her eyes for so long that Lalie felt as if she were falling, being pulled into a dark vortex of mystery, need, and heat. She drew a shaking breath and her fingers tightened on his arm to steady herself.

"Don't ask this," he said gruffly. "You won't like the answer."

"Tell me."

Addison continued to examine her face, then he shook his head and glanced toward shore. "Rivaldi believes Percy seduced Truda," he said finally. "By giving you to Sarto, Rivaldi was sending Percy a message and taking his revenge."

"No," Lalie whispered, feeling the blood rush from her

cheeks. Her hand dropped and she stumbled backward a step. "That isn't true. Percival and Mrs. Rivaldi? No."

But suddenly, chillingly, she heard voices murmuring in her head. "Yes, I've—seen—Percy." And ". . . an eye for an eye . . . what's done to mine shall be done to his, only worse, far worse."

Lifting a hand, Lalie covered her eyes and sank abruptly to one of the stools beside Maria's oven. "Percival isn't like that. He wouldn't . . ." Truda Rivaldi's seductive gaze shimmered in her memory. Truda and Percival? She lifted her hands as if thrusting the image away.

"I don't know if Truda Rivaldi and Percy are guilty of an indiscretion or not, Lalie." Addison's hand pressed her shoulder. "But that's the rumor, and apparently Gunter believes it."

Lalie touched his hand with her fingertips and gazed back downriver. The *Raider* was a dot bobbing in the distance. Because she felt March's sympathy, because she wasn't facing him, she could say what she did.

"March?" she whispered. "What if going to Hiberalta is a mistake? What if I'm wrong . . . ?"

He didn't seize on her moment of doubt as she feared he would. Neither did he gloat or use the moment to renew his assault on Sir Percival's character.

"Then I'll take you home," he said simply.

March placed his boot on the shelf beneath the glass window and rested his elbow on his knee, staring straight ahead at the river. Above Manaus the river turned a silt-rich tawny color and was called the Solimões. Despite the hundreds of small tributaries that poured into the Solimões, the thousand-mile stretch between Manaus and Leticia was sparsely populated. Long before Leticia, however, they would turn into one of the tributaries and follow it to Ipta, a muddy settlement that marked the beginning of the overland portion of the journey.

"It's good to have Missy back," Fredo said without shifting his gaze from the surface of the river.

March made a grunting sound and pretended he didn't notice Fredo's smile.

"Sarto's right, Cabo," Fredo said, still watching the river. Skillfully he avoided colliding with a floating grass island. "Rivaldi be waiting with gunboats."

"We've got plenty to worry about before then. Percy won't be too happy either after we steal a few of his slaves."

Fredo grinned. "Like the good old days, Cabo." Before entering Addison's employ, Fredo had smuggled guns into Brazil from Colombia and Peru.

March laughed. "You get us safely back to Pará, and the *Addison Beal* is yours. A farewell gift to you, Maria, and Joao." The ship would make Fredo independent, a wealthy man by Brazilian standards.

"I get you back alive, Cabo." Fredo lifted his black eyes from the river. "That's my farewell gift to you."

Returning to the *Addison Beal* was like coming home to familiar routines and comforts, but with a difference.

Maria found a piece of string to tie back Lalie's hair, and Joao strung a tarpaulin over her corner. When they dropped anchor for the night, the familiar swarms of mosquitoes and gnats appeared in a cloud over Lalie's table.

"No pretty dishes, Missy," Maria said sadly, placing a tin bowl in front of Lalie. She lit the kerosene lamp on Lalie's table then touched Lalie's shoulder with a shy gesture. "Good to have you home again, Missy."

Instead of taking offense that a menial had extended a gesture of familiarity, Lalie pressed Maria's hand in return. "I'm glad to be here," she said softly. "Maria," she called when the woman turned to rejoin the others eating beside the earthenware stove. "Is there any news?"

she asked with a meaningful glance at Maria's flat stomach.

"No, Missy," Maria said sadly. "No baby."

Lalie ate her black beans and rice slowly, straining to hear the conversation around the stove. They were talking about today's excitement, laughing and teasing, congratulating themselves on their planning, execution, and final victory.

Lalie felt very much alone. That her isolation was self-imposed and unquestionably proper behavior for a lady did not ease her dejection at being excluded. Suddenly she felt ridiculous.

She was eating the same meal out of the same crude tin bowls as the others were. At this point Maria owned more clothing than she. She had no money, no possessions, she was dependent on the generosity of others.

Frowning, Lalie stared down at her beans and rice. She had committed a stupid blunder by agreeing to board the *Raider* because she hadn't wished to offend Gunter Rivaldi, a man who had deliberately sent her to be raped or possibly killed. She had treated that vile man with every polite courtesy.

Yet she held herself apart from the people who had saved her honor and conceivably her life, people who had unfailingly treated her with generosity, kindness, and respect.

If it was proper to dine with the Rivaldis of the world and reproachable to dine with the Fredos, Marias, and Joaos—especially after they had saved her life—then there was something dreadfully amiss with propriety.

Before she could examine her logic and perhaps commit another stupidity, Lalie stood and carried her bowl to the group sitting around the stove. No one looked at her as she pulled a stool forward, sat, put her bowl in her lap, and continued to eat. But a hush descended over the conversation.

"So," Lalie said brightly. "Did Fredo engage in any fights in Manaus? And how many hearts did Joao break?"

Several eager voices spoke at once, relating Fredo's exploits and teasing Joao about his romances.

And through it all, Lalie felt March Addison's speculative gaze studying her. She felt his surprise and the unmistakable warmth of his approval.

Later, they lay side by side in their hammocks, listening to the buzz of insects, the slap of water against the hull, and the faint sounds of Maria and Fredo murmuring on the lower deck.

When Lalie finally realized she was still much too upset to sleep, she said in a low voice, "I saw you at the opera."

Addison wasn't asleep, either. "I saw you, too."

"Miss Botega is very beautiful."

"Yes, she is."

Waiting, Lalie prayed he would satisfy her curiosity about Miss Botega, but he said nothing more. A hundred jealous questions burned in her mind, but she couldn't bring herself to ask any of them. After a moment she reluctantly raised another subject.

"I met a gentleman at the opera who disagrees with your conclusions about the Amazon. He claims the prosperity will never end. He believes Malaya's entry into the rubber market will make no difference to the Amazon's future."

"He is wrong," Addison said simply. "Your friend has fallen victim to the dream."

"The dream?" Shifting onto her side, Lalie peered through the layers of netting wishing she could see his face.

"Everyone comes to the river with a dream, Miss Pritchard. For most it is a dream of riches, of amassing great wealth. Others dream of fame. For some the dream promises adventure or romance. Once the dream takes hold it won't be dislodged. The dream drives men—and women—to continue striving even in the face of failure and despair."

"What is your dream, Mr. Addison?" She couldn't see his features, but she could see that he had turned toward her. A peculiar feeling fluttered through her stomach as she realized husbands and wives faced each other like this at the end of a day. A wave of heat colored her throat and cheeks and she wet her lips and swallowed.

"In the beginning I dreamed of riches, Miss Pritchard. And perhaps of adventure. Later I dreamed of justice, of righting wrongs and changing men's prejudices. Now I dream only of leaving."

Speaking into the darkness, trying to focus on something other than March Addison, Lalie haltingly told him about Truda Rivaldi's pet Indian girl. Across the small distance that separated them she felt the tension of his anger and outrage. "Men's prejudices are not easily overcome. I suspect it will be years, perhaps generations, before the people along the Amazon conquer their fear and hatred of the Indians."

Lalie was almost asleep before she realized Addison had not inquired about her dream. But her dream was obvious. She dreamed of love and romance; she dreamed of life lived to the fullest, not merely endured.

But tonight her dreams shimmered with sensual images of a dark-haired man with eyes like midnight and skin like bronze, a man who crushed her in his powerful arms and clasped her in a passionate embrace against a body whose strength and urgency demanded surrender.

Dreams and memory tangled, leaving her restless when morning came and acutely aware of March Addison. With a shiver of confusion Lalie realized she had been acutely aware of March Addison for a very long time. Upset and confused, she watched him move about the boat. She didn't know what it meant that she felt nervous and fluttery in his presence, empty and depressed when she was not.

Fanning at the heat, she frowned and commanded herself not to think about it. Think about Percival, she told herself over and over. But to her despair, she could no longer remember the face of the man who waited for her in Hiberalta.

Chapter 15

As March swung the axe over his head, chopping fallen logs into lengths that would fit inside the boiler, he thought about Miss Eulalie Pritchard. To his regret, thinking about Miss Eulalie Pritchard was not unusual. He thought about her twenty-four hours a day, and had done so since he'd rescued her from Sarto nearly a week before. Today he was thinking how drastically he had revised his original impression of her.

Eulalie Pritchard was not the typical English young lady he had originally dismissed her as being. The vast majority of young ladies did not cast off the yoke of parental authority, run away from home, and chase after the man of their choice. Though March made the concession with reluctance, he admired Eulalie Pritchard's spirit. Right or wrong, her actions distinguished her as a remarkable young woman.

Moreover, he agreed with her reasoning. He sure as hell would not have permitted anyone to select a bride for him. Why should Miss Pritchard allow someone to choose or reject a husband for her?

Of course March believed Dr. Pritchard was correct in considering Percival Sterling a disastrous selection. But still the choice should belong to Lalie. If Lalie chose to throw herself away on a bastard like Sterling, so be it.

Pausing, March shoved back his hat, wiped the sweat from his brow, and glanced at the ship anchored a few yards offshore. Miss Pritchard was standing at the rail watching him with an expression he couldn't read.

Since her luggage had been lost aboard the *Raider,* Lalie wore one of Maria's loose cotton shifts. It was green and blue and enhanced her extraordinary eyes. The hem fluttered against her shapely calves, well above her ankles. A length of string tied back her hair, but long coppery curls fell forward over her shoulder. Her small feet were bare. March stiffened, aching inside at the sight of her beauty.

Staring at her without realizing it, he tried to recall if he had ever spent this much time with a woman without becoming bored or wishing to extricate himself. Eulalie Pritchard irritated him, drove him half-mad with desire, but she did not bore him. Right or wrong, logical or illogical, she held an opinion on everything under the sun. She was well read and intelligent. Her observations were fresh and often amusing. Finally, he was fascinated by the changes her character had undergone since the beginning of the journey.

On first meeting her, he had believed her to be entirely superficial. He had been mistaken. She was also stronger than he had originally believed, perhaps stronger of character than she herself suspected.

"Cabo?" Emerging from the dense jungle foliage, Joao dropped a load of branches at his feet. "We have enough wood now?"

"What?" Startled, he pulled his gaze from Lalie and blinked. Then he cursed. Instead of finishing the chopping, he was standing like a moonstruck swain admiring the play of sun and shadow across a woman's cheek.

He stared back at Eulalie Pritchard and his dark eyes

narrowed. Handing her over to Percy Sterling was going to be the hardest thing he ever did.

No one tarried after eating the evening meal. Since they had entered the tributary leading to Ipta, swarms of biting black flies had enveloped them. Long before anyone was genuinely sleepy, they took to their hammocks, seeking refuge beneath the folds of netting.

Lalie tried to read in the dim lantern light that filtered through her netting but soon gave up. Tossing aside the book Addison had lent her, she lay back in her hammock and blotted the perspiration from her throat and brow. The damp, sweltering night made her feel fidgety and restless. She couldn't find a comfortable position within her hammock; the enclosing folds felt hot and confining.

"When will we reach Ipta?" she asked, trying to stir a breeze with her palm fan.

"Possibly tomorrow. At most, the morning after."

Addison too had abandoned the effort to read. He lay in his hammock smoking. The fragrance of cigar smoke hung on the still night air, not entirely unpleasant, Lalie decided, surprised by the realization.

"Then five days overland?" she asked.

"More like three. Starting at Ipta instead of Xlanti gives us a shortcut. When we reach Tupati, the major settlement on the Yaki, we'll hire a boat. Then one more day, two at the most, and you'll be in Hiberalta."

Lalie folded her hands behind her head and stared at the lacy shadows cast on the deck roof by her netting. Her long journey was nearing its conclusion. She should have been wildly happy, but instead her spirits were low and she felt vaguely troubled. Her feelings regarding Hiberalta and Sir Percival had become much more complex and confusing than she had believed possible. In the beginning everything had appeared so simple and straightforward. There had been no doubts, no apprehension or ambiguous flutterings of dread. Now, everything was different.

"Mr. Addison . . . do you think I've changed?" she asked abruptly. The question was awkwardly personal, but the concern had occupied her mind of late and there was no one else to ask.

"Yes," he responded without an instant's hesitation.

Lalie sighed. That's what she had feared. Yet she didn't see how it could possibly be otherwise. She couldn't experience all she had lived through and remain the same person who had departed England.

"Sometimes I don't know who I am anymore," she whispered. "Pieces of me are slipping away." Addison didn't comment but she sensed he listened with interest. "I didn't understand this before, but . . . I think I've spent most of my life trying to be like my mother, trying to fill the void her death created, trying to be what I thought she would have wanted me to be. But at the same time"—she drew a breath—"at the same time I wanted to be different from her, I wanted something more from life."

"And what would that be?" Addison asked quietly, shifting in his hammock to face her.

"I wanted to live my life to the fullest, without knowing what that meant. I thought I knew, but now I realize I didn't." She was silent for several minutes. "I guess I thought living a life to the fullest meant creating upheaval, doing something daring and unconventional."

"There's nothing wrong with living a conventional life, Miss Pritchard. The world is filled with conventional lives," Addison said. "Even extraordinary lives are often based around routine. Whether or not one 'lives' one's life is not a function of where or with whom one lives, but a function of happiness, isn't it? People can be unhappy in Paradise. Others find happiness in conditions that would make you or me shudder."

She nodded, feeling her throat grow tight. "I saw that in Tilwe's village. The Indians have very few of the things so many of us believe we require. Yet they're happy."

"To me living one's life to the fullest means doing what

one wants instead of living by imposed restrictions. Sometimes that places one outside the bounds of convention, sometimes it does not. In the end, you are the only person who genuinely knows what makes you happy. You are the one who must alter your circumstances or accept them to find that happiness. Whether or not your life is satisfactory and full depends solely on you."

"You're saying we can't look to other people to provide our happiness." A tear trickled from the corner of Lalie's eye. She had no idea why she was weepy tonight.

For no particular reason she recalled watching Addison chopping wood on the shore. Her restlessness had begun then with the strange fluttery feeling she couldn't put a name to. She remembered the sweat glistening on his naked chest like warm oil, remembered the definition of muscle and tendon and the concentration tightening his rugged features. She had thought what a beautiful man he was. And suddenly she had realized how painful it was going to be to finally say good-bye to him, to accept that she would never see him again. The depth of her distress depressed her.

Tossing aside the netting, Lalie swung her bare feet to the deck and slipped out of her hammock. "I need . . ." She didn't know what she needed. "I'm think I'm thirsty."

In a moment Addison had dropped from his hammock and was by her side, dressed only in his trousers. Reaching, he turned out the kerosene lantern. "The light attracts insects." He passed her in the sudden darkness, moving toward the crates near Maria's stove. "There should be an opened bottle of champagne."

"Thank you." In a moment her eyes adjusted to the dim starlight and she followed him across the deck. While Addison searched for the champagne, Lalie stood at the railing listening to the rush and hiss of the river and wishing for a breeze.

The night was sultry and still, the sounds from the jungle subdued and secretive. Not a whisper of breeze rustled the foliage or stirred the hot night air. Even at this late hour Lalie noticed a gleam of perspiration on Addison's bare chest and could feel Maria's shift sticking to her own heat-damp body.

Addison appeared beside her. When she took the cup from him their fingers touched and it seemed that heat lightning jumped between them, shimmering, scorching, paralyzing her.

Lalie should have stepped away from him, but she couldn't move. She stood as unmoving as a statue, listening to the wild acceleration of her heartbeat, looking at his broad, naked chest, inhaling his subtle male scent. Her mouth dried and a vast weakness opened in the pit of her stomach and spread. Only the electric tension following in its wake held her upright. When she raised helpless eyes to his, she was trembling and her breast rose and fell in quickened breaths.

March was staring at her, as paralyzed as she. A low groan issued from his throat as her lips parted. The cup of champagne slipped from Lalie's fingers and fell unnoticed to the deck. Slowly, helplessly, she stared at the dark, damp hair covering his chest. She saw the pulse beating in the hollow of his throat, felt her own pulse drumming against her temples, her wrists, the back of her bare knees. Then she raised her gaze to his clenched jaw, his hard mouth, and finally defenseless, she surrendered to the dark eyes burning down into hers. Their stares locked and held. Her breast rose and trembled on a dry, scorching breath. A yearning sound almost like a sob caught in her throat.

And she wanted. Needed. A floodgate opened within and bathed her in sweet, dewy heat. The world narrowed to the few inches that separated them. Lalie's lashes dropped and she swayed on her feet. If he didn't touch her, she would faint.

Touch me, touch me, she urged silently. *Lock me in your arms.*

When his shaking fingertips caressed her throat, she cried out softly, her voice a moan, and she felt an explosion ignite inside. Large, helpless eyes gazed up at him; her lips parted and a tremor of longing swept her body. Too weak with desire to stand, she swayed against him, sucking in a quivering breath when her hot face touched his skin.

March's arms slipped around her and he crushed her against his body so tightly that she could hear his heart thudding beneath her ear. Her head fell backward and she lifted her mouth, her quickened breath mingling with his in the sultry darkness.

As if possessed of a need and energy of its own, her body arched against his, fitting hip to hip, seeking the power and urgency of his hard strength. Trembling, shaking, feeling faint with needs she didn't fully understand, Lalie wrapped her arms around his waist, feeling the rock-hard smoothness of his skin beneath her palms. She waited, waited, her lips parted in invitation, her heart hammering in her breast.

"Lalie." Slowly, his hands slid up her sides, molding her body, the heels of his palms brushing her breasts, his touch forcing a low cry of longing from her throat.

He cupped her face between his hands, his hot, dark eyes hungry on her trembling mouth. Then with agonizing slowness he bent his head and kissed her, slowly and deliberately then with increasing passion.

Her body moved against his; her hands rose and she buried her fingers in his thick hair as her mouth opened beneath his to receive his plundering tongue. Gasping, almost sobbing with the bliss and relief of finally knowing his kiss, Lalie clung to him, pulled him closer, closer, as if she could absorb him, as if by holding tightly she could make this feverish moment last forever.

When his lips released her, his arms tightened around her in a crushing embrace, catching her as she collapsed against his body. "Oh God, Lalie. I've imagined this moment a thousand times," he whispered hoarsely against her hair. His hands encircled her waist, clasping her tightly against him.

"March. Oh March. March." She whispered his name against his throat, breathing his alluring scent, greedy for his touch. Her fingers flew over his taut skin and tangled his hair. She explored the shape of his strong shoulders, his throat, his jaw.

When he tilted her face up again, she closed her eyes and her lips opened, anticipating, eagerly wanting his kiss again and again and again. But he cupped her face between his palms and licked the sweat off her throat and her upper lip, licked her until she could bear the exquisite torment no longer and pulled his mouth to hers, straining against him in the steamy darkness, her body trembling and hot and urgent with a need for something more.

He swept her up in his arms, cradling her against his naked chest. There was no thought in Lalie's mind except March and her feverish need for him. Hands clasped to his shoulders, her mouth locked to his, she gave no thought to where he was taking her until he gently laid her in her hammock.

Bending over the hammock, he kissed her deeply, his mouth alternately tender then roughly possessive. His fingers trembled over her cheek, paused to cup her breast and brush the hard bud of her nipple. Then his hand moved lower, halting on her stomach. Lalie's body arched involuntarily, thrusting against the steady pressure, and she gasped and writhed in the hammock. Her legs parted slightly and her breast lifted. Her every nerve leapt at his touch.

When he slowly withdrew his hand, a cry of frustration and loss broke from her lips.

"I have never wanted a woman as much as I want you now. If I don't leave this instant, I'll dishonor you." His voice was hoarse and unsteady. In the dim starlight, his eyes looked black and hot with desire. "Leaving you now is the hardest thing I have ever done."

"March . . . please." Tears spilled down her cheeks. Her body was on fire, her skin a tingling mass of feverish nerves. Her thighs ached for his touch, her breast trembled for his tongue. Her lips were swollen and aflame.

His hand lifted and she felt his fingertips brush her cheek, wiping the tears away. He brought his fingers to his mouth and tasted her tears.

Then he opened his eyes and kissed her again, a savagely possessive kiss that crushed her and the hammock to his chest, a kiss that left her gasping and sobbing with need.

Then he was gone, stumbling away in the hot darkness. Lalie heard a splash alongside the ship. And she wrapped her arms around her shaking body and wept because March Addison was an honorable man. But she had discovered she possessed no honor at all. The river had stripped her of that, too. Tonight she was a shameless wanton, trembling and aflame with her frustrated passion for the wrong man.

Sometime near dawn March returned to the upper deck. Sleepless and devastated with shame, Lalie sensed him standing beside her hammock for what seemed a very long time before he turned away and slipped into his own hammock.

She released a long, convulsive breath and wept silently.

In the morning she ate her farinha and turtle eggs with the others, but she didn't look up from her stool. With all her heart she hoped March would pretend last night had never happened. But that was impossible. How could he forget when she herself could think of nothing else?

She felt his gaze; it seemed to burn into her. Her body tensed and finally she abandoned the effort to eat. Her breakfast tasted like straw; she couldn't swallow.

Shortly after Fredo cast off, March came out of the wheelhouse and walked to the oven where Lalie sat watching listlessly as Maria kneaded a bowl of bread dough.

"We have to talk," March said in a low voice.

Lalie shook her head and turned her face away from him. "Please. I beg you," she whispered. "Don't speak of it."

Bending, he raised her by her elbows, then took her arm and led her toward the stern, away from the kitchen and the wheelhouse door. If Lalie had believed last night's fever had burned itself out, she was wrong. His hand on her arm set her body on fire.

"Oh dear God," she murmured helplessly. Tears blurred her vision, but that was good because it meant she could not see his features clearly. Maybe she could gaze at him without seeing the lips that had demanded hers, without remembering his tongue licking her skin.

March leaned on the railing, staring at the narrowing tributary, at the tree branches overhanging the water. "I won't apologize, Lalie. Any apology would be a lie."

She lifted a shaking hand to cover her eyes. "I betrayed Percival. He trusted me enough to ask for my hand, and I've proved unworthy."

March didn't look at her. He continued to frown at the water below. "Has it occurred to you that this journey was a mistake? That you don't love Sterling enough to marry him?"

A terrible thought jolted her. "Was that the reason behind last night? You were trying to show me—"

"Don't be a fool," he said sharply, still not looking at her. "Last night had nothing to do with Percival Sterling. Last night is something you and I have been building toward for a long time. I think you recognize that, too. What you have to decide is whether last night changes anything."

She turned aside to pull down the brim of the old hat of Joao's that she was wearing, using the motion to conceal the tears in her eyes. She didn't answer until she was certain her voice would be steady, then she spoke in a quiet, expressionless tone.

"You still don't understand. If I allow myself to doubt my feelings for Sir Percival even once, then . . . then I've betrayed my father's trust and wounded him for nothing. I've traveled halfway around the world and two thousand miles up this damned river for nothing. I will have frightened myself, will have submitted to sunburn and insects and indignities for—nothing. I will have sacrificed my good reputation, will have disgraced my father's house, will have shattered my self-esteem, and all for absolutely nothing. If I didn't trust my love for Sir Percival, if I didn't believe it was real, then I should have stayed home and kept my reputation intact."

Now he straightened and looked down at her, his dark eyes penetrating. "Then how do you explain what happened last night?" he asked softly. "How do you justify coming into my arms? I didn't imagine it, Lalie. You wanted me, too."

"I don't know," she whispered, her voice a moan of self-reproach. "Please, March. I'm so confused and upset." She bit her lip. "Somehow—without either of us recognizing it—we became friends." She raised eyes that pleaded with him to agree. "I think perhaps you're the best friend I've ever had." With a sense of shock, she realized this was true. "And . . . and maybe, given our circumstances, we've mistaken friendship for something else."

"That's bloody damned nonsense, Lalie."

She gasped and frowned, not sure how to respond.

"Last night I wanted you more than I've ever wanted any woman. And you wanted me. Neither of us was looking for friendship or a pleasant companion. Whatever we were looking for, we found passion. Raw animal passion."

She winced as if he had struck her, and she stumbled backward a step, covering her face with her hands.

Instantly March moved up beside her and dragged her hands away from her face. "There's nothing to be ashamed of, Lalie, passion is as natural as breathing, it's part of being alive." His dark eyes glittered down into hers, taking her breath away. "You haven't betrayed Sterling by simply being alive. All you've done is awaken to yourself. Is that so terrible?"

"You're my friend," she whispered, losing herself in his eyes and his touch. She wet her lips. "You know it was more. You know I betrayed him."

"No I don't. You didn't betray anything simply by letting your body come to life."

Lalie drew a long, shuddering breath and made herself look away from his lips and eyes. Forcing herself, she tugged her hands free and stepped back from him.

She swallowed, straightened her spine, then met his eyes. "That is bloody damned nonsense, Mr. Addison."

He stared for a few seconds then threw back his head in a burst of laughter. He laughed until tears dampened his eyes and Fredo leaned his head out of the wheelhouse and smiled.

"Miss Pritchard," he said when he could speak, "you are a remarkable woman. I never believed a day would ever dawn that I would envy Percival Sterling." His fingertips briefly touched her throat then fell away. "But I do."

Crimson spread across her throat and cheeks. "That's a lovely compliment, Mr. Addison. Thank you."

"About last night—"

Hastily, Lalie raised a hand, frowned and shook her head. "Neither of us can explain what happened last night." She drew a deep breath. "But we can agree it mustn't happen again."

Addison's dark gaze examined her face. "Is that what you want?"

"Yes," she whispered. But her heart sank and her traitorous body rebelled at her resolve. Even now memory caused her breast to quicken, her skin to heat. Confused, she flicked her tongue over dry lips then started when March made a low sound deep in his throat. She stiffened, holding herself as erect as if she wore one of her corsets. "Please, March," she ended simply. "Please don't make this harder for me than it is already."

For a long moment he stared at her. "You are like a fever in my blood. A question that has no answer," he said, speaking in a low, intense voice. "You are a mystery that reveals bits of itself while always concealing the final solution. I think of you every minute of every day. I can't sleep at night for wanting you, for knowing you're there beside me and yet as far away as the stars."

Lalie's knees threatened to collapse and she threw out a hand to clutch the railing. "Don't," she whispered. But he expressed her thoughts and feelings as well as his own.

"I count the minutes until I can deliver you to Hiberalta and end this torment. At the same time I cannot bear the thought of that bastard putting his hands on you, kissing you, possessing you."

"Please stop," Lalie whispered. She had never thought of herself as weak. But she was. That she had come within a breath of betraying Percival devastated her. That she had *wanted* to betray him, had longed to betray him, that it had been March and not she who had walked away, caused her an agony of shame.

And worse. She gazed into his hard eyes and understood that she longed for him even now. Now, in the full, blazing sunlight. Now, on the heels of her insistence that she loved Percival. Now, now, now.

Dropping her head, she covered her face with shaking hands. She was untrustworthy, a woman without morals or honor. She was mere days from her beloved, perhaps no more than a week from her wedding day—and she burned with desire for another man. The gates she had opened would not be closed again.

"Listen to me, Lalie." March spoke near her ear, but thank God he did not touch her. "I will deliver you to

Hiberalta, to that son of a bitch, Sterling. I will do my business, find Tilwe's people, and I'll leave." Between her fingers, she saw his clenched fists. "I will not say or do anything to cause you a moment's discomfort with Percy. You need have no fear on that count no matter what happens between you and me."

She stared up at him.

"But these last three or four days are ours." Reaching, he gently removed her hands from her face, holding them between his own. "These last days are a window in your life and mine, opened for a brief span then forever closed. What happens in the frame of this window is up to you, Lalie."

"I . . ." His dark eyes seemed to see right through her. She was drowning in dark heat, in a whirlpool that tossed her emotions like bits of twig and leaf. "I understand what you're saying, March, but . . . but I can't." She closed her eyes. "I can't, I can't."

"But you want to," he said softly, drawing her closer until she could sense his desire and feel the heat from his body. "For now, that is enough."

She sagged against the railing, watching him walk across the deck toward the wheelhouse. Her heart pounded in her chest, her breath scalded the back of her throat.

"Help me," she whispered to the God she wasn't sure existed. "Help me," she repeated. But God was busy elsewhere that day, and she received no answer.

Lalie gazed ahead, staring into the window that March had described, and his face filled the frame.

They reached Ipta at midday. Through the veil of a soft, steady drizzle Lalie could see the settlement was no more than a collection of tin-roofed shacks sitting on stilts above a muddy garbage-strewn bank. Steaming jungle foliage crowded the edge of the shacks and straggled through the cracks of a decaying wharf.

A row of Indian men sat beneath a tumbledown lean-to near the end of the dock. Two of the men rose to their feet as Fredo cut the engine of the *Addison Beal* and guided the ship toward a rotting post. Hunched against the drizzle, protected by shapeless bark-skin capes, one of the Indian men caught the rope Joao threw and tied it to a post.

Now Lalie understood why Maria had assured her it was not necessary to don her one remaining civilized ensemble. No one in Ipta would care that she stood barefoot and wore a thin calf-length cotton shift.

Near the wharf was a rusting metal sign that announced the post office shared the same gray building as Ipta's only cantina. Another sign hanging from one hinge announced the presence of a tiny dry-goods store. The final place of business boasted the only freshly painted, easily readable sign. It read: Whores.

Lalie looked toward the dripping jungle as the drizzle diminished and the sun struggled to reappear. The thick foliage appeared impenetrable. The listless ambience of Ipta depressed her spirits and she felt as gray as the weathered boards.

"The first thing we'll do is buy you some jungle boots," March said, appearing at her side. He scanned the collection of buildings. "Maria and Joao will remain here with the *Addison Beal.* You, Fredo, and I will leave immediately."

Lalie nodded, staring at the row of mules. "Do you remember worrying how many mules we'd need to transport my luggage?" She smiled humorlessly. "That seems a lifetime ago."

March's gaze held her eyes. "I remember everything."

The memory of starlit kisses burst across her mind; she remembered a hot day in the lagoon. For an instant Lalie saw again the glow of sunset on March's naked, glistening shoulders, felt his powerful body wrapping around her. She wet her lips as a familiar weakness opened in the pit of her stomach. "Yes," she whispered. She too remembered everything. She always would.

Swallowing hard, she turned away from him and inspected the mules that would take her within a day's journey of the man she would marry.

And sudden tears glistened in her eyes.

Chapter 16

Most of the items in the cramped dry-goods store had turned gray with mildew and jungle rot, but Lalie found a small pair of men's boots that were still in serviceable condition. She also selected a pair of heavy stockings and a rubberized cape to protect her from rain on the trail.

When March inquired about quinine tablets, the proprietor shrugged and informed him there would be no more quinine until the next shipment upriver. Lalie's consternation was immediate.

"You've been giving me your tablets, haven't you?"

"We can't have the bride falling ill with jungle fever, can we? What would people think?"

Lalie's frown deepened as she followed him outside the dry-goods store and across the planks laid over the mud. And she silently cursed herself for being thoughtless and unobservant. Her quinine supply had vanished along with her luggage on board the *Raider* but whether or not the *Addison Beal* carried enough quinine for everyone was a question that had not entered her mind. "March, listen to me. We can split the tablets. We can—"

He stopped suddenly, turning to grip her by the shoulders. Anger flared in his eyes. "No, you listen to me. You're going to take the quinine tablets. And we're going to buy you all the suitable clothing we can find in Tupati. I'm not going to deliver you sick and half-naked to Percy."

"Don't be a fool," she snapped. "Partial protection is better than no protection. How much help will you be to Tilwe's people if you become ill?"

It was the first time she had allowed herself to admit that March might find Tilwe's people at Hiberalta. But neither of them paused to reflect on the implications of her doubt.

"I don't want any argument on this, Lalie. Yes, I could agree to share the tablets. And maybe half-doses would be protection enough for both of us. But suppose it isn't? Suppose you fall ill with malaria. For the rest of my life I'd question my motives. I won't take that risk with your health or my peace of mind." His teeth clenched. "You are, by God, going to arrive at Hiberalta in good health. Your son-of-a-bitch future husband will have nothing to complain about." He spun around and stalked toward the decaying wharf.

She followed him, interrupting his instructions to the Indian men who loaded the mules' packs.

"Is my peace of mind of no consequence?" she demanded angrily. "How peacefully do you suppose I'll rest if you become ill? Or if I'm the reason Tilwe's people can't be rescued—because you're too ill to manage it?"

"You're in the way." Glaring, he stepped around her. "Put on your boots and the cape we bought. I expect to get under way in"—he glanced at the sun flaring over the edge of the clouds—"fifteen minutes. We have about six hours of daylight."

"You are the most stubborn, intractable, uncompromising man I have ever met! You get an idea in your head and nothing on earth will budge you!"

"You're wrong. Now get out of the way, Miss Pritchard. These men are trying to work and they're having to do it around you." He pushed back his hat and scowled. "Go!"

Sputtering, she turned on her heel and marched back to the *Addison Beal.*

Packing her few belongings required less than five minutes. When she finished, Lalie stood in the center of the *Addison Beal*'s upper deck and revolved in a slow circle, engraving on her memory the steamer that had served as her home for months.

"We'll miss you, Missy," Joao said shyly. He hesitated then extended his hand and Lalie shook it. He drew a breath and spoke in a formal tone, having rehearsed his farewell speech. "I wish you every happiness in your future life."

"Thank you," Lalie whispered. "I hope you find a wonderful young lady, and when you do, I wish you many sons." Leaning forward, she pressed her good lace handkerchief into his hand. "I wish I had something more to give you."

Then it was time to say good-bye to Maria. The two women faced one another, each with tears in her eyes. By now they knew each other very well and in many ways were as close as sisters.

"Oh Maria." Blindly Lalie opened her arms and they embraced, clinging to one another. "I shall miss you dreadfully." After they stepped apart to wipe their eyes, Lalie placed her mother's pink brooch in Maria's palm and closed her fingers over it. The brooch was the only piece of jewelry she had worn the day she boarded the *Raider.* It was all she had to give.

Maria stared at the treasure. "I can't accept this, Missy."

"You must. I want you to have it."

With shy pride Maria carefully pinned the brooch to her cotton shift then she lifted Lalie's hand and placed a tiny vial in her palm.

Lalie examined the red fluid inside the vial with a puzzled expression. She smiled in bewilderment. "What is it?"

Leaning forward, Maria whispered in her ear.

"To sprinkle on the sheets on my wedding night?" Lalie repeated, her eyebrows soaring. Then she understood. And because she knew Maria's kindness she didn't take offense. "I won't need this," she protested gently, extending the vial to Maria.

Maria tucked the red fluid inside Lalie's bundle. "If you marry Sir Percy, you need it, Missy," she said firmly. A wise look entered her brown eyes. "Remember the eye of the *boto,* Missy? The *boto* will come to you." She patted Lalie's bundle and the vial within. "Now no one will know but you."

Lalie's cheeks flamed and she bit her lip, looking toward the row of mules on the shore. March beckoned to her. "I have to leave now."

Maria took both her hands. "Not my business, Missy, but . . ." She hesitated then made up her mind to speak her thoughts. "You make big mistake. Cabo love you. And you love Cabo." Her brown eyes softened with warmth and sympathy. "Big *bagunça* if you marry Sir Percy. Break Maria's heart. You see Cabo through the eye of the *boto.* You belong to him."

Suddenly Lalie wished her letter had never reached Hiberalta. If Percival hadn't known she was in the Amazon . . . Her eyes swept the docks and settled on March. How differently her life might have gone. She would have been free to make decisions she didn't now dare to consider.

The crimson deepened on Lalie's throat and cheeks. "Mr. Addison and I are friends, but—"

"Miss Pritchard," March roared from the shore. "Get down here right now or we're leaving without you!"

Lalie looked at Maria and both women smiled. Then they embraced again before Lalie ran down the plank and hurried toward the waiting men and mules.

She waved until she could no longer see Ipta or the *Addison Beal.*

* * *

Romexi, one of the men March had hired for the journey to Hiberalta, scouted ahead of the mule train, then came Fredo, then a pack mule in front of Lalie and another behind, then the Indian called Termo. March rode at the rear.

The trail was visible to those with eyes to see and followed a narrow rock-strewn creek. Occasionally the stream plunged down a stony crevasse and they lost sight of it for several miles. Then, even to March, it seemed the jungle closed around them with oppressive denseness.

A discomfiting silence signaled their presence had been noted and was being observed. Pasé and Ymana tribes inhabited this area. At least they had before the demand for cheap labor decimated the nearby tribes. March suspected not all the Indians had been captured. But he felt confident that whoever peered at them through the thick, damp foliage would not interfere with their passage out of fear of drawing attention to themselves.

Occasionally overhanging ferns or lianas blocked Lalie from sight, but for the most part his view was unobstructed. He could see the back of Joao's old hat and the flaming coils that swung beneath it, the only spot of color amid the unrelieved green and brown of the jungle. She wore the shapeless rubberized cape against the damp chill in the air, and her heavy men's boots stuck out on either side of her mule.

March smiled and drew on his cigar. He guessed Eulalie Pritchard knew she didn't cut a very feminine figure in her outlandish attire. But she hadn't complained and he liked her for that.

Or maybe she believed he would find her less appealing. If so, she was wrong. He enjoyed observing women in their lace and satins, magnificent at their decorative best, but in the jungle the beauty of character emerged. And in his opinion, character was a woman's most splendid ornament.

When they halted to set up camp, March studied her as

he fashioned a rock pit then kindled a fire. Now he saw the strength in a jawline he had previously considered delicate. He identified breeding in the thin, sculpted line of her nose, but breeding freed of stiffness and arrogance. There was a new softness in the seductive curve of her lips, a new fullness in her unfettered figure. And in the depths of her jeweled eyes he read loyalty and honor and inner struggle.

When he finished unloading the stew Maria had prepared and sent with them, he placed the pot in the fire then straightened beside her. She stood with her palms extended to the flames, gazing into the fire.

"Are you warm enough?" A twilight chill had settled over the forest. A burst of activity and chattering exploded in the canopy above, then an illusion of silence returned. Firelight danced on her golden skin. For a moment March remembered the sweetness of that skin, the exquisite taste when his tongue had touched it.

"What did you mean when you spoke of a window in our lives?" Lalie asked in a low voice, not looking at him.

"This will warm you," he said, pouring her a cup of *cachaça.* She tasted it, made a face, then swallowed again. Stepping back from the fire, he sat on a fallen cedar log and lit a cigar. "We'll reach Tupati the day after tomorrow. We'll spend the night there, and the following day I'll deliver you to Hiberalta." Saying the words made his chest ache. "From that moment forward your life and your behavior will be prescribed. As Lady Sterling there will be things you can do and more things you cannot do."

Still gazing into the fire, she murmured, "I suspect Mrs. Wilkie's rules are about to reenter my life."

He smiled and blew a smoke ring toward the fire. "These few days are a window of time between the life you once led and the life you will live in the future."

"Sometimes I think this entire journey has been a window in my life."

"Have you spent the time as you wished?" he asked

softly. "Have you used this period of freedom to do all the things you may never have the opportunity to do again?"

"Are you asking if I've really lived my life—within this window of time?"

"Have you?"

She turned to look at him, examining his face. "I don't know," she admitted in a quiet tone. "Perhaps I haven't done all I might have wished." It appeared to March that color flooded her face, but the warmth may have been reflected firelight.

"Be selfish, Lalie. You may never have this chance again."

They studied each other for several minutes, and March would have offered ten years of his life to know what thoughts opened behind those sad blue-green eyes.

Fredo broke the spell. He approached the fire, rubbing his palms together.

"Missy's lean-to is finished, Cabo."

"Good."

Lalie ladled stew into the tin bowls Romexi fetched from the mule packs, and after they ate, Fredo passed around a bottle of *cachaça*. March sat on a blanket on the spongy ground, his back propped against a log, smoking while Fredo played a melancholy tune on his mouth harp.

Without speaking Lalie came to him. She hesitated a moment, her face in shadow. Then she released a long breath and sat beside him. When he wordlessly opened his arm, she moved closer and leaned against him, resting her head on his shoulder.

"I . . . I'm chilled and I thought—"

"It isn't necessary to explain," he murmured against her silky hair. "Be selfish, remember?" He closed his arm around her, not assuming liberties she hadn't offered, content to have her body next to his.

They sat together, facing the fire, immersed in thought.

"I used to hate cigar smoke," she said after the fire had burned low.

"Used to?" He smiled when she squirmed against him, and he imagined her frowning. But she surprised him with a soft laugh.

"Do you suppose the scent changed, or did I?"

"I think you did," he said, his voice gruff. His arm was beginning to fall asleep but he didn't remove it from around her shoulders.

She rested her chin on his sleeve and looked at the embers. "Perhaps you're right. Once I would have been shocked by the idea of sitting like this, practically on your lap."

He heard the smile in her voice and felt absurdly happy. One by one Fredo and the two Indians slipped away to their sleeping pallets, but March didn't move. The night grew darker and he felt enclosed by the trees above and the foliage that pressed around them. Night creatures rustled in the underbrush and once a bat swooped over their heads. Neither of them moved.

They sat together in a loose embrace, seldom speaking, sharing each other's warmth until the embers dimmed to an orange glow.

"I'll help you to your lean-to," he said eventually, making no effort to rise.

She pressed her forehead against his arm and spoke so softly he had to lean his cheek next to hers to hear.

"There are things—selfish, dishonorable things—that I long to do, March. But I can't." A tremble swept her small body. "Please try to understand. I wish I could . . . but I can't. I would hate myself."

Standing, he assisted her to her feet then held her gently. Only by great effort of will did he restrain himself from crushing her tightly against his body. The darkness was so thick that even after he tilted her face upward, he could see only a pale, oval blur.

"Will you hate yourself if you don't?" Her throat was like warm satin beneath his fingertips, her lifted mouth a siren call of temptation. "Will you look back with regret? Will you spend the rest of your life wondering? As I will?"

"It's so hard to do the right thing," she whispered. He could feel her holding herself away from him, trembling beneath the touch of his hand.

"And what is the right thing, Lalie? Right for whom?" He brushed a strand of hair from her breast. His stomach tightened and his voice turned hoarse. "Will you think of me in the future and remember me as I will remember you? Will my image haunt your dreams as your image will haunt mine? Will you lie in Sterling's arms and think of me? Will you wonder what it would have been like with me?"

"Please, March, I beg you," she whispered. "Please don't say these things." Her shaking fingers covered his lips.

He kissed her fingertips, and sucked her little finger into his mouth, making her gasp. "These last days are mine, Lalie, and I will say these things. Because the memory of you will torment me all the rest of my life. Whenever I see a flame-haired woman I will think of you and I will wonder what it would have been like to make love to you."

A sound like a sob broke from her throat. She tried to pull away from him, but he held her against his body, letting her feel the power and need between his thighs.

"On those hot nights when sleep won't come, I'll lie in my bed and remember the softness of your breast, the sweet curve of your waist. I'll remember the lagoon, the sunshine on your eyelids. I'll remember the taste of your skin and the scent of your hair . . . and I'll wonder."

"Oh God, March . . . please."

"I'll hear laughter that reminds me of you and I'll wonder. I'll smell the fragrance of lilac or verbena and I'll ache for you, and I'll wonder."

Tears slipped down Lalie's cheeks. She dropped her head to his chest and gripped his arms. She felt weak and faint.

"I'll make love to other women, Lalie, but they won't be you. I'll feel that loss and wonder. All my life I will remember you and regret that I didn't have you. All my life I will wonder at the feel and taste and touch and scent of you. I will wonder if you would have cried my name. I will wonder if I would have given you pleasure. I will wonder and mourn my loss."

"Stop. Please, stop! You're tormenting me." Even in the darkness he could see that she covered her face as she pulled away from him, that she swayed on her feet. "Don't you think I wonder, too?" Her voice emerged as a fierce, raw whisper. "Don't you think I torture myself with the same yearning curiosity? Don't you understand that I'm half-crazy with the shame of my own thoughts? I can't look at you without wondering. I can't hear your voice without trembling. I can't think of you without remembering and wondering! I . . . I . . . oh God!"

Turning, she stumbled into her lean-to and fell across her pallet. March stood in the damp chill and listened to her wild sobbing.

He couldn't guess how long he stood in the black forest waiting for her to call his name. But she didn't. Finally, aching with desire for her, he returned to his own pallet.

In the morning Lalie ate her cold farinha and warmed-over stew without speaking. She knew she looked pale and tired from passing a sleepless night. But for all the sleepless hours of confusion and feverish longing she had resolved nothing.

After Fredo helped her up onto her mule, she passed a hand across her eyes and tried to calm her febrile thoughts, hoping the shafts of bright sunlight would clarify her thinking and strengthen her resolve to preserve her tattered honor.

But her resolve ebbed low, weakened by the longings of a body that didn't know it was pledged to another man, by a passion that consumed her mind and flesh.

And with every plodding step Lalie's mule took, her window of time closed another inch.

In two and a half days she would stand in the arms of a man whose face she could no longer recall. Perhaps a week later she would be his wife, sharing his bed and a life she knew little about. She didn't know if Percival Sterling dreamed. She didn't know his moods or his character. She didn't know if his touch would be gentle or demanding, tender or awkward. She didn't know what they would say to one another or if silence would become an enemy. She didn't know if they would be friends as well as lovers and companions.

And always—always she would remember and wonder about the man who rode behind her. The man whose gaze she felt on her back, her hips, the nape of her neck. The man who had awakened her and brought her body to feverish life. A man whose voice alone could flood her secret areas with liquid heat. Whose gaze penetrated and stirred. Whose touch was sweet fire on her skin.

Always, she would wonder.

Always, she would look back with regret that she hadn't dared to live fully, to experience fully when the opportunity was hers. While the window of time was still open.

And one day, perhaps a month from now, perhaps years from now, she would gaze into the mirror and whisper, Poor Eulalie, your courage failed you. You could have satisfied your need to know and laid the demon to rest but you lacked the courage.

Such thoughts led to madness. She shook her head violently and tried to erase her shameful longings. If she seized her window of time, she would then have to live with the knowledge that she had betrayed Percival within days of her wedding. For the rest of her life she would live with a secret too terrible to contemplate.

But how could she say good-bye to March without knowing? Without experiencing all of him?

Despair twisted her features and she was glad he could

not glimpse her face, could not see the tears that slipped from her eyes.

When they halted for the night, she sat across the fire from him, drowning in her misery. And very much aware that her window was now half-closed. The next day they would arrive at Tupati on the Yaki River. The day after that March would deliver her to Hiberalta.

And then, she thought, raising her eyes to the firelight playing across March's bronzed face, the long journey that once had seemed endless would finally end. They would shake hands like strangers and murmur polite farewells.

March stared back at her across the dying fire. He sat on the ground, leaning against a fallen log, smoking, one knee raised, his hat pushed back on his dark hair. His trousers and shirt were soiled by rain and earth and bore streaks of foliage green. As usual, his collar was open and she could glimpse the soft, dark hair on his chest, as well as one of his scars.

"How did you get the third scar?" Suddenly it seemed crucially important that she learn about the third scar.

Though she spoke quietly and they sat across the fire from each other, he heard her and smiled. "The tale is embarrassingly mundane."

"I want to know."

"I fell out of a tree when I was nine and landed on the gardener's wheelbarrow." He shrugged and smiled.

But she saw him in her mind as a child. Dark, tousled hair, intent, curious eyes, a compact, muscular body. Adventurous. Stubborn. Going his own way even then.

"I wish I could have heard you play the violin again," she said softly. "Right now, sitting in the middle of a dark jungle, I think I must have imagined you playing. I'm afraid I'll always picture you with a machete in your hand instead of a bow."

He grinned and drained his cup of *cachaça*. "That's how I'd prefer to be remembered, thank you."

Fredo stood, yawned, waved then disappeared toward

his pallet. The Indians were already asleep, sitting against tree trunks, wrapped within their bark-skin capes.

"I'll never see you again, will I?" Lalie asked, staring at him. A sting of moisture heated her eyelids.

"Not unless you and your husband visit Malaya."

Several minutes passed before she could speak again. Clenching her fists so tightly that her nails bit into her palms, she asked, "And there is no possibility you might change your mind and stay in Brazil."

"None. At my direction, my solicitor has already purchased an estate in Malaya. Many of the rubber trees are already planted. It sounds as if the house needs to be knocked down and a new one built, but I would have done that anyway."

The embers had cooled until only a dim glow remained. Lalie thought of the long day ahead of them and knew she should get some sleep. But she pulled her blanket tighter around her shoulders and made no motion to rise.

"Tell me about the house you'll build," she requested, thinking of Sir Percival's opulent mansion in Manaus.

He studied her face before answering, straining to see through the darkness. "The house will be much like my house in Pará. Two-story, tile-roofed, large airy rooms simply furnished. The terraces will face the coast to catch the breeze. I'll have a courtyard, plantings."

"Fireplaces?"

"In Malaya?" He smiled. "No."

"Tell me about the furnishings."

He remained silent for a moment then said, "Why are you asking these questions?"

Because she felt a hunger to know every small detail about him, about his life. Because she wanted to visualize his surroundings. She wanted to learn about his future in Malaya, about his past in England. A look of despair tightened her features. She wanted to know everything about March Addison, all the tiny details that knit together to form who and what he was.

"I don't know," she whispered. "I do know we need sleep."

Pushing to her feet, she hesitated beside the firepit, waiting to discover if he would follow. Wanting him to follow. Wanting him to overpower her objections and take her into his arms and bathe her in kisses. That was the solution of course—if he overpowered her and took her despite her protests, she could absolve herself of all blame.

His voice floated out of the darkness, speaking as though he had read her thoughts. "I won't force you, Lalie, or pressure you to do anything you don't want to do. If you and I are to be spared a lifetime of regret and wonder—it must be at your invitation. But our time together is nearly ended."

"I know," she whispered. Tears of frustration and misery welled in her eyes as she stumbled into her lean-to. His sense of honor would not permit him to overwhelm her objections; just as her sense of honor would not permit her to surrender. Soon they would go their separate ways and March Addison would be forever lost to her.

The final thought rang in her ears. Forever lost.

Could she face the rest of her life without knowing the rapture of March Addison's lovemaking? Could she face the rest of her life knowing that he was half a world away from her?

Once again Lalie wept herself to sleep.

Chapter 17

The mule train emerged from the jungle forest at midday, leaving the dripping coolness behind and entering a scorching heat so intense that Lalie was limp and bathed in perspiration before they reached the outskirts of Tupati.

In size and design Tupati was reminiscent of Quantos. A church spire pointed to the blazing sun, clay-baked streets wound away from a central plaza. Near a palm-studded sea wall, market vendors dozed within the shade of their stands, awaiting a breeze and the return of the fishing boats that plied the Yaki.

After settling Lalie beneath the shade of a palm drooping over a plaza bench, March made arrangements with Romexi and Termo for the return journey, then he issued instructions to Fredo. Fredo nodded and departed, leading the mules down a lane winding away from the plaza. Finally March returned to Lalie and placed his hands on his hips.

"On your feet, Miss Pritchard. We have some shopping to do."

Groaning, Lalie waved at the mosquitoes with Joao's old hat. "All I want is a bath and a nap." It seemed impossible but once she would have been mortally embarrassed to utter the word "bath" in front of a man. Had she really been that silly and artificial?

"You may have a bath and a nap after we assemble a wardrobe." Reaching down, he caught her hand and pulled her to her feet, releasing her hand almost immediately.

Lalie resisted the urge to press her hand to her lips. "I have no funds for clothing. And you've been far too generous already. I wouldn't feel comfortable accepting more from you."

"I am not going to deliver you to Hiberalta with no more luggage than the clothes on your back, Miss Pritchard. If it will ease your pride, consider a new wardrobe as your wedding gift."

Turning away, Lalie shaded her eyes and gazed down the only cobbled street, noticing a surprising number of shopfronts. It occurred to her that Percival had undoubtedly visited Tupati on numerous occasions. Perhaps he had stood where they were standing now. Perhaps he had enjoyed a *cafezinho* in a café or purchased a hat from the haberdasher at the end of the street.

Raising her head, Lalie gazed toward the river, toward Hiberalta. By this time tomorrow she would be standing on Hiberalta's dock. The rest of her life would begin.

Eagerness should have lit her eyes. She should have felt happy and excited. Instead, a gray knot of apprehension tightened behind her chest and she felt like weeping.

"I can't go shopping," she said finally, glancing pointedly at Maria's soiled shift and the jungle boots she was wearing. She lifted a strand of tangled hair and let it fall. "I look like hell."

March rolled his eyes toward the heat-white sky. He made a show of summoning patience. "That is why we are going shopping, my dear Miss Pritchard. So you *won't* look like hell."

"I can't go shopping dressed like this."

He raised an eyebrow. "I see. You're worried what the shopgirls might think?"

She glared at him, then a sheepish look melted her scowl. Finally she laughed.

"You're not going to allow me to backslide, are you?"

He grinned down at her, but then a look of speculation narrowed his dark eyes. "Although, I must concede—you truly do look rather awful. Maybe we should stop in at a café so you could wash your face and"—he made a stirring motion with his finger—"and maybe pin up your hair."

"Sorry, Mr. Addison." She shoved Joao's hat firmly on her head. "I don't have any hairpins, remember? Besides, you made your point too well. The shopgirls will have to take me as I am. Who cares what they think?" Tilting her head, she raised an eyebrow and pursed her lips. "You know, you look rather disreputable yourself. It strikes me you're in urgent need of a shave, a bath, and fresh clothing."

Dark stubble shaded his chin and cheeks. His jungle boots were scuffed and scratched, his clothes soiled and stained with sweat.

"In fact," she said, setting off down the cobbled street. "You look like hell, too."

He fell into step beside her. "It occurs to me, Miss Pritchard, that your language has deteriorated remarkably since I first made your acquaintance. Could it be you're developing human characteristics?"

She leveled a mock scowl up at him. "I wonder—do you suppose making your acquaintance and the deterioration of my language could be related?"

After peering inside a shop window, he opened the door for her and ushered her inside with a smile. "I'd like to think I may claim some of the credit." When she made a face, he laughed then turned to a dark-eyed shopgirl, addressing her in Portuguese.

For a moment the shopgirl didn't move. She stood immobile in front of a table holding folded petticoats and stared at March. At once Lalie saw him as the shopgirl did.

Tall, powerfully muscled, a bronzed river pirate recently emerged from the steaming jungle, potently virile and devastatingly handsome.

The shopgirl said something to March in a faint, breathless voice and he responded, then she began laying out stockings and garters and petticoats and beribboned corsets and chemises. She continued to gaze at March, paying Lalie no attention.

Lalie examined the items displayed for her inspection, surprised to discover petticoats of the finest nainsook and Indian muslin. She also felt a burst of heat radiating in her cheeks. "I've never shopped for small clothes with a man before," she murmured, glancing at March. Her voice was as unsteady as the shopgirl's.

"Shall I assist you?" he asked, eyeing one of the lacy chemises. He then looked at her breasts as if measuring for size and fit. His dark eyes sparkled and danced.

Lalie's chin rose and she tossed her head. "Of course not. I merely offered a comment." Stiffening her spine, she briskly set about her business, ignoring him and the mild flirtation he conducted with the shopgirl.

After she selected the items she preferred, they went to the next shop and then the next, acquiring so many parcels that March had to hire a mulatto boy and his cart to transport them all.

Surprisingly, most of the shops in Tupati offered items of faultless quality. All but her dresses were of the same caliber Lalie would have purchased at home. The few ready-made dresses she found were sewn with slapdash workmanship and were disastrously out of fashion. The simple gowns would serve, however, until she could return to the modistes in Manaus.

In the last shop at the end of the cobbled street, she discovered an ivory-colored silk gown that flowed through her fingers like fine spun gossamer. It was the first truly lovely gown she had observed and the only gown in Tupati that might conceivably serve as a wedding gown.

"Buy it," March said in a gruff tone near her ear. She closed her eyes, feeling his warm breath on her cheek. "It will look beautiful on you."

"No." Under no circumstances could she allow March Addison to purchase her wedding gown. "I'll send back for it," she whispered.

Something very like pain tightened his expression and he stepped away from her. "I see . . ."

The light, bantering mood they had established vanished like steam rising from the jungle. They departed the shop without speaking and March gestured for the mulatto boy to follow.

"Where are we staying?" Lalie inquired as they passed the plaza. Her cheeks were flushed and she had begun to pant from the heat.

"The firm leases a house here. We're almost there. Yavita, the housekeeper, should have your bath ready by the time we arrive."

"That sounds like heaven." But she wondered uneasily how it would sound to Sir Percival. Still, she hadn't observed any hotels or inns in Tupati during their shopping excursion. She bit her lip and looked at March doubtfully. "Knowing how gossip travels on the Amazon . . . is it likely to assume Percival will learn you purchased my trousseau?"

"You're already worrying what Percy thinks?" March didn't glance at her. "I imagine you'd be wise to explain the circumstances before Percy learns the story from someone else. And yes, he will learn who paid for your garters and stockings. And no, he won't be pleased."

She considered his advice. "I'm sure Percival will understand," she said finally.

March didn't comment. Bending, he pushed an iron gate that opened into a stuccoed wall. Behind the high wall sat a lovely small house surrounded by ferns and flowers, shaded by sweet eucalyptus and cedar trees. Lalie heard the tinkle of a fountain within an inner courtyard.

"It's lovely," she breathed, grateful to escape the sun.

Fredo was waiting for them. Stepping onto the veranda, he paid the mulatto boy and took charge of Lalie's parcels. Yavita, a smiling, dark-eyed woman, led Lalie up a short flight of stairs and showed her into a shaded bedroom. A tub filled with fragrant water was waiting.

With a cry of pleasure, Lalie threw off the soiled shift and her boots then stepped into the tub. Yavita reappeared with a tall pitcher of mango and papaya juice, and left a jar of oil to rub into her skin.

Sighing with pleasure, Lalie closed her eyes and relaxed in the water, inhaling the welcome scents of soap and sweet oil. After a time the thought floated through her mind that Percival was only a day's journey away. The reminder offered much to consider: their reunion, her forthcoming wedding, her new home.

Oddly, none of these items were invested with a sense of reality. They remained as distant a dream as when she had begun her long journey. Only this moment was real. She couldn't force her mind to move forward.

When Lalie realized she was dozing, she made herself rise from the water and towel her body. Then she smoothed the fragrant oil over her legs, shoulders, and breasts before she pulled back vanilla-scented sheets covering a high feather bed. She felt certain she would be asleep the instant her head touched the pillow.

But she was wrong.

While the imminent appearance of Sir Percival and Hiberalta didn't yet seem real, her impending farewell to March felt very real. Tonight would be their last evening alone. Their long journey together was nearly ended. The window had almost closed.

The pain of loss was also very real.

When Lalie awoke, she discovered Yavita had laid out her clothing for dinner. Yawning, she rubbed her eyes then blinked in disbelief. She turned back to the array of ribbons and silks and gasped. The ivory-colored gown she had not purchased gleamed in the sunset rays that slanted through her bedroom window.

Slowly, she slipped out of bed and moved to touch the gown, swallowing a lump in the back of her throat. She didn't know whether to be pleased that March had sent for the gown, or angry that he expected her to wear her wedding gown to dinner with him.

Sighing, she held the dress against her body, surprised at how eager she was to wear something soft and feminine again, and by how easily she gave in to the provocative whisper of silk. Surely she could find another gown for her wedding, she told herself.

Seating herself before a slim vanity mirror, Lalie felt a nervous flutter in her stomach. She dressed her hair and powdered her shoulders. Yavita laced her corset and assisted her into the ivory-colored gown, then they both stepped back to inspect Lalie's reflection in the mirror.

Tonight her hair, piled on top of her head, glowed like spun copper. The tiny puffed sleeves of ivory silk gleamed against her shoulders. The dress was cut low and a delicate webbing of lace curved over her breasts, running to a point where drifts of airy silk blossomed forth like pale petals.

"Do you think he'll—" An explosion of nervous tension agitated her stomach.

"You look beautiful, senhorita." Bending to a tray on the table near the door, Yavita removed a cloth cover and revealed a stunning surprise. "Mr. Addison, he say you wear these tonight."

Lalie gasped and her fingertips flew to her mouth as she stared at a magnificent emerald necklace and earring set.

"He shouldn't . . . no, I, I can't . . ."

Gently Yavita pressed her back onto the chair before the vanity mirror and clasped the necklace around her throat. "Mr. Addison, he say you will protest. He say pay no attention. You wear these tonight. He say you should always wear emeralds." She studied Lalie's white-faced reflection. "Mr. Addison, he right. Emeralds make you eyes look green. Look plenty good with you pretty hair."

Lalie stared at herself in the mirror. It was hard to believe the elegant, bejeweled woman who looked back at her was the same person who had arrived in Tupati, smudged, soiled, and wearing a shapeless cotton shift and heavy jungle boots.

Lifting a trembling hand, she touched the sparkling emeralds at her throat and experienced a dizzying moment of confusion. This was how she had envisioned her wedding night. A leisurely bath followed by careful grooming, a gown of ivory silk, a gift from her beloved followed by an intimate dinner during which they murmured endearments and planned their future together before they . . .

It was happening exactly as she had dreamed it. Except with the wrong man. A man who existed only within a window of time that would soon close forever, leaving her to wonder for the rest of her life.

Suddenly Lalie understood she would never observe a trader steamer without searching for March Addison on its deck. She would never inhale the scent of cigar smoke without being transported back to the sultry nights aboard the *Addison Beal.* She would look for him on the rubber barges that passed Hiberalta; she would seek him on the crowded streets of Manaus. She would long for his company when she read a book she wished to discuss, would gasp his name when something unexpectedly delighted her.

He would be the unsolved mystery in her life because she lacked the courage to live and to experience fully. She would never be able to forget him. For the rest of her life March Addison would occupy her mind as an item of unfinished business. He would be her one regret.

Lalie stared at her image in the mirror. "If I . . . But how could I live with such a secret?" she whispered. Moisture shone in her eyes.

"Did you speak, senhorita?"

"Oh Yavita. What if I'm making a terrible, terrible mistake?" Closing her eyes, Lalie pressed both hands to her breast in an attempt to quell the surge of panic that threatened to choke her. "But it's too late to turn back."

Yavita touched her shoulder with a timid hand. "Mr. Addison, he care for you, senhorita. If you no want dinner with him, is not too late to say. He understand. He wish to please you."

"I didn't mean Mr. Addison, I meant—" She bit off the name.

Her pounding heart told her the choice was between concealing a shameful secret for the rest of her days or facing a lifetime of torturous regret. And she had to decide immediately. Tonight. Before the window closed forever and this magical interlude was lost.

Standing abruptly, she turned away from the vanity mirror, unable to meet her eyes in the glass.

Silver candelabra cast a mellow glow over delicate silver-rimmed china and heavy silver flatware. Small jungle orchids floated in a crystal bowl. The damask-draped table had been placed beside the bubbling courtyard fountain. The scent of jasmine pervaded the air. A million stars shone in the tropical sky, twinkling behind clusters of palm fronds. As if on command, a full moon began its slow rise.

But Lalie saw only March Addison. His dark hair dropped in a wave over his deeply tanned forehead. His cheeks were close shaven and his mustache trimmed to reveal his sensual upper lip. He wore Irish linen so white against his bronzed skin that the contrast dazzled. A snowy cravat was tied above a silver waistcoat. But it was his eyes that halted Lalie's forward step, that stopped her breath in her throat. He stared at her with narrowed, hungry eyes that slowly examined her hair, her throat, the swell of her breasts.

"Good God. Do you have any idea how beautiful you are?" he whispered.

Lalie swallowed and touched her fingertips to the pulse thudding in the hollow of her throat. "The emeralds . . . March, I can't accept them."

"I hoped the emeralds would match your eyes. But the brilliance of your eyes eclipses mere jewels."

"I'll leave them with Yavita," she said weakly.

"The emeralds are yours. If you won't accept them now, I'll post them to your father before we leave tomorrow. They'll be waiting when you return to London to visit."

They stood apart, the moment stretching toward eternity, staring at one another as if to capture and hold this memory against the emptiness ahead. Finally, self-conscious and light-headed, Lalie walked to the fountain, feeling the silk mold her thighs as she moved.

"It's a lovely night," she murmured. The statement was mundane, one she might have made when first they met. But she was suddenly at a loss for conversation. Her throat had dried.

"No lovelier than you," March said from directly behind her. Bending his dark head, he kissed her bare shoulder.

A shudder passed through Lalie's body, and for a moment she surrendered to the weakness that shot from his warm lips through her. Leaning back against him, she closed her eyes and tried to breathe. "March, please. I beg you not to do this. Help me be strong." Her shoulder burned where his lips had pressed, and the intoxicating scent of his cologne clouded her mind.

Powerful hands circled her waist and he held her against him. He spoke near her ear. "I won't force you to do anything you don't want," he promised in a husky whisper. "If I press too far, you have only to say no and I'll respect your wishes." Warm breath flowed across her cheek and shoulder, his lips brushed her earlobe. "But tonight is mine. I won't make decisions for you, and I won't help you."

To test him, Lalie summoned her strength and stepped forward. The instant she moved, he released her. But the circle of heat left by his hands remained on her waist like a manacle. Swallowing with difficulty, aware that her breathing was shallow and rapid, Lalie approached a tray on a serving table beside the fountain. She poured wine into crystal goblets, her fingers shaking. And she left his wine on the silver tray rather than risk touching him again.

Without speaking they strolled the perimeters of the courtyard, passing in and out of the sylvan moonlight, slowly allowing themselves to become intoxicated by the wine, the heavy scent of tropical blossoms, by each other.

"We've come so far," Lalie murmured. As they turned at the end wall of the courtyard, she noticed Yavita emerge from the house bearing trays of food. "Do you remember when we met?" Dropping her gaze, she smiled into her wine glass. "You labeled me stupid and ignorant. Now you offer compliments that would turn the head of any woman."

His smile made her heart skip a beat as he pulled back her chair and seated her at the table. Before he returned to his own seat, he caressed her shoulders and the sides of her throat. "You were ignorant, but never stupid." He gazed at her through the glow of candlelight. "And always you were beautiful."

"I made you angry so many times," she said, trying not to think about his caress.

He laughed. "That you did, my dear Miss Pritchard. Once or twice I considered hurling you overboard."

"There were times when I wanted to throw you overboard too, if I'd thought I could do it."

Silently, moving like a wraith, Yavita refilled their wine glasses then served their dinner.

Lalie smiled. "Do you remember ordering the *pato no tucupi* that first night?"

"It was a dirty trick," he admitted, looking sheepish.

"Which you don't regret for an instant," Lalie accused him, laughing. He grinned, looking wonderfully, impossibly handsome. Although she would always remember him as a hard-muscled river man, his intent dark eyes scanning the river's surface, his powerful thighs braced apart, tonight he was the gentleman. Looking at him, it was difficult to believe he had ever dined from anything but the finest china and the heaviest silver; difficult to imagine him wearing anything but formal linen and impossible to imagine she had ever thought him crude or ill mannered.

Together they remembered the first moment Lalie had glimpsed an anaconda and the incident with the bushmaster. They laughed over the dozens of events that had happened during their time together on the *Addison Beal.*

"And the day we all swam in the lagoon, do you remember?" Lalie asked finally, smiling softly. "It was so hot that day."

"I remember," he said. Pinpoints of candlelight reflected in his dark eyes.

Her stomach tightened and her chest ached. When she looked down she discovered she had hardly eaten a bite. "Oh March," she whispered, raising her eyes to him. "We're saying good-bye, aren't we?"

For a moment he didn't speak, then he touched his cravat and stood. "I have a surprise for you." From behind one of the arches leading into the courtyard, he removed a violin he had placed there earlier.

Lalie's eyes widened. "Where on earth did you find a violin in Tupati?"

Standing in the shadows, not moving his gaze from where she sat in a pool of moonlight, he played Chopin for her. The achingly sweet strains floated through the warm night like a caress, winding around her, enclosing her, speaking to her with a loveliness that raised a lump in her throat. When darkness absorbed the last notes, Lalie discovered her cheeks were wet with tears.

She couldn't speak as he laid the violin aside then bowed before her. "May I have the pleasure of this waltz, Miss Pritchard?"

Smiling around the lump scalding her throat, she stood and gave him her hand. "I would be delighted, Mr. Addison."

For a moment he stood with his hand on her waist, her fingers wrapped in his, looking down at her. And she wondered helplessly if her legs would support her when he stepped forward.

But they moved in perfect accord, dancing as if they had always danced together to a lilting waltz only they could hear. March whirled her over the courtyard tiles, round and around the tinkling fountain. Her skirts billowed behind her, shimmering in the moonlight; her eyes glowed like the emeralds at her throat.

Then suddenly, hungrily, she was in his arms, surrendering to his mouth, his hands, the sweet kisses that plundered her mouth and left her shaking and breathless and unsatisfied. Her trembling hands flew over his face, touched his lips, discovered the strong racing beat of his heart. Her nerves tingled with tension and fire and need.

When she collapsed against him, faint with desire and drunk with kisses, her body aflame, he swept her into his arms. "Say no, Lalie, and it ends here," he said in a hoarse voice. "Tell me this isn't what you want."

But she could not speak. She simply wrapped her arms around his neck and pressed her forehead to his cheek.

"Tell me, Lalie."

"I want you, too," she whispered. "Oh March. I want you, too."

And as he carried her into the house and up the staircase, she understood with a sense of helpless joy that the outcome had never been in doubt. Tonight was as inevitable as the river currents. From the moment they'd met they had been moving inexorably toward each other and this moment.

The balcony doors were open. Gauzy curtains fluttered softly in the moonlight beneath the teasing whisper of a breeze. Drifts of scent rose from the pots of jasmine and the music of falling water splashed in the courtyard below.

March placed her on her feet beside the white coverlet draping the bed. Framing her face between his hands, he kissed her tenderly at first then with mounting passion. His fingers fumbled with the buttons running down her back until she moved to provide easier access, reaching to remove her hairpins as the ivory gown opened down her back.

When he turned her so he could push her sleeves down and guide the ivory silk over her hips, she saw he had removed his jacket and stood before her in his trousers and waistcoat. With bold, shaking fingers, she reached to untie his cravat, letting it drop to the floor along with her gown.

He stared at the hourglass curve of her body clad in a beribboned corset and frothy petticoats. A low groan issued from his throat. With one finger he traced the curve of her breasts swelling above the ribbons, then bent his head and kissed the warm, scented flesh. Lalie gripped his shoulders and swayed, her eyes closing as she moaned softly.

As he opened her lacings, kissing each inch of flesh as it was revealed, she unbuttoned his waistcoat and pushed it off his shoulders, letting it drop to the floor.

He slid her petticoats off her hips, his hands gentle and hot, then he removed his shirt. Moonlight gleamed on his naked shoulders and heavily muscled chest and Lalie sucked in a strangled breath.

His mouth, hot and possessive, claimed her lips and drank deep of the girl she had been and the woman she was about to become. Then as she sat, he knelt beside her and rolled her garter down and off. As he slowly peeled down her stocking, his lips explored her thigh, the back of her knee, her calf, and her ankle. When he sucked her toes into his mouth, Lalie thought she would faint from the force of the explosion that erupted through her body. He did the same to her other leg, stripping it of garter and stocking, licking and tasting her flesh until she felt a scream of urgent longing building in the back of her throat, until her body trembled with shudder after exquisite shudder.

When he stood she gazed at him with shy expectancy, desperate with yearning for whatever would happen next. But he didn't remove her chemise or knickers as she half expected. Instead, he gently guided her onto the bed and stretched out beside her, gathering her into his arms and pressing her firmly against his hard length.

He kissed her deeply, deliberately, before he smoothed her hair back from her face and gazed into her eyes. "We'll go slowly, my dearest. We won't proceed before you're ready, and I'll try not to hurt you."

But the pain he alluded to was the exquisite pain she longed to experience. As he kissed her her heated mind spun in a frenzy of urgency. Arching against him, moaning, she yearned to merge with him into one being, desired the mysteries to open to her and lie revealed.

"Slowly, my sweet love, slowly," he murmured, bending over her to kiss her eyelids, her lips, the pulse that thudded wildly in her throat. With tormenting deliberation his hand stroked upward from her waist to cup the breast that strained against his chest. The sudden heat of his palm wrested a cry from her lips, her voice a sob of longing. Her nipple stiffened into a small pink stone, thrusting against the thin material of her chemise. And it was she who tore off her chemise so his lips could suckle her naked breasts.

He groaned when his tongue, hot and slightly rough, encircled her nipple, teasing her until she cried out in frustration and buried her hands in his thick hair. He sucked her nipple into his mouth and stroked it with his tongue. And while he made love to her breasts, his hand curved over her hip, across her tight lower stomach, then skillfully stroked between her legs until she wanted to scream in pleasure and desire.

All shame forgotten, modesty burned away in a blaze of need, Lalie reached for the buttons on his trousers and began to open them.

"Lalie," he murmured, his voice hoarse with passion. "Oh God, Lalie." Helping her, he ripped open his trousers and threw them off, then drew her knickers down her hips and legs. For a moment he leaned over her, staring at her. She was naked except for the sparkle of emeralds, except for the dew of perspiration glistening in the pale moonlight. "You are so beautiful," he moaned.

Almost with awe, he brushed his palm across the auburn triangle between her thighs and she strained upward against his hand, writhing beneath his gaze and his touch, desiring him to the exclusion of all other thought.

Her mind narrowed to the urgent demands of her wakened body. Liquid heat scalded her, burned on her skin. A terrible, wonderful tension drew her body tight. She ached for relief and believed if he didn't come to her immediately she would surely die.

And then finally he was guiding her thighs apart. He moved slowly, gently, as if eternity belonged to them, touching her, checking her with fingers that scorched and enflamed.

"Now!" she gasped, thrashing beneath him, her hands flying over his chest, his shoulders. "Please now, please, please, March. Oh March!"

Blindly, she reached and found him, heard him suck in a sharp breath when her fingers clasped his rigid thickness, and with a cry of joy she guided him into her.

For an instant there was pain, a sharp, piercing pain, swiftly followed by sweet, savage ecstasy such as she had never dreamed could exist. Her fingers gripped his shoulders and her throat arched backward under his kisses. Her hips moved with his, giving and seeking the pleasures of a mystery now revealed.

"Did I hurt you?" he murmured hoarsely against her lips.

"Don't stop," she whispered mindlessly, wrapping her arms around his neck, holding him tightly so she could feel his heart beat against her swollen breasts. "Oh March, don't stop. I feel . . . I feel . . ."

As if he understood her incoherent cries, he increased the pace of his thrusts, faster, deeper, until she felt the tension swirl in her body, gathering, building, building, and finally erupting in a gasping, euphoric explosion. It seemed to her that her universe contracted then erupted outward again in waves of blissful release.

When her eyes fluttered open, he was smiling down at her, smoothing strands of wet hair away from her cheeks.

"Is it always like that?" Lalie whispered, lifting shaking fingertips to trace his lips. Her eyes were radiant. "Is it always that wonderful?"

He laughed softly then stretched beside her, his darkly tanned skin a stunning contrast against the white sheets. He stroked her body lightly. "Kiss me, Lalie."

She came into his arms willingly, languorously. She held his head between her hands and covered his face with soft kisses. She kissed his eyelids, the corner of his lips, his jaw, his throat; she buried her lips in the hair on his chest and traced his scars with the tip of her tongue.

And she saw the stirring her kisses aroused and dared to take him in her hand. She marveled as he grew and swelled against her palm. First she was amazed then lost in fresh waves of passion when he guided her atop and then onto him, rocking her hips between his powerful hands.

Afterward they dozed then drank champagne in bed, offering their naked bodies to the warm breeze that meandered past the balcony doors. They stared deeply into one another's eyes and leisurely explored one another's bodies with awe and wonder and quickening desire. And March showed her aspects of lovemaking she hadn't dreamed of, awakened her to raptures that left her weak and shaking and gasping his name.

Toward dawn, Lalie slipped from his arms and stood beside the gauze curtains at the balcony door, smiling softly at a light rain. The world was green in the pale dawn, the rain like sparkling drops of emerald. Lalie touched the gems at her throat and ears and knew she would never again see or think about emeralds without remembering this night of ecstasy.

"Lalie? Come back to me."

Smiling, she returned to the bed and they lay in each other's arms, gloriously exhausted but not wanting the night to end. March gathered her close to him and pillowed her head on his shoulder.

"I love you," he said quietly, resting his cheek against the top of her tousled head. "I ask nothing from you, expect nothing. Tonight is an interlude in your life, that's all it was intended to be and all it can be. A window that opened for a time then closed. You will continue with the life you have chosen, and I accept that."

She stiffened in his arms, but said nothing. Tears welled in her eyes and she turned her face against his chest.

"But for me, you are more than an interlude. You are a miracle I never expected to happen. I can't close this window, Lalie. I love you. I always will. The only way I can give you to Sterling is knowing he's what you truly want and that you're happy."

"Oh March, I—"

"No, don't speak. There's nothing you can say that wouldn't be painful to one of us." He tilted her face toward his and kissed her. "Now lie still, my darling, and let me love you. Let me say good-bye to you in my own way."

This time when he made love to her, slowly and with exquisite beauty and tenderness, Lalie wept in his arms.

Chapter 18

Lalie covered her eyes when Yavita opened the bedroom curtains to a burst of sunshine. Outside on the balcony rail, a flock of multicolored parrots squawked and quarreled. A steamer's whistle called from the river. Yawning, Lalie sat up, noticing the sun had risen well above the morning horizon. She also noticed her new clothing had been packed and was waiting in the portmanteau beside her door.

"Mr. Addison, he go to the docks. He say Fredo bring you when you ready," Yavita murmured, placing a breakfast tray across Lalie's lap after mounding the pillows behind her.

After Yavita withdrew, Lalie set the tray aside, taking only a cup of strong Brazilian coffee. Her hands trembled as she raised the cup to her bruised lips.

In the blaze of clear morning sunlight, the night of passion she had shared with March seemed distant and dreamlike. Except it wasn't a dream. A tiny moan tightened her throat as she remembered his skilled hands caressing her, his mouth exploring her breasts, her thighs, teasing her very center.

Almost dropping the coffee cup, Lalie returned it to the tray then covered her face with her hands. What had she done? She'd been a fool to believe the window would close and then she would forget March and blithely go on with her life. Windows were made of glass. Always she would see through the panes to a night of splendor and magic, a night of fulfillment more intense than she had thought possible.

A night of blinding betrayal.

Twisting on the bed, she pushed her face into the pillows and groaned. How could she face Percival, knowing she had betrayed him mere hours before arriving at Hiberalta as his bride? How could she have done such a thing? She who tried to live her life with honor? She had made a mockery of honor.

And yet—and the knowledge devastated her—she regretted nothing. In her heart she knew she would rather carry the burden of betrayal than have denied herself March Addison's love. Not to have known his body and his passion would have opened a void inside her that would have lasted the rest of her days.

And he loved her. Confusion and misery created havoc in her heart. At a time when she should have been joyously happy, bewildered tears brimmed in her eyes. March Addison loved her.

More troubled and confused than at any point in her life, Lalie climbed out of bed and attempted to focus on the impending reunion with the man she had chosen to be her husband. If only he had never received her letter. Because he had, she was left with no choice but to continue to Hiberalta.

March leaned on the wheel of the boat he had rented, watching as Fredo helped Lalie out of a mule-drawn cart.

She wore the puffed blouse and dark skirt she had worn aboard the *Raider*, primly covered from throat to ankles. Today she wore her magnificent hair pulled severely away from her face and twisted into a knot on her neck. The wide-brimmed straw hat was one of several they had purchased the day before.

"Good morning, Miss Pritchard." Extending his hand, he assisted her on board the boat. "Watch your step, please."

Although it was difficult, he kept his tone politely distant and betrayed no hint of intimacy. He would keep his word. The window had closed; he would not embarrass her by referring to the fiery passion that continued to rage in his blood.

"Thank you," she murmured. Like his, her tone remained carefully expressionless. But crimson burned on her cheeks and she turned her face away after taking the seat he indicated.

"It's ten o'clock," he said, consulting his pocket watch. "I estimate we'll put in to Hiberalta near three. Yavita sent a basket if you feel hungry, and there's champagne if you're thirsty." For one blinding instant he remembered licking droplets of champagne from between her rose-tipped breasts. "Cast off, Fredo," he commanded abruptly.

Taking a position in the bow, he made himself stay there, keeping his back turned to her. But he sensed her presence; he could still taste her and feel the lush imprint of her body on his.

"Watch out for that log," he snarled.

"I see it, Cabo," Fredo replied calmly. He didn't look at March. "And I see the rapids ahead to the left. And the rubber barge coming toward us."

March released a breath and wiped the sweat from his brow. The humidity overhanging the river was as thick as the relentless heat. "I'm sorry."

Fredo shrugged but didn't take his eyes from the rippling green surface of the water. "We stay long at Hiberalta, Cabo?"

March scowled at the sunshine bouncing off the river, his fists clenching and unclenching. "No more than a week, probably less. If we haven't found Tilwe's people by then, we won't find them."

Fredo's dark eyes glanced toward him. "Someone going to slit Sterling's throat one day . . ."

"Not us," March said at length. The reply was long in coming, but he spoke with quiet firmness. "Sterling is the man she wants," he added softly.

"Maybe," Fredo said, lighting a short cigar with one hand.

He glanced at Fredo's walnut-dark face, then turned toward the lacy foliage overhanging the banks of the Yaki.

He had believed one night with Lalie would slake his passion and satisfy his need for her. But he was wrong. She burned like a fever in his blood. He was like a man dying of thirst who discovered one swallow—no matter how sweet—was not enough. He suspected he would never have enough of her; he would still desire and need her years from now.

When March turned again, he discovered she was watching him and moisture glistened in her splendid eyes. Tears of regret? Tears of anger? Sadness? Her expression revealed nothing.

Because he had given his word to cause her no complications, he tipped his hat then turned back to the river.

No one ever truly adjusted to the heat and humidity smothering the Amazon basin. By the time Hiberalta came into view, Lalie felt limp and damp, numbed by the brutality of the sun and the hours on the river. For most of the voyage she had welcomed the numbness, believing it the only thing that prevented her from leaping up and throwing herself into March's arms.

Now she twisted in her seat and, with pounding heart, strained to inspect Hiberalta as it gradually appeared in front of the boat.

Her heart thudded against her corset stays then dipped toward her toes.

As had happened when she'd arrived at so many of the river settlements, she smelled Hiberalta before the boat approached its graying docks. The sulfurous smell of rubber pervaded every breath, but beneath the wild rubber drifted the stink of burning garbage and smoke from a section of forest being cleared to the north of the compound.

As the boat closed the distance to the dock, Lalie examined a collection of thatch huts arranged around a patch of raw red earth that someone had tried to plant with palms and shrubs. The palms were a sickly yellow, dying in the heat. What leaves remained on the shrubs had curled and turned brown.

The main house could be termed a mansion only in comparison to the sagging buildings that surrounded it. The large rectangular building was, as March had said, roofed with thatch. A covered veranda circled both stories. The windows on the lower floor were glassed, but the upper-story windows were open to the air and closed with shutters during storms.

Lalie gasped and her heart lurched as a man appeared on the lower veranda at the sound of the approaching boat. When he stepped off the stairs and the sun struck his golden hair, she recognized Sir Percival Sterling.

She watched him with wide eyes, her mind blank, until the boat drifted toward the dock and Percival, who stood on higher ground, was lost to view. But three men carrying rifles stepped onto the dock.

"Addison? We thought it was you," one of them said. He shifted his cigar to the other side of his mouth. "You got no business here."

March threw out a rope. "Tell Percy I've brought his bride." His dark eyes narrowed on the men. "Move, gentlemen."

They studied March with unblinking stares, then examined Lalie. Finally one of them climbed the slope toward the compound.

Heart pounding, Lalie accepted Fredo's assistance to the dock while March secured the boat then placed her portmanteau near her feet.

Suddenly she realized this was the end. But there were so many things they had left unsaid. "March—"

"What the hell are you doing on my property, Addison?"

Whirling, Lalie shaded her eyes and stared up the slope. Relief flooded her mind as she realized Percival Sterling had not changed. He was still tanned and golden, with pale, cool eyes and clean-shaven skin. His nose was thin and aristocratic, his mouth full and poetic. He wore full business dress despite the blistering heat that left his dark suit rumpled and wrinkled. It was an odd first thought, but it struck Lalie that Percival's attire would have been faultless in London but bordered on ridiculous here. Surely he would have felt more comfortable dressed as March was, in light trousers and opened shirt.

Then Percival saw her and his eyes shone. "Lalie!"

Hurrying, he rushed to the dock and clasped both her hands in his. He was too much the gentleman to kiss or embrace her, for which she was grateful, but his expression proclaimed his pleasure. "I'm delighted that you've finally arrived." He glanced at March. "But I expected Gunter to be with you."

"It's a long story," she murmured, acutely aware that March was watching her intently. Stepping back, she waved a hand, including him in the reunion. "I'm deeply indebted to Mr. Addison. Without his assistance I would never have reached Hiberalta."

For several seconds Percival and March studied each other. "I see," Percival said finally. He jerked his head at one of his men. "Jose, go up to the house and prepare for our guests. You know what I mean." Taking Lalie's hand, he wrapped it around his arm, pressing her close to him. But he continued to return March's steady stare. "It appears I am also in your debt for making this happy day possible. I hope you'll accept the full range of Hiberalta's hospitality for as long as you wish to stay." The invitation was stiff and grudging, accompanied by an undisguised hope of refusal.

"I accept your invitation with pleasure," March answered between his teeth. "A week of rest and refreshment will be welcome."

Lalie bit her lip and fixed her gaze on the garbage-littered slope before her. It was Percival's body her arm rested against, but it was March to whom she responded, feeling his gaze on the back of her neck. She sensed his mood, felt his anger as a tangible force. In a dismaying complication she had not foreseen, she experienced a sting of betrayal that she stood by Percival's side and not March's. A headache instigated by confusion and heat pounded behind her temples.

"My dearest, you're trembling," Percival said, bending to peer beneath the brim of her hat. "But I'm being thoughtless. We need to move you inside out of the sun."

They passed the palms dying in the center of the compound just as a woman's angry scream sounded from within the house. Halting, Lalie's grip tightened on Percival's arm and she then turned to him in consternation.

Percival's free hand moved in a gesture of indifference and dismissal. "It's nothing, my dear. Only a maid. Don't be concerned." His eyes swept her face in a way that had thrilled her in London. Then she had looked at him and had seen romance and faraway places. Now . . .

Lalie dropped her head and felt a blush rise on her cheeks. She glanced at March's thinned lips then quickly looked away. But not before she noticed his dark, vivid coloring made Percival's pale features seem faded and diminished by comparison. Biting her lips, she hurried forward.

The interior of the house was dim and almost cool. Percival led Lalie and March into a large parlor crowded with heavy furniture. For an instant Lalie could have believed she had been transported home to England. Overstuffed chairs flanked an upholstered sofa, scarves and bibelots and silver-framed portraits crowded every surface. Tasseled lamp shades ornamented the lanterns, Turkish carpets decorated the floor. Feeling slightly overwhelmed, Lalie seated herself on the sofa.

Percival rang for champagne, which was served by a white-coated Indian man who dragged one foot in a limp.

Staring at Lalie as if she were a vision that might disappear if he looked away, Percival raised his glass. "To my future bride. You have made me the envy of all men."

Lalie couldn't speak, was afraid she could not swallow. March's eyes burned on her like dark twin suns. Never in her life had she believed she would one day be sitting in a room with her lover and her future husband. The thought devastated her. She didn't know which man to look at, so she dropped her gaze to her lap and felt a blush of confusion and shame flare on her cheeks.

Percival smiled. "To the future Lady Sterling."

When Lalie reluctantly raised her eyes, March was staring at her. He lifted his glass and drank. Something deep inside twisted and Lalie looked at him in a plea for . . . for what? Understanding? Forgiveness? She didn't know.

But Percival saw the exchange and he scowled. "Perhaps you'll be good enough to explain under what circumstances you chose Mr. Addison to carry you upriver."

Lalie heard the disapproval and controlled anger beneath his tone. Drawing a breath, she related her story in a halting voice that steadied as she progressed.

"So you see, I didn't exaggerate when I stated my debt to Mr. Addison," she finished, noting the sky was streaked with sunset color. The telling had taken longer than she realized. "Mr. Addison has seen to my welfare from the beginning and has borne all my expenses. I'm indebted to him even for my clothing." Hastily she reminded Percival that her trousseau had been dispatched to Pará through a misunderstanding.

Percival turned a speculative gaze on March. "Naturally I shall reimburse you for Miss Pritchard's expenses."

"That won't be necessary," March said, watching Lalie.

"I insist," Percival stated coldly. "You may present an invoice or I'll estimate the amount. In either case, my estate manager will have a bank draft ready for you by morning."

Standing abruptly, Lalie made a fluttery gesture toward the parlor door. "I . . . I wonder if I might be shown to my room before dinner . . ."

She couldn't bear to remain in the same room with March and Percival for another minute. She could not glance at March without recalling the rapture they had shared. And she couldn't look at Percival without bowing her head beneath the weight of her betrayal. Moreover, the men's mutual dislike thickened the air; their statements to each other were barely civil.

"Of course." Percival jumped to his feet and rang the servants' bell. Taking her arm, he guided her to the door, then in full view of March and before Lalie could guess his intention, he pulled her to him and kissed her passionately on the mouth as if they were lovers of long standing.

"I'm so glad you've come, my dearest Lalie."

When he released her, Lalie stumbled backward, her eyes wide with shock, her face white.

In the last weeks and months she had realized there was much about Percival Sterling that she did not know. But she did know his manners were impeccable. This kiss was an inexplicable departure, a stunning lapse of proper behavior.

"You belong to me now," he said, smiling tenderly at her expression. And suddenly Lalie suspected the kiss had been for March's benefit more than her own. "I will attend to your welfare now, and I will bear your expenses."

Lifting a hand, he touched his fingertips to her pale cheek. "From now on you will depend solely on me. I shall not fail you, my dear."

The tender assurance stabbed her with guilt.

Spinning, Lalie caught up her skirts and almost ran up the staircase.

March lit a cigar and moved to stand in front of the parlor window. If he didn't leave this house in the next few minutes, the chances were excellent that he would smash his fist into Percival's arrogant face. God knew he wanted to.

From this vantage he could see the business office across the compound, part of the barracks, one of the rubber warehouses, and a portion of the dock. He could not see the labor camp, though he could smell the stink of it through the opened windows.

Having been to Hiberalta before, he knew the labor camp was located in the jungle about half a mile from the main compound. And he knew what he would find there, the holding pens, the whipping posts, the squalor.

"All right, Addison," Percival said from behind him. "I want the truth. If you laid a hand on my property, I'll kill you."

March turned from the window and clamped his teeth on the cigar. "If you mean Miss Pritchard, I suggest you ask her if I've given cause for offense."

Percival set aside his champagne and poured a tumbler of *cachaça* from a decanter on the serving cart. "Don't tell me you kept your hands off her," he said, sneering. "She's a stunningly beautiful woman."

"If you believe I forced myself on Miss Pritchard, then I invite you to step outside right now." March's eyes narrowed in a challenge.

Percival's smile was slow and insulting. "You tried and she refused you, didn't she?"

March ground his teeth. "Miss Pritchard deserves better than to have her honor sullied with your accusations."

"You surprise me. Am I to conclude you've raised your sights since last we met? You're defending ladies now instead of whores?"

March reminded himself that Sterling was his host. He couldn't rescue Tilwe's people if he were ordered out of Hiberalta. "There's something Miss Pritchard neglected to mention regarding Rivaldi's arrangements for the final portion of her journey. Rivaldi sent you a message."

"What message?"

In a few short sentences, March related the incident with Lum Sarto and the *Raider*. "Rivaldi said an eye for eye, Sterling. Your indiscreet dalliance with Truda Rivaldi damned near got your future bride raped and beaten."

Percival touched his tie and shrugged. "Rivaldi can be managed; I'll take care of him. And you know Truda. Is there any man in the Amazon basin for whom she hasn't spread her legs?"

"I can think of one."

"You sanctimonious son of a bitch. Someday you and I will settle our differences once and for all, Addison."

March watched his cigar smoke drift through the window. "Word has it your men are running slaving expeditions as far downriver as Santarém. I have reason to believe you stole men from a village of friendlies. They were taken aboard a steamer displaying the rose and the stag."

"What of it?" Percival tossed back his *cachaça*. "Labor is becoming harder to find."

"I'm not leaving Hiberalta until I've made a thorough search. If Tilwe's people are here—I'm taking them."

Percival smiled, his expression mixing a blend of slyness and calculation. "You'll *buy* them, you mean." He shrugged again. "If you find the savages you're seeking, I might let you have them. For a price."

"Agreed."

Percival watched him stride toward the door. "You and your man can sleep in the barracks and take your meals there. You've got five days to finish your business, no more. Then I want you off my property."

March paused to glance up the staircase and imagined a lingering hint of lilac and verbena. Swearing under his breath, he strode out of the house.

Lalie was both relieved and disappointed to discover March would not join them for dinner. Surprising herself with an attack of timidity, she entered the dining room with a hesitant step and discovered the candlelit room as crowded with oppressively heavy furniture as the parlor. The long table and sideboard were carved from dark, heavy wood, as were the tapestry-covered chairs. The windows had been closed against the nightly invasion of insects. As a result, the room was stiflingly hot.

Percival stepped out of the shadows near the sideboard, and Lalie recognized immediately that none of the gowns she had purchased in Tupati were elegant enough for dinner at Hiberalta. Percival wore full formal attire as if they were dining in London prior to attending a ball. Smoothing her palms over the skirt of a cool muslin gown, she blushed and murmured an apology.

"Your beauty transcends your apparel, my dear," Percival said. But she noticed a flicker of disapproval. "We'll acquire proper attire for you when we return to Manaus."

"Do you dress for dinner every evening?" she inquired as he seated her, his hands brushing her shoulders.

One pale eyebrow rose in surprise. "Of course. Naturally we do our best to uphold standards." Lalie felt another flush of heat infuse her cheeks. "It appears we have a great deal to discuss, my dear."

"I realize there were gaps in my story—"

"And eventually I want to hear a full account." He snapped his fingers and the white-coated man with the limp hastened forward to fill their wine glasses. "But I was referring to *our* plans." Another snap of his fingers brought a man scurrying from the serving pantry. He placed steaming bowls of turtle soup before them. "Unfortunately, Father Franklin is downriver assisting at an outbreak of yellow fever. He isn't expected back for several weeks."

Lalie was so nervous she found it difficult to swallow. "Father Franklin's absence may be fortunate." It was dismaying to be thrust into wedding plans so quickly. "A delay will provide us an opportunity to become reacquainted before we . . . It's been nearly eight months since we've seen each other, Percival. I do think we need some time together." Giving up, she set down her spoon and abandoned the effort to eat. "Forgive me for speaking so bluntly, but . . . I've assumed a great deal coming to you as I have. Is it possible your intentions have altered?"

The moment she asked the question, Lalie understood the truth. She hoped he would admit he no longer wished to wed her.

Whatever she had once loved in him, she could not find it now. As she recalled, his manners—except for the kiss in the foyer—were faultless. And he was as handsome as she remembered. But now she suspected his protectiveness would be smothering instead of thrilling. The elegance she had loved seemed slightly foolish here, his wit more self-serving than she remembered.

The thought of sharing this stranger's bed sent a wave of panic through her mind.

"I shall speak as bluntly as you," he said, studying her face. "After receiving your letter, I asked myself that very question. And the answer is no, my dearest, my intentions have not altered." Candlelight washed all color from his eyes and Lalie had the unnerving impression that his irises had melted in the night heat. "I care for you, Lalie. I believe we can be happy together."

Guilt bowed her head. He was so earnest; his voice so

tender. "People will say you married beneath yourself. Out of your class," she whispered.

"I believe you'll perform brilliantly as Lady Sterling and give no cause for complaint." He shrugged. "As long as we're speaking frankly, I'll remind you that with a large enough fortune, my dearest, one can marry whomever one chooses and the rest of the world must accept one's choice." Smiling, he sliced into his *tucunaré* steak. "I rather prefer it that you're innocent of society. I shall have the great pleasure of corrupting you myself."

Lalie returned his smile, but it was an odd joke. When she thought of Truda and Gunter, she couldn't be certain it was a joke at all. Her smile faltered.

Percival talked through dinner, through coffee, and throughout the stroll they took afterward, circling the dying palms in the center of the compound that he referred to as the plaza. He spoke of the fortune he was amassing, of the esteem he had earned in the Amazon. He told her of the palace he was building in Manaus, expanded on the unblemished future of rubber. He spoke of powerful friends and his own considerable influence.

Not once did he solicit Lalie's opinion. With a shock of recognition, she realized he had not solicited her opinion in London, either. She had been so dazzled by his golden good looks and his exotic background that she had failed to notice. But she had been a different person then, too unsure of herself to readily voice her thoughts or to notice that her opinions went unrequested. She had been content for Percival to speak for them both and to make all decisions. She had viewed his instinct to do so as a strength.

He waved a hand to encompass all of Hiberalta, which he smilingly referred to as his kingdom, then identified the buildings for her, all but a small house standing near the barracks. "You'll meet Mr. Jonpesson, my estate manager, and the rest of the management staff over the next week," he informed her.

"Are there any women living here with whom I might anticipate a friendship?"

"Jonpesson's wife is hardly in our class, my dear. You won't wish to spend more time with her than duty requires." He patted Lalie's gloved hand and his fingers accidentally brushed against her breast. "You'll be quite occupied running the house and entertaining when business associates stop at Hiberalta."

"Percival—I noticed all the servants are Indians." She drew a breath. "They look miserable."

He frowned angrily. "I was wondering if Addison had infected you with his radical ideas." Stopping, he turned to face her. "Rabble-rousers like March Addison erroneously believe the savages are people like you and me. Believe me, they are not. They are beasts. Filthy, deceitful, lying, stealing animals! You can beat them to death before they will turn a decent day's work. They run off the minute the overseer's back is turned. They don't respect their betters. They don't respect themselves! Listen to me, Eulalie. I will not tolerate any softness toward the savages. You may think you're displaying a warm heart and womanly virtues by exhibiting pity, but I assure you that you will only contribute to their laziness by exercising any misguided sympathy. The savages require a firm hand and a regular taste of the lash."

She stared at him. "Can you really believe that?"

"And you will, too."

It was a command. "Some of the Indians," she said, choosing her words with care, "may have been taken from their villages against their will. In such circumstances, it seems reasonable to suppose they might attempt to escape. They might resent tasks that seem alien or pointless to their way of life."

"It seems more reasonable to suppose a thinking creature would accept his situation and labor to please his captor, does it not? Self-interest alone should propel the savages to learn new tasks to avoid punishment. One would think so, but human logic is not applicable to the jungle beasts."

"The woman who brought my tea . . . she seemed so sad." Lalie bit her lower lip. "So downtrodden and sad."

Dropping his hands from her shoulders, he took her arm and resumed walking. "You'll learn. When you try to keep a clean house, when your scones arrive with teeth marks in them or missing entirely, when your jewelry is stolen, you'll learn." Lifting an arm, he pointed toward the distant glow of pit fires. "That's the labor camp. I don't want you going there, Eulalie. Spare us both any misguided ideas of the lady of the manor distributing charity or largess. The savages are unworthy of your concern."

They returned to the house without further conversation. Lalie overheard shouts and coarse laughter rising from the barracks. Someone played a piano inside the Jonpessons' residence. A low roar sounded from the nearby jungle followed by the shrieking of monkeys.

At the foot of the veranda steps, Lalie paused beside one of the smudge pots wafting black smoke to drive away the mosquitoes. Turning aside from Percival, she scanned the moon-washed plaza.

The small house in Tupati seemed a million miles away.

"What reason did Mr. Addison give for not joining us at dinner?" she asked in a low voice.

"He was not invited." Lalie heard the scrape of a match then inhaled the scent of Percival's cigar. Oddly, cigar smoke had again become unpleasant. "I don't hold you to blame for engaging March Addison to carry you upriver," Percival said. But his tone suggested otherwise. "Clearly you had no true grasp of Addison's lack of character. But it must be obvious to you now that March Addison is not our kind."

"And the Rivaldis are?"

"Exactly," he agreed in an approving tone. A brief hesitation preceded his next words. "I understand some fence-mending is necessary with Gunter. But whatever reason Addison may have suggested for our current misunderstanding is a lie. My differences with Gunter Rivaldi are strictly of a business nature. The melodramatic nonsense relating to the *Raider* was entirely unnecessary." He made a sound of disgust. "I assure you, you were never in any danger whatsoever. As usual Addison exaggerated and exploited a situation to make himself appear heroic. I trust you saw through his ploy once you recovered from the peril he induced you to believe you faced."

"Those were terrible men, Percival," Lalie insisted quietly. "They meant to—harm—me. And I believe they had Gunter Rivaldi's permission if not his instruction to do so."

Percival dismissed her words with a gesture and a patronizing smile. "Your imagination may have led you to believe so, but you were quite mistaken, my dear. And I'm sure you'll agree we mustn't speak poorly of our friends the Rivaldis. You yourself related that Gunter instructed Captain Sarto to treat you as he would treat his own daughter. I fear you do Gunter grave injustice to imply he wished you ill."

The moonlight turned his hair to burnished gold. Lalie remembered a sleigh ride across the snowy back roads of Hackney when he had removed his hat and moonlight had lit his hair as it did at this moment. She had felt her heart race and had thought him as handsome as a fairy-tale prince.

With all her despairing heart Lalie wished she could view him the same way now.

"Sherry, my dear?" he asked, waving his hand toward the steps.

"Thank you, but I believe I'll retire." The hours alone with him had left her confused and upset. A dozen dismaying thoughts spun through her mind, not the least of which was her resentment at his insistence on dictating how she would think. That he had probably always done so only added to her dismay.

Before she could anticipate his intentions, Percival awkwardly drew her against his body. As she opened her lips to speak, his mouth came down over hers in an eager kiss that bruised her lips. In a startling display of intimacy, his hands cupped her buttocks and crushed her body against his.

When he released her, Lalie stumbled back from him. "Please, Percival, it's too soon," she whispered. "I need time; we hardly know each other. Please don't rush me." Six months ago she would not have believed he would be so insensitive.

He took her hand between his and gazed down at her. "You didn't travel thousands of miles to be ignored," he said in a thick voice. "We're going to be married. It's not as if my intentions are in question. I'm not dallying with you, Lalie."

She turned her face aside when he tried to kiss her again. For a moment of panic she worried that he wouldn't release her, but he did. Feeling the worst of hypocrites, feeling like a low cheat, she drew a breath then said, "But we're not married yet . . . Please, grant us time for a mutual affection to take root and grow."

Whirling, she ran upstairs and shut her bedroom door behind her. For a moment she stood against it, listening to the thud of her heart. As she had returned unexpectedly, no lamp was lit and she was glad. Moving almost in a trance, she walked to the window and stared out at the moonlit night.

"What have I done?" she murmured helplessly.

Drawing a handkerchief from her sleeve, she pressed it to her eyelids, then blinked hard, clearing the moisture from her eyes in time to see Percival stride across the plaza toward the small house he had not identified. He mounted the porch steps and opened the door without rapping. For an instant Lalie glimpsed a woman's form then the door closed.

She raised swimming eyes to the velvety night sky and thought of moonlit waltzes, of hearts and minds of one accord.

"Oh March," she whispered. Then she buried her face in her hands.

March and Fredo stood at the fringe of the jungle watching as the labor camp settled for the night. The stench of open sewer trenches and rotting garbage was almost unbearable. They had already inspected the punishment pens and found men squeezed into small boxes that prohibited them from standing or sitting. They squatted in an agonizingly cramped position, their eyes as dead as they wished themselves to be. One man hung unconscious from the whipping post, his back in bloody tatters.

For all that, the conditions at Hiberalta were not as horrifying as the conditions in other camps that March had observed. He and Fredo had searched behind Sterling's labor camp for the infamous Amazon body pits without finding one. They located a shockingly large cemetery, but at least the laborers weren't tossed into an open lime pit when they died.

The workers' food was also better than March had observed at many rubber estates. He had expected the meat to be half-rotted and wormy, and it was, but the quantity of manioc cake and farinha exceeded the rations he had expected. The camp also received fruits and vegetables too small or spoiled to be of use in the main house. The laborers could purchase manioc beer or *cachaça* at an exorbitant price, the sum added to their credit account before they were locked into windowless barracks for the night.

Few of the Indian laborers appeared extremely malnourished, but none were fully healthy. Exhaustion wiped their eyes of expression. Symptoms of disease were readily evident. Most bore the scars of lash marks across their backs. Many were mutilated in some manner, missing one ear or both, breathing through slit noses, or showing scars and scabs on limbs and torsos.

"I saw Tomli, one of Tilwe's men," Fredo revealed in a low voice. He drew on his cigar and watched the sparks shooting from the chimney of one of the twenty-four-hour smokehouses. The sulfurous stink of congealing rubber permeated the night.

March nodded. "If we point him out now, he'll disappear before we've located the others." Despite Percival's apparent acquiescence, March was certain it would not be easy to take Tilwe's people out of Hiberalta.

Together he and Fredo turned onto the path leading to the barracks in the main compound. They would sleep lightly tonight, their weapons in the hammocks beside them.

Before they reached the barracks, they passed a small house set back from the other residences. March overheard a man and woman arguing; the voices were familiar though he couldn't place them. A woman's sobs followed the sound of a heavy slap.

Neither he nor Fredo spoke. When they emerged into the central clearing, March glanced toward the main house. Light spilled over the smudge pots smoking on the veranda but the upper story was dark. He scanned the windows, then flung his cigar into the jungle.

Swearing softly, wanting to hit someone, he strode toward the barracks and a sleepless night.

Chapter 19

In the morning Percival rearranged his schedule and conducted Lalie on a mounted tour of the nearest *seringal.* She was able to see for herself how the milky latex was collected from widely scattered hevea trees. March had not exaggerated. Collecting the latex, carrying it for miles through dense jungle growth, smoking the heavy balls over a slow-burning palm fire was tedious, grueling labor.

Twice they passed *seringueiros* in the jungle, carrying fifty-pound balls of rubber on their backs, staggering toward the compound and the warehouses where the balls would be inspected and weighed. The unwieldy lumps of raw rubber reminded Lalie of giant black wasp's nests.

Percival pulled his horse into a shaft of sunlight beside Lalie's mare and directed her attention to a graceful ashen-barked tree. Angled slashes scarred the trunk along which a creamy sap dripped down into a tin bucket. As they watched, a man who was bleeding from infected insect bites changed the buckets. After attaching the filled tin to one end of his shoulder yoke, he tottered backward a step then righted himself and set off through the jungle.

"Usually the rubber is referred to as black gold," Percival explained. "But I think of it as white gold, like the sap."

Biting her lip, Lalie gazed at the ferns and dense undergrowth through which the *seringueiro* had vanished. "That man requires medical attention."

"I beg your pardon?" Percival blinked at her with a genuine lack of comprehension. He had no idea what she referred to. He hadn't even noticed the *seringueiro.* When Lalie described the man's oozing sores, he smiled. "Spoken like a true doctor's daughter. He can purchase salves and unguents at Hiberalta's general store if he feels he needs them. Most likely the sores don't trouble him much."

It was inconceivable that anyone could dismiss another man's misery in so offhand a manner. Lalie began to grasp the reasons behind her father's opposition to Percival's suit. Her father had seen dark truths she had been too moonstruck to notice.

After they returned to Hiberalta and finished a light midday repast, Lalie asked to visit the compound's general store. Her request amused Percival. Teasing her about wishing to shop so soon after her arrival, he waited for her to fetch a parasol then accompanied her to a building near the warehouses.

Inside Lalie saw bins of cooking utensils, iron hatchets, axes, sewing kits, candles and matches, tobacco, crates of *cachaça,* and shelves of ointments and liniments. The outrageously exorbitant prices shocked her.

"But this small jar of ointment costs twenty times what it would cost in Tupati!"

The proprietor, a giant sausage of a man named Mr. Leo, leaned on the countertop and winked at Sir Percival. "We have to make a profit, now don't we, ma'am?"

"But—" Distress darkened her eyes. "How can the laborers afford any of this?" She waved at sacks of insect-infested manioc flour that were priced as dear as gold. The cheapest item in the store was *cachaça,* and it too was priced several times higher than it could be purchased in any of the river settlements.

"Well now, that isn't our problem, is it?" Mr. Leo smiled, exposing crooked, yellowing teeth. "It should ease your heart, ma'am, to know we give the little bastards credit when they need it." One fat finger tapped a thick sheaf of credit slips. "Sir Percival's generosity is legendary. Why, some of them monkeys are in so deep they won't receive a pay envelope for years. That's how far the boss is willing to lend a helping hand. Yes, sir."

He and Sir Percival exchanged a smile.

Lalie marched out of the general store and snapped open her parasol. Anger gleamed in her eyes, and she managed to control it only with difficulty. "Do I understand correctly? The *seringueiros* must purchase their own tools to harvest your rubber, and their own food and supplies to sustain them while they do it? And these items must be purchased at Hiberalta's store at prices so extreme you must extend them credit that they have little hope of repaying? In effect, your labor force costs no more than a few twists of tobacco and a few crates of *cachaça!*"

Percival raised an eyebrow. "You needn't trouble your pretty head about business matters, my dear. Women and business are an unseemly mix, don't you agree?" Taking her arm, he guided her forward. "I have some matters to attend to with Mr. Jonpesson, so I'll leave you now. I'm sure you want your afternoon nap."

Angry and silent, Lalie allowed him to lead her back to the main house. He had an irritating habit of couching commands in such a way as to sound thoughtful and concerned with her welfare. In truth he was instructing her how to think, what to wear, whom she might choose as a friend, and when to nap. He blithely expected her to turn a blind eye toward the labor camp and the general store, and to praise his business cunning. He expected her to accept his interpretation of events despite the evidence of her own eyes and intellect.

Gazing into the future, Lalie saw herself fading into a

dim subservient shadow. As Lady Sterling, she would be Sir Percival's hostess and his ornament, his uncritical audience and the mother of his heir. And that was all. Intellect was not wanted, neither was independent thought.

At the foot of the veranda steps, Percival halted and raised her fingertips to his lips. "I've invited the Jonpessons to dinner tonight." He frowned before he said, "I suppose we should include Addison . . . he is our guest."

Lalie glanced up at the house. "But I haven't inspected the pantry stores or thought about menus or—"

He smiled and patted her hand. "The arrangements have been made. I could hardly expect you to assume your duties on your second day in residence. Ah yes. There it is." Leading her up the steps, he walked along the veranda to a large wicker cage containing a brightly colored parrot. "A present for you."

"Thank you," she said after a minute.

But it wasn't the parrot that arrested her attention. She stared at the bars enclosing the cage.

Wearing the ivory-colored silk gown was a mistake; Lalie knew it before March entered the parlor and stopped short at the sight of her. Biting her lip, she looked at him helplessly. There had been no choice. Percival had come to her room and personally selected the only gown he judged suitable for entertaining company.

"Good evening, Mr. Addison," she murmured, dropping her gaze.

"You look well, Miss Pritchard. It strikes me that emeralds are all that's wanted to complete your ensemble." He bowed over her gloved hand, pretending not to notice her sudden gasp.

Percival, who was welcoming the Jonpessons, swung around and stared at Lalie as if only now realizing she wore no jewelry. At the same moment Mrs. Jonpesson noticed Lalie's bare ears and throat and tactfully removed her own modest earrings.

Frank Jonpesson, Sir Percival's estate manager, ambled forward to be presented. He was a ruddy-faced man of middle years who would never tan but would continue to burn and peel throughout his employment in the tropics. Sober and earnest of demeanor, he was infinitely more comfortable with numbers and ledgers than in the presence of company.

Judith Jonpesson deferred to Lalie as if she'd already become Lady Sterling. A lively intelligence twinkled in Mrs. Jonpesson's eyes, and from time to time it looked as if she might be suppressing an irreverent remark. Lalie suspected that if circumstances had allowed, she and Mrs. Jonpesson would have developed a fulfilling friendship. Instead they would respect the lines drawn by their husbands. They would live in the same confined area, nod to one another at a distance, and silently suffer the lack of female companionship.

Throughout dinner Lalie sensed Mrs. Jonpesson's curiosity. And at least once she discovered the woman watching her with an expression resembling sympathy. The look of commiseration would have given her pause if she hadn't been seated beside March. But she could think of little but March Addison.

Aside from his formal attire and the *de rigueur* compliments he paid Lalie and Mrs. Jonpesson, March exerted no particular effort to be congenial. He flatly refuted Percival's and Jonpesson's claim that the Amazon rubber boom would continue unabated as far into the future as a man could dream. He actually thanked the Indian servant who served the meal. He deliberately mentioned that Percy had been disqualified in last season's tapir hunt.

Lalie concealed a helpless smile behind her napkin. March was simply being himself, indulging a sour mood and stopping just short of goading Percival into ordering him from the house. It was obvious Percival was annoyed.

But Addison's rudeness and Percival's irritation were not the only things that made the dinner difficult. Sitting near to March and being unable to touch him or to speak naturally and freely was agony for Lalie. Even when she was not looking at him directly, she was intensely aware of every movement he made, each comment he uttered. She sensed his mood as if it were her own. She knew when he was amused, when he was irritated. Knew when he believed he had scored his point and when he felt bested. Twice she guessed what he would say before he spoke, and correctly anticipated the expression on his darkly handsome face.

She knew him as well as she knew herself. The dawning realization sent waves of confusion rolling through her mind.

Not wanting to leave Percival and March alone together, she stood at the end of the meal and forced a smile. "Mrs. Jonpesson has confided she holds no more objection to cigar smoke than I." She didn't glance at March, but sensed his amusement. "Therefore, gentlemen, I invite you to join the ladies in the parlor for your brandy and cigars."

Percival's disapproval was swift and readily evident, but he supported her decision before their guests by taking her arm and leading toward the parlor. It seemed to Lalie that he gripped her arm with rather more force than necessary.

"Perhaps you've forgotten, my dear. But I believe I did mention we observe proper form at Hiberalta."

"Your reprimand is noted," she murmured, her cheeks flaming.

March observed the exchange and guessed its content. Standing in the door to the veranda, he lit a cigar and blew a stream of smoke toward the milky night sky. His mood had been foul all day, and was worsened by seeing Percival's arm on Lalie's waist. The instant he saw her, wearing the ivory silk, memory flooded his mind with passionate images. Once again he held her in his arms and whirled her across the courtyard tiles, watching the moonlight caress her high cheekbones and soft eyes. Once again he lifted her and carried her to his bed, heard the whisper of silk gliding over her hips and floating to the floor.

"You have such a peculiar look on your face," Mrs. Jonpesson remarked at his elbow. "A penny for your thoughts, Mr. Addison."

He smiled without humor and raised his brandy. "I was thinking how eager I am to depart for Malaya, Mrs. Jonpesson."

A long sigh escaped her lips as she waved at a swarm of insects. "Some days I long for home. I yearn to leave the tropics. But Mr. Jonpesson has two more years on his contract." She glanced over her shoulder to where Jonpesson and Sterling chatted with Lalie. "I understand you refused to accept reimbursement for Miss Pritchard's travel expenses. May I assume that indicates you are a relative or a friend?"

"A friend of the family," he said.

Mrs. Jonpesson bit her lip, glanced at Lalie and the two men, then spoke in a low, hesitant voice. "Perhaps as a friend of the family you might speak to Miss Pritchard about . . . that is, I wonder if she is truly committed to . . . oh dear. I don't wish to sound disloyal to Sir Percival," she amended hastily. "It's just that . . ." Crimson flooded her cheeks and she looked as if she wished she had not begun this conversation. "Well, things are not as idyllic here as they may seem," she finished uncomfortably.

Things were hardly idyllic at Hiberalta, March thought, drawing on his cigar. There were the obvious abuses, of course. Moreover there was the woman in the small house. Now he knew her identity, though he had not spoken to her. Her anger at being removed from the main house minutes after Lalie's arrival was known to the entire compound. It was her scream they had overheard walking up to the house.

March gazed at Lalie's fresh beauty and felt the ache of wanting her, the desire to protect her from her fate. Sooner or later she would learn of the abuses occurring at Hiberalta. Eventually she would discover that Sterling's mistress had set up housekeeping not a hundred yards from her door.

Knowing the indefatigable Miss Pritchard, he suspected her discoveries would come sooner rather than later.

The moment the Jonpessons said good night, Lalie pleaded a headache and rushed upstairs to her bedroom in order to escape Percival's attempts to cover her with wet kisses. Perhaps to underscore his displeasure at her relaxed etiquette, he made no effort to detain her. Instead he bid her good night at the foot of the staircase, then reached for his hat and stick and left by the front door.

From her upstairs window Lalie watched him cross his "plaza" and enter the door of the small, isolated house. Sighing, she swung her gaze toward the moonlit thatch of the barracks roof and wondered if March had returned there.

She hadn't exchanged a single private word with him tonight. Each time she hoped they might have a conversation, Percival had appeared at her elbow, clasping her in a light embrace as if to taunt March. There were so many things she wished to say, yet she had no right to seek him out. Most especially she had no right to yearn for him as she did.

Sighing, she turned from the window and stepped out of the ivory-colored silk. She picked up her nightdress, stared at it for a few seconds and put it down again. A look of resolve on her face, she put on a simple dark skirt and blouse and left the room.

As she slipped down the staircase and soundlessly closed the front door behind her, Lalie told herself that all she wanted was a bit of exercise before bed. If March should chance to see her strolling around the plaza and wish to join her . . . well, that wouldn't be her fault, would it?

She hurried down the veranda steps then slowed her pace. She circled the moon-drenched plaza once then twice, beginning to feel foolish. Waves of laughing or cursing burst from the direction of the barracks. She heard the tinkle of Mrs. Jonpesson's piano. Someone played a mouth harp near the docks. There were the usual jungle sounds. But no one wandered within sight of the central clearing. She spotted one of the men who patrolled Hiberalta then he too disappeared. It occurred to Lalie that Hiberalta could be a very lonely place.

On her third turn around the clutch of sagging palms, she heard the sounds of an argument coming from the small house nestled against the edge of the jungle. It was Percy's voice, and the person he was arguing with was a woman. Her footsteps carried her away from the plaza and along a dark path that passed close to the small house.

As she approached, placing each step carefully in the darkness, the argument became louder. Lalie cast a quick glance behind her, blushing with shame for her behavior, then she stepped off the path and crept through the foliage toward the light seeping past a shuttered window. Her heart was pounding, and she couldn't believe she actually intended to eavesdrop.

"Please," the woman's voice sobbed. "Percy, I love you. Don't send me away."

"Oh, for Christ's sake. It isn't forever. Just until you're rid of it."

Lalie heard the scrape of a match, then the scent of

Percival's cigar. Hardly daring to breathe, she stood stone-still in the darkness beside the shuttered window and tried to understand what she was overhearing.

The woman spoke between wrenching sobs. "This is *her* fault! You were happy with me before *she* came!"

With a shock, Lalie realized the woman was talking about her.

The sound of a rough slap cracked through the night, then a cry and a heavy thud as the woman fell to the floor. Lalie gasped and her fingertips flew to her lips. Percival had *struck* a woman.

"You knew she was coming to Hiberalta and you didn't say a damned thing, you slut. I should give you to Lum Sarto and his men. That's what you deserve."

Fresh shock widened Lalie's eyes before she closed them and slumped against the wall of the house. Percival *did* know Lum Sarto's reputation. But . . . how could the sobbing woman have known about Lalie or guessed she was journeying to Hiberalta?

"I make you happy. You know I make you happy. Let me stay. I beg you, please. Please don't make me give it away. I'll do anything you ask . . ."

"Of course." Percival's laugh was harsh and ugly. His voice hardened. "As soon as Addison departs, I'll send you to Tupati. You'll stay there until it's over, then you can return. Alone. In the meantime I don't want you showing your face outside this door. Keep the windows shuttered, is that understood?"

"So *she* won't see me?" the woman cried bitterly. "Percy, I beg you. We can be a family! No! Percy, please. Don't leave."

Lifting on her tiptoes, Lalie peeked through the shutter slats and drew a sharp breath. The woman's back was to her and Lalie could not glimpse her face. But she could see Percival's ugly expression. His face was red, his eyes feverish.

He twisted his hands in the woman's black hair and

jerked her face close to his. "What is it about you?" he snarled into the woman's face. "You infuriate me; you're worth nothing, but still I want you."

"Then send *her* away. Marry me. Marry me, and—"

His laugh was grating and offensive. "Marry you?" Bending, he ground his mouth down on the woman's lips then looked at her. "Marry a whore? You make me laugh!"

Lalie turned away from the shutters as Percival moved his hands over the woman's breasts. She stood without daring to breathe; shocked, she stared at nothing. She couldn't think.

When the door of the small house slammed, Lalie's heart jumped and she sucked in a sharp breath. Closing her eyes in dread, she waited to be discovered. Instead, she heard Percival's steps moving toward the plaza. Inside the house, the woman had dissolved in a storm of fresh sobs.

Now, Lalie thought, straightening her spine, do it now before you have a chance to think this through.

Slipping around the side of the house, she stepped up on the porch and pushed the door open with trembling fingers.

Clea Paralta looked up with eyes filled with hope. When she saw it was Lalie, she dropped her head in her hands and moaned.

Her face was bruised and her lip bloody. And she was very pregnant.

"He'll kill us both if he discovers you came here," Clea warned.

Lalie poured cups of *cachaça* from the bottle Percival had left behind and offered one to Clea.

"Is the baby . . . is it Percival's?" Lalie asked quietly. She tried not to stare at Clea's blackened eye or the bruises discoloring her jaw, shoulders, and wrists.

"Sim." Raising a hand, Clea shoved back a tangled wave

of black hair. "You ask yourself how I know this. I have not been with another man since Percy returned to Pará."

"Then you were with child when—"

"When I met you. *Sim.* But I didn't know until just before you sailed that you had come to marry Percy." Fresh tears slipped down her cheeks and her dark stare glittered. "I hate you!"

Lalie reached over and caught Clea's hand in both of hers, holding tightly when Clea tried to jerk away from her grasp. "You don't hate me, Clea," she said softly. "Even if I hadn't come to the Amazon, Sir Percival would not have married you. In your heart, I think you know that."

A sob caught in Clea's throat and her shoulders sagged. "All I want is for him to admit the baby is his." Gently she disengaged her hand and dropped it to her swollen stomach. Tears glistened in her eyes. "If Percy would agree to provide for the little one, my baby could have a life!"

"Oh Clea. I don't think he ever will." Sympathy softened Lalie's gaze. "How did this happen?"

After wiping her eyes on her sleeve, Clea looked up at the roof beams. "I met Percy several years ago. He was . . . not like the others." She shrugged and met Lalie's gaze. "When Percy stayed in Pará, I was his alone. His woman." A flicker of pride momentarily eclipsed the hopelessness in her eyes. "March can tell you. Once, he and Percy fought over me. March was wrong—he should not have interfered."

Mind racing, Lalie frowned. "The scar . . ."

"*Sim.* In his groin."

Lalie had meant March, not Percival. "I know some of that story," Lalie said sadly. "Percival was beating you."

"It is his way." Her eyes flashed defiantly. "I love him. And even though he hits me, he loves me, too."

Although she didn't argue the woman's claim, Lalie's gaze rested for a moment on the blackened eye and Clea's bruises. "You hurried upriver when you learned about me," she said, working it out in her mind. "The *Addison Beal* made several stops along the way, so you arrived well in advance of me."

Clea's chin lifted. "I knew I had only a short time to convince him to give my child his name."

"Oh Clea," Lalie said. Pity moistened her eyes and softened her voice. "Don't you understand? Sir Percival will never marry you or acknowledge your child. Forgive me for speaking bluntly, but Percival will never place himself in a position where people could say that he had wed a river prostitute. I doubt he will ever admit your child could be his. Can you understand that?"

"Miss Pritchard—"

"Lalie."

Staring at Lalie over the candle flame, Clea drank the rest of her *cachaça*. "You have changed," she said finally. "You are not the same woman I met in Pará."

"There's nothing here for you but heartache. Go home to Pará with March. Start over. You can build a good life for yourself and your child. You're a beautiful woman, Clea. Eventually you'll find a man who will appreciate you, who won't abuse you or hurt you."

"You know what love is," Clea whispered. A helpless shrug lifted her shoulders. "You came all this way for him. You love him, too. Could you leave him as easily as you advise me to?"

If Lalie had learned anything in the last two days, she had learned that she did not love Sir Percival Sterling. She could never love a man like him.

"We're not discussing me," she said firmly. "Clea—will you do this? Will you speak to March? March is your friend. You know he won't lie to you. Ask him if you have a future at Hiberalta. Ask him if Percival will ever acknowledge your child."

For a long moment, Clea stared at her. "If Percy discovered I'd spoken to March, he'd . . ." She shuddered.

"Listen to the fear in your voice. Look in your mirror. Percival beats you. He left you in Pará even though he knew you carried his child. Clea, all he wants from you is . . ." Lalie blushed furiously and knew she couldn't bring herself to say more. "Let March help you."

They spoke for a few minutes longer before Lalie stood. "Promise me you'll think about what we've discussed."

"I . . . I'll think about it."

Mind reeling, Lalie stepped onto the dark porch and expelled a long breath. It was inconceivable that the people living at Hiberalta did not know about Clea. The Jonpessons would certainly know Percival's pregnant mistress was on the premises. Mr. Leo knew. The guards knew. Everyone knew.

Suddenly her heart skipped a beat. She inhaled the pungent odor of smoke an instant before she saw the glow of a cigar and a man's shadowy form standing beside her on the porch.

"Miss Pritchard, you are a surprising woman. You never fail to amaze me."

"March! You frightened the life half out of me!" She pressed a fist to her thudding breast. "What are you doing here?"

"More to the point—what are you?"

"I . . . I just . . . Were you eavesdropping?"

"Absolutely. Before that I was spying. I saw you listening at the shutters, my dear Miss Pritchard. Then watched you slip inside. I agree with everything you said." Even in the shadowed blackness, she saw his mouth tighten. "I'll convince Clea to return with me. I won't leave Hiberalta without her."

"March . . . tell me about the labor camp." Lalie spoke in a low, urgent voice. "I have to know." When he finished speaking, she dropped her head and closed her eyes. A horrified shudder convulsed her body.

"Do as Percival instructed, Lalie. Don't visit the camp. It will only shock and sicken you."

This was the moment Lalie had been seeking, an opportunity to confide what lay in her heart. But she gazed up at him and her mouth dried. A vast weakness of longing spread through her body.

"When are you leaving?" she whispered, supporting herself against the porch post.

"Two of Tilwe's people are dead. The healing woman died on the whipping post, another man by his own hand," March said bluntly. "Fredo and I have contacted the other two. We'll leave Hiberalta tomorrow night."

"March, I—"

His hand rose to her mouth and he placed his fingertips against her lips. "There are a thousand things I wish to say to you. But I gave my word that I would not say or do anything to cause you distress. I ask the same of you, Lalie. Don't tell me we'll always be friends. Don't tell me that you'll think of me often. You might believe such platitudes will make losing you less painful, but they won't. We said our good-byes in Tupati."

The door opened and Clea peered at them. "*Mãe de Dios!* Everyone will hear you! You," she said to Lalie, "go before someone sees you." She tugged March's sleeve. "Come inside. Please."

Stepping forward, March caught Clea in his arms, and she began to sob. "I'm so glad to see you, my friend. Tell me what to do."

But first March turned back to Lalie, who twisted her hands in front of her skirts. "Good night," he said quietly. He touched her cheek with his fingertips then Clea pulled him inside.

"I love you," Lalie whispered, staring at the door. Her admission rocked her like an earthquake, and was followed by a feeling of profound dismay that it had taken her so long to admit the truth, even to herself.

Adding to her self-reproach was the knowledge that Sir Percival Sterling had not changed. He was the same man she had known in England, facile, charming, possessed of faultless manners, handsome and golden.

But now Lalie could see his dark side as well, the side she had never known existed. She saw Percival's tyranny, saw his insensitivity, his casual brutality and his appalling lack of moral conscience.

She also saw March Addison, a man she had once believed crude, mannerless, and lacking in redeeming qualities. Beneath his impatience and relaxed conduct was a good and decent man. A compassionate man, a man of conscience and high principle.

Neither man had changed. Both were just as they were when she first met them. It was she who had changed, she who had learned how to see below the surface.

And she loved March Addison. In the joy of allowing herself to admit the truth, she understood she had loved him for a long time.

Chapter 20

Lalie rose early following a sleepless night and packed her clothing then replaced her portmanteau behind the bedroom door. Not until dawn did she finally accept that she had no choice but to leave Hiberalta without confronting Percival and explaining in person that she had made a mistake. It seemed a cowardly act, but an honorable approach would imperil the rescue of Tilwe's men.

After breakfast in her room, Lalie wrote a long letter reminding Percival they did not share the same philosophy or the same traits. In the event he might mistakenly believe their differences were reconcilable, she confessed her love for March. The next page apologized for her failure to recognize earlier where her heart lay, and she apologized for the embarrassment and awkwardness her decision would surely cause him.

When Lalie reread the letter, her sentiments impressed her as wooden and stilted. But that couldn't be helped. Her growing dislike for Percival made it impossible to sound remorseful about her decision. After a moment's thought, she tucked the letter within the folds of her bedspread where the pages would be found by the maid the next day.

Then, heart brimming with anticipation, she hurried in

search of March Addison, almost running in her eagerness. She didn't find him, but she located Fredo at the boat, inspecting a large wooden crate he had constructed near the stern.

"Cabo go to steal Tomli and Jono, Tilwe's men. They hide in this box until tonight," Fredo said out of the side of his mouth when Lalie inquired as to March's whereabouts. He inspected the slope and what he could glimpse of the compound. All was quiet, wilting in the morning heat.

"Fredo, please, this is very important," Lalie said. "March can't leave Hiberalta without me."

Fredo's head jerked up and he stared at her. Then a slow smile thinned his lips. "Will be dangerous, Missy." His gaze flicked to the row of vessels tied at the docks and a yawning man who wandered into view carrying a Winchester. "I'll disable the boats, but Sterling's men will come. They chase us maybe as far as Ipta. Rivaldi will be waiting in Manaus."

"I love him, Fredo."

He grinned. "I know, little Missy. You look each other through the eye of the *boto.*"

Lalie smiled. "Tell him."

"I say little Missy want to talk." He returned her smile. "The rest Cabo hear from you."

Then the waiting began.

Not wanting to be seen with Fredo by Percival's guards, Lalie left the boat and returned to the main house. She passed the small house. Her steps slowed. She looked at it uncertainly, wondering if she dared speak to Clea again. The temptation was strong to do so, but it was much too risky. Someone might see her. The sun climbed in the sky. Luncheon arrived and passed. At least three times Lalie rushed to her bedroom and nervously peered out the window toward the dock, fearing March had departed without her. She was only partially reassured when she sighted the bow of his boat bobbing in the river.

Wherever March was, Lalie understood he had placed himself at considerable risk. It would not be easy to move Tomli and Jono around the compound and down to the boat without being sighted. She didn't know what would happen if March were discovered attempting to steal two laborers from Hiberalta, but she suspected Percival's retribution would be swift and terrible.

By the time she heard the parlor bell announce tea, Lalie was beside herself with nervousness. What if March didn't come to her? Or what if he were apprehended trying to conceal Tomli and Jono aboard the boat?

Her anxiety was relieved on the last question when she descended the staircase and joined Percival in the parlor for tea. If March's plot had been uncovered, Percival's anger would have been impossible to conceal.

"You look particularly enticing today," Percival commented, taking a seat beside her on the sofa. Pale, speculative eyes studied her. He spoke in a silky tone. "I'd forgotten what beautiful eyes you have. Dare I say, come-hither eyes?"

Immediately, Lalie set down her teacup and rose to her feet. She moved to the door leading onto the veranda. "How much rubber does each warehouse contain?" she inquired uneasily, seeking to focus his attention on something other than herself.

Heat waves shimmered above the red earth exposed in the center of the compound. The palm fronds had begun to brown and curl at the edges. But Lalie could not see the dock from this angle. Where was March?

Percival's sudden approach startled her and she jumped as his hands circled her waist and he bent his head to nuzzle her neck. "I can think of a more interesting way to pass a hot afternoon than discussing rubber . . ."

"Please don't," Lalie whispered, stiffening.

His mouth moved to her ear and his wet tongue tickled her lobe. "It will be weeks before Father Franklin returns to Tupati . . . it's foolish to deny ourselves until then. Why should we torture ourselves by waiting?"

Even now he possessed the ability to shock her. Never had Lalie expected this sort of insinuation from Sir Percival, who placed such stock in proper form. Surely he understood his blatant disrespect was objectionable and insulting. Even if she had loved him, she would have taken offense.

When his perspiring hands slipped up her rib cage and cupped her breasts, Lalie gasped and instantly moved to step out of his embrace. But his grasp tightened and he jerked her back against his body. His hands moved over her breasts, probing, fumbling to open the buttons on her shirtwaist.

"Stop this at once!" she commanded. Lalie struggled to pull away from him. "I mean what I say, Percival. Don't!"

"Your nod to propriety is duly noted," he said, panting against her neck. Roughly, he spun her to face him and jerked her hips against his so she could feel his hard state of readiness. Wet kisses rained over her face, her throat. "I've wanted you from the moment I saw you." With one hand he clasped her against his body, the other hand kneaded her breast.

"Percival, you're hurting me!" Feeling a bite of panic, Lalie tried to shove him away, but he grabbed her hips and thrust his body roughly against hers.

Capturing one of her hands, he pushed it down between them and pressed her fingers around his erection. "I won't be denied, Lalie," he muttered against the side of her face. His own face was flushed and ugly with determination.

Wrenching her hand away from him, Lalie slapped him. For a moment neither of them moved. They stared at each other in silence, aware that events had spiraled out of control.

Strange heat glowed in Percival's blue eyes. "So that's how you like it. What a pleasant surprise." He slapped her so hard that Lalie crashed to the floor, knocking over a cluttered whatnot table as she fell. A small porcelain figurine shattered near her hand. Flowers spilled over the carpet.

Shock and pain widened her eyes. Her fingers flew to the hand print flaming on her cheek and she stared up at him, too stunned to react. Then he loomed over her and ripped open her shirtwaist. Buttons popped over the parlor carpet, and Lalie gasped with sudden fear.

She understood she was in serious trouble. The lust burning behind Percival's eyes told her he had passed the boundaries of reason. None of his men would respond to her screams. The servants would not help her. Lalie wet her lips and whispered, "Percival, I beg you. Don't do this."

"Is that your game?" he whispered in a raw voice. "You women like to be overpowered." He shoved her flat on the floor, then he straddled her body so she couldn't roll away from him. After throwing off his coat, his eyes fixed on her breast swelling over her exposed corset ribbons, he pushed down his suspenders and opened the front of his trousers.

Lalie frantically tried to crawl out from under him. Then she screamed as his fingers caught her hair and he jerked her head back. In a second he was on the floor, pushing her onto her back and shoving her flat again. His knee slammed down between her legs, forcing her thighs apart.

Lalie fought like a wild creature, summoning every ounce of strength she had. Scratching and hitting, she struggled beneath him. To her horror, her resistance only aroused him, inflamed him. Blood dripped from the scratches she clawed down his cheek, but he didn't appear to notice. Ripping up her skirt, he dug brutal fingers into her flesh, seeking the band of her knickers. Tears of rage streamed down her cheeks and she kicked and pounded at him.

"Get off her, you son of a bitch, or I'll blow your brains over that wall!" The voice was low and deep and filled with fury.

Lalie didn't hesitate. She seized Percival's moment of surprise to scramble out from under him. Crawling, tripping over her hem, she scurried out of his reach then grabbed the arm of the sofa and pulled to her feet. Tremors racked her body. Her hair had tumbled to her waist and her clothing hung in shreds.

"Thank God you came!" Shoving back her hair, she darted a quick glance in March's direction. He stood over Percival, his finger on the trigger of his Winchester. The knots running up his jaw looked like pebbles of steel.

"Get Clea and go to the launch. Now!"

"You just signed your death warrant, Addison," Percival snarled.

Turning on her heel, Lalie ran toward the front door. On her way out, she caught up a cloak she had spotted earlier and draped it over her torn clothing. Running, she cut across the baked earth of the plaza and darted up the path to the small house.

One of Percival's men stepped onto the path in front of her, blocking her passage. "You no go here, Missy."

"Get the hell out of my way, you bastard, or I'll claw your eyes out of your ugly head!" she screamed.

The man's jaw dropped when she shoved her elbow into his ribs and rushed past him. He stared after her then turned an uncertain expression toward the main house. It was better to know nothing than to have failed in carrying out an order. He melted into the jungle foliage in the direction of the labor camp.

Lalie pounded her fists on the door. When Clea appeared, Lalie dragged her out onto the porch. "We're leaving now! Hurry!"

"What? But I . . . now? March said I had until tonight to decide." Clea's dark eyes swept Lalie's open cloak, and she gasped at the sight of her exposed corset and ripped skirt.

Lalie met her eyes. "Percival would have raped me if March hadn't intervened. You must decide now, Clea, right this minute. Every second we delay imperils our escape."

They both spun toward the plaza at the sound of a gunshot.

"Decide!" Lalie nearly screamed.

Clea hesitated only a second then she nodded and hurried down the porch steps. Lalie's heart sank. Until now, she hadn't realized exactly how heavily pregnant Clea was. Even her shapeless cotton shift was stretched taut. She looked as if she were due any moment.

Rushing after her, Lalie caught her arm. "Lean on me if you need to."

Together they made their way toward the boat, just as a melee erupted around them. Men ran toward the main house, shouting questions at each other, trying to learn what was happening. Another gunshot sounded at the edge of the jungle.

"Walk," Lalie urged. "Try to appear at ease, as if nothing is wrong."

Clea glanced at her. "You crazy? The mistress and the bride go for a stroll together in the middle of gunshots and all this confusion, and you think nobody will notice?"

Lalie fixed her gaze on the dock area and walked steadily toward it, wishing Clea could move faster. She could see Fredo darting from vessel to vessel, looking back over his shoulder toward the main house. Where was March? Oh God, was he still in the house? With everyone in the compound running to surround it?

"Halt!" A dark-faced man swung around the side of the general store and leveled his Winchester at them.

"Get out of our way," Lalie commanded imperiously.

But this time her act didn't work. The man didn't budge. His narrowed black eyes swept from Lalie to Clea and he tightened his grip on the gun. "You stay here. No move."

Behind him, Lalie could see Fredo running toward the boat. Perspiration trickled down her cheeks.

Then a rifle butt swung out of the foliage and smashed against the side of the man's head. He dropped to the ground. "To the boat. Run!" March ordered, swinging around to face the compound, his Winchester ready to fire.

"Clea can't run!"

"Then walk fast, Miss Pritchard, walk very fast," he said. "And do it now, damn it. Go!"

Before she slipped an arm around Clea's swollen waist and hurried her forward, Lalie glanced back at the house in time to see Percival run onto the veranda jerking rope from his wrists. She could hear his enraged shouts, but not what he was saying.

Then she rushed Clea toward the boat. Gunfire erupted behind her, and a bullet smacked into a dock post as she helped Clea across the plank. Fredo pulled Clea into the boat and shoved her down on the deck, then reached for Lalie.

The instant Lalie's feet touched the deck, she threw off the cloak so she could move freely and snatched Fredo's Winchester from his hands. "I know how to use this. You take the wheel and get us out of here!"

Fredo hesitated, but as Lalie raised the gun to her shoulder he nodded sharply and dashed to the wheel.

Gunfire blazed at the top of the slope, then March appeared running toward them. Squinting, Lalie prayed that she remembered the shooting lessons her father had taught her. She squeezed the trigger and shot at the men pouring out of the compound behind him. The boat had begun to drift from the dock by the time March reached them. He made a flying jump and landed hard beside Lalie.

A hail of bullets smacked the water and the sides of the boat as it leapt forward. Lalie fired as fast as she could load the cartridges Clea handed up to her, and so did March. A stream of men poured down the slope, jumping over fallen comrades and running toward the line of vessels.

Two minutes passed, then three. Percival's men discovered their vessels were disabled, and the boat sailed out of range of the bullets that slapped the surface of the water.

March dropped a hand on Lalie's shoulder. Her concentration was total, she didn't immediately understand his signal. She continued frantically shoving cartridges into the chamber.

"It's over," March shouted above the roar of the motor. Placing both hands on her shoulders, he leaned to look into her wide, angry eyes. "Lalie, it's over! At least for the present."

After shaking the hair out of her face, Lalie stared back at the small antlike figures racing around the Hiberalta dock. Spinning, she looked at Fredo who maneuvered the boat down the river.

March pulled open the lid of the box Fredo had built at the stern and two pairs of terrified dark eyes peeked out.

"I'll get Tomli and Jono out of here," March said. "You see to Clea."

First Lalie closed her eyes and sucked in a deep breath of the cooler river air. Her entire body began to tremble. She wondered if she had wounded or killed any of the men running after March. The possibility made her feel sick. When she opened her eyes and pried her fingers away from the Winchester, her hands were stiff and shaking.

She placed the gun on the deck then looked at Clea, who lay sprawled against the side of the boat. Her eyes were closed and her face was the color of chalk.

"Clea! Oh my God. March? March!"

Dropping to her knees, Lalie reached a hand to the blood spreading in a widening stain across Clea's shoulder. Clea opened her eyes and managed an expression that might have been a grimace or a faint smile. Biting her lip, Lalie ripped Clea's shift away from the wound. When she looked up, March was bending at Clea's back and a hard frown pinched his lips.

"The bullet passed through," he said grimly. "That's good." Clea leaned back against him and closed her eyes again. "When we reach Tupati, we'll—"

"No." Clea's dark head moved against his shoulder. "Don't leave me in Tupati. He'll find me there," she whispered. "Take me home, March."

March met Lalie's eyes above Clea's head. A wounded pregnant woman would slow their pace tremendously.

"We'll take you home," Lalie murmured, placing her shaking hand against Clea's cheek.

Clea caught her hand and held it in a painful grip. "I need *cachaça,*" she said. March quickly produced a bottle and removed the cork with his teeth. Clea took a gulp and gasped.

Lalie drew a breath. "We'll stop in Tupati long enough to buy medication and then—"

"No delays," Clea pleaded. She stared at Lalie. "Percy will come, Miss Pritchard. He'll follow us as far as Pará if he has to. He won't give up. If we're going to have a chance, we can't stop for anything." Wincing in pain, she raised the bottle of *cachaça* to her lips and drank deeply.

"She's right," March agreed quietly. When Lalie protested, he nodded toward Tomli and Jono, who sat silently in the stern of the boat. "As soon as we're in the jungle, I'll ask them to prepare something to ease her pain."

They did what they could to make Clea as comfortable as possible. Lalie tore strips from her petticoat and bound Clea's shoulder. They fashioned a crude awning from the cloak Lalie had taken and positioned Clea beneath it. Already half-intoxicated, Clea curled on her side, cradling the bottle between her breasts.

"Don' worry 'bout me," she murmured sleepily.

While March spoke to Fredo, Lalie poured cups of water for everyone. Then there was nothing to do but wait as they traveled down the Yaki.

When March sat beside her, Lalie drew up her knees to make room for him then tried to tug her buttonless shirtwaist over her corset. March observed the effort with twinkling eyes.

"Let me guess. Once again you have nothing to wear. Has it occurred to you, Miss Pritchard, that you are littering the Amazon basin with cast-off clothing? Keeping you supplied with stockings and dresses bears signs of becoming a full-time occupation."

After arranging her shirtwaist as decently as she could, Lalie lifted her head to meet his eyes. "I was never so glad to see anyone in my life," she said in a low voice. A shudder convulsed her shoulders. "If you'd arrived just minutes later . . ."

His fingertips moved across her cheek, brushing back her hair so he could see her face. "I almost didn't go to the main house. But Fredo insisted you had something important to say and insisted I had to hear it."

"I love you."

He stared into her eyes as if he didn't understand her words.

"I asked Fredo to beg you not to leave Hiberalta without me." She drew a deep breath. "I've thought about it, and I've made up my mind. I love you and I want to be with you. If you won't take me to Malaya, then I'll follow on my own." A mischievous glint diminished her threat. "As you know, I have a history of chasing after men."

"Wait a minute. You're saying you intended to leave with me all along?"

She nodded. "I knew immediately it would be a disaster to marry Percival. I—"

"And you really love me?" His fingers tightened on her shoulders as he turned her to face him.

"Oh March." She stared into his warm, dark eyes, feeling the world spin around her. "Tell me you haven't changed your mind. Tell me you love me! That's all I could think about last night. I was so afraid that you wouldn't want me anymore. I had a terrible nightmare that—"

His mouth came down over hers, possessively, and he kissed her until her heart hammered against her corset stays and her mind swam with joy. Drawing her into his arms, he held her tightly, his fingers tangling in her hair. Sighing with happiness, Lalie clung to him, feeling safe in his strong embrace.

"I love you, my very dear Miss Pritchard," he murmured against her temple. "You have made me the happiest man on earth." After a moment he gently eased her away from him and lowered his head to gaze into her eyes. "Unless I've misunderstood—you did just propose to me, didn't you?"

"What?" A burst of scarlet bloomed in her cheeks, then she laughed. "Yes, Mr. Addison. I believe I did."

He grinned. "Now what do you imagine Mrs. Wilkie's etiquette book would say about that?"

She returned his grin. "The truth? I don't give a damn. More important—what do you say?"

His laughter rang across the Yaki and his arms tightened around her. "Miss Pritchard, I do love you!"

Twenty minutes before they reached the bend below Tupati where March had arranged to meet Romexi and Termo and the mules, Lalie remembered to inquire about Percival.

"Sterling jumped me and we struggled," March said. "I'd like to tell you the bastard is dead, but he's too damned lucky to die. The gun went off and the bullet missed him by inches. I tied him up."

"You could have killed him," Lalie said slowly. "But you let him live instead."

"Unfortunately, I'm not one who can kill in cold blood."

"I'm glad," she whispered.

She scanned the inlet the boat was heading toward. She didn't glimpse Romexi or Termo, but she sensed they were present, watching from the concealment of the dense jungle foliage.

"Clea's correct, isn't she? Percival will come after us."

"I stole his bride, his mistress, and two of his laborers," March said, standing and looking toward the jungle banks as Fredo cut the motor and the boat drifted toward the shore. "Sterling won't be satisfied until one of us is dead."

Lalie frowned up at him, noticing how pale he appeared beneath his tan. "March, are you feeling well?" she asked.

"Just a headache. I'll carry Clea. You bring the cloak and my Winchester."

She stared up at him a moment then did as he asked. A few feet behind the wall of ferns and heavy jungle leaves Romexi and Termo were waiting. They offered no comment regarding the party's early arrival; March's plan had provided for the unexpected. Silently the Indians faded into the jungle, following a path only they could see to where they had tethered the mules.

After Fredo set the boat adrift, he followed Romexi and Termo, swinging a machete to widen the path for March, who carried a half-delirious Clea. Tomli and Jono followed Lalie.

Already Lalie grasped how drastically her presence and Clea's slowed the group's flight. And Fredo's machete left a broad path that even she could have recognized and followed.

The journey quickly became for Lalie a waking nightmare; it seemed to go on forever and was totally exhausting. An hour before each dawn, she pulled her stiff and aching body up from the damp ground and mounted her mule, riding until it was too dark to see in front of her. Before she curled into an exhausted ball at night, oblivious to insects both crawling or airborne, she ate what was placed before her, drank *cachaça* without wincing, swallowed the quinine tablets March gave her, and did what she could for Clea.

As March had promised, Tomli and Jono disappeared into the jungle and returned with medicinal items. March packed Clea's wounds with the downy cotton from a Sumaúma tree while Tomli roasted *guaraná* nuts then ground them into powder against a flat rock. When a large dose was stirred with water, the *guaraná* powder created a strong narcotic that made it possible for Clea to rest comfortably. On the trail Romexi and Termo carried her in a hammock strung on a pole and supported over their shoulders.

When they finally straggled out of the dripping jungle and into Ipta, Lalie lifted her face to the broiling sun and went limp with joy and relief that the worst lay behind them.

The instant Maria spied them, she ran toward them, her arms open to embrace Lalie, who slid to the ground exhausted.

"I knew you come home!" Maria's brown hands flew over her, touching her dirty man's shirt, her shredded skirt, her tangled hair matted with twigs, leaves, and dirt. Maria's black eyes widened with concern and curiosity, but she realized now was not the time for questions. She rushed to the woman March was helping out of the hammock. "Clea!" Maria exclaimed as Clea's heavy body, bruised face, and blood-stained shift emerged from the hammock. Maria slipped her arm around Clea's waist, taking command, assisting her toward the *Addison Beal*.

Fredo and March grasped Lalie's arms and rushed her down to the dock. Smoke streamed from the stacks and soon the *Addison Beal* was ready to depart Ipta. Fredo ran up the plank and raced toward the wheelhouse. Joao passed him, moving in the opposite direction to the boiler room.

March paused long enough to make sure the two Indians had safely boarded and to string a hammock between two support posts for Clea. Then he shook his head as if to clear it before he moved unsteadily toward the wheelhouse. At the door he looked back at Lalie and she gasped.

Sweat poured from his face and body, his eyes looked slightly unfocused. He gave her a thumbs-up sign and a wobbly grin before he lurched into the wheelhouse.

Lalie stared at the wheelhouse door as the steamer's whistle blasted and the *Addison Beal* nosed toward the tributary currents.

March was seriously ill.

Maria called in a soft voice, requesting Lalie's assistance while she changed Clea's dressing. Like a sleepwalker, Lalie approached the stools circled around Maria's stove.

Maria looked very worried. "She going to have baby soon, Missy. Very soon." With reverence, she placed her hand over Clea's swollen stomach.

"Soon," Clea agreed in a dreamy, intoxicated voice.

Lalie looked at the wheelhouse door then back to Clea. "Oh my God," she whispered.

Chapter 21

Maria coaxed Clea into eating something while she applied resin from the *grado* tree to the woman's shoulder wounds. The blood of the *grado,* as Maria called the resin, formed an elastic skin that held the edges of the wounds together. After Clea drank a mild dose of *guaraná* to help her rest, Lalie and Maria assisted her into one of Maria's clean shifts then into the hammock.

Standing beside the railing watching the emerald shore roll past, Lalie thought that the *Addison Beal* nearly flew down the tributary. Then she realized it was because on this, their return journey, they moved with the currents instead of against them. They reached the confluence with the Solimões shortly before twilight. Instead of seeking safe harbor for the night, Fredo steered the *Addison Beal* into the swift currents far offshore. The boat continued downriver long after darkness descended, with Fredo navigating by the light of a waning moon.

The men ate in shifts, first March, who only toyed with his food and Joao, then Tomli and Jono, and finally Fredo. Lalie fidgeted on a stool beside him, impatiently waiting until Fredo finished his rice and beans before a tumble of words poured from her heart. Fredo listened, then handed his tin plate to Maria.

"*Sim,* Missy. Cabo has the white man's fever." After lighting a cigar, Fredo narrowed his gaze and watched the smoke sail backward into the darkness. "Going to get very bad."

Her mind racing, Lalie recalled March giving her and Clea his quinine tablets. There hadn't been enough tablets for everyone as neither she nor Clea had been expected on the return trip. And March had also given her many of his tablets during their journey through the jungle to Hiberalta, she remembered. "Malaria," she whispered.

"Could be." Fredo stared into the smoke puffing from the stacks. The kerosene lantern above his head illuminated his expressionless face. "Many bad fevers in the Amazon, Missy."

Most likely it was malaria. Lalie frowned toward the wheelhouse door. "He should be in bed," she stated. She stood and got the boat's medicine box. The large corked bottle of quinine was nearly empty. For a moment she weighed the bottle in her hand, looking toward Clea's hammock. Then she marched toward the wheelhouse with a resolute step.

"Here," she said firmly, extending the bottle to March. "Swallow two of these tablets right now."

Starlight reflecting on the water provided the only light in the wheelhouse. When March turned at the sound of her voice, he saw her silhouetted in the doorway.

Smiling, he raised his sleeve to blot the sweat trickling down the sides of his face, then he turned to peer through the glass windows at the rippling dark surface of the water.

"You look very fetching in Joao's clothes, Miss Pritchard, my love." Blinking, he cut back the throttle and tried to decide if he was looking at a sandbar looming on the right or if the darker patch in the water was an illusion. "Those trousers never looked so enticing."

"I mean it, March. Swallow these tablets at once!"

"There aren't enough for everyone."

"That's the point, you idiot! Therefore we should use the tablets we have where they might do a little good."

A sliver of moon slipped from behind a cloud and now March could see the sandbank was real. A shudder groaned through the ship as he jerked the wheel hard to the left. Lalie stumbled and he caught her, her body cool against his hot skin.

As the sandbar passed harmlessly to the right, he held her in his arms, brushing his lips across her forehead. She clung to him a moment then her hands raced over his shoulders and up to his jaw, settling against his forehead.

"You're burning up! Damn it, March! You've been giving the tablets to us and not taking any yourself. That is the most idiotic thing I ever heard of!" Angry tears choked her voice.

When he was certain the surface ahead was clear of obstruction, he tightened his arms around her and kissed her nose, ignoring the worry dampening her magnificent eyes.

He smoothed a strand of hair back from her cool, silky throat. "I'd never forgive myself if you or Clea came down with malaria."

"Chivalry has no place here," she snapped, dashing a hand across her eyes and pushing out of his arms. "Not now, not in these circumstances. If Clea or I fall ill it endangers no one but ourselves. But if *you* are incapacitated, we'll *all* suffer for it!"

"Little Missy speaks true," Fredo said from the doorway. Entering the wheelhouse, he stepped up beside March and edged him away from the wheel. "Do as she say, Cabo."

Taking him by the hand, Lalie pulled him out of the wheelhouse and led him to the hammock she had instructed Joao to hang. In the light of the kerosene lamp,

March looked pale and clammy. His shirt was soaked with sweat. Lalie's heart fluttered as she argued him into his hammock then made him swallow two of the quinine tablets.

He frowned up at her through the netting. "I've had attacks of malaria before. Eventually it runs its course. I want you and Clea to split the remaining tablets between you. They'll provide at least a little protection until we reach Manaus and can replenish our supply."

"Now there's a stubborn and well-reasoned plan," Lalie said sharply, glaring through the netting at his sweat-slick face. "We protect the nurses and let the patient die. I'm sorry, my darling idiotic Mr. Addison. But that is not how we're going to proceed. We don't have enough quinine to effect a cure, but we have enough to keep you functional at least until we reach Manaus. That's what we're going to do."

"Don't be an ass, my dear self-righteous Miss Pritchard. At the moment we have one wounded and one ill. We don't need another person—you—also falling ill."

"March—we need you on your feet and functional," she said simply, peering through the netting. "Fredo can't pilot the *Addison Beal* by himself. He has to eat; he needs rest. No one else is a navigator. If you aren't able to help us outrun Percival and avoid Rivaldi, what will happen to Tomli and Jono? Or Clea? Or me?"

For a long moment he didn't speak. When he did, his voice was weary. "I'll take the damned tablets."

"Good. Now rest, darling." Slipping her hand beneath the netting, she stroked his hot cheek. "Get well."

When they finally dropped anchor for the night, Fredo staggered out of the wheelhouse and tottered directly to his hammock, so exhausted he was almost asleep on his feet. Long after the men were snoring in their hammocks, Maria and Lalie sat in the darkness beside the stove, sipping *cafezinho* and talking quietly.

"We get more quinine in Manaus," Maria promised after a period of worried silence.

"Yes."

Neither mentioned Gunter Rivaldi, as if pretending he was not a threat would make it so. But both women knew Rivaldi's henchmen were just ahead. And Percival was somewhere behind.

And Lalie had believed the worst was over when they straggled out of the jungle. Tilting her head back, she gazed up at the distant stars. She suspected the worst was yet to come.

While waiting for March to return from Hiberalta, Joao had stocked the *Addison Beal* with wood for the boiler. The entire lower deck was filled with lengths of wood split into boiler size. Joao, Tomli, and Jono spelled each other in the stifling boiler room feeding the fire.

Freed of the necessity to stop for wood, Fredo and March kept the *Addison Beal* in the swift, powerful currents far offshore. The ship quickly traveled downriver, seizing the advantage of breeze and currents that cut their time significantly. When Lalie inquired, March estimated they would reach Manaus in a third of the time it had taken them to travel in the opposite direction.

Deeply concerned, Lalie studied March's countenance with the same objective eye she once had trained on the patients who came into her father's office. Today his skin looked hot and dry, chalky beneath his tan. His eyes were dull. She noticed he pushed his midday meal around his plate, hardly touching the food.

"You have to eat something," she urged.

The quinine tablets diminished his symptoms and kept him on his feet, but there weren't enough tablets to vanquish the illness. He alternated between periods of low fever and mild chills, a continual headache furrowed his brow. His weariness and waning vitality were becoming increasingly evident.

"Lalie, please." Before saying more, March passed a hand over his forehead and clenched his jaw. "I know you're trying to help, but your constant fussing is driving me mad. If you must fuss, fuss over Clea."

Frowning, she turned toward a long bank of clouds boiling up from the south. By now Lalie knew the reddening sky, the gray and purple clouds, signaled an approaching deluge. Flashes of lightning speared distant treetops. The air grew hot and still. Every trace of a breeze disappeared. Even from a mile offshore Lalie could smell the rank odor of the jungle, rotting leaves, logs, and moist earth.

She sighed, watching the storm rush toward them. "I thought this was supposed to be the dry season," she said, choosing not to take offense at March's earlier remark. Of course he was irritable. He was working long, stressful hours when he should have been in bed. His head hurt; he ached all over.

"There's no such thing as a dry season, not really," March said, managing a smile as he stood and gave his untouched plate to Maria. "Just less wet." He too focused on the approaching wall of clouds. The southern sky flared red then shaded toward black. A breeze returned, bending the treetops and increasing in intensity. "This is going to be a big one," he commented after a moment. Frowning, he rubbed his eyes. "Maria, you'd better tie down your kitchen. Lalie, instruct Joao to secure a safe spot on the lower deck for you and Clea and Maria."

Nodding, Lalie watched him return to the wheelhouse, his step unsteady. Then she leaned over the railing and peered downriver, her expression reflecting growing unease. This section of the Solimões cut through the jungle forest like a razor slash. There were no obstructions to deflect the rising wind and no place along shore where the *Addison Beal* might seek shelter from the rapidly approaching storm. They would be at the mercy of the sky and the river.

Working quickly, Lalie helped Maria rope down her supplies and secure the kitchen area before she went in search of Joao, leaving Maria to prepare Clea to move to the lower deck.

Having anticipated the need, Joao had already draped heavy netting over the stacks of wood to prevent them from rolling down on the small nestlike area he had prepared for the women. Over the netting he arranged voluminous tarpaulins to keep the wood dry. When Lalie appeared, he paused to wipe his forehead and glance at the swelling black clouds. The breeze stiffened and a light chop stippled the river's surface. Whitecaps appeared on long rolling swells as a crack of lightning splintered the sky and a growl of thunder rolled across the hot silence.

"We may need help getting Clea down the stairs," Lalie said, glancing at the rings and rope with which they would tie themselves to the boiler-room wall.

Joao peered at the rapidly vanishing sliver of sunlight. "We do it now," he urged uneasily. "The storm moving very fast."

The first raindrops pelted them as they dashed up the staircase, the large drops cool against heated skin. They arrived to find March and Maria helping a white-faced Clea out of her hammock.

Maria cast a worried glance toward Lalie then slipped her arm around Clea's swollen waist, careful not to jostle her bandaged shoulder.

"The baby come now," Maria explained as Clea smothered a groan.

"Now?" Lalie gasped and stared at Clea.

When the contraction eased, Clea raised a pale, apologetic smile. "I'm sorry."

"Don't worry," Lalie said unconvincingly. "Everything will work out fine." A drumroll of raindrops tattooed the roof of the deck, falling faster and heavier by the second. The upper deck swayed as the water roughened. A sheet of spindrift floated across the deck, drenching hair and clothing. "Maria, you and Joao take Clea below. I'll bring the blankets."

Before she followed them to the lower deck, she met March's gaze. His skin looked pale; he had clenched his teeth to keep them from chattering. Lalie's heart skipped a beat as she recognized the signals of approaching chill.

With an expression that brooked no argument, she draped one of the blankets around his shoulders and pulled his face down to hers. "Listen to me, March Addison. Stay inside the wheelhouse and keep dry. Maria left you a jug of hot *cafezinho.* Warm your hands and face in the steam." Shoulders sagging, she looked at him helplessly. "Oh God, March. You're ill, Clea's having a baby, and the storm—it's going to be bad, isn't it?"

He tried to smile. She saw a tremor pass down his body. "Do you have a knife?" he asked, raising his voice to be heard above the gusting wind. They both knew the knife was to cut the ropes if the *Addison Beal* capsized. When she nodded, he gave his head a shake as if to toss aside the terrible possibility of losing her. "I love you, Lalie," he said, holding her by the shoulders and staring down at her.

"I love you, too," she whispered. Wind whipped the ends of her hair. The shoreline was no longer visible through the black rain and tossing waves.

"Do what you can for Clea," he urged. The words were almost lost in the din of rain pounding the deck roof. "And keep yourself safe for me." Quickly he embraced her, holding her for one long moment against his heart, drawing warmth from her yielding body. She framed his face between her small hands, met his gaze, then kissed him fiercely before she spun out of his arms and ran toward the staircase.

He stood unmoving, his legs wide and braced against the heavy sway of the ship, until she reached the staircase. For an instant she looked back and their eyes met, then she plunged down the steps and disappeared from view.

Only then did March surrender to a violent fit of shivering. He closed his eyes and lowered his chin into the folds of the blanket until the tremors eased. From experience he knew the chills would pass in about thirty minutes and would be followed by flushes of heat. Swearing, he pushed his aching body back to the wheelhouse.

A bolt of lightning turned the jungle white and Fredo glanced at him in the sudden light. "You shaking very bad, Cabo. Can you steer?" he asked in a level voice.

"Better than I can see," March admitted.

"Then you be the hands, and I be the eyes."

The men exchanged places as a wall of water crashed over the bow. The battle began.

"We're safe here, snug as bugs," Lalie shouted in a falsely bright voice as she wrapped a wet blanket around Clea's upper body.

They had braced Clea against the warm boiler-room wall, enclosing her in a cocoon of blankets after tying the rope under her armpits. Lalie and Maria were tethered at the waist, giving them greater freedom of movement. They watched in anxious silence as Clea bent forward again, clutched her stomach and moaned. While they waited, listening to the roar of wind and water, Lalie braced her back against the stack of wood, wiped the water from her eyes, and scanned their supplies for the hundredth time.

In a waterproof packet Maria had stowed one warm, dry blanket for the baby, and they had tied a covered bucket of clean water to one of the wall rings. Finally, Maria had given her birthing-bite to Clea, as she had mournfully abandoned hope of ever needing it herself.

When Clea's contraction eased and she lay back panting, Lalie removed the birthing-bite from between Clea's teeth. It was a lovingly carved piece of soft, smooth wood, now bearing the repeated imprint of Clea's bite. The birthing-bite had been Fredo's wedding gift to Maria and she had counted it among her most precious possessions. That Maria offered the birthing-bite to Clea signified a heart-wrenching death of her dreams. The recognition made Lalie's chest ache.

Leaning forward on her knees, Lalie wiped sweat and rain from Clea's brow, watching as Maria passed a hand over Clea's stomach then nodded to signal all was going well. The women tried to ignore the wall of water that suddenly soared up near the railing then fell with a sickening crash back to the river. They were drenched to the skin and shivering.

"You're doing fine," Lalie shouted. But when she rearranged the blankets over Clea's breast, she noticed Clea's exertion had opened her shoulder wound and a streak of pink had appeared on her wet shift.

Clea stared up at her, her eyes wide with pain and fear. "I love him," she whispered. Her tears mixed with the thick spray tossed up by the foaming waves. "He was not good to me, but—but, oh God, I love him."

"I know," Lalie said grimly. She slipped the birthing-bite back into Clea's mouth. Another contraction came as lightning opened the sky, and before the brilliant flash blinded her, Lalie saw Clea's contorted features, saw Maria's hands pushing, helping. And she also lurched hard toward the rail as the *Addison Beal* struck something, dipped and shuddered.

The wind roared down the straight slash of the Solimões, whipping the river into giant walls of foam and water. Just as Clea fell back, gasping, a tower of water smashed over the lower deck, deluging them before it ran hissing and foaming out from beneath the railing. Choking and coughing, Lalie wiped her face then Clea's before she removed the birthing-bite from Clea's mouth.

"Why couldn't he have loved me and kept me with him?" Clea gasped, holding her stomach. She peered up at Lalie with bewildered dark eyes. "I'm going to die," she said, repeating the words over and over. "I don't want to live."

Maria pushed past Lalie to grip Clea's shoulders and give her a hard shake. "You have your baby to live for!" she shouted. Her eyes blazed.

"I'm a whore!" Clea moaned. "What kind of life can a whore give a child?" Despair drained the color from her lips and eyes as she stared up at Lalie and Maria, panting for breath. "He would never have married me. He would never have admitted my baby was his!"

Lalie was spared a reply as the *Addison Beal* pitched into a sudden hard list. A scream tore from her throat as she hurtled toward the railing and a hissing, foaming nightmare of water. The rope bit into her waist, catching her. Then she was flung backward again, striking her head against the boiler-room wall.

Clea screamed. Lightning cracked and thunder roared. Once a dugout was flung onto the lower deck, narrowly missing Maria's legs. When the women cleared their eyes and mouths, the dugout was gone. A snake slithered from between Lalie's feet and vanished in the blackness.

Wind swallowed Clea's screams and snatched at Lalie's words of encouragement. One hour merged into another and still the storm raged and new life fought to emerge.

"I see the head!" Maria shouted finally, shaking wet hair back from her face. Determination erased the weariness in her gaze. "Push, Clea! Push!"

Blood gushed from between Clea's thighs and streamed from her wound as she sat forward, gathered her strength, then ground her teeth down on the birthing-bite and gripped Lalie's hand.

"Again! We're almost there. Again!"

Braced as best they could, the three women fought the pitch and roll of the ship and the terrifying power of rampaging nature. Water streamed from their faces. Wind whipped the waves into frenzied peaks and tore the words from their lips.

"Now! Now! Oh God!" Tears and rain washed Clea's face. She looked too weak and exhausted to make the final effort, but she clenched her teeth and bore down.

"Sim!" Maria cried joyfully. She pressed down on Clea's contracting stomach.

And Lalie, tears stinging her eyes, oblivious to the water swirling around her knees, guided the baby into her hands. She stared at it, then hunched over the small form to protect it as a massive wave crashed over her and knocked her on her side. When the flood rushed away, she struggled up and hastily brushed the water from the infant's tiny face. A small, lusty cry shouted against the wind and Lalie laughed out loud. Maria handed her a cloth and together they cleaned the baby and wrapped it in the dry blanket before Lalie placed the infant in Clea's trembling arms.

"You have a son, Clea."

She didn't know if Clea heard above the roar and shriek of wind and water and wailing ship's timbers, but for a moment Clea's weary expression softened to a smile, and she closed her eyes then pressed her lips to the baby's cap of downy dark hair.

It was now, as the tension began to lift, that Lalie finally noticed the scarlet pool drenching the hem of Clea's shift. Water swirled over the deck and drained away, but the rush of blood swiftly pooled again. Horror stiffened Lalie's body. Clea was hemorrhaging, and there was nothing anyone could do.

When Lalie lifted stricken eyes, she knew Clea understood she was dying.

"No!" Lalie cried, shaking her head violently.

"Give my child to someone who will love him as I would have loved him," Clea whispered. Someone who will teach him . . . to love the river."

Lightning ripped the sky, and in the flash, Lalie saw the stream of blood had widened. Swallowing a scream that threatened to strangle her, she gripped Clea's hand and leaned close to hear her whisper.

"When my son is old enough, tell him . . ." Clea's eyes, fluttered and closed. "Tell him . . ."

"No!" Lalie screamed. "Oh God, no!" When she frantically dashed the water from her eyes and looked again, Clea was gone.

As fast as it had come, the storm ended. Hot sunlight bored through the thinning overcast and lit the jungle with glistening vibrant green. During the storm the *Addison Beal* had been thrown toward the shore, and Lalie could see hanging and broken leaves, heavy with crystal droplets. Brilliantly colored birds emerged and shook themselves dry. Thousands of insects resumed their symphony. A sodden monkey clung to a dangling liana inspecting a patch of raw red earth along the altered shoreline and the muddy swirl beneath it.

Lalie sat with her back against the boiler-room wall, cradling Clea's baby in her arms, her eyes red from weeping. She didn't feel the temperature rise or her chilled skin begin to warm, didn't remember Maria leaving her or Joao and Fredo coming to take Clea's body away. She stared unseeing at the rare twin rainbows that lit the southern bank of the Solimões.

"Lalie?" March knelt beside her and touched her pale, wet cheek.

"Clea is dead," she murmured, her voice expressionless.

"I know," he said gently.

"Percival Sterling killed her as surely as if he held a gun to her head," she said between her teeth, staring at him.

"Come with me, dearest. You're cold and soaked to the skin." He cut the rope that bound her waist then helped her to her feet. "You and the baby need dry clothes."

Her mind cleared then and she looked at him for the

first time. "Oh March," she whispered. He was dreadfully ill, shaking with chills while at the same time flushed with fever. His face was hot and burning when she touched his skin, but his hands were like blocks of ice. Tremors racked his body despite his efforts to control them.

By the time they reached the debris-strewn upper deck, Maria had strung March's hammock and had a cup of steaming *guaraná* waiting. "Drink this and put on these dry clothes then get into the hammock, Cabo. No argument."

That he obeyed sent a chill down Lalie's spine. She watched with fearful eyes as he silently stripped off his wet clothing, his splendid body shaking with chills, then pulled on the trousers and heavy shirt Maria pushed into his hands. He looked at Lalie apologetically, then rolled into his hammock.

"Oh March," she said softly, peering through the netting at him. Fear constricted her chest and made it hard to breathe. Wrapping her arms around the infant, she rocked back and forth, not taking her gaze from March's face.

"So much work to do . . . sorry . . ." he murmured, looking up at her. "Feel like a damned . . . fool!"

"Just rest," Lalie whispered, trying to keep the fear out of her voice. "Sleep is the best thing, darling. Sleep and get well. We'll manage without you."

His effort to grin wrenched her heart. "Just what . . . I feared."

After Fredo assured himself that the *Addison Beal* had sustained no incapacitating damage, he ordered Joao to stoke the boiler and immediately they got under way again. They stayed near the shoreline, seeking a river hamlet. When they spotted a few stilt houses, they dropped anchor, and there they buried Clea on a bluff overlooking the river. Once they were back on the river, Tomli and Jono silently went about cleaning the storm debris, while Joao built a pen on the lower deck for the goat they had purchased in the hamlet to provide milk for the baby.

When the baby slept, Lalie gently placed him in the rocker she and Maria had earlier made from a champagne crate, placing the crate near the warmth of Maria's stove. After giving him the sugar tit Maria prepared, she pressed Maria's shoulder then went to the wheelhouse to stand beside Fredo. They looked out at the river and waves that were still white-tipped and choppy.

"How much farther to Manaus?" she asked quietly, bracing her legs against the roll of the ship.

"If we get early start tomorrow, we reach Manaus late afternoon."

"What will happen then?"

"Maybe," Fredo said slowly after a lengthy pause, "Joao can slip in and out and Rivaldi's men not see him. We get quinine then run downriver."

"Is it likely that Rivaldi's men will fail to spot us or Joao?" Lalie asked after an equally long pause.

Fredo frowned and he squinted over a curl of smoke drifting from his cigar. "We going to find out, Missy."

They stood together, watching the river, alert to sandbars that had changed position during the storm, watching for tree limbs and roots and other debris from the storm. Lalie sensed the river as a living entity and knew Fredo did the same. They could not see beneath the river's surface but could sense the life there and the currents that ran like arteries beneath their bare feet.

"March needs complete bed rest. If he . . ." She bit her lip. "Can you get Tomli and Jono to their village if you have to do it alone?" Lalie asked. Their pace was grueling and even Fredo had begun to show the effect of the strain. Red lines mapped the whites of his eyes. Exhaustion had leached the rich walnut hue of his skin to a gray muddy shade.

"I will do it, Missy."

She nodded. "What can I do to help?"

He smiled. "Shoot any bastard who tries to stop us." The smile hardened on his lips. "Cabo too sick to shoot straight. Tomli and Jono have never held a gun. Maria, she scared of guns. Me, I be here at the wheel. You and Joao—you the only guns we got, Missy."

"Good God," Lalie breathed, staring at him. She thought of Lum Sarto and his men, thought about the numbers Rivaldi could throw against them and a shudder rippled down her spine.

Then she straightened her shoulders and her gaze narrowed. Her bare toes curled against the deck and her fists clenched against her trousers. A half-dozen plans formed and faded and formed again in her mind. Bending, she lifted March's Winchester and broke it open over her arm, inspected the chamber then snapped it shut.

"You can count on me," she said firmly. "No one is going to stop us."

The woman who had left Manaus was not the woman who would return to it.

Chapter 22

March struggled out of a vivid *guaraná*-induced dream. Confused and disoriented, he looked around, realizing that reality itself had assumed nightmarish qualities.

A string of swear words burst from the wheelhouse then running feet pounded across the deck. When he tried to sit up, his head spun painfully and he discovered some idiot had lashed him to the wheelhouse wall and surrounded him with sandbags. More astonishing still, he had a baby tied in a sling across his chest. He blinked at the sleeping infant with an incredulous expression and shook his head, trying to clear it.

In some dim corner of his mind he comprehended that the tiny newborn's presence should not astonish him. But try as he would, he could not recall where the baby might have come from. Clea's image flickered in his mind followed by a sense of loss, but he couldn't pull the puzzle together. Surely the baby must belong to Maria but he couldn't remember her being pregnant. He could not fathom why Maria would have tied her baby in a sling around his chest or why he was roped to the wall so tightly he could hardly move.

"They're waiting! There! Guns on the seawall, and a gunboat coming up fast from behind that passenger liner!"

Lalie's voice? Fog swirled in his head. Trying not to disturb the baby, March lifted on one elbow and attempted to peer over the surrounding sandbags.

Beneath his body, the deck vibrated as the *Addison Beal*'s engine rumbled to full throttle. From the lower deck, he heard Joao shout to someone in the boiler room. A choking cloud of smoke belched from the stacks and the *Addison Beal* began to pick up speed. They were at Manaus, March realized dully. He got a glimpse of church spires and the golden dome of the opera house. And he saw sunlight glint across the barrels of guns arranged along the seawall. There weren't the usual number of ships and steamers docked at the wharf and what vessels there were seemed deserted.

As if he were still dreaming, he calmly watched flashes of light blossom from the gun barrels, felt the ship sway as bullets smacked into the side. A half-dozen splintered holes appeared in the support post nearest him. Answering shots sounded from the lower deck and again from a position not far from where March strained to see.

Rising further, he saw Lalie and Maria leaning against a barrier of sandbags that had been stacked against the railing. Maria sat with her back against the bags, handing cartridges up to Lalie, who was kneeling on a stool, firing March's Winchester over the rail into the hail of gunfire.

He blinked and stared, no longer calm, frantically trying to understand what he was seeing and hearing. Lalie wore a pair of men's trousers that rounded over her buttocks in a provocative curve. Her hair was braided and fell down her back like a rope of fire. But this was not as strange as the fact that she was firing the Winchester as fast as she could load, her hands sure and her mouth set in a hard, cold line. Bullets whizzed past her head but she took no notice, continuing to fire the Winchester as if life depended on it.

The baby shifted in the sling tied over his chest and he

dropped his head to stare at it and wonder where it had come from. Then a bullet hit one of his sandbags and his arms instinctively folded around the infant. It penetrated his fogged mind that people were shooting at them. Shooting at Lalie.

Swearing and straining against the ropes that held him, he fought to rise and failed. Cursing with frustration, he shoved upward as far as he could, looking over the sandbags to see the river and a little of the shore as the *Addison Beal* swerved away from Manaus and ran for the deep currents.

"Behind us!" Lalie screamed, jumping up from her stool. As she raced past him toward the stern, she saw he was conscious. "Keep your head down," she shouted. His jaw dropped as she ran out of his line of sight.

When March realized the action was now behind them and he could see nothing more, he dropped back, cradling the amazing baby against his chest while he tried to twist free of the ropes. He couldn't make himself understand what was happening, but he knew he should be part of it, knew they were in danger. He had no knife to cut the ropes that bound him and was too weak to break free. All he could do was listen and feel the *Addison Beal* shudder as it strained to capacity. The smell of smoke from the stacks and the acrid odor of gunfire stung his nostrils. The sound of shots went on and on.

Sweat poured from his body, soaking the sling holding the sleeping baby. He tried to keep his eyes open but he couldn't. Reality and dream blended in his fevered mind. The fox's red tail flashed in front of him and he urged his horse forward. The English countryside smelled of rain. Some fool fired at the fox without a care for the yapping dogs and March turned his head to scowl. Astonishingly he saw a baby and smelled one, too. Who on earth had been foolish enough to bring a baby to a hunt?

The scene tilted in confusion and he realized he wasn't

chasing a fox, he was hunting tapir. The scents of the forest surrounded him, and the chill, suddenly giving way to the scent of gunpowder.

"March? Darling, wake up." A gentle hand shook his shoulder and his eyes fluttered.

"Lalie," he whispered, staring up into the oval face leaning over him. "You are so beautiful. So hauntingly lovely. Your eyes are like emerald rain."

"Can you stand? Lean on me." Anxiety choked her voice.

For a moment he didn't move anything but his eyes. The sandbags were gone as was the baby. He thought he must have imagined them until he glanced toward Maria's stove and saw her sitting in a pool of lantern light, smiling down at a bundle in her arms. A tiny fist waved above the blanket.

"The ship's moving," he said, frowning as Lalie helped him to his feet. It was dangerous to run the Amazon at night. Every captain could relate a dozen stories about foolhardy idiots who had been wrecked on the sandbars by attempting to navigate in the darkness.

"Fredo is almost certain we've outrun them, but he wants to be sure. We'll drop anchor in another hour or so."

Her arm was cool around his waist. He inhaled the fragrance of her hair. When she made him sit on the side of his hammock and instructed him to eat a bowl of food floating in a soapy-looking broth, he made a face and pushed the food away then tilted his head and studied her.

Smoke darkened her cheeks and the man's shirt she wore. Loose strands of hair had pulled free from her braid and floated about her face. She was so luminous and beautiful that she stopped the breath in his chest. He stared at a smear of blood streaked across the thigh of her trousers, straining to understand why she was dressed as she was and how the blood came to be there.

"It's nothing," she said softly. Her fingertips fluttered

in a gesture of dismissal. "The bullet hardly touched me. Eat. Then you can rest."

"Bullet," he repeated, frowning. He could not work it out in his mind. "You said we outran them. Who did we outrun?"

Leaning against the support post beneath a lantern, she pushed the loose hair back from her face. A look of grim satisfaction shone in her eyes. Had any other woman ever had such splendid eyes? He didn't think it possible.

"We made the mistake of stopping above the bend outside Manaus to assess our situation and fill the sandbags." He continued to stare at her clothing, unable to imagine why Miss Pritchard was dressed in male attire, but he liked the way the shirt molded the top of her breasts and the trousers shaped her hips and calves. "We must have been spotted because Rivaldi's men were waiting for us."

Rivaldi. His frown intensified and his head jerked up. "Rivaldi's men were firing at us!"

She nodded. "We held our own. A stack of wood fell on Tomli, but he isn't hurt badly. Joao and I had a couple of close calls, but nothing serious." A proud smile exposed small, pearly teeth. "We did more damage than we received." At this statement her smile wavered. She gave her head a shake and he could almost see her thoughts shift forcibly away from guns and bullets. "Fredo was magnificent," she said with a grin. "He mounted wings on the *Addison Beal.* We flew out of the Manaus harbor."

March's gaze darted toward the stern and the river behind them. The starlit ribbon of water was empty of traffic.

Miss Pritchard took the plate from his hands and gently pressed him back into the hammock. "The good news is they've abandoned the chase. Fredo thinks Rivaldi is satisfied to close the harbor to us and chase us away. Such honor as he possesses is appeased." Leaning over the hammock, she placed her hand on his hot face and alarm brimmed in her eyes. She spoke in a quiet voice. "The bad news is we didn't get your quinine."

Finally he understood. After wetting his lips with his tongue, he drank the *guaraná* she gave him, watching her all the while. "I'm ill," he said, handing back the cup. "The fever." That explained his confusion. He couldn't recall ever having a bout this intense.

"Very ill," she agreed in a soft, worried voice. "We'll stop in Parintins for quinine before we return Tomli and Jono to their village. Hang on until then, darling. At the pace Fredo is maintaining, it won't be long." Leaning, she kissed him lightly on the lips then dropped the netting around him.

March stared in wonder as she extinguished the lantern then moved toward the others gathered around Maria's stove. Her Majesty had called him darling and she had kissed him. He blinked at the hot darkness in amazement. He suspected his illness and the resultant confusion masked one hell of a lot of wonderful changes. Cursing his fever and headache, he impatiently wished himself instantly cured and his memory restored.

Then the *guaraná* wove its magic and he drifted into a drugged sleep. He dreamed of a moon-dappled courtyard and ivory-colored silk billowing around him. A satiny curtain of reddish-gold hair fell across his naked chest and long, slender legs wrapped around his waist. Lilac and verbena teased his senses.

When he next roused himself, it was daylight. Groggily, head aching, he struggled upward and lifted the netting draping his hammock. The *Addison Beal* was running the swift, powerful currents in the center of the river. Only by squinting could March make out a strip of green signaling the distant shore.

Blinking, fighting to focus his thoughts, he turned his head toward the wheelhouse and saw Miss Pritchard standing in the doorway holding a baby in her arms. Sunlight slanted across the deck, shimmering on her coppery hair and caressing her golden skin. Reassured, he dropped the netting and fell back into the hammock.

Lalie sat quietly, her hands clasped tightly in her lap, watching Maria cooing over the baby, which she had named Luis Alfredo in honor of Fredo's father. Last night Lalie had formally presented Clea's baby to Maria and Fredo and asked if they would raise the boy as their own son. The joy in the couple's eyes had eased the pain Lalie had felt at relinquishing the infant.

For nearly a week Lalie had wrestled with the question, longing to find a way to keep Luis Alfredo herself. Finally, she had faced what her heart had known from the beginning. Clea's baby was a child of the Amazon. Clea had wanted her son to remain on the river and to love it. She would have been pleased to know Fredo would raise the boy to be a river captain. And Fredo would be a far better father than the man whose blue eyes gazed out of Luis Alfredo's tiny face.

Lalie sighed then turned a worried gaze toward March's hammock. She wished she could have discussed the baby's future with him, and hoped he would approve her decision. But a coherent discussion was only intermittently possible.

March was fearfully weak. He drifted in and out of lucidity. Sometimes he was coherent for long periods, aware of the present and past and able to advise on the future. More often he lapsed into feverish mumblings and had no memory of previous conversations or events.

The fever flared with a vengeance from time to time, always followed by drenching sweats. Trying not to think what his frighteningly rapid pulse and breathing might mean, Lalie fanned March when the burning sweats erupted and packed blankets around him during the teeth-chattering chills. Twice a day she massaged cedar oil into his aching muscles and joints, weeping as her hands moved over his naked body.

As the days wore on Lalie became terrified that March was dying.

Dropping her head one day, she covered her face with her hands and drew long, shuddering breaths. "Don't die," she commanded silently. "Don't leave me now that I've found you!"

Maria's hand pressed her shoulder. "Is bad luck that we find so little quinine in Parintins."

The muddy little river settlement had yielded only a quarter of a bottle of quinine, not enough to provide more than momentary relief. They had stayed in Parintins only long enough to reprovision. Then had headed down the river again in search of the medicine they needed to save March's life.

Lalie raised her head and gave Maria a miserable look. "God forgive me but I wish we could just leave Tomli and Jono at the tributary and race for Santarém. I'm so afraid for March."

"Even flying with the currents, Missy, Santarém is almost two weeks from the tributary."

They both cast anxious frowns toward March's hammock, not noticing Tomli until he coughed. Careful not to meet their gaze directly, Tomli spoke in a rapid flow of Tupi, pointing toward March's hammock then to the shore. The urgency in his tone frustrated Lalie as much as her lack of comprehension. Finally she lifted her palms and shook her head then strode toward the wheelhouse, gesturing to Tomli to follow.

Fredo listened intently as Tomli spoke.

"Fredo—what did he say?" Lalie demanded impatiently.

"He say Cabo very sick. He say we carry Cabo to Tilwe's village. Healing woman make him well."

"Is that possible?" Lalie asked doubtfully. "Didn't the

healing woman die at Hiberalta? And would the Indians have quinine?"

Fredo spoke to Tomli, then addressed Lalie. "He say the healing woman's apprentice fix up Cabo. She has bark from the cinchona tree. Tomli say the bark good for fever."

Lalie gasped and her eyes shone with hope. "Quinine is made from the cinchona tree!"

Fredo glanced at her. "Whatever the healing woman have, Missy, it won't be like the quinine in the bottles."

"But it's quinine!" She gripped his arm and stared into his black eyes. "I don't know if March can make it to Santarém," she said urgently. "He's so weak. Fredo, we have to take him to Tilwe's village. That may be his only chance."

Fredo patted her hand and nodded. "Then we carry him to the village, Missy."

His jaw tightened as he considered what the decision might mean. It was impossible to know if Sterling's men still pursued them, but he had to assume they did. Therefore he could not leave Maria, the baby, and Joao behind on the *Addison Beal* while he took Cabo and Missy to the healing woman. They would all have to go to the village. And they might have to remain there for some time, until Cabo was well enough to resume travel.

This being the case, he navigated the *Addison Beal* as far up the tributary as possible before the river bottom rose dangerously high and he feared running aground. That night, even though Tomli and Jono quivered with impatience to slip away into the jungle, Fredo enlisted their aid in camouflaging the *Addison Beal* as best they could with netting, leaves, and branches.

In the morning he discovered Tomli and Jono had gone. Their departure surprised no one. It was, in fact, reassuring to know the village would be expecting them.

Lalie, Fredo, and Joao assisted a half-delirious March

down the plank and laid him in one of the dugouts. After they had arranged him as comfortably as possible in the cramped quarters and fashioned an awning to shade him, Fredo returned for Maria and Luis Alfredo, settling them in the second dugout, which Joao would paddle.

"Can you paddle?" he asked Lalie, taking his position in the dugout that carried March.

"I can learn," she said firmly.

They made a wobbly, uncertain start, but Lalie eventually got the hang of it, and the two dugouts moved up the waters of the tributary. In short order Lalie learned that paddling was hard, exhausting work. Her shoulder and back muscles shrieked in protest at every stroke.

As the water continued to narrow and the jungle foliage closed around them March rambled deliriously and Lalie listened to his weak voice with an aching heart.

"You have to get well," she whispered through a shimmer of tears. "You must, my darling!"

A dozen Mundurukú warriors waited for them. Their tattooed faces and painted bodies emerged from the foliage as the dugouts approached the shore. Silently, they waded into the water and pulled the dugouts up onto the pebbled beach.

Although Lalie displayed the good manners not to gaze at the naked Indians directly, from the corner of her eye she recognized Tilwe and Buti, Irikina's husband. They placed March into a hammock and swung the poles over their shoulders before they entered the jungle forest. Leaving Fredo and Joao to see to Maria and the baby, Lalie plunged into the cool, dense forest after the warriors, running to keep pace with them.

By the time they reached the village, she was panting and sweating. Thorns had scratched her arms and clothing. One of the small, naked women rushed forward and pushed a gourd of manioc beer into Lalie's hand. She nodded gratefully but didn't pause to drink until they passed the central *maloca* and approached the healing woman's thatched hut.

The new healing woman waited beside the doorway. She was so slender that Lalie almost mistook her for a boy until she drew near and noticed the woman's painted breasts. Spirals of red and black dye circled her breasts, winding around her body and up over her face. A single red feather pierced one ear; she wore a necklace made of jaguar teeth. Pointing a bony finger, she directed the warriors carrying March to a narrow sleeping platform surrounded on all sides by small fires.

Lalie followed the warriors inside the hut and immediately broke into a profuse sweat. The interior of the hut was horribly hot, smoky and malodorous. A clay pot hung suspended over each fire, its bubbling contents emitting a stench that stung her eyes and nostrils.

Once March had been placed on the platform, the healing woman's glance drove the warriors out. For a long moment her challenging gaze fixed on Lalie.

"I'm not leaving," Lalie said quietly, meeting the healing woman's black eyes.

The healing woman did not comprehend the words, but she understood Lalie's stance and stubborn expression. Finally she pointed to Lalie then to a bark mat on the floor. She then set to work, thereafter ignoring Lalie's presence.

First the healing woman peeled off March's clothing. Lalie's heart ached at how thin he had become. The scars on his chest curved over his ribs as if the muscle beneath had melted away. Biting her lip, she gazed at his sweat-drenched skin glistening in the firelight. She remembered him sweeping her easily into his arms and carrying her up the stairs to a moon-bathed room, where his powerful body had so completely dominated hers. Tears glittered in her blue-green eyes, but she did not allow them to fall.

Next the healing woman bathed March with a sharp-smelling dark liquid. When that was done, she painted his groin, chest, and forehead with swirls, taking care to obtain exactly the symbols she wanted. Afterward, she lifted his damp head and spooned liquid from one of the clay pots between his lips. Then she lowered herself to a cross-legged position on a bark mat beside him, drank from a bowl she had placed there, closed her eyes, and began to sway and sing in a low monotone.

Lalie stared and her spirits plummeted. Her disappointment was like a knife plunged into her heart. She had invested all hope in the Mundurukú healing woman, pinning her faith on some kind of primitive Indian magic. But this was not magic nor was it medicine. This was nothing. Suffocating heat, painted symbols, and chanting would not cure malaria.

"Quinine!" she shouted, bending over the healing woman, her body shaking. "Where is the quinine?"

Continuing her chant, the healing woman ignored her.

Lalie ground her fists against her eyelids, fighting the scream that clawed at her throat. She sucked in a long draught of the smoky, foul-smelling air, then she spun on her heels and ran to the back of the hut. On the shelves behind the healing woman's stew pot were rows and rows of seeds, twigs and leaves, animal skins, stacks of bark strips and tubers, mushrooms, dried fish scales, webs of fungus, and other items Lalie didn't recognize.

Which bark came from the cinchona tree? Was one of the piles of powder the quinine she sought? Tears of desperation swam in her eyes. Despairing, she lifted one bark strip then another, unable to discern any but the most obvious differences and even then ignorant of what she was seeing. Was the cinchona bark this strip, or that? Dropping her head into her hands, she tried to breathe past the vise tightening around her chest. Then she spun back to the healing woman.

"Quinine!" she shouted. "Help me! I need quinine!"

The healing woman's trance had taken her beyond hearing. She continued to sway and chant. Her eyes reflected the fires as she stared at a vision revealed to her alone.

With a cry of frustration, Lalie stumbled from the hut, emerging into the blistering sunlight. She sank to her knees in front of the doorway, blind to all but her own despair.

Only gradually did she become aware of the silent women surrounding her and the village opening in front of her.

Finally she saw the women working in their manioc gardens behind the central *maloca,* and smelled the smoke from the cooking fires. Two children played with a pet monkey to her left. To her right a small painted man painstakingly carved darts for his blowgun.

Children ran laughing and shrieking through the clearing. A group of warriors demonstrated their bows for Fredo and Joao. Maria stood among a cluster of women rocking Luis Alfredo in a hammock strung between the *maloca* posts. Chickens pecked the hard-packed ground; parrots preened themselves in the thatch. Old men dozed in the shade of the huts.

"He's dying," Lalie whispered, her voice cracking. She wanted to scream at them to stop and share her grief. Stop placing fish on racks to dry; stop passing manioc beer as if this day were like any other. "My love is dying!" she cried.

A shy hand touched her shoulder. She wiped her eyes then blinked up at a young woman cradling a fat baby in the crook of her arm.

"Irikina."

The woman smiled timidly then drew Lalie to her feet and attempted to lead her away from the healing woman's hut. Gently, Lalie resisted. She had to stay near March, she could not leave him.

Fredo noticed her distress and came to her side to

interpret for her. The women listened, pity in their eyes. They knew the hardship of living without a man. One by one they slipped away, leaving only Irikina.

Irikina sat on the ground beside Lalie outside the healing woman's hut. The women brought them manioc beer, and Lalie held the baby she had delivered. Irikina stayed with her the entire day. Listening to Lalie's incomprehensible words, offering solace and encouragement, sharing Lalie's pain.

Lalie found herself telling Irikina all about herself and March and the love they shared. It mattered not at all that the Indian woman understood none of it. It only mattered that she had someone to speak to.

When darkness had descended, they still sat in front of the hut. Men told hunting stories around the fires and children dozed in their mothers' arms. Lalie discovered Maria had joined her. She and Irikina sat beside Lalie, holding their babies, trying to comfort her.

At length Irikina stood and offered her hand. This time Lalie grasped it and followed her to the stew pot in Buti's hut.

One day followed another as alike as the waves that bathed the shores of the Amazon.

Lalie rose before dawn each morning. She slipped from her platform in Buti's hut, washed her face and hands, then crossed the dewy clearing to the healing woman's hut, praying that March would be better. Having gradually earned the healing woman's trust, she was permitted to bathe March each morning, and spoon the healing woman's concoctions between his lips. She spent the day by his side, swaying in the steaming heat inside the hut, feeling her sanity waver as she watched the healing woman's ministrations.

The healing woman chanted. She painted symbols on March's body and on her own. One day she covered his nakedness with twigs and dried leaves. Another day, she applied her lips to his body, sucking out evil spirits. She ground powders and stirred them into bitter brews. She chewed leaves into paste and patted the paste into cakes that she fed to the delirious man on the platform. She spread cooling mud over his body then washed it away with smears of wild honey. Nothing made sense to the doctor's daughter who watched.

Lalie sat on the bark mat beside March and observed the healing woman with fading hope. Hysteria threatened to overwhelm her from time to time, but she fought it off. Today was different, however. Today she sensed an approaching crisis.

Suddenly the healing woman straightened from where she had been kneeling beside March's naked, unconscious body. As if only now becoming aware of Lalie, she spread her long, bony arms and advanced, her eyes glaring out of the black and red circles. The angry words she shouted were unintelligible, but their meaning was clear.

And today Lalie was too exhausted, too filled with despair to fight. Standing, she pressed a hand to her eyelids, then, doing as the healing woman insisted, she stumbled out of the dark, sweltering hut into the sunshine. When her eyes adjusted to the glare, she scanned the clearing then drew a breath and set off through the forest, welcoming the cooler, damp air.

Almost at once she understood what she was seeking and eventually she stumbled across the waterfall March had once taken her to. For several minutes she stood with her face lifted to the sun while she remembered March standing here. Then she dropped to her knees beside the lily pond and scooped cool water over her face and throat.

"Let him live," she murmured, closing her eyes. "Please." She had never believed that hearts could actually break. Now she knew it was true. Falling forward, she lay in the ferns and sobbed.

Fredo and Joao found her as the sun was slipping below the forest canopy. She lay on her back in a tangle of ferns. When they called her name, she stirred and opened swollen eyes.

"You've come to tell me that he's dead," she whispered, her voice splintering.

Fredo gently lifted her to her feet. "Come."

Gripping his shoulders, she peered into his dark eyes, trying desperately to read his expression. "Tell me," she begged. "Tell me!" But he struck off through the forest toward the clearing. "Joao?"

"Missy come." And he too turned into the twilight forest.

Turning, Lalie forced herself to walk into the forest, her feet dragging. Then, without realizing it, she began to quicken her pace. Finally she was running, slapping the ferns and leaves out of her path, her heart pounding as she burst into the clearing. She raced past Fredo and Joao, her swimming eyes fixed on the entrance to the healing woman's hut.

Gasping, panting for breath, she sped to the doorway then collapsed against the post. Tears were streaming down her cheeks as she stared inside.

March smiled weakly up at her. "You did say you love me . . . I didn't dream that, did I?"

He was shockingly thin and naked except for a strip of bark cloth across his lap, but he was sitting up and drinking manioc beer from a gourd bowl. Beneath a three-week growth of beard his cheeks were drawn and gaunt, his dark eyes hollowed and tired.

But those eyes glowed at the sight of her. He was alive. And the glazed vacancy had departed; he was lucid. He had returned to her.

"Oh God," Lalie whispered, staring at him. "Oh dear God."

One eyebrow lifted in amusement. "No, Miss Pritchard, it's: Oh dear March." He smiled. "Come here."

Laughing and crying, she flew to him and flung herself down on the platform next to him, burying her face in the hollow of his throat. Her hands raced over his body, as if by touching him she could assure herself that she wasn't dreaming. His skin was warm and dry and smelled like wild honey. When he kissed her, he tasted of manioc beer and something bitter and medicinal. His beard tickled her chin and upper lip.

When Lalie opened her eyes, the healing woman was sitting on the bark mat beside the platform smiling at her.

"Thank you," she whispered through tears of joy. "From the bottom of my heart, I thank you!"

The healing woman acknowledged Lalie's joyful gratitude with a nod of her head. She understood. The language of the heart was universal.

The crisis had passed, and March would survive, but he was far from well.

"No," Lalie said several days later, scowling as she pressed him back to the platform. "First you need to rebuild your strength. Then you can get up."

He glared at her and demanded, "Are you going to bully me the rest of our lives?"

"Yes. Now eat your fish."

They smiled at each other.

Gradually their smiles faded and Lalie felt a blush of heat rising in her throat and cheeks. She became aware of her nipples thrusting against her shirt at the same moment she noticed a stirring beneath March's trousers. "You *are* feeling better," she murmured, looking down.

But when he laughed and reached for her, she felt the lack of strength in his arms and knew he was still a long way from regaining his full vitality.

Since the day the fever broke she had nursed him tirelessly, never leaving his side. Tilwe's warriors had moved March from the healing woman's hut to Buti and Irikina's hut, and while March slept, which was often, Lalie helped Irikina peel and pound manioc and she watched Irikina's baby while the Indian woman tended her garden. Maria spent the days with them, and in the evenings they drank manioc beer together, praised the babies, and fussed over March, shaving him, bathing him, feeding him though he was able to feed himself. He grinned and called them his harem.

At night Lalie slept in his arms, offering her warmth against the damp forest chill, and longing for the moment when he would be strong enough to make love again.

"Soon," he said one day in a husky voice, reading her thoughts. He gripped her hand and gazed at her ripe mouth. "Soon, my darling."

They had been so absorbed in each other that neither had noticed the commotion erupting outside in the clearing. But when they heard a gunshot and screams, they both jumped. March jerked upright on the platform; Lalie spun to face the entrance of the hut in time to see a man enter—a white man with golden hair, a man carrying a gun.

"What a touching little domestic scene," Percival snarled from the doorway. Stepping into the hut, he looked at Lalie, sneering at the sight of her trousers and shapeless shirt, her hair tied back with a length of hemp.

Then his cold gaze fixed on March. "You are a dead man, Addison."

Chapter 23

Jumping to her feet, Lalie positioned herself between March and Percival. "Put the gun down. Can't you see he's ill?"

"Stay out of this, Lalie." Swinging his thin legs over the edge of the platform, March pushed to his feet and lurched against the support post, holding himself upright. His black eyes narrowed contemptuously on Percival.

"I've come for my property, Addison. Killing you will be my reward for perseverance." Percival jerked Lalie to his side. His pale eyes glittered, reflecting the sunset rays that streamed through the doorway as he bent his head to her. "You and I have some unfinished business to attend to."

Revulsion twisted her face, and she shoved free of his grasp. Desperately afraid for March, she turned to face Percival well out of his reach. "No Englishman would shoot an unarmed man!"

Sterling's cold eyes assessed the situation at a glance, absorbing March's debilitated state, the medicinal pots arrayed beside the platform.

He smiled arrogantly. "The very suggestion is offensive, my dear." One golden eyebrow arched in derision as he studied the hatred blazing in March's eyes. "Naturally, I propose we settle our differences as gentlemen."

"And the stakes?" March snarled.

"Winner take all," Percival snapped. When March glanced at Lalie, he smiled. "I'll take my bride and every savage who looks as if he or she can deliver a day's work."

For a moment Lalie didn't understand, then she grasped they were arranging the terms of a duel. Her fingers flew to her lips and she stared at March.

"No," she whispered. "This is madness. March, today is the first time you've stood upright in weeks!" His legs were shaking with the effort and his mouth was pressed in a tight line of determination. A sheen of sweat appeared on his chest and brow. Whirling, she appealed to Percival. "A duel would be the same as murder! He can hardly stand!"

"And if I win?" March asked, speaking between his teeth.

The blood drained from Lalie's face as she jerked toward him. "March, no!"

Percival shrugged. His confident smile indicated the unlikelihood of March's triumph. "Then you win our offensively garbed Eulalie, and your precious savages earn a reprieve."

"Done." Swaying, March gripped the support post. "Pistols. In the clearing at dawn."

"Agreed."

"Oh my God." Lalie's knees collapsed and she sank to the edge of the platform, staring up at them.

In contrast to March, Percival appeared robust and carelessly menacing. He stood tall and golden in the doorway, vivid next to March's pallor. Where March's trousers dropped loosely to his hips, Percival wore crisply tailored breeches, a snowy linen shirt, and a panama hat.

Smiling, Percival caught Lalie's hand and raised her limp fingers to his lips. "I shall expect you to join me for dinner in a quarter of an hour, my dear. I shall also expect you to discard that scandalous attire and garb yourself more suitably."

"This is all I have," she said in a dull voice. In the span

of a few moments the world had gone mad. Yet Percival believed the moment appropriate to discuss the propriety of her apparel. Lalie's mind spun, trying to comprehend what was happening.

"How shocking. We'll purchase appropriate attire in Parintins on our return journey. You won't want to show yourself on deck until we correct this offense." Before he dropped her fingers, he rotated her hand and flicked his tongue across her palm. A speculative smile heated the depths of his pale eyes. "I'll expect you in a quarter of an hour."

The instant Percival turned away, Lalie rubbed her hand on her trousers then jumped toward March, ducking under his arm. "Lean on me," she urged, tugging him toward the platform.

First he wiped the sweat from his brow, then gave his head a shake as if to clear it. He let her help him to the platform but only to fetch Buti's blowgun. Removing his arm from Lalie's shoulders, he leaned on the blowgun as a cane and stumbled up and down the hut, practicing walking.

"Oh March," Lalie whispered. His legs trembled with the effort, fresh sweat flooded his brow and upper lip. "You're too weak to attempt this. You're shaking." When he said nothing, concentrating on remaining upright, she began to plead. "We can escape. Tonight, when everyone is sleeping—"

"No, Lalie." Pausing, he placed a fist on his heaving chest and blinked at the thatch overhead. The exertion of walking had exhausted him. "Sterling would enslave every able-bodied man and woman in the village."

Tears glistened in her eyes. "Damn it, March! Look at you. You're exhausted after ten steps." Standing, she gripped his arms. "You can't win! He'll kill you, damn it, don't you understand? He'll kill you!" Hot tears scalded her cheeks.

Struggling from her grasp, he leaned against the support post to gather his strength, then grimly resumed walking, leaning heavily on the blowgun.

"I have tonight to prepare."

"You *can't* prepare! March—you were desperately ill for over six weeks! This is the first moment you've stood on your feet. You cannot win! Please, I beg you not to do this!"

Ignoring her, he wobbled dizzily toward the Winchester propped against the thatch. After fighting to regain his breath, he bent to raise it in his arms. The weight of the barrel dragged the bore down until it pointed to the ground. March raised his head and stared at nothing.

"Leave me, Lalie."

"Call off the duel! Tell Percival you've changed your mind. Surely we can reach some other—"

"No."

"There must be something you can do to give yourself more time," she begged.

But he wasn't listening. He was struggling to raise the Winchester, staring in disgust at his shaking arms. She didn't think he noticed when she stumbled out of the hut.

A charged silence overhung the central clearing. No children darted in play around the cooking fires. There were no shouts of warriors' laughter or the contented murmur of women. Even the chickens and dogs had fallen silent.

After seizing their weapons, Percival's men had herded the warriors into the main *maloca*, Fredo and Joao among them. Though twilight shadowed the interior of the *maloca*, Lalie could glimpse the warriors' expressionless faces. At this moment the small brown men no longer appeared fierce to her. They looked helpless and vulnerable in their nakedness, no match for the burly Spaniards holding them at gunpoint.

Following the direction of the Spaniards' grins, Lalie turned, and a rush of acid flooded the back of her throat. The men not guarding the warriors were raping whatever woman caught their fancy. Their only concession to decency was their avoidance of aged women and women with babies at their breast. Through her horror, Lalie thanked God that Maria and Irikina were not among the women being brutalized in full view of the compound.

Fighting waves of nausea, she stumbled toward the stool placed beside a bonfire where Percival waited. He stood at her approach and bowed then indicated the stool beside his. His display of politeness amid brutality sickened her.

"Stop them," she demanded in a shaking voice.

"The men have earned a bit of pleasure. Even if is with monkeys." Having disposed of the subject, he gestured to the dishes arrayed on fresh banana leaves. "I can recommend the smoked piranha, but I would avoid the carambola if I were you. Bruised fruit offends the senses, don't you agree?"

"You make me want to vomit," she whispered. Until now she had visualized Satan as dark and ugly. But the evil angel could be handsome, with hair of gold and eyes of cold, clear blue; he could smile with a tender mouth.

Percival loomed over her, smiling into her eyes. One hand caressed her cheek and then caught her head when she tried to jerk away from him. "You will call my name and scream with pleasure. You will beg me to possess you." She shuddered with revulsion. "Now sit down, my dear. Melodrama is seldom conducive to good appetite."

Because she had no choice Lalie sat beside him, averting her gaze from the ongoing brutality enjoyed by his men. Their shouts and the crackle of the bonfire were the only sounds in the village. The women endured what was done to them in silence. No sound rose from the men held prisoner in the *maloca.*

Lalie squeezed a mango between trembling fingers. When she could bear the silence no longer, she said in a low voice, "March is dangerously weak. If you will spare his life, I'll return with you to Hiberalta. I . . . I'll do anything you wish. Just spare his life and leave these people in peace."

Percival laughed. Pinpoints of firelight danced in his pale eyes. "I'll have you in any case. And I'll have the savages. *And* I'll have the pleasure of killing Addison."

"I beg you," Lalie whispered.

His fingers cupped her chin. "You'll beg me often. You have a very great deal to atone for, don't you?" His other hand rose to his cheek to remind her of the way she had scratched him. Slowly his hand slipped from her throat to fondle her breast. When she jerked away, he laughed and refilled a crystal glass from the champagne bottle near his boots.

In agonized silence she listened to a bizarre one-sided conversation that made her mind reel. Percival remarked on the sultry night in a tone as pleasantly bland as if a mass rape were not being conducted within their sight, as if his men were not clubbing one of the warriors for sport. He reviewed the last opera he had attended in Manaus, inquired if she was comfortable, offered his views on Darwin's work, pressed her to sample the smoked piranha, speculated on the rising price of rubber.

Through it all, Lalie stared into the flames, her hands gripped tightly in her lap, and her heart cried out to March in anger and despair. His foolhardy courage, the sense of honor that would not permit him to escape and abandon the villagers, would end in his death. The thought was unbearable.

At the conclusion of the meal, during which she ate nothing and drank nothing, she stood when Percival did, not looking at him for fear she would spit in his face.

"Clea is dead," she said finally. After a moment he shrugged. "She was carrying your child."

When he laughed, she cringed. "Don't be a fool. God only knows whose child she carried."

Lalie stared up at him then. "Don't you care that she's dead? Clea loved you."

"Clea was a whore."

There was nothing she could say to him. No words would penetrate his perversity. When Lalie opened her eyes, she said, "I would like a word with Maria." To present the request in terms he would understand, she added that Maria was her maid. She knew he would never permit her to speak to Fredo. Both would be frantic to know what was happening.

Percival granted her request with a magnanimous gesture, but he gripped her around the waist before she left him, and crushed her against his body. "Tomorrow we'll finish what we began in Hiberalta," he promised before his mouth closed over hers in a bruising kiss.

Shoving away from him, Lalie deliberately wiped the back of her hand across her lips then spat on the ground. His hard laughter followed her across the compound to the hut where the mothers and babies were sequestered.

Maria and Irikina rushed forward the moment Lalie entered the hut, and begged for news. Watching their faces pale, she explained the terms of the duel. After Maria did her best to interpret, Irikina explained to the others that March had refused to attempt escape. He would duel Sterling in an attempt to save the villagers. They gazed at Lalie without hope, knowing as she did that March was too weak to win.

"Irikina asks if the men know of this duel," Maria said.

"What good would it do if they knew? Their weapons have been confiscated, they're prisoners."

The hope died from Maria's gaze and she bent her dark head over Luis Alfredo's tiny body. She said nothing, but Lalie knew she was worrying about Fredo, knowing he too would end as a slave in the *seringais* at Hiberalta. If he lived.

After embracing Maria and Irikina, Lalie turned to the doorway to return to March, but a mustachioed Spaniard lowered his Winchester and barred her way.

"Señor boss say you no leave. You stay here."

Lalie's head jerked and she stared past the Spaniard's shoulder to where Percival stood beside the fire. Their eyes met and she understood an appeal would be futile.

During the long, sleepless night, three of the women disappeared with their babies through a flap in the thatched wall. Lalie watched, and shook her head when Irikina gestured that she too should make an escape. She was not wise to the ways of the jungle; she would not survive long in the primitive wilds. And she would not desert March.

"Irikina is going with the others," Maria said in a tired voice, straining to understand Irikina's whispered urgency. "She hopes to find some way to help the men."

Lalie nodded then leaned her head back against the thatch and closed her eyes. She longed for March. There were so many things she wanted to say to him. Near dawn a bittersweet memory rose to taunt her. Once she had believed March Addison lacked honor and that Percival Sterling possessed it.

Milky wisps of mist drifted across the compound, smothering sound, chilling the gray morning air. Lalie felt the dampness as she stood and flexed stiff shoulders when one of the Spaniards shouted at her and gestured with the barrel of his gun.

"Señor boss man say you come now. You watch."

Without speaking, she combed her fingers through her hair then followed the Spaniard to a bonfire sputtering against the hazy wisps.

"Good morning, my dear." Percival removed his hat and offered her a steaming cup of thick coffee, which she refused. He looked well rested and refreshed, dressed as he had been yesterday in tailored trousers and shirt and freshly polished boots. "An invigorating morning, don't you agree? A bit damp, but the fog will burn off before long, I'll wager."

"Percival, stop this madness. It's murder."

"Don't be tedious, dear Eulalie." The words were muted by the clouds of mist. "Are you warm enough?" He snapped his fingers at one of the Spaniards. "Give the lady your jacket."

"I don't want it."

"As you wish." He shrugged, tilting the coffee to his lips.

Lalie extended her palms to the fire and shivered in the eerie silence. In her overwrought state it seemed that ghostly figures flitted in the mist, strange nightmarish creatures with rope hair and rust-colored bodies. In an instant they were gone.

When she again opened her eyes, she saw March emerge from a wisp of fog, proceeding toward them on unsteady legs, his expression grim and determined. She bit her lip to keep from crying out. He was perspiring heavily at the effort to stride forward. His eyes looked hot and feverish.

For a moment his gaze met hers, silently affirming his love for her. Saying good-bye. Then he turned to Percival.

"The pistols?"

At a snap of Percival's fingers one of the Spaniards hurried forward and flipped open a pistol case. Percival bowed slightly from the waist, his smile mocking the gesture. "Your choice."

Lalie sat hard on the stool Percival had vacated, her eyes wide with the horror of what she was witnessing. Her throat worked and she tried to scream, but no sound emerged from her frozen lips.

March selected one of the pistols, raised it and sighted down the barrel. Still without speaking, he accepted three cartridges from the Spaniard's dirty palm.

Percival did the same. "I've taken the liberty of providing only three shots. I propose a three-shot limit at fifteen paces."

Lalie smothered a cry. March would be fortunate if he could remain upright long enough to fire one shot. As for

Percival—at fifteen paces only a blind man or one as ill as March could fail to deliver a lethal shot. She began to tremble, and tears filled her eyes.

"Agreed," March said in a firm voice. "In the event no fatal shot is scored, I propose the man left standing be declared winner. The man down shall abide by the terms as agreed."

Hysteria made Lalie dizzy. March could hardly stand yet he could envision himself as the victor. She gazed at him with incredulity, and never had she loved him more.

Percival inclined his head and made a flourish with his hand. "Shall we?"

March nodded, weighing the pistol in his hand. Before he followed Percival into the swirls of mist, he looked at Lalie.

"I love you, Miss Pritchard."

Standing, she gazed into his wonderful dark eyes, reading the love and warmth that was for her alone. "I love you, Mr. Addison," she whispered.

They gazed at each other for a moment longer, then March followed Percival away from the fire and Lalie and the Spaniards hastened after them.

Although Lalie could not glimpse the treetops through the mist, she felt their towering presence in the eerie hush. Milky vapor floated around them, obscuring the huts and the forest. Her skin jumped when an unseen monkey shrieked. She tilted her head and stared up at the fog, at the pale disc struggling to break through the damp drifts. She told herself she would not watch what was about to occur.

But she did. Blinking with despair, she lowered her head as the two men positioned themselves back to back and raised their pistols. Percival did so in a confident, insouciant manner, his expression relaxed. March stared straight ahead, his mouth pressed in a hard line. He didn't glance at the pistol in his trembling hand.

"Please," Lalie whispered, her mouth dry. Her fingernails dug into her palms. A drop of blood appeared on her lip beneath her teeth.

"Uno . . . dos . . . tres . . ." One of the Spaniards began the count and each man stepped forward.

Swaying in horror, unable to breathe, Lalie peered through the mist, first at one man then the other. Without being aware she moved, she collapsed to her knees on the damp, packed earth. Her chest burned for want of air; her eyes stung but she didn't dare blink. The count continued. Eleven, twelve, thirteen. She saw March's body tense, preparing to turn, swung her wild eyes to Percival, who was turning on the count of fourteen and raising his pistol.

She started to scream, but before a sound could issue from her mouth, a dart struck Percival's throat and an arrow quivered in his chest. Shock widened his eyes and the pistol fell as he raised his hand and peered down at the arrow in amazement.

March spun on the Spaniard's count of fifteen and fired. He missed Percival by several feet. As he shot, a blizzard of arrows flew out of the mist.

Percival's body jerked with the impact as a dozen arrows pierced his body. The Spaniards standing on either side of Lalie fell to the ground. She stared down at them, absurdly thinking they looked like pincushions, struck through with feathered arrows and painted darts. In the distance she heard soft thuds as other bodies fell.

Behind her a gun fired, then screams split the silence. A shaft of sunlight filtered through the haze and Lalie saw men running out of the forest. But they didn't look like men, they looked like creatures drawn from a nightmare. They wore coarse yellow wigs woven from palm fiber, some wore crowns of red and yellow toucan feathers. Their bodies were covered entirely by black and orange patterns; their eyes blazed with hatred. They ran past her screaming, waving bows and arrows, blowguns, and machetes. At once Lalie realized what had happened: the women who had escaped the night before had sought the help of a neighboring tribe.

When March's arm circled her waist, she pushed her face against his sweat-soaked shirt and surrendered to a series of deep shudders. Behind her she heard screams and another gunshot.

Then Irikina and two women appeared, pushing Fredo, Joao, and Maria toward them. Irikina stroked Lalie's cheek, then she spun and ran back to the slaughter taking place behind the mist.

Rushing forward, Fredo and Joao draped March's arms over their shoulders. "Run, Missy," Fredo called, dragging March forward. "They got the blood lust. When they finish Sterling's men, they come after us. Not even respect for Cabo save us if we're still here!"

Pushing Maria ahead of her, Lalie sped after them, hoping to God Fredo could find the tributary and the dugouts in the fog.

It was a nightmare flight. Once Lalie thought she and Maria were lost. Heart pounding in panic, she halted and tried to hear the men crashing through the foliage, willing the wild hammering of her pulse to cease. Then the mist parted and she glimpsed them ahead and hurried Maria and the baby after them. Thorns clawed at their clothing; cold droplets dripped from the branches overhead. A roar sounded in the undergrowth. And behind them came screams and shrieks and shouts of savage triumph.

When she and Maria stumbled out of the forest and onto the pebbled shore, Fredo already had March in one of the dugouts. His face was white, his teeth clenched. He opened his eyes as Lalie waded to the dugout and tumbled inside, scrambling to her place in the stern and reaching for the paddle.

"I'm not injured," she assured him hastily, looking behind to see Joao pulling Maria and the baby into the second dugout. "Go," she shouted to Fredo, digging her paddle into the water. "You," she said to March when they had gained the center of the stream and were flying with the current, "you rest!"

A weak smile of admiration trembled on his lips. "Do you remember . . ." He paused for breath. "Wondering if you had courage?" Although his eyes closed, his smile widened. "You are such a fraud, my love. You have enough courage for two."

Paddling furiously, she said, "I believe that's the nicest compliment you've ever paid me. I even think it may be true. It's possible I do possess a wee bit of courage." She gazed at him with the soft eyes of love. "And so do you, you wonderful idiot."

"You do have a way with words, Miss Pritchard."

"Rest, my darling Mr. Addison," she said between strokes. "Some of us have work to do."

"I'll make this up to you," March murmured, closing his eyes again.

"Damned right you will," she agreed, smiling. Then she settled into the task, concentrating on matching Fredo's strokes.

When they reached the *Addison Beal,* they discovered Percival's men had smashed the wheelhouse, taken hammers to the engine and vandalized the boiler room.

After insisting that March swallow a cup of *guaraná* and waiting until he slept in his hammock, Fredo, Joao, and Lalie grimly inspected the damage.

"Big *bagunça,"* Fredo said, shoving back his straw hat and scratching his head. Joao agreed, his expression glum.

"Can the damage be repaired?" Lalie asked.

Instead of answering, Fredo narrowed his eyes on the broken shoreline. "Percy's boat is here somewhere," he said finally.

"Yes!" Lalie's face lit up. "We can take Percival's boat and tow the *Addison Beal."* She gripped Fredo's arm with excitement. "There may be quinine on Percy's boat."

"Quinine like gold, Missy. White man carry it with

him." When he saw her face, his voice softened, then he said, "But we can look."

That night when they gathered around March's hammock after a meal of freshly caught fish and toasted manioc, he insisted on sharing a cup of the *cachaça* Percival's men had overlooked. But he was too weak to sit up and grip the cup.

Swearing and sputtering, he apologized. "I've never felt so damned helpless in my life!" His eyelids fluttered in the lantern light and he dropped his hands. "There's work to do, and—"

"Hush," Lalie interrupted, placing a fingertip over his lips. "We're managing. Joao found Percival's boat hidden a quarter of a mile upriver. We're going to move aboard it and tow the *Addison Beal.* We'll be underway soon." Bending, she kissed his brow. "We found a few tins of milk on Percy's boat but no quinine. We'll buy some in Santarém. Once we're there, we'll tuck you into bed where you will stay until you've regained your strength. I mean it, March. I don't want an argument on this."

"Well, you're going to get one." March's dark eyes narrowed on her face. "As it appears you've forgotten, let me remind you that I am still captain of this ship." His gaze shifted to meet Fredo's. "We are going home. To Pará. All I need is rest and I'll do it in my own bed, thank you. Is that understood?"

Fredo grinned. "Understood, Cabo. I make Percy's boat fly. We go like hell."

"March Addison," Lalie whispered, laying her palm against his hot cheek. "You are the most stubborn, ill-tempered man alive! Will you never learn to be patient?"

"If you care a jot for my welfare, darling girl, you will open the hidden panel behind the wheel—Fredo will show you—and you will bring me a cigar," he said, gazing up at her from the depths of his hammock. "Do you know how long it's been since I've had a smoke?"

She stared at him, then she laughed.

But she wasn't laughing when she returned with his cigar to find him tossing in his hammock, semidelirious and sweating with fever. The progress he had made in the healing woman's hut had evaporated in the mist. During the next week she alternated between nursing March and standing beside Fredo in the wheelhouse, silently urging the coupled boats to fly.

On the tenth day, she sank to a stool beside Fredo after they dropped anchor near midnight. He sat with his back to the rail, holding Luis Alfredo on his chest, a cigar clamped between his teeth.

"We can't go on," Lalie said quietly. "We're all exhausted. Joao is half-dead from the heat and the work in the boiler room. We're out of food. You are asleep on your feet. And March desperately needs clean water, quinine, and medical care. We should have stopped in Santarém as I wanted to."

Fredo opened his eyes and stared at her. Dark circles rimmed her steady gaze. She was thinner than he remembered.

"Cabo say we don't stop until Pará."

"I say we stop at Quantos. That's the next town, isn't it?" Despite her exhaustion she managed to smile. "You know I won't give you a moment's peace until you agree."

Fredo thought for a moment, sighed and said, "We go to Quantos." He smiled. "We're going to miss you, Little Missy."

"I'm going to miss you, too," Lalie whispered. She remembered a time in another life when she had refused to share a meal with Fredo, Maria, and Joao. "I love all of you so much."

Chapter 24

Late afternoon sunlight tinted the river a rich golden-caramel color. Overhead the blue sky arched toward a strip of land that glowed emerald on the opposite shore. Brown, blue, and green—Lalie would never again observe those shades without recalling the Amazon, without memory teasing her senses with the fragrance of sunshine and water and riotous foliage.

Crossing her arms on top of the Quantos seawall, she leaned her chin against her hands and watched a ribbon of dark smoke trailing from the stacks of a passenger steamer bound upriver for Manaus. A tiny figure appeared on deck and waved to her, or maybe the woman waved to all of Quantos. Lalie waved back, envying the woman her trip upriver and the experiences it would bring. Smiling through a shine of tears, she watched until the steamer rounded a broad curve and the last puff of dark smoke was lost to view. Then Lalie's thoughts drifted backward to her own voyage of discovery.

She had been devoured by insects, sunburned repeatedly, battered by storms, and frightened half out of her wits. She had been shot at, wounded, and had possibly killed several men. She had delivered two babies, lived in an Indian village, had eaten things that made her shudder to remember. She had been too hot, too cold, too wet, too angry, too sad, and happier than she had dreamed was possible. She had met wonderful people, horrible people, and people whom she would remember all the days of her life. The river had claimed her and changed her in ways she would still be discovering for years to come.

Closing her eyes, she listened to the lazy rattle of the palm fronds overhead, the steady rush and murmur of brown waters.

The first time she had visited Quantos she had been a different person, priggish, self-righteous, and lacking confidence.

The river had returned another woman to Quantos, a stronger woman. The future held no fear for this woman. Whatever challenges waited in the years ahead, Lalie would face them with confidence and enthusiasm. Just as important, she had toppled the barriers she once had erected between herself and those people who were different from her. And her life was richer for it. Richer for not requiring others to conform and for no longer needing to conform herself.

The river had washed away everything that was inessential or artificial and left only that which was strong and true.

"A penny for your thoughts." Father Emil smiled and leaned his elbows on the seawall beside her.

She gazed at his thin, handsome profile then faced back to the river. In an ever-shifting pattern, the caramel ripples had deepened to a darker hue. "When we first met I couldn't comprehend how you could be content to spend your life here, in a dusty backwater river settlement."

"Now you understand." It wasn't a question. He knew what she was feeling because he felt it, too.

"Will the Pahang River be like this one?" she asked after a while. At this moment the Amazon sang in her blood and Malaya seemed impossibly far away.

"Each river has its own mood and character," Father Emil mused, gazing over the sunlit surface. "But in the end we must shape our rivers ourselves. We form them around the stuff of dreams." Removing his pipe, he turned to look at her. "Did you find your dream, Lalie?"

"Oh yes," she said softly, thinking of the man napping in Father Emil's guest house. "I found my dream and more, much more."

"I'm glad." For a while they were silent, enjoying each other's company and the magic of the river. "I expect you'll be leaving soon. March has recovered enough to upset half the town with his impatient bellowing." He smiled and glanced toward the church spire and the small guest house to the right of the rectory. "As March is a notoriously poor correspondent, I hope you'll write regularly and tell me of Malaya and how you both fare." He smiled at her trousers, man's shirt, and sandals, at the glorious stream of coppery hair catching fire in the sun. "I predict you will cut a dash along the Pahang, dearest Lalie."

She laughed and accepted his arm as they strolled past the palm-shaded plaza toward the guesthouse. "I've discovered the secret you gentlemen have been concealing from us ladies for centuries. Trousers are enormously more convenient and more comfortable than long skirts and a multitude of petticoats."

He grinned and lifted a fold of his cassock. "Now if someone would share that revelation with the church . . ."

Smiling, she informed him that she had ordered a full wardrobe from Pará to be delivered tomorrow or the following day. "You needn't fear I'll embarrass March. By the time we reach Pará I'll be wearing proper lady's attire."

Father Emil rolled his eyes toward heaven. "To think. I have lived long enough to hear someone worry about embarrassing March Addison."

Laughing, Lalie entered the cool, shadowed foyer of the

guest house, stopping when she realized the priest was not behind her. "Are you coming?"

"Well, now that March is nearly recovered I thought you might like . . . Ah, that is, I have an appointment with—with whom?—with Senhora, I can never recall her name, it's—" An infusion of scarlet rose like a wave from his collar to his forehead.

Smiling with affection, Lalie placed her hand on his cheek. "Dear, understanding Father Emil. It would be lovely if your appointment lasted until dinnertime." Pink blossomed on her own cheeks. He was a priest, after all. The Voice of Propriety rose from the grave long enough to deliver a weak tweak to her conscience.

"If the two of you decide . . . I would be honored to perform the ceremony . . . that is, I mean . . ."

Lalie laughed and leaned forward to kiss him. "I'll tell March." She gazed into his eyes. "Thank you, Father Emil."

After preparing a tea tray she carried it upstairs to March's room and pushed the door open with her shoulder. Corner windows caught the river breeze and white curtains floated in front of the shades. Afternoon shadows slanted across the polished floor. Finally, like saving a sweetmeat for last, she let herself look at the bed, feeling a surge of happiness at the sight of the man she loved.

A lock of dark hair fell over his brow. March was not as deeply tanned now, but vibrant and glowing with health. He sat against a mound of embroidered pillows, his long legs crossed at the ankle on top of the coverlet. A linen shirt was open to the waist, revealing a tangle of dark hair and the edge of an old scar. The sight of him accelerated her heartbeat and stopped her breath.

"You're awake."

Tossing aside the book he had been reading, he smiled and patted the bed beside him. "Put down that tray and come talk to me."

She arched an eyebrow in a parody of the prudish

girl who had passed through Quantos a lifetime ago. "Mr. Addison. Are you suggesting I sit beside you on the—dare I say the word—bed?"

A heated gaze moved slowly from her ankles to her calves and hips then lingered on her breasts before ascending to her lips and finally to her sparkling eyes.

"Come here, Miss Pritchard," he said in a low, husky voice.

Smiling, she put down the tea tray and jumped on the bed beside him, settling against the pillows in expectation. She looked at March in surprise when he didn't immediately reach for her.

He drew a breath then folded his hands across his chest and looked at their feet, side by side on the coverlet.

"I have an idea you are about to deliver a speech," she murmured, moving closer to him. He smelled like starch and shaving soap, warm good smells that she loved.

"I can't remember when I last smoked a cigar," he said. "Did you know that? And do you know why I am not enjoying a cigar right now? I'll tell you why. I am forgoing that immense pleasure because *you* object to cigar smoke, that's why. Women change a man. You all do it. Sometimes you don't even mean to do it, but you do it."

"If you want a cigar, then for heaven's sake, smoke a cigar." Raising his arm, she dropped it around her shoulders and leaned her head against him, smiling. "I've gotten accustomed to cigar smoke. In fact, I rather like it."

"And I know what's coming next. You've already proposed, so you're going to insist that we get married. That's exactly what women do."

"I'm going with you to Malaya in any case. It's up to you whether we go as husband and wife or as lovers. But I'm going with you and that's that."

"I had a tidy, well-ordered life, Miss Pritchard, before you came along. I thought I was content. Now I'm about to get married and spend the rest of my life buying women's clothes for a woman who keeps losing hers. And—I suppose you're going to want a gigantic wedding with all the fuss and feathers that entails. I won't have a thing to say about it." He turned to face her across the pillows. His dark eyes made love to her mouth and his hand slipped to her thigh.

"Father Emil will marry us and the ceremony will be simple. We'll have a small affair, just you, me, Fredo, Maria, Joao, the baby, and the town of Quantos." Raising her hand, she slipped her fingers inside his shirt and pressed her palm against his warm skin, the contact sending a thrill through her yearning body.

His strong hands framed her hips and guided her against him. Closing his eyes, he kissed her nose then the corner of her parted lips. "After that you'll want a house . . ."

"Any house you live in will be fine with me," she said, parting his shirt and kissing his chest.

"Then it will be children . . ." His fingers opened the buttons down her shirt and he sucked in a breath as her breasts arched up to him.

"At least three, I think." Winding her arms around his neck, she pressed against him and gasped softly as his lips spread fire across her skin.

"Before all that, you'll insist on a trip to London. You have rather a lot of explaining to do to your father, and you'll probably want me to have a hand in it." His hands peeled down her trousers and fumbled with the buttons on his own.

"My father is going to be delighted by how things turned out." Pressing him back on the bed, she leaned over him and covered his throat and chest with kisses, circling his nipples with her tongue.

"What are you doing, you wanton hussy?" he groaned, reaching for her. "We're trying to make plans and have a conversation here."

Laughing softly, she moved on top of him and he stared at her breasts and groaned again. "We have the rest of our lives to talk. Hush now, my dearest Mr. Addison, and love me."

His arms closed around her, crushing her against him with the same thrilling strength and power she remembered. "I love you more than life itself," he whispered against her hair. "I'm never going to let you go."

Sunlight dappled the room, glowing on their naked bodies. Lalie fell back on the pillows and cupped his face between her hands, covering his mouth with kisses.

Through the opened windows she could hear the singing lullaby of the river and recognized its rhythm as her own. Its currents were the currents that quickened her veins. Its power and strength had wakened her from a long slumber and had given her new life.

Afterward, sated and blissful, she rested in March's arms, her tousled head nestled on his shoulder. And it seemed to her that a long-ago voice floated on the river breeze: "Poor Rose, she never really lived."

"I will live for us both, Mama," she whispered, her eyes wet with happiness. "I have already begun."

Then there was only the murmur of the river and soft laughter and the joy of two hearts beating as one.